HAIL TO OUR CAMP

ED COHEN

outskirts press

Outskirts Press, Inc.
http://www.outskirtspress.com

ISBN: 978-1-9772-1537-6

Cover Image by Paul Sundick

PRINTED IN THE UNITED STATES OF AMERICA

TO ARI AND JOSH
WHO'VE HEARD ALL THE STORIES BEFORE
IF YOU HAVE NO STORIES TO TELL, YOU
HAVEN'T LIVED LIFE.

TO PAM
FOR HER SUPPORT AND LOVE

TO MY PARENTS
WHO HAVE ALWAYS BELIEVED

1

I followed my mother as if I was a slalom water skier. She was a sleek motorboat, just purring over the burning cement sidewalk in front of Van Buren High School. She cut a swath so smooth that her powerful wake parted the multitude of humanity and I walked unmolested in its path. Children and parents awaited word to board the buses that would take us away to camp. It was the summer of 1969, the last few days of June, and the warm muggy morning portended possible thunderstorms by the afternoon.

My mother was dressed in her skimpy tennis outfit, clinging tightly to her athletic body, accentuating the six pack that she had feverishly worked on every morning. Her V neck allowed her perfectly rounded breasts to bounce around, daring the world to stare upon them, and the shortness of her skirt inched upward with each step, revealing tight, muscular thighs and the daintiest of pink panties. In the crowd fathers and grandfathers started salivating, and the mothers and grandmothers jabbed their spouses in the ribs while directing the eyes of their young and impressionable boys to other things.

Me? I just followed calmly behind her, surrendering to the moment. My father, dressed in his golf outfit, dodged the mass of humanity as he tried to keep up. He was lost in thought, constantly checking his watch, hoping he would be able to get to the country club and his awaiting tee time.

"Mother! I don't want to go. For God's sake, will you ever listen to me?"

"Where is bus number eight?" was all she asked. We were only in front of Bus One. Nine coaches lined the street like dormant snakes waiting to slither away.

My mother pushed forward. Maybe it was her hubris that caused people to jump out of the way, with her knowing that her beauty could part the Red Sea. She definitely had chutzpah, thus the belief that she was the center of the universe and it was either you kissed her ass, or you didn't exist. Suddenly, and I knew it was going to happen sooner or later...there it was...

"Man, I'd love to fuck her!"

That little gem, which seems to always follow my mother wherever she ambles, came from one of the counselors in his blue Camp Tonkawa staff shirt, clipboard in hand, giggling and ogling my mother. Other counselors seemed to agree.

My mother just turned and smiled. She loved the attention.

How do you think I felt? I was about to turn thirteen years old and all I ever heard in life was how every warm-blooded male wanted to fuck my mother, and why not? She was beautiful. I was reminded of this every day in school, listening to my male classmates talking behind my back and my female classmates teasing me about the dress they saw her wearing at the mall. Her stash of mini skirts were bought with the sole purpose of corrupting the minds of the innocent. She was the perennial champion of the club's singles and doubles tennis tournament while my father won the club golf tournament at the same time. Fortunately I inherited their athletic DNA.

Maybe that was my saving grace. This was not my first summer away. My parents shipped me off to my first sleepaway camp when I was five, and for the next eight years I traveled the East Coast from one summer camp for entitled Jewish children to another camp for Jewish brats. I could never find a summer home, one I could attend every year. I was a nomad, an orphan, thrown out of my home at such a tender age. I sometimes surprised myself with my sense of survival. I disliked summer camp, and I would always complain about the camp I had just attended. My parents would then search for another summer camp where they could dump me. I never had a choice.

The summers belonged to my mother and father and their

endless days and nights at the country club, where my father would linger till midnight after a day on Wall Street. If he got home early enough to play nine holes he would play and then drink with his friends till he stumbled home around ten or eleven that night.

My mother took yoga in the mornings, followed by tennis lessons where I do believe she was fucking her instructor. Then she would head to the club to drink and gossip with the other women in the neighborhood. There was no room for me.

I, Jason Rosen am an only child, and here's my story in a nutshell. I have an 'A' average in school. When I come home from school I either study, or in the warmer months I head out to the tennis court in our backyard, set up the ball machine, and practice my strokes in solitude. The tennis court is tucked into the corner of our immense backyard, just a few yards from our kidney-shaped pool, where I prefer to be every summer. I want to be home, alone, never having to mingle with other kids.

I have one, maybe two acquaintances whom I met on the first day of first grade, but I keep them at arms length. I have trouble making friends, much less liking them.

It may seem like I have everything a boy could want... everything but the love he craves from his parents.

I don't trust people. Especially new bunkmates who tend to steal from me. Somehow at every camp they're always finding the small stash of money that I've hidden in my cubby or my trunk. Normally I'm a punching bag for the first week of camp. Everyone taking swipes at me, either with their fists or with socks filled with tennis balls and I just take it because I'm so damn easy going. When I finally get to prove my athletic prowess on the fields of battle I suddenly realize that everyone wants to befriend me. It's too late. I never make amends--it's too late, you blew it. I'm one and done for the summer.

I've seen the entire East Coast, from Maine, to the Berkshires, to the Poconos to the Adirondacks, and now Pennsylvania. My parents usually throw me on a train down to Grand Central station where I navigate my way through the rush hour crowds and find the train that will take me to a distant summer camp. Sometimes I'm thrown into a limo and driven to wherever we need to muster for the summer deployment. Thus my shock at my parents accompanying me to Queens, New York for this new venture.

"Mother, will you listen to me, Man is going to walk on the moon this summer and I want to see it."

"Jason, it's over-rated. Besides you'll see it over and over in the future."

"But I want to see it live. I want to be in front of a TV watching it. Please let me stay home. I promise I won't bother you. All I want to do is read by our pool and watch a little TV at night. I won't get in your way."

My mother stopped in her tracks and turned to face me. Her jewelry, which she collected like I collected baseball cards, glistened like morning dew. Her blond hair, almost as brilliant as the sun, whipped into her eyes, and she bent down to face me eye to eye.

"Do you know how lucky you are to be going away to camp? Do you realize how many children wish they could be in your shoes? You have no friends. You're a hermit, you need to get out and socialize. Jason, you need to live life. What good is staying at home and being by yourself?"

"We could go and see a movie together once in a while..."

"We're busy. We have our own lives with our friends. You have nothing."

I never wanted to go to camp. All I ever desired was for them to come home and pet me on the head like they do with our dog. Would a little kiss on the keppie kill them? A hug? Instead i'm discarded every summer and sent to some expensive sleepaway camp, when all I beg for are a few crumbs of affection.

And on we moved. My mother carving her way deftly through the crowd. I marveled at what I was seeing, a camp of wealthy spoiled children. Boys were carrying their own water skis, and golf bags that were bigger and heavier than they could afford to lug around. The younger girls were dragging stuffed teddy bears that were twice their size, and the older girls were more concerned with their curling irons and cosmetic kits than with the simple joys of the summer.

I love sound. Sometimes I just like sitting in the back yard listening to the bees zipping near my ear, or the sound of sprinklers going off somewhere in our vast neighborhood and I have come to savor those moments. I collect 45s, and love every bit of rock and roll and Motown that blares over the radio.

My thoughts of hearing music were drowned by some children sobbing as they prepared to leave their parents. This was vanquished by the sound of girls squealing in delight upon seeing their camp friends after the long winter. And yet, through the cacophonous blizzard of emotions I could still hear the comments about my Mom.

We finally arrived at Bus 8. My mother approached the counselor who was busy studying his clipboard, checking off the names of those who had arrived. He looked so official in his dark blue Banlon shirt with CAMP TONKAWA etched over his right breast. Even with the three buttons open, the stifling material was making him drip sweat onto his clipboard.

"Jason Rosen is here," my mother announced.

The counselor didn't look up, so my mother started to tap her talon red nails on his clipboard till he raised his eyes. First he was annoyed, but this melted into wonderment at the sight in front of him. His mouth dropped open, and drool started to form in the corners of his ever-widening smile. Instead of checking for my name he started to gawk at my mother's cleavage. My mother gently placed her hand, palm open, under his chin and closed his mouth and then wiped the drool off his shirt.

"Son, I have a tennis match in an hour and a half and my husband has a tee time in an hour so we have to get going. Now can you please check in Jason Rosen?"

The counselor snapped out of it, checked off my name and peeled off a name tag that was slapped over my right breast:

HELLO

MY NAME IS

The counselor scribbled Jason in the space provided.

"Here's fifty dollars," my father said as he slapped a single crisp bill into my hand.

He shook my hand, and my mother kissed my cheek. I slipped the bill into the pocket of my cut off jean shorts, and stowed my small backpack under the bowels of the bus. When I turned around my parents were gone.

2

hy is it that when the new kids in camp are lumped to-gether in a bunk the majority of times this little clique is a regurgitated group of nerds and geeks.

HEAR ME NOW, I am not a GEEK nor a Nerd. I am a loner! I live and thrive on being left alone, an island, a solitary lily pad floating on a lake. I'd rather read a novel at night, instead of watching a lot of television, safely ensconced in my bed. It's the same when I'm shipped off to a camp. I always find myself huddling under my blanket, flashlight in hand, reading a novel instead of a comic book.

Returning campers greet old friends, and take advantage of the system. They know which metal cots (disguised as beds) are best, and how to gain favor with the counselors. They know how to wea-sel their way out of cleaning the bunk. New campers have to fend for themselves.

So it came as no surprise when I spied a strange little boy trudg-ing down the aisle of the bus heading straight toward me. His back-pack was twice the size of his body. He was stooped low and could barely lift his head as the backpack dragged him down.

I was seated by the window, the seat next to me was empty. The gnome of a boy asked if he could sit there. I shrugged my accep-tance and watched as he struggled to take his backpack off and put it above the seats in the provided rack. I was afraid that he would topple over and the backpack would smack me in the face so I got up to help him. Upon turning around I found him sitting in my seat.

My mistake as always. Sometimes I realize I do too many fa-vors for people and get nothing in return. I didn't complain because that's my nature and I'm too easy going for my own good.

I considered him a gnome because he looked like one. His tiny body was dwarfed by a large round head that was overshadowed by immense Dumbo ears. His large round eyes portrayed a sadness seldom seen in a kid my age. His nose was long, thick and wide, not even close to fitting on his face, and of course he had to have a large wart sitting right on the tip. A wart so obvious that it stared at you like a third eye. You couldn't look away. I wondered how he could spend every single day of his life looking out over his nose with that disfigurement at the end.

He turned and caught me staring at him, and thrust his hand into mine. "Hi, I'm Harris Beckerman."

"I know, I read your name tag."

"I hate these things," he said, as he ripped it off his shirt. "Think they're going to shoot me if I don't have this on? Anyway, it's nice to meet you, Jason. This is my first year here. What about you?"

"Same here, " I said with a heavy heart as I too peeled my name tag off and crumpled it into a tiny ball.

"Hey, maybe we'll be in the same bunk," Harris said with a touch of hope in his voice. It was exactly what I was afraid of.

"Do you know what Tonkawa means?"

"No, what does it mean?" I really didn't want to know but Harris seemed intent on telling me anyway.

"It's an American Indian tribe and it also means 'Staying together'. I sort of like that."

Harris turned back to the window, searching for someone. The counselor who had ogled my mother's breasts shouted "time to go," and he politely threw off the last vestiges of parents who had lingered on the bus. Excitement built to a pitch as the cargo doors under the bus were closed, and the driver turned over the engine.

See, I knew it. I knew I was going to be in the same bunk as this gnome. Not that it was written in stone, but you knew the cosmic gods would have us assigned as bunkmates. We would know for certain when we arrived in camp, but I was resigned to the fact that Harris would be attached to my hip for the summer like a leech.

He would look to me for advice. He'd seek my aid and protection when others would most assuredly pick on him. He was chum for the sharks. All I wanted was to be left alone for the entire summer.

It was time to depart. Parents backed away from the luxury liner buses and began to wave goodbye. Some of the younger children started to cry, but if they were lucky they had older siblings on the bus who would calm their fears. For the most part the sobbing was drowned out by campers cheering our departure.

Suddenly a woman from the crowd, pale and emaciated and whose head was covered with a red bandana, dashed toward the bus. She slammed her hand against the window where Harris was sitting, her fingers reaching and yearning for him. Tears streamed down her cheeks from behind her thick, and darkly tinted sunglasses. Her fingers desperately tried to dig through the glass pane as she grasped for Harris.

Harris pressed his mouth to the window and kissed the fingers, and then he pressed his hand and forehead to the window and spread his fingers as wide as they would go, begging to reach the woman's hands.

The bus started to pull out, but neither would let go of their desire to be in contact. The woman tried to keep up with the bus, but she stumbled and fell to the ground. In the reflection of the window I saw Harris mouth, "I love you, Mom."

A man rushed to the side of the fallen woman, and he kneeled down next to her. He pulled the sobbing being warmly to his chest, and kissed her with warmth and affection. I had never seen such a melodramatic scene at any departure, and it made me wonder what I was missing about Harris.

Fifteen minutes into the drive Harris finally pulled his face away from the window. A dried river bed of tears had etched a path down his face.

3

slept. I slept through the Bronx with its burned out buildings. The sun blazed bright and played "peek a boo" through the gaping holes where windows used to exist.

I slept as the caravan headed north on the Thruway. The Palisades bade us a welcome from the other side of the Hudson as we headed north on 87. The caravan approached the Tappan Zee Bridge making good time.

I dreamed about summers past. Summers at a sleepaway camp.

It's a phenomena in itself. Thousands of Jewish children being shipped to far off places, to a variety of sleepaway camps.

There are the Jewish Federation camps, the rustic, affordable no frills camp for those on a tight budget. Others were able to find what they needed in the religious summer camps, where a strict kosher kitchen was maintained and Saturdays were spent celebrating the Sabbath. No activities, just a day of rest sandwiched between services and studying.

What many parents desired for their children were the 'Cadillac Camps'. Expensive, pristine, and an all-encompassing package of every traditional camp delight. Canoe trips, camping trips, numerous softball fields and basketball courts. And of course the food had to be beyond edible.

These were always 'kosher style'; no milk products found it's way to the tables when we were having meat. If they were really a traditional camp the boys side recited blessings before every meal, and on Friday nights the blessing was made over the Challah, and the girls would light the Sabbath candles. Every Friday evening there would be services where one or two prayers were uttered followed by a sermon.

'Cadillac Camps' were my venue. One summer I was sent to a camp in Maine. A limo driver picked me up at home, escorted me to a ticket counter at Laguardia airport where a stewardess escorted me onto the plane. I threw up in those tiny little bags, and entered the camp looking greener than a martian. I was treated like I had a horrible infectious disease, and I cried every night. By the end of the first week I was numb to the entire experience.

Yet all these sleepaway camps shared two cultures that permeated their souls; the military and Native American traditions. The military theme was found in the bugle calls, lineups, bunk inspections, rallying around the flag as we raised it in the morning with our hands over our hearts, and lowered it in the evening before dinner.

Native American traditions flourished throughout all camps. You had campfires, sleepouts, canoe trips, bunks named after Indian tribes, and then during Color War you would participate in the 'Apache Relay', the 'Hatchet Hunt', and 'Rope Burns'.

Most of my life I've been alone. People sometimes think I'm spoiled. They believe I may be jaded. Some even have uttered that I'm ungrateful for all that my parents have provided for me. It may seem I have everything, but I know there's a Grand Canyon-sized hole in my heart. See... all I want is a little quality time with my parents. I think that's what they call it—quality time.

Three types of children are sent off to camp every summer. There are those campers whose parents had a wonderful experience at sleepaway camp and want their children to experience the same.

These parents believe that the summer away from home will prepare their child for college, and the soon to beckon real world. There was no better opportunity to gain self esteem and independence at an early age. Lesson one, analyze the situation and overcome the obstacles.

The second child is the troubled child. They are the wild child, the campers who can't sit still and are constantly creating mischief. I have heard the name Ritalin and I assume it's a panacea to help these campers attain some sort of concentration needed to make it through the day instead of bouncing off walls. Their parents are frazzled, and desperate to not have their children home all summer. Camp was much more a respite for the parents, a vacation so to speak, than it was for the child.

The third child is the one who is sent away because their parents just don't want to be bothered with them. They are the children who are treated as a nuisance in life. They float through life ignored by their parents and will always wonder why they were born.

I am a child of the third tribe.

I was in a deep sleep as the buses slithered across the Tappan Zee Bridge, and lumbered up the Thruway to the tollbooths in Woodbury. From there they veered onto Route 17 and headed towards the Catskills, better known as the Borscht Belt. We all knew the names of these famous hotels; The Concord, Kutshers, Grossingers, etc. Many bungalow colonies were also sprinkled across this landscape.

We left Route 17 at exit 104, the Monticello exit, and the buses from New York mustered in front of the Monticello Racetrack, as they awaited the two buses from New Jersey. It was imperative that all the campers arrived at the same time.

I was still asleep when the New Jersey buses pulled up, allowing the caravan to proceed down Route 17B. I finally woke up to see the racetrack disappear around a bend, as we lumbered down the two lane road toward the town of White Lake.

In White Lake, Chassidic men walked along the side of the road with hands clasped behind their backs. Their black hats shielded them from the sun. Some talked amongst themselves while others seemed to be hidden in deep thought or prayer. Their spouses, pushing baby carriages, wore long skirts and stockings, with their hair hidden underneath scarves or their sheitels. I wondered how they could withstand the heat, dressed in their full length garb. You could see the yellow stained arm pits of those men who walked without their black jackets on. I could only imagine the body odor that wafted off their souls.

I fell asleep again, my best protection against having to talk to Harris. We passed the small hamlets of Bethel and then Fosterdale. Suddenly I was rudely awakened by the sound of each and every bus blasting their horns.

"Where are we?" I asked.

"In Cochecton. You slept the entire way up. Want a Milk Dud?"

The kid sitting across the aisle from me extended a hand that was covered with melted chocolate, as were his lips. He looked like he was wearing chocolate lipstick. He was rotund, chubby, but not weak chubby, muscular chubby and he looked about my age.

"Come on man, have a Milk Dud. I have all this candy and I don't want those counselors taking it away from me, so I'm sharing."

He opened his backpack to show me his stash of chocolate candy. Then I realized that the floor of the bus was littered with wrappers.

"I'm okay. Not much into chocolate"

"Suit yourself," he said as he tilted his head back and dropped two Milk Duds into his mouth.

"You're such a pig," said the tiny girl sitting next to him.

"Oh shut up. You're such a pain in the ass," he shouted, pushing her away and getting a chocolate stained fingerprint on her white Camp Tonkawa t-shirt. She started to cry and bang her little hands against his body.

"She's my sister and I can't take her anymore. She's only eight years old, but she acts like she's sixteen."

"Why did we slow down? Why are the buses blowing their horns?" I asked, knowing that this wasn't his first year at camp. He wasn't wearing a Camp Tonkawa t-shirt, which was taboo for any returning campers.

"Look outside. There's this steep S turn the buses have to make to get under that stone train trestle. Only one vehicle at a time, so they have to honk to make sure no other car is heading through at the same time."

We inched our way forward and moved under the bridge which looked like it would collapse with the slightest touch. We emerged into Cochecton, a two lane dirt town. Off to the left was a sign for the DEW DROP INN, a bar that served food. If you blinked twice you would miss the town with its one general store, a lonely laundromat, and the ubiquitous liquor store. The bus convoy picked up speed and started to cross a metal truss bridge that spanned the river.

"We are crossing the Delaware River now. In the middle of the bridge we'll be in Pennsylvania. The river is low, see how the townies are wading into the middle of it? It's only up to their knees... that's not good for our canoe trip."

I leaned over Harris, who had his nose glued to the window, and studied the sparkling, dirty water of the Delaware. The children in the river were wearing torn jean shorts, their pale bodies begging for the summer sun. One or two waved hello, but the rest of the group of teenage boys and girls were flipping us the middle finger.

"I can't believe this. They're cursing us out, flipping us the bird," Harris shouted. "Why would they do that?"

"Because the Jews are back for the summer. They hate us," the chubby kid said as he leaned over me. I tried my best to avoid being tagged with his chocolate markings.

"Hey kid, what's the matter with your nose? What's that turd on the end of it?"

Harris just blinked his eyes in disbelief, and turned back to looking out of the bus.

"I'm Richard Mandelbaum, and if that geek is in my bunk this summer he's dead meat."

He tried to shake my hand again but I refused to touch him.

"You know, you have chocolate all over your face and hands."

"So what's it to you? What do you care? What are you, my father? You going to slap me in the head now? Just leave me alone and go fuck yourself," he said as he turned his back to me and unwrapped a Milky Way bar and shoved it into his mouth.

The buses shifted gears and trudged up a steep hill, past a large green sign that announced we were now entering Pennsylvania.

"We're only fifteen minutes from camp," the chocolate monster announced as he started to arrange his backpack.

The convoy picked up speed as the buses flew down hills and yet strained to climb the next ones they faced. It felt like we were on a roller coaster ride. We zipped through another town called Damascus, which was even smaller than Cochecton, with its one church, its liquor store and one gas station that housed a number of yellow school buses.

"Swan Lake is a piece of shit, Swan Lake is a piece of shit," Mandelbaum screamed. I thought he was crazy, but then he explained his chant.

"That's Billy May's bus fleet. In the winter he is the bus line for the school system in Damascus, and in the summer he supplies the buses for Camp Swan Lake and Tonkawa. Swan Lake is right behind the gas station. We play Camp Swan Lake in inter-camp games, and they always cheat in every sport."

"Oh, this summer is going to suck," Harris muttered. "All I wanted was to stay home this summer and watch the moon landing." For a moment I felt the tiniest of bonds with Harris as I tried to suppress a smile.

Harris put down the novel he was reading, CATCH-22, and looked at me. He was searching, yearning to see if I would be his friend this summer.

"Have you read this book?" he asked.

"Yes, last summer. One of my favorites along with CATCHER IN THE RYE"

"I agree. Maybe we'll be in the same bunk."

I just turned away. I had nothing to say. We trudged up one last incline and then flew down its backside and suddenly, off to the right, was a lake. It sat splendidly between the woods and the base of a steep hill. At the top of the hill was a three story white mansion that looked so out of place on a hill in the middle of nowhere.

"That's Grayson Hall, where the owner lives. All of the married counselors and group leaders live there too. The lake at the bottom of the hill is our water ski lake. Wait till you see our swimming lake," Mandelbaum told us as he wiped off the chocolate around his mouth with the sleeve of his shirt.

"How many years have you been coming here?" Harris asked.

"This is my seventh summer."

"I hope we won't be in the same bunk," Harris muttered softly.

"I hear everything, asshole, and God, I hope we're not," Mandelbaum said.

4

Abner Dingle waved each bus into camp.

"He's the caretaker. We all love him. He lives in that house across the road and takes care of the camp in the winter and you wouldn't believe the shit he does around here in the summer," Mandelbaum told us. "Look at his arms... he's so fucking strong."

Abner Dingle was indeed strong. He was wearing a flannel shirt that had the top four buttons open, revealing a massive chest. The sleeves of the shirt were torn off, and as he waved each bus in, he flexed his biceps. You just knew this man was someone you didn't want to mess with.

"He's over sixty years old," Mandelbaum told us. "He's so old."

Dingle smiled at our bus, and you immediately noticed that he was missing his two top front teeth. He wore thick round-framed glasses, and his hair was a nice comb over. You could call him a country geek, but then you realized that he was a tad over six feet tall, and his incredibly massive biceps looked like they could move mountains. The buses slowed to a crawl as they passed the gate house. They navigated their way down a narrow gravel road.

Of all of the camps I have been in, none matched the natural beauty of this one. It used to be a country club during the years after World War II, and its manicured fields attested to its past grandeur.

Pine trees lined the white gravel road, reaching toward the sky. Branches bowed over the road, like fingers clasping each other in prayer. It formed a tunnel of green that filtered the bright sunlight. The branches scraped against the roof of the buses, making a high pitched sound like fingernails being drawn over a blackboard. Every now and then you'd hear branches crack and fall to the wayside.

Off to the left was a softball field in pristine condition. The base-paths were meticulous, raked and rolled so not even a pebble was out of place. The outfield and infield grass were deep-green and lush, with nary a weed to be seen.

"Reminds you of the first time time you went to Shea Stadium, doesn't it?" Mandelbaum asked.

"I was only there once when I was very young, before my grand-father died." I've never been back to Shea Stadium since.

Each side of the backstop had a team bench and behind each bench was a small wooden grandstand of five rows. A small score-board, the kind you had to hang numbers on, sat behind first base.

"That's the girls softball field, but we use it more than they do. There are three more ball fields beyond this one." Mandelbaum said as he pointed off into the distance.

A few yards past the softball field was the Social Hall. It was a large white building with a red shingled roof. Barn-style slid-ing doors were situated on each side of the building. The door in the back of the Social Hall led to a large porch which wrapped around its rear. Across from the Social Hall, on the opposite side of the gravel road, was a smaller structure that turned out to be the Canteen. Every camp had a Canteen... a small gathering place for socials, and the spot where the counselors could hang out at night. Counselors could purchase burgers from the grill and quench their thirst with soft drinks from the soda fountain. It was also where the candy was safely secured. Campers were allowed to purchase candy twice a week. We were given Canteen books, filled with little stubs worth ten and twenty-five cents. This from a fund our parents provided. They were our bank books for the summer.

The road bisected the camp in two. We inched forward. Basketball courts for the boys camp were on the left and just beyond that on the right was Grayson Hall. With its two white columns accentuating the porch the mansion looked more southern gothic than eerie. It was Spartan living at its best. No air conditioners and only one or two televisions with lousy reception. The end of the gravel road was near.

Only a few yards beyond Grayson Hall was the Boys Arts and Crafts shack followed by the Girls Arts and Crafts. A small circle with a ceramic vase nestled in the center of this tiny island of green marked the end of the road. Our bus turned off its engine and and lay dormant right in front of the Mess Hall, the one building that stood between the boys and girls camp. The second lake, the swimming lake was right behind it and stretched across the boys campus. We were finally able to step out into the fresh air, groggy from the three hour trip.

"That's bunk number One and Two on the boys side, right there against the road. The youngest kids in camp sleep there, ... you know, five and six year old kids." Mandelbaum said as he pointed to the bunk that sat on the edge of the road across from the Girls Arts and Crafts shack.

"Girls camp is right there?" Harris asked as he pointed to a small shady campus.

"Yup, crazy isn't it?" Mandelbaum said.

I knew what he meant because most camps have their girls camp separated from boys camp by either a lake, woods, or a mile of road. At Camp Tonkawa you could spit across the gravel road and hit the girls camp.

"Makes it easy every Friday night when we have brother and sister visiting hour, and you have to visit your pain in the ass sister," Mandelbaum said as he jabbed his elbow into his sister.

"At all the other camps I've been to you take your life into your hands if you tried to sneak onto girls side. This looks like a breeze," I said.

"Don't bet on it," Mandelbaum told us. "You take your life into your hands here too. It's almost like the road is electrified. Joe Geisinger, the owner, patrols the camp almost all night, and when he goes to bed his bouncers take over."

"Bouncers?" Harris asked.

"Big guys, football coaches, ex-football players,.. gym teachers from Brooklyn. They scare the crap out of you. Just be aware that when you hear the owner's Cadillac start up you better not be found anywhere but in bed. "

The legend of the gravel road piqued my interest. Would this be the summer that I decided to ruin my pure snow white image and dare to be …. bad? Would I dare cross the gravel road?

The hatch to the storage space under the bus opened and campers were grabbing their golf clubs, water skis, huge stuffed dolls, and…. fishing rods?

"Can you believe how many nerds have fishing rods?" I said to Harris as I pulled my bag out of the bowels of the bus.

"What did you say?" Harris asked, fishing rod in hand.

"I said… where are we supposed to go now?"

Harris nodded toward the expansive and majestic lawn that lay on the other side of the buses. The girls were headed to their campus, which was small in stature and hidden under a canopy of trees. Boys camp was massive and open, sloping gently down to the boys and girls waterfront at the edge of the second lake. A long line of bunks sat atop the hill, in an inverted 'L 'pattern, with the ninety degree angle at the farthest edge of camp.

We followed a migration of boys dragging their paraphernalia as they crossed onto boys camp, heading towards a little white shack that sat in the center of the campus. We must have looked like our ancestors, being forced into exile from a shtetl, carrying all of their earthly belongings.

"I bet that's where we're going to be this summer," Mandelbaum said in passing as he pointed towards two bunks that sat at the farthest reaches of the camp, a right angle to the line of bunks. Mandelbaum explained that the oldest kids, the fourteen and fifteen year old campers live in 'Senior Hall', a larger bunk that was split up into eight rooms of varying sizes, and sat between all the bunks.

The screen door to the shack squealed open and slammed shut like a hammer hitting a nail. A man emerged from the HCO and we knew we were almost home.

5

We sat waiting. The gaggle of three hundred boys buzzing with excitement. The thick luscious green grass begged to be trampled on. Noise, laughter, camaraderie. Harris knelt beside me feeling as alienated in the moment as I felt. It was like a secret society we happened upon, looking in from the fringes, wondering if we would ever be a part of this eight week world.

When the screen door squealed open on its rusted hinges an immense man emerged and demanded our full attention. He had thick muscular arms and a short crew cut and his square jaw and bushy eyebrows made him look angry. In his green Lacoste shirt he resembled the Jolly Green Giant. With his two pinky fingers thrust into the corners of his mouth he whistled. Short and shrill. Everyone stopped talking. Harris and I sat on the outskirts of the throng of campers, not knowing what to expect.

"My name is Ed Barnett and I'm the boys Head Counselor. When I stand in front of you I expect all noise to stop. Is that understood?"

Most of the campers nodded in agreement, but the older campers just snickered.

"This little shack here is known as the HCO. This is where you can find me, or my assistant, Irv, any time of the day." he said as he pointed to a small, stocky handsome man next to him. Suddenly he shot a glance at Irv and shook his head in disgust. "Why does he always do this to me?"

All eyes turned to the top of the hill where we watched a bull of a man charging toward us. He was dressed in a bright red Banlon golf shirt. His close cropped silver hair reminded me of a knight's armor, and contrasted sharply with his deep dark tan. He was stocky and muscular and he sort of looked like a bull, in a complimentary way, as he floated down the hill. He bullied his way through the crowd of children, pushing away campers who rushed to greet the owner of the camp.

"At least it wasn't false advertising," Harris shouted. He was standing and jumping up and down like he was in the front row of a rock concert.

"What are you talking about?" I asked, realizing that Joe Geisinger was pushing his way toward us.

"He said he would be wearing a red shirt, and there he is, in his red shirt," Harris shouted in glee as Joe approached us. His smile was dazzling, and on the first day of camp there was a radiance in his eyes that signified his love of camp. By the end of the summer that brilliance, that radiance, would be diminished and almost doused to non-existence.

Now Joe and I never got off to an auspicious start. He had scheduled an evening with my parents. He came by to present himself and the camp by showing us a slide show. He rang the doorbell and I answered it and invited him in. He asked where he could set up his projector for the slide show and I showed him to the basement den.

I grabbed two sodas, and met him downstairs.

"Where are your parents, Jason?"

"Out."

"What?"

"Out. They don't care what you have to present. They heard it's a great camp and that's all they care about. You're the one who insisted on coming over to make a presentation. My parents have better things to do."

Joe was exasperated. He seethed as he paced around in a circle. He furiously packed up his projector and slides. When he turned around he stopped in his tracks as he saw me standing there with a check and a pen in my hand.

"My father left this signed check made out to Camp Tonkawa. I just have to fill out the amount."

"Why... why... well... I'm not sure I'm interested in..."

"My father said I should offer you twice as much as the normal tuition. So how much should I make the check out for?" The rest is history.

Joe grabbed Harris and put him in a head lock.

"Hey..." Joe started to shout, "Harris.... Harris, how are you doing?"

Joe knocked Harris to the ground and continued to grab children in a teasing headlock, as he made his way through the crowd. The younger boys charged and jumped on Joe, cheering him wildly as if he were a rock star. Joe threw them all to the ground with a hearty laugh. He loved this. He loved camp. When he broke through the crowd he turned to Ed Barnett and shouted "Carry on!" then charged towards girls camp.

"He remembered my name... he remembered my name. I can't believe it," Harris sputtered.

"Don't be a fool," I told him. "When he had you in a headlock he pulled back your t shirt and read your name tag."

I so wanted to burst his little bubble... the little bubble that he sat on at this exact moment. He was feeling so magnificent, thinking he was special because the owner remembered his name... but I had to prick it. Send the little gnome into free fall.

"What name tag?" he asked, trying to reach around and pull his shirt in front of his eyes.

"The one your mother sewed on the back of your clothing so it wouldn't get lost in the weekly laundry."

"Oh... " and suddenly there was a silence. "My mother didn't sew anything. I guess she sent it out to someone to have them sew it on."

"Well, the same with my mother. She would never do anything so menial. She might prick her fingers, and actually bleed and show she's human."

It was a rare moment of honesty.

Again, the shrill pinky whistle. Ed Barnett called us to attention and gave us the instructions as to our bunk assignments. When our names were called we would walk to our bunks. We would unpack our trunks and duffles which lay dormant in the center aisle of the bunk. We would make our beds, and then carry the trunks with our duffle bags packed inside, out onto the lawn to be picked up.

The older boys, aged fourteen and fifteen, were the first to be called, and they made a mad dash up the hill toward the largest bunk on campus. Then it was the thirteen-year-old boys, and just as I had predicted, Harris and I were in the same bunk as our names were called out in sequence. Seven or eight other names were also called and they were now sprinting up the hill toward Bunk 18.

I knew there was no reason to rush. It's one of the Laws of the Summer. Being new to a camp you had no say on where you were going to sleep. The returning campers had dibs, they knew where they wanted to sleep, and they knew who they wanted to sleep next to. It was no use fighting the fight on the first day. Experience. I just had to accept what was given to me.

We were walking side by side up the hill when we heard our names called.

"Hey… Hey.. the two of you." It was a nasal whiny shout. "Yeah, you, Harris, and Jason… wait up."

We turned around to see an old man in baggy yellow shorts and a white t shirt trudging up the hill next to a chubby, round-headed boy who sprouted a mean crew cut. Who was this guy? He looked older than my grandfather. He was a short stocky balding man, I mean I was almost as tall as he was. His legs were so bowed that you could fit a bowling ball between them with ease. It was almost as if he was born and raised on a horse. His thick glasses were completely fogged, and beads of sweat glistened off his forehead. He walked up to us, and cleaned off his glasses with his t shirt.

"Hey, what's the matter with the two of you, didn't you hear me calling?"

"How did you know our names?" Harris asked.

"Ehhhh…. (again that nasal whine. It was going to drive me crazy all summer)… I know everything. I'm Saul Kamins, but everyone calls me Chick. So you don't ponder the question too long I'll tell you how I got that name. My father always called me "boychick", and sooner or later I was just called Chick. I'm your group leader. Now, how did I know your names? There are only three new kids in Bunk 18, and Oliver here is one of them, so I just assumed you were the other two, since I know everyone else in the bunk. I don't know who's who between the two of you, but I do know that this is your first summer. Now who's who?"

I introduced myself, but saw Harris just staring at Chick's chest, mesmerized by...

"What on earth are you staring at?" Chick asked.

"You have the biggest nipples I've ever seen on a man or a woman." Harris blurted out, and even though Harris was correct with his observation, I would never have said anything.

"And how many women's nipples have you ever seen?"

"Well, in Playboy... "

"Eh... you haven't seen anything yet ... Listen, I need you to help Oliver carry his stuff up to the bunk," Chick commanded.

Oliver had placed himself comfortably on top of his big suit-case, the one that Chick had been dragging for him. Oliver's breathing was labored, every breath he sucked in with desperation. He reached into his pocket and took out an inhaler, jabbed it into his mouth and took a shot. His head jolted, his body eased, and his breathing became rhythmic and smooth.

"I have asthma," was all he said.

To me, Oliver looked like he was from another planet. His lips were thick slabs of bacon and he constantly wiggled them so that he looked like my long dead gold fish, the one that circled the dirty little bowl I had kept him in. I would sit for hours and stare at that fish pursing its lips, and that's what I was reminded of while staring at Oliver.

He had a perfectly symmetrical head, a round face, and a nose that was too tiny for his face. He had long fingers with bulbous tips that looked like suction cups. He just didn't look human.

Suddenly I was upset, and it took everything to hide what was building up inside of me. Why on earth would parents send such lambs, at the age of thirteen, to summer camp for the first time ? Most children start camp life at the age of nine, and friendships have been consummated and the vagaries of surviving the summer have been finely honed. To be thrown into such an environment at such a late stage of camp life was cruel. At least I had the camp experience from an early age so I knew what to expect.

Now I was stuck, forged into this relationship with two novices who I knew I would have to defend and protect. This was not the role I wanted for the summer. All I wanted was to be left alone. That was the only way I survived every July and August.

"What are you waiting for?" Chick whined. "Be good kids and pick up his luggage. I have to go and check on my bunk. If you need me for anything I'll be in bunk 20."

Chick sauntered off, wobbling from side to side, his bowed legs making it impossible to walk in a normal gait.

6

We walked into the bunk and everyone stopped unpacking their trunks, all talking ceased, and we were dissected for nearly thirty seconds.

"Shit, what the fuck do we have here?"

That was the only comment I heard, but I didn't know who muttered it. Everyone went back to unpacking. They haphazardly threw their clothing into the cubbies above their beds. For the moment we were ignored.

It felt like a scene from a Western movie. Strangers enter a saloon, and a paralysis ensues while everyone fingers their guns. The saloon inhabitants have to decide if the strangers are harmless.

Harris surveyed the scene for two seconds and went for his trunk, picking one of the three beds left open. His aggressiveness in moving forward surprised me. I was a bit disappointed in my hesitation because now there were only two beds left, and one was under the double decker. I stepped forward for my trunk when Oliver touched my arm.

"I'm sorry," he whispered, "I just wanted to let you know that due to my asthma I can't sleep under a double decker. I have a doctor's note stating so. You can try to grab that last bed, but you'll only have to move at a later date."

I would normally disregard such a threat, but Oliver looked as if he was turning blue in front of my eyes, and his anxiety caused him to reach for his inhaler. I told him to put it away, and that I would abide by his request.

In previous camps the bunks were separate units, but not here at Camp Tonkawa. Bunk 18 was under the same roof as Bunk17, a wall dividing it in half. We shared one large porch. There were ten to eleven campers in most bunks, and the small metal cots were separated into cubicles of two. Each had two shelved wooden cubbies over and between the beds. Only room for underwear, socks, some shorts and t shirts. The rest of our wardrobe was to be stored in larger cubbies in the back room where the two toilets and plastic stall shower were situated.

Three large windows on the right side of the bunk punctuated each cubicle. Rays of light danced with dust particles which had laid dormant for the winter months and were now being swept into the air.

Oliver dragged his trunk and duffle over to his bed, which was in the same cubicle as the double decker. I studied my bunkmates. It was a method I had developed from previous summers. A quick need to analyze who were the troubled kids, who was part of a clique and who I could rely on to be totally benign. I wasn't looking for a friend for the summer. Only when this information was processed could I proceed.

But then again, I play another game. I imagine what each camper will be like as an adult. It was looking good for the Proctology field because almost everyone looked like an asshole.

There really was only room for one trunk in a cubicle, so I stood my ground in the center of the bunk while I watched Oliver slowly remove his meticulously packed clothing from his trunk. His parents had sealed his clothing in plastic.

"My mother wanted to make sure that my clothing was dust free upon arrival. I mean after all the trunks were picked up two weeks ago, and who knows what could get inside" Oliver said as he caught me staring at him. "But then you walk into this bunk, and what's the difference... I'm starting to choke on the dust." He started hacking up some solid phlegm in his coughing spat.

The sound of trunks being slammed shut and dragged down the middle of the bunk brought me back to reality. Half my bunkmates had already unpacked and were now ready to run out to the basketball courts. The parade stopped in front of Harris' bed, and Harris stopped and turned around to face some of the bunkmates

"See, that's the Geek I was telling you about," Richard Mandelbaum said as he pointed at Harris. He still had a Milky Way bar in his mouth and a chocolate stain jigsaw puzzle covered most of his shirt.

"Well, he's a slob, and we'll just have to have him do it all over again, until he gets it right." A skeletal-framed boy stepped forward and brushed Harris aside. His ribs were protruding to a prominence so profound that it made me wince. He began to toss each meticulously folded t shirt over his shoulder. They fluttered to the ground like parachutes.

"Hey,..." was all Harris could say, as he stood there in a stunned silence, his mouth still frozen on the only word that he could utter.

"You tell him, Mickey Hardon," Richard Mandelbaum shouted.

"Got to get it right from the start... otherwise you're going to fall into some bad habits," this kid said, sneering with satanic glee.

He continued to indiscriminately toss white underwear and socks onto the floor. He then attacked the neatly stacked shorts. In a matter of seconds the floor of the bunk was littered with a mosaic of clothing. Hardon then marched out of the bunk, bouncing his basketball . He was followed by Mandlebaum, and in succession a tall frizzy-haired geeky looking kid, and a couple of other bunkmates. As the last trunk was dragged across the floor, and the screen door slammed shut we could hear Hardon shouting at someone.

"Who the fuck are you?" he asked

"Your counselor, Mike Stocum."

"Well, Slow Scum... don't be such a jerk off. We're going up to the basketball court." And then I heard the dull sound of a basketball hitting grass instead of concrete. The pack moved away from the bunk, heading to the basketball courts.

The screen door opened softly and Mike Stocum entered. He was never going to last as our counselor. This I surmised in the matter of a second. He was too shy.

He wore a college basketball shirt, some small school in

Pennsylvania. I was sure he was a member of that school's basketball team because he stood taller than six feet. He had a smile that was both swarmy and smirky and yet shy, and was basically the smile of someone uncomfortable being in a situation. I don't think he was ever in a space with so many Jewish kids and he just didn't feel comfortable. His bed was already made. He flopped down on the top of the double decker. When he saw me drag my trunk over toward the double decker he jumped down off the bed, slid into the doorway and slithered out onto the porch where he sat down on the boot box. (Yes... just what it sounds like, a small box that also serves as a bench, but when you lift the cover it serves as a storage place for our rubbers or boots.)

Harris was sniveling, trying not to cry wholeheartedly. He commenced the process of folding and storing all his clothing.

The first thing I felt I had to do was get out of my Camp Tonkawa shirt. I reached into my duffle, and took out my lime green shorts and orange t shirt. I liked the clash of colors. Then I quickly made my bed, with no help from our counselor. Moving a double decker is difficult, and I didn't do a good job of tucking in the back sheet and blanket which now lay against the wall. Nobody looks back there during morning inspections. After I finished tightening up my bed I looked across the bunk to see two blue eyes just staring at me. He was the coolest kid I had ever seen. He was smiling as he got off his bed, and crossed over to my bed.

"Jericho Baker," he said shaking my hand. "I can see you've been to other camps before."

"You're right, I've been to too many. How could you tell?"

"You make a good hospital corner. Look at the crappy hospital corners on all the other beds. Yours is crisp, and yet I don't blame you for not tucking in the bed tightly on the other side. Double deckers suck. Don't know how you got dealt that shit hole bed?"

"Oliver, has a note."

"Ohhhhhh... a note," Jericho said as he looked over at Oliver.

Oliver smiled and waved his note in the air, as an offer to let him read it.

"Well Oliver, just don't tell anyone else about that note, because as you can tell the bunk will not let you live that down. Mickey Hardon, the one who tore down that cubby," he said nodding toward Harris, " is just a maladjusted asshole. Never trust someone who prefers to wear a crew cut. Oh,.. and Oliver, definitely don't let the counselors see that note. They're all sarcastic sadists, and they'll use that note to rip you apart all summer,"

Jericho paused and looked me up and down.

"Jason," I was able to mutter. I shook his hand, but found myself in a stupefied awe upon meeting Jericho.

"So you're probably wondering about the names of our bunk-mates. Well, they like being called the Jewish Mafia... they've been summer friends for years."

Jericho tapped me on the shoulder and motioned for me to follow him down the center aisle of the bunk. He stopped at the cubicles next to the backroom.

"That thin-looking kid with the big head... the one who looks like a walking and talking penis is the leader of the group. His real name is Benjy Goodman, but he likes to be known as Mickey Cohen. So people call him Mickey, but because he's such a prick the counselors added Hardon as part of his name... You can call him either Mickey or Hardon, or Mickey Hardon, but nobody ever calls him Benjy. He's also a big pussy at heart."

"How do you know that?"

"I just know it. So Mickey Hardon had his Bar Mitzvah this year... we all had our Bar Mitzvha's this spring... and you know who he had at his Bar Mitzvah? A couple of New York Knicks!"

"Wow.... that's so cool," Harris cooed.

Then Jericho pointed to the bed against the wall, the other bed in the cubicle shared with Mickey Hardon.

"That tall goofy nerdy-looking kid with the Brillo hair? He's the brains behind the Jewish Mafia. He's the judge, lawyer... whatever you want to say. But he's just like his dad who's some big time lawyer in the city.. His real name is Stevie Rothstein, so he's named after Arnold "The Brain" Rothstein..... He wants to be called The Brain but the counselors all call him Felix, after Felix the Cat. You know, the cartoon character whose eyes are always rolling around in his head. That's Stevie Rothstein to a T..... his mind is always running in circles... so sometimes he's called the Brain and sometimes he's called Felix. And he's a big pussy."

"And who did he have at his Bar Mitzvah?" Oliver asked.

"Playboy Bunnies!"

"Get the fuck out of here... how did he get them?" I was the one amazed at this information.

"Told you.. .his dad is one of the top lawyers in the city, and he knows Hugh Hefner!"

"What about the others?" Harris had finished picking all his clothing off the floor and joined us.

" I think the two of you already met Mandelbaum on the ride up. Well, Mandelbaum is Meyer Lansky, but the counselors just call him The Mayor."

Jericho pointed at Mandelbaum's bed. He slept next to Mickey Hardon, but in the next cubicle.

"The other chunky goon in the bunk is Stuart Greenberg, but affectionally known as Hooky."

"Hooky... what's a Hooky?" asked Oliver.

"Hooky was Meyer Lansky's right hand man. Hooky and The Mayor are like two mountain rams. Stubborn as all hell, and angry. They're always charging into each other, always butting heads. I'm waiting for one of them to knock the other out. They're perfect for each other. Hooky and the Mayor. And they're both Pussies."

Harris snorted. "Sounds like a T.V. show."

"It is.. the two of them could be a major comedy show if they weren't pathological."

"And who did they have at their bar mitzvahs?"

"Nobody special. A couple of Mets, a couple of Yankees."

"The Yankees suck," I said, trying not to be jealous.

"Yeah, for once the Mets are better," Jericho said.

Jericho then walked over to the bed against the wall, the one next to Hooky's bed. He pointed at the neatly folded clothing.

"See anything strange?" he asked.

"It's neat. Almost perfect," I told him.

"This is the bed and cubby of a little weasel. See any T shirts, outside of the Camp Tonkawa T shirts? All Izod shirts. This little puke is preppie all the way. Goes to Horace Mann."

I shrugged my shoulders, acknowledging that I had no idea what he was talking about.

"Horace Mann is a top Prep School in the city. The kid's dad has more money than God. He's spoiled beyond belief. Dresses too clean and sterile for me. You know, chinos at the socials. I don't think he owns a pair of bell bottoms or jeans."

"I don't own a pair."

Jericho stepped back and looked me up and down.

"I do admire your balls in wearing that outfit. You're making quite a statement with purple and orange. But you want to know something.... I'll make a hippie out of you yet," Jericho told me.

"What if..."

"Oh, you need to ... trust me. Now, this preppie kid's father is the CEO of some major corporation. Big bucks! Wealthy beyond belief. His father comes up to visiting day in a helicopter. He dresses sharp and thinks he's hot shit but he's really cold diarrhea. They call him Bugsy... after..."

"Bugsy Siegel," Oliver chimed in. He had neatly stacked his clothing.

"So Bugsy is a liar.. he always makes up stories... especially when things get tough...when a counselor is about to pick on him... he starts crying and makes up a story. So like last year, when one of those asshole counselors I was telling you about was coming down on him hard, he started crying... He told us that his mother lost both her eyes... not that she went blind, but she lost both her eyes."

"Out of her head? Off of her face?" Harris was in shock.

"Yes... that's what he told us. And he cried all night.. Then the next day was visiting day and there was his mother with the nicest green eyes you've ever seen."

"And who did he have at his Bar Mitzvah?" I asked.

"A movie star," and then Jericho whispered her name.

"That's unbelievable," Oliver squealed.

"Who is she?" Harris asked.

"She's going to be so big! She was just in a movie! What's the matter with all of you?"

"Bugsy's dad pay for that?" I asked.

"No..get this.. His mother, the one with the cat green eyes... she was this stars neighbor growing up in Brooklyn. Sometimes this 'star' would babysit for Bugsy's aunt, so she was invited, and she sang a tune or two," Jericho told us.

"But you said Bugsy always lies. Maybe he was lying about this too?"

"Nope... I was there... the obligatory having to invite all your bunkmates to the bar mitzvah routine. I didn't want to go... but I was forced to by my mom. And I had to invite them to my bar mitzvah. "

"I haven't had mine yet. It's at the end of the year, and we're not doing anything big at all," I said.

"I didn't have a big one either," Jericho answered.

"So, our bunk... all they are just a big bunch of pussies?"

" Yup... biggest bunch of pussies you'll ever see."

Jericho pointed to two other beds.

"So that's the bunk...except the two quiet kids who just tag along...Cahn,...who has a nice left hand jump shot...plays tennis left handed.. hits and throws left handed..."

"Why isn't his nickname Leftie?" I asked.

"Because he's not a part of the Jewish Mafia.. he's just a good kid who hangs close to his friend from home."

"And who's that?"

"The kid sleeping in the same alcove as Harris."

"I didn't even notice a kid next to me," Harris told us.

"The kid next to you is Cahn's friend. His name is Beckett

Studberg. He's another nice kid who just minds his own business, except..."

Jericho paused, and looked around to make sure nobody was eavesdropping.

"What? He has some sort of disease?"

"No... he just imitates Marv Albert every second of the day. It's going to drive you crazy."

"What do you mean?"

"He'll be like Marv Albert... you know.. calling the game! He'll sit on the bench when he's not playing and pretend that he's talking into a microphone. He has it down pretty good....

'Jason passes it off to Jericho in the corner, who takes one dribble to his left, and lets fly a rainbow of a shot.. and YES!!!'... and that's Beckett's Marv Albert imitation"

"So maybe he wants to go into T.V. or radio when he gets older?"

"By the middle of the summer he's calling everything. I mean... you'll be walking down the center of the bunk to take a shit and Beckett will start in again and you'll hear...**'Jericho is striding boldly toward the back room. He's looking for the back door pass.. or is he just looking to take a dump?'"**

"You have to stop him," I said, starting to laugh.

"Then he'll describe every move at breakfast, lunch, and dinner. 'And Hooky has dribbled ketchup down his chin and onto his shirt... a double dribble."

"And what about you? How come they seem to ignore you?" I asked.

"I'm not a Pussy."

"Meaning?"

Jericho sighed, and fingered the peace symbol that hung around his neck. Then he flashed us the V sign with his fingers.

"Peace, love and understanding, man... that's what I believe in. Peace.... but there's one time last summer when I couldn't take it anymore. Summer of '68, last summer. I started wearing my hair a bit longer... and started doing other things. Mickey

Hardon was on my case about everything. Our counselor didn't care. He looked the other way. After visiting day he started talking shit about my parents and my older brother. Started talking about my girlfriend up here…. and then I snapped. Before I knew it I was jumping from one bed to another, finally flinging myself through the air…" he paused and smiled as the memory poured forth.

"And what happened?" Harris asked, his mouth dropping open in wonder.

"I was actually flying. I flew through the air, tackled Hardon, and pummeled him badly. He never cried. Maybe he would have, if the counselor didn't finally pull me off. Whatever, .. He was bloodied. Like I said I don't believe in violence anymore, but everyone has a breaking point."

"And you lost it," Harris said

"Look, they're all bullies, and bullies are just pussies who are scared. All you have to do is slap a pussy in the face and he'll back down. Maybe even cry. Sometimes you just have to stand up for yourself. Hardon never approached me again."

"And since everyone else in the bunk is a pussy, nobody in the bunk touches you?" I asked.

"Exactly."

I couldn't say it. I wanted to, but I didn't want to sound like a geek right off the bat. Jericho had long wavy brown hair that reached the back of his neck. He was always brushing his hair back over his ears as he talked. He had the sharpest blue eyes I had ever seen, and the hint of a cheesy white peach fuzz mustache. And damn him.. I hated him because he had one of those young teenage athletic bodies with a thin waist, and muscular hairless chest. The "peace" symbol that hung around his neck on a long piece of leather just made him God-like.

"My brother gave me this before they shipped him over to 'Nam'. I didn't want to come back to this place, but my parents wanted me out of the house so I couldn't hear any news about the war...like it matters. My brother writes me every day. And my summer girlfriend begged me to come back, so I did," he said smiling.

"You have a summer and a winter girlfriend?" Harris couldn't believe what he was hearing.

"Well, yeah... my winter girlfriend isn't Jewish so she'd never come here. Not that I didn't ask her to, but it's a different mentality. Jewish parents understand sleepaway camp where others may not. She also happens to be in the same grade as me and the same school... so much easier. Beth is my summer girlfriend, and I'll see her a few times during the year. I really like her though. I'm thinking of dumping my home girlfriend."

Definitely the coolest kid. Great smile, two girlfriends, and an older brother he could share life with. There was a Kennedy charisma that seemed to flow on ethereal waves, and it made me succumb to his charm.

Jericho proceeded to help Oliver finish putting away his clothing, and then he turned to help me. Jericho dragged my trunk across the floor, and after I opened the lock, he began to hand me my clothing. Everything was so efficient. I was done in a matter of minutes.

Jericho Baker shook my hand, and then went over to help Harris finish with his cubby. I had never felt the need for a friend, nor desire for someone to befriend me.... until this moment.

7

had to now worry about the Jewish Mafia. I never knew Jews had a Mafia that they were proud of. I guess it was the need to feel tough in a world that didn't expect Jews to be gangsters. I would have to look these characters up when I got home from the summer.

The five members had all started in bunk three at the age of six. It was the summer of 1962. Since that summer they returned like flocks of birds in the spring. Each year a handful of new campers would enter the bunk, be tormented, and never return for the next summer. Then Jericho joined the bunk in 1967 and they quickly found out they couldn't break him.

After I had carried my trunk out onto the lawn, the Jewish Mafia returned . Seems Ed Barnett caught them on the basketball courts and told them to return to their bunk.

Mickey Hardon was a motor-mouth of energy. He never stopped talking. Always moving, always flailing his arms as he spoke. He would spit as he unleashed a tirade of nastiness. From the beginning he cursed Stocum up and down, and then he gave the counselor the finger, but this only after Stocum turned his back to Mickey.

I tried not to laugh every time I looked at him. It was true! Mickey Hardon's head was shaped like a penis. His neck was thin, and it led to his bulbous head. Then there was the bald line down the middle of his head. His extreme crew cut highlighted that bald line. His head did look like a penis!

Mickey Hardon's lore was his dancing spit. He could hack up a wad of spit, and let it slowly drip toward the floor, and when this spider strong web of saliva was about to touch the ground he would suck it back up into his mouth. He told the bunk that he perfected the dancing spit so he could capture a fly, just like a lizard's tongue.

Hardon always had a basketball in his hand, and this sport was his passion. He bragged of his prowess, and was constantly reaching for the ball and bouncing it in the bunk.

The Brain was always lying on his bed reading his Richie Rich, and Archie comic books. Jericho was right, because The Brain's eyes were always moving. They were shifty eyes, always peeking over what he was reading. He always flashed a huge sly smile, just to throw you off kilter... like he was letting you know he was plotting something against you.

The counselors were correct in saying that he looked like Felix the Cat, except for the hair. It seems every summer he comes up with some "magic bag" that he's constantly pulling shit out of. Little things, like Chinese Handcuffs, or plastic bladders that you would blow up and then sit on to make a fart sound. Nobody ever knows how he keeps that bag stocked.

The Brain was the tallest kid in the bunk, but he was harmless. I could tell immediately that he had no athletic skills, and yet the Jewish Mafia seemed to revere him. I knew he was a deeper thinker than he let on. I happened to have spied a couple of paperbacks lying under the stack of comics on his bed. Kafka. He was reading Kafka for freaking sake.

When I returned to my bed, Jericho sat down next to me with a deck of cards and started to deal a game of poker.

"I don't feel like playing poker."

"Good... then I won't have to worry about you, because that's the favorite game of the Jewish Mafia."

"I love poker," Harris added as he sat down on Oliver's bed without asking Oliver's permission. Oliver looked a bit pissed off, but he moved over anyway.

"Now don't get caught in a game with them," Jericho warned. "They'll cheat and demand their money that you lost to them."

"Money? Who has money?" Harris asked.

"Canteen money, silly. They bet their canteen money, and they pay up once a week when we get our canteen books for purchasing candy."

So basically this ritual of card playing was the same at every camp I've been to. "What else should we look out for?" Oliver asked as Jericho started to shuffle the cards.

"One more thing... very important."

"What?"

"Whatever you do, don't use the sugar on our table when you get to the Mess Hall."

"And why not?"

"Hooky likes to take live flies that are trapped on the fly paper and pull their wings off. Then he dumps them into the sugar containers on our table. They look like little raisins at first."

"Lovely," Oliver moaned.

When the record player at the HCO blew the bugle call for assembly, we gathered outside our bunks and waited to be called down to the Mess Hall for lunch. Chick stood in front of us with the counselors in our group standing behind him. Stocum stood off to the side, an outsider to the nth degree. So were two other counselors who were new to the camp. They looked like nice guys, football players from Hamilton College, but they just didn't fit in.

The other counselors in the group were their own little cabal, having grown up through the ranks. They were campers, then waiters, and now counselors.

All the counselors were dressed in different fashions, almost like Brooklyn with its numerous and colorful neighborhoods. The football players wore cut off jean shorts and t shirts that were ripped in half, exposing their muscular bellies which fell under the shadow of their massive chests. The basketball players were dressed in tank tops and skimpy basketball shorts. The basketball shorts didn't have pockets so those counselors all had their hands buried down the front of their shorts. They looked like they were feeling their balls all day long. One counselor was wearing shorts with an elastic band that was stretched to the limits. He wasn't obese.... just a tad flabby... a bit overweight... oh hell... his flab would wiggle if he ran or laughed. You could just tell. To top off the uniform was the necklace which was adorned around every counselors' neck. The one with a whistle that was looped around a lanyard or sneaker lace.

"You want to see what douche bags are? We have a douche bag extravaganza for counselors this year," Jericho said without looking toward Chick.

"How so?"

"Those two shmucks near Chick are nasty narcissistic assholes. The one with the perfect nose, the perfect body, the chiseled face, is Asa Rosen. Obvious nose job, blond hair, six pack abs—fucking guy is in love with himself. He thinks he's a god because he's a basketball junkie. When he jumps he can touch the top of the backboard but only when he has a running start. Not bad for someone under six feet tall. I mean he thinks all the girls love him... with his blond hair and thin body... but that nose.. it's perfect,"

If this Asa was perfect then how did Jericho see himself? He was pretty near perfect to me. Do those blessed with good looks never worry about their appearance. Their only worry is that someone will eclipse their beautiful image ? Meanwhile the rest of us poor souls always pine for a moment of recognition that we may also possess a touch of beauty, be it inward or physical? What was it like to never worry about how you look because naturally you're what every girl is looking for? Jericho didn't realize how lucky he was.

"So stay away from Asa?" I asked.

"Yeah, ignore him and his college roommate, the guy who is standing next to him. That's Samson Goldberg. He's about 6'5" and plays on the same college team. Premature baldness, but never mention his hair. He's sensitive about that. Asa is the guard, Samson the forward. Whatever you do, don't call him Sammy. He'll beat the shit out of you. They love to just torture you all day long."

Jericho then pointed to the chunky counselor behind Chick.

"The chubby one, the one with the cheesy mustache. That's Lenny Lipschitz. He never likes taking his shirt off because he's flabby and you can see stretch marks, and he can't stop sweating. When he runs it's like a balloon bouncing away, lopping from one foot to the other in slow motion.... almost like he's floating on air. Look at him, the fog condensing on his horn-rimmed glasses, beads of sweat pouring down his forehead. Constantly bites the back of his hand. When he gets close, look at the back of his hands. Check out how raw they are. He's a mess. Yet he's the one who dishes out all the degrading and disgusting nicknames that kids have. He shouldn't have the right to make fun of anyone."

"They do sound like douche bags," I said. This brought a smirk to Jericho.

"And that thin counselor next to Lenny is Spanky," Jericho continued.

"Named after the Lil Rascals character?"

"Nah, they caught him jerking off as a camper. You know, he was spanking the monkey... so they called him Spanky and it's stayed with him ever since."

"So all I need to remember is that our counselors are all douche bags?" I asked.

"Well, those two football players look like nice guys, and Spanky isn't that bad, but the rest are douche bags."

"What's a douche bag?" I asked.

The call for lunch sounded and our group walked in single file across the campus. Jericho explained what a douche bag was before we hit the Mess Hall. We were the Sub Senior group, and most of us were thirteen years old. The next oldest group, the Senior boys, fourteen and fifteen years of age, followed us in. They were allowed to walk en masse.

"So, if you're fourteen you're mature enough to walk as a group and not in single file?" I asked Jericho.

"Yes. It sucks. It's funny how fourteen is the maturity line at this camp."

"Listen, this is the first camp I've ever been to that's not a uniform camp."

"What's a uniform camp?" Jericho asked.

"Where they tell you what to wear every day. Reveille blows and they announce if you're going to wear blue or white, or whatever the camps colors are. "Good morning Camp Kee Wah, you will wear blue shorts and your blue Camp Kee Wah shirt today."

"I don't think I could make it past one day in that type of camp," Jericho said, as he tried to shake that thought out of his mind.

When the entire boys' side had entered the Mess Hall, a camper recited the blessing over the bread in Hebrew. Everyone covered their heads with a hand, a make shift Yarmulka. The only ones not covering their heads were the counselors who weren't Jewish, like Stocum and the football players.

The Jewish Mafia had rushed to our assigned table the second they broke through the Mess Hall doors. I found myself sitting near the head of the table next to Stocum. Harris was across from me with a huge smile across his face.

"What are you grinning at? " I asked him.

"We're at the head of the table. We'll get the food first," he said.

"Yes, but you don't understand 'The Rules of the Summer'. Every camp, same rules. You don't change the seats you are sitting in from the first day on. So we're at the head of the table and what that means is that we stack!"

"Stack? What does that mean?" Harris asked.

I saw Oliver was waiting for an answer. He was sitting next to me, and I could sense his fear creeping toward me.

"Stack... meaning that when everyone's done they just pass their plates up to the front, and you and I scrape the uneaten food into the plastic bins that are at the foot of the table. Then we stack the dirty dishes and cups so the waiter can take them into the kitchen."

"That's not fair!" Harris said.

"I'm not allowed to touch those dirty dishes," Oliver announced. And that was the fear I sensed wafting through Oliver.

"Do you have a note for that too?" asked Jericho who was sitting next to me.

"As a matter of fact I do," Oliver said, and he was about to take out his note, when the waiters, all dressed in khaki pants and a white t shirt, started marching down the aisles of the boys' side.

Hamburgers and French Fries on the first day of camp. One always eats well on the first day of camp so we have something nice to write home about.

"Here are your dump trucks!" The waiter shouted as he tossed the square metal bowl onto the table. French Fries flew all over the table, and the Jewish Mafia scrambled to fill their plates with as many as they could grab. The Brain threw the metal bowl back to the waiter who ran back into the kitchen for seconds.

"Why do they call French fries 'dump trucks'? I asked.

"Because they arrive in those little square metal containers that look like dump trucks. Then they 'dump' the fries on the table so they can run back into the kitchen to get seconds. The food's not that bad here, but sometimes you have to watch out for some meals." Jericho said. You knew he was relishing the role of being our mentor.

"Like what?"

"Elephant balls."

"What are elephant balls?" Harris asked.

"They're not hamburgers, and not meatloaf. Just huge balls of meat that look like a bear's turd, or an elephant's balls. Eat one and you'll be constipated for a week. Also don't eat the beets, they'll stain your teeth. And every Friday night we have greasy chicken. You'll never eat it after you see it swimming in all the grease."

In the meantime Stocum was holding the platter of burgers, and helping himself to four shiny patties. He then tried to hand the platter to Harris when suddenly The Mayor leapt from his seat and intercepted the handoff. It caused a complete fumble. He giggled as he took one burger and then passed it off to the rest of Jewish Mafia. By the time the tray made its way back up to the front of the table there were no more burgers left. Oliver and Harris were stunned but I was angry.

"This is fucked up," I cursed. I was looking at four blank plates while the rest of the bunk enjoyed their meal.

"We didn't get any!" Oliver whined.

"Is this part of the rules of the summer?" Harris asked. "We don't get to eat?"

"Usually, the counselor doesn't take first" Jericho screamed, as he stared at Stocum whose only concern was to continue to munch away on his hamburger.

"Well, this sucks!" Harris shouted, looking down at the far end of the table only to find The Brain smiling back at him and giving him the middle finger.

Suddenly a hush fell over boys side. Most of the counselors and some of the older campers turned their attention to the other end of the Mess Hall. Girls camp began to file in, and where the girls were busy gabbing with one another, the boys couldn't take their eyes off the parade.

"See any new fresh meat?" Asa asked Samson.

"Not yet.. got to wait till tonight," Samson answered.

"What assholes." Jericho whispered.

"Why do the girls come in after we do?" I asked.

"So there's no mass hysteria in the kitchen. Everything is cooked and served in a precise, orderly manner and the waiters aren't charging into each other in the kitchen." Jericho told me.

The counselors and Jericho in particular were craning their necks looking at the girls walking in.

"I just saw my girlfriend walk in. Haven't seen her in two months. Like I said we get together a couple of times during the year. She lives in Westchester and I'm on Long Island."

"I'm in Westchester too," I told him. Why was I feeling excited about this fact? I never get excited about anything. "I live in Scarsdale."

"North of there. She lives in Katonah. I mean it's not far, and as my dad always says, it's only one bridge to cross."

I was going to ask him what he meant, but our waiter was

chugging down the aisle with a new stack of burgers and fries. This time Stocum took three more burgers and before the Mayor could steal the tray I grabbed it and dished out food for those of us who missed out on the first helping. Maybe it was time I needed to assert myself because if I didn't, I would probably be hungry all summer.

8

I feared the first night.

It was always the first night at camp that would dictate the personality of the summer. The rest of the afternoon and early evening went according to the summer camp playbook. We had to write letters home to our parents after lunch during a period of time known as Rest Hour. We had to tell them how great the trip up was, how wonderful lunch was, and how beautiful camp is. Then we played some ball in the afternoon.

We would be broken up into teams for daily competitive activity, but for now we would play bunk versus bunk. It was our equivalent of the New York Mets spring training camp. I knew I was being observed by both the counselors and my peers, just as any rookie would be scrutinized.

As I planned…. and as I had done in other camps that weren't uniform camps, the first impression I made was in what I wore in that initial game of softball. Still in my light lime green shorts with an orange t shirt, I now donned a purple baseball cap. I was ready to play. If I didn't stand out now, then the camp had to be color blind.

Mickey Hardon was the appointed captain of the team and during our softball game he stationed me in right field. Me? Right field? Hardon placed himself at shortstop, and the Mayor was our first baseman. Bugsy was our pitcher. Jericho was stationed out in left, looking as cool as ever in his blue tinted sunglasses. They were small square frames that fit perfectly on his face and the sun seemed to highlight his blond hair. He stood defiantly in left, arms crossed. He was either bored or playing possum. Maybe he was hoping that someone would mistake his nonchalant attitude for laziness, only to pounce on any fly ball hit to him... just too cool.

The rest of the bunk displayed such inadequacies as athletes that I stood in right field totally mortified. Mickey Hardon put me in right field just to humiliate me. I pretended not to care, so I stood silent as a monument to this travesty. My hands crossed over my knees and my glove hung limply in my left hand. Only one ball was hit toward me and I made a running catch look routine. The rest of the game saw the infield commit error after error.

However, my position in right field allowed me to survey the camp from a different vantage point. Right behind the softball field were the boys' tennis courts. Another ball field lay just beyond the reaches of the softball field that we were playing on. This field had ninety foot basepaths, perfect for baseball. Laying at the edge of both outfields was the gravel pit where the counselors parked their cars.

Every inch of grass was manicured, cut to perfection. The dirt roads were raked clean and lined with wooden barrels that were graced with flowers of exotic colors. Not a branch on a pine tree was out of place.

And under these pines sitting on a bench was Oliver, who spent the entire moments after rest hour lathering his body with sun tan lotion. He seemed to enjoy watching since he wasn't able to participate. This was going to be the case for any other strenuous activities.

"Hey Oliver, why so much lotion? You look like a fat cock covered with sperm,"

Lenny shouted from his position as the umpire behind home plate. He barely moved when making calls as he leaned against the backstop as a crutch.

"Look at Sperm... he looks like someone just shot his wad all over his body.... Hey Sperm, what's with all the sun tan lotion?" Lenny continued.

It was now a taunt, and I knew the bullying repertoire would soon ensue. I stood idly by, just wanting to resume the softball game.

Oliver's nickname for the summer was born. Lenny was so

proud of himself, that he couldn't stop calling Oliver "Sperm."

"My mother warned me that my skin was very fair..." Oliver started to say.

"Did you say fairy? Are you a fairy?" asked Lenny.

"My skin is fair, and I get burned easily, and my mother wants to make sure I don't get skin cancer," Oliver said defiantly.

"That's bullshit," Lenny taunted him. "How can the sun harm you?"

"She says it can cause melanomas. So I have always been careful in the sun."

"Well, you look like sperm," Lenny mocked as he strutted in front of the backstop, proud of his creative stroke of genius.

"Well, at least I don't look like a Sperm Whale," Oliver shouted.

Everyone, and I mean everyone stopped talking. We were stunned into silence and we waited for the reaction. Suddenly Jericho started applauding. Slow, loud and thunderous claps. I followed suit. The two of us, applauding Oliver's brilliant retort.

Lenny didn't hesitate. He took the softball and threw it as hard as he could, just missing Oliver's head. Oliver didn't even have time to flinch. The ball ricocheted off the pine trees. It looked like a pinball machine except the trees weren't lighting up and instead of pings there were only dull thuds.

"Just watch yourself, Sperm," Lenny threatened.

Oliver sat quietly on the bench, safely under the shade of the pine trees. His skin was still a sticky white. The Jewish Mafia began calling him Sperm. . It was strange though, because it sort of fit.

"Hey Sperm, why are you in the shade?" Hardon screamed.

"What's the matter, Sperm? Don't want to play?" Lenny asked.

"He can't, he's got a note from mommy!" Hardon shouted.

There was an eruption of laughter that finally forced Oliver off the bench. He positioned himself against a pine tree, with his back to the game. I'm sure he was crying. Oliver would be the only kid to use sunscreen all summer. Nobody else wore any protection. Nobody ever thought we had to.

On this day I thought I taught that little shit Mickey Hardon a lesson. To further humiliate me, he batted me last in the order, right behind Harris. Our bunk had only two hits the entire day. Jericho had lined a single into left field for the first hit. I then proceeded to stroke the second hit of the game for our bunk. To be more exact it was a home run. I hit it so far past the leftfielder that it rolled past the mound of the adjacent baseball field.

We lost the game 14-2.

"What kind of fucking outfit are you wearing?" Hardon spit out. I knew he was livid at my home run. "You look like a clown."

"At least I don't play like one."

Mickey Hardon threw his glove at my feet, hoping to make me trip. It didn't work.

"I told you that you look ridiculous," Jericho whispered as we walked back to the bunk after the game.

'Yeah, well... this way the counselors will remember me."

"Trust me... they're never going to forget you now."

An afternoon swim continued my humiliation. My friendship with Jericho was solidified when he asked me to be his swim buddy. However, when swimming in the deep end, you had to swim with a buddy. Before entering the water you had to take numbered tags from one pegboard under the pavilion, and hang them from a pegboard on the dock in the deep end. That was the number you were assigned for the swim.

Once in the water, when the whistle was blown, all talking ceased. If you weren't on one of the two outer rafts that floated about 25 yards out from the dock you had to tread water, while counting down, starting from ONE. Only duets sang out. If only one voice was heard all hell broke loose.

After the swim period ended we had to return our tags to the pegboard under the pavilion and if a tag wasn't returned a major search ensued.

Alas, I was forced to decline the buddy request because I had not yet taken the deep water test. I was relegated to the crib, the shallow area that was surrounded by the dock. Here the water was at best three feet deep, and you could feel the mud squish between your toes as you waded in.

Harris was my buddy, and we stood around like morons unable to enjoy an afternoon swim in a refreshing lake. Half of the camp was at the waterfront, and the crib area was tiny and crowded. Younger campers who didn't know how to swim were relegated to the crib. New campers like yours truly who had not taken the deep water test were not allowed out of the crib. We would have to wait a day or two to take that test.

I hated the crib area. We didn't swim. We just stood around like morons while younger, idiot campers, splashed around us like hooked fish that were fighting for their lives.

"Have you noticed that there are warm spots all around us?" Harris asked as he stood next to me.

"Oh God…"

"What?"

"I've got to get out of this crib area," I told him, as I started to swim toward the ladder.

"Where are you going?" Harris asked, as he started to follow me.

"The counselors will tell you that the warm spots are where the fish are peeing, but there are no fish in the crib… all the little kids are peeing in the lake."

Harris beat me to the ladder and climbed onto the dock. I didn't know he could swim that fast.

Dinner found the evening tray of chicken hijacked once again, and Stocum remained silent. The frustration building in Harris surprised me. In a sense I admired his indignation, but wondered what he was going to do to fight this. I just rode with the flow.

After dinner there was forty-five minute period of freedom called Free Play. Most of the bunk headed to the basketball court. Jericho disappeared around the side of the bunk and headed into the woods behind us. I sat on the boot box with Harris and Oliver, each of us with our reading material. I sat back and started "One Flew Over the Cuckoo's Nest" and Harris started to peruse his way through a pile of Batman and Superman comic books. I looked at Oliver, whose nose was deep into the pages of a UFO magazine. A couple of books on UFOs and Extraterrestrials sat on the floor between his feet.

"You don't believe in all that?" I asked.

"I don't know yet. I'm hoping there is life on another planet."

"Why? You planning to visit it?" I snorted.

"Look at me. I can barely breathe. I'm weak. I can't exercise, and sometimes life is just not fun. At least the belief in UFOs gives me some hope that there's a better world beyond earth."

"What? You're talking about heaven?" Harris said, putting down his comic book. He stared at Oliver.

"Life on another planet. Just a dream that they'll come down, take me away to another planet where I don't have to worry about my health. Maybe they'd have some machine that would cure all my ills, or just take me out of this body and replace it with a healthy one. I can always dream."

There was no evening activity, so they allowed Free Play to last a bit longer. Counselors manned every inch of the camp, but for an hour there were no official activities. Counselors were to keep the peace and prevent injuries. That was the extent of the supervision.

Campers ran off to play tennis, basketball, and some bunks even had four or five steps leading to the porch which made them conducive for legendary stoop ball games. The 'Great Lawn' was dotted with counselors having frisbee and softball catches with their campers.

Then there were the few of us who just sat on the boot boxes and read. I did get up for a little while and I took a long walk down along the lake.

The road led me to the Mess Hall and up the main road of camp, where I stood mesmerized on the outer boundry of the girls campus, looking in from the outside. Girls side seemed content on staying inside their bunks while boys side resembeled a free-for-all. You could hear the giddiness on boys side, probably from the realization that we no longer had to abide by true parental rule. Recall was finally blown at 8:30, and everyone staggered back to their bunks.

And then the first night came upon us.

Stocum watched us undress as we had to get into our pajamas. That was our evening uniform, pajamas instead of underwear and a t shirt. These were the rules set forth by Joe Geisinger. If Chick came in and saw we weren't in pajamas he would wake us and force us to don the PJ's.

Taps sounded and Stocum turned off the lights to the bunk and headed up to the Social Hall for a counselors meeting. The Head Counselors would discuss the 'Rules of the Summer', and how they expected the staff to behave. I bet bullying was never discussed. It never was. Maybe they were warned to never lay a hand on a camper, but I bet nobody ever discussed that verbal bullying was as damaging as physical abuse. Sadly, counselors were never trained to detect the signs of bullying amongst bunkmates. What would they think if someone brought up what Lenny did to Oliver earlier in the day?

Our OD (On Duty) coverage that night was Chick. The old man would have to cover four bunks. An O.D. was basically a glorified baby sitter. I knew the night wasn't going to end well.

At first everything was peaceful. Hardon, The Brain, the Mayor and Bugsy were busy playing poker on The Brain's bed. Jericho had already fallen asleep. He was curiously mellow after Free Play, barely saying anything to me. He had a soft smile and just went about his business without anyone bothering him.

I found myself reading along with Harris and Oliver, but this time by flashlight. There was a feeling of solitude under the double decker, as if I was removed from the bunk. I felt like I was in a cocoon, but of course this was without a counselor sleeping above me. There was very little air circulation in my corner. I could sense the staleness, and the evening hadn't cooled off the humidity in the bunk so there was still a musty taste in the air. Oliver couldn't have survived in this bed.

I knew from previous summers that it was imperative to stay awake, or at least to stay awake longer than the clowns in the corner. I didn't say anything to Oliver when he turned off his flashlight and buried himself under his blankets and I didn't warn Harris when he turned in. I should have, but decided to remain silent.

I kept dozing off, feeling my head drop to my chest, and each time suddenly waking in fear. I don't know how much time had passed since Harris fell asleep, but I could tell something was going down by the whispering that emanated from the back corner of the bunk.

With a stealth rarely seen amongst thirteen-year-old boys, the Jewish Mafia moved toward Harris. The Mayor had gone into the back room and emerged with a cup. It was the warm water trick. Not that I've ever seen this work, but it was always attempted. Bugsy positioned himself at the foot of my bed, serving as a lookout to make sure Chick wasn't going to walk into the bunk. I stared at him, not sure what I would do if the bunk turned on me. I was hoping that my angry look threatened them.

Harris had fallen asleep with one hand hanging limply outside his blankets. The Brain softly took Harris' hand and positioned his fingers into the cup of warm water. The Mayor held the cup steady. This was supposed to make him pee in his bed. They stood around giggling, but it was obvious that nothing was happening.

The Mayor finally put the cup down. He and Hooky then positioned themselves at the head of the bed. Hardon took his flashlight and jumped on top of Harris. Shining the flashlight into Harris' eyes he started screaming "TRUCK."

Harris shot up in fear. The Mayor and Hooky grabbed his arms and forced him back down on the bed. He was pinned. Bugsy kept looking at me, to see if I was going to come to Harris' aid, but I just kept reading.

Mickey Hardon now straddled Harris, sitting on his chest. Harris kept crying that he couldn't breathe, but Hardon kept laughing, and then he did his dancing spit.

A wad, thick and juicy crept from his mouth. It inched slowly down toward Harris who kept fighting valiantly but to no avail. The Mayor pinched Harris's nostrils closed and Harris could barely breathe. He opened his mouth which allowed Pinhead to drop his dancing spit squarely down the dwarf's mouth, sucking it back up before Harris started to gag.

The Brain, who was standing silently behind everyone, then approached. Harris was still gagging and didn't notice the Brain coming in for the kill. The Brain pulled something from behind his back. It was a swath of flypaper. It looked more like a strip of Candy Buttons, but that wasn't candy on the paper. I could make out about fifteen flies. Most were dead, but I could see that some were still alive. Mickey Hardon assisted in keeping Harris' head pinned while The Brain proceeded to wrap the flypaper around the poor kid's mouth.

Oliver heard everything. He had his pillow over his head and was crying into it, trying to muffle the sound. The rest of the bunk was asleep except for...

"Yesssss... and The Brain has just beaten his record from last summer and applied the fly paper in record time," Beckett whispered into a fake microphone.

And I was ashamed. I was angry at myself, that I wasn't coming to his aid, but I just didn't want to take on the entire bunk. This was not my battle. I was motionless, squeezing the life out of the book in my hand. I kept staring at Bugsy, hoping my glare was a warning to stay away. Bugsy ignored me, and kept looking out the bunk,.

I just never could understand why there was so much hatred and anger in boys, why they received enjoyment out of torturing others. It was no different than at any other camp I ever attended. There was always that posse that picked on the weak, the defenseless. They enjoyed it, reveled in the agony of others, and I'm sure they would laugh about it for years to come as if it were a sport.

"Chick, " Bugsy whispered loudly.

The bunk jumped off Harris and scrambled back into their beds, pretending to be asleep. Harris catapulted out of his bed and made a mad dash into the back room. He untangled the flypaper that was twisted around his face. You could hear strands of hair being ripped from the back of his scalp as the flypaper fell to the floor. He flew into one of the stalls, puking his guts out.

Chick walked into the bunk. He heard Harris in the backroom, but to his eyes, everyone seemed to be asleep. He looked over at me and said, "Put that flashlight out and go to sleep now." I did as I was asked.

Harris staggered out of the backroom crying, and wiping the puke from his mouth.

"Hey, what are you doing out of bed?" Chick asked in his nasal whine.

"They... they...put flypaper around ... " Harris kept trying to say between sobs that were so painful to hear that I buried my head under my pillow just like Oliver had done.

"Ehhhh.... stop your crying and grow up. Now get back into bed and we'll talk about it in the morning," Chick shouted. You could hear the rest of the bunk giggling into their pillows. "Now shut up and go to sleep. You had a long day."

Chick waited until Harris shuffled back into bed, still sobbing, and then he left.

I feared the first night. I was usually the brunt of the attack, but at this camp there were two other rookies who were my inferiors. Yet I was a kindred, tortured spirit with Harris. I never could understand what made people pick on others.

From under my pillow I could hear the whispered laughter and the sobbing, and I closed my eyes as hard as I could, hoping that everything would just go away. I wish I could say that I slept through the night. That was not going to happen. I stayed awake for as long as I could. I remember outlasting Mickey Hardon and Bugsy, but then I must have fallen asleep...... until.....

I heard the screen door squeal open.

There are night sounds in camp that crackle through the darkness. Sounds only heard when you're in a desolate area. The thick black of night split open by the hum of a car miles away, piercing the air on deserted roads. The hum dissolves into a rush, almost like a gust of wind, as the car approaches the road outside of camp. Just as quickly as the sound rushes forth, it slowly dissipates into the horizon. On certain nights this flow of sound is interrupted by squealing tires that are desperately attempting to grip the road as the brakes are applied. Often this is too late and it's followed by the explosion of a car meeting a deer.

The constant deep bellows of frogs communicating in the night often keeps me awake. I always wonder what they're saying to each other, and question when they sleep. Sometimes the croaking of frogs was welcomed as my mind would race back to the winters at home, where I would hear the sounds of my parents copulating. The moans would creep under my door as I lay in bed.

There is the silence of sleeping boys, except for the creak and yaw of bed springs with every twist and turn. Stocum had not returned yet, or at least he wasn't in bed. I knew this because there was no sag in the mattress. If Stocum was back it would look like a big pimple about ready to pop.

Then there is the eerie quiet of a bunk right before counselors sneak in during the night. At first I heard the screen door open, squeal and then gently shut, but then I saw the basketball sneakers and knew it wasn't Chick walking in. The pair of counselors walked down the center aisle and I could see it was Asa and Samson. Samson had a cigarette in his right hand, and it looked like a hot poker. Samson was making sure that no ash was flicked. Asa had a broom in his hands.

They stopped at Hardon's bed. Asa tied a gag around Hardon's mouth. Hardon suddenly shot up in bed. He tried to struggle, but Samson pushed him back down.

"This is your warning for the summer Hardon... We don't want any trouble from you... so we're just going to warm up here by playing some pool with your testicles," Asa whispered.

"You can either struggle or make it easy for us. All we want to do is shoot a little pool," Samson said.

Hardon quit struggling, and Asa pulled off the gag. Hardon was laughing. It sounded almost like he was going to enjoy this.

"Come on... I promise I won't fuck up this summer," Hardon squeaked out.

"Too late, Hardon. We need to shoot some pool so quit squirming." Asa commanded as he pulled off Hardon's pajama bottoms.

Asa clamped his hands on Hardon's legs and lifted the camper's torso into the air. Hardon's balls were dangling free from his body and Samson took aim. With the brush end of the broom against his chest Samson crooked his fingers around the stick and drew it back like a pool cue.

He took dead aim at the right testicle, and in a smooth professional motion slid the broom handle forward for a perfect strike on Hardon's right gonad. Mickey Hardon screamed and somewhat begged for forgiveness because I wasn't sure if he was laughing or crying.

"Left ball in the corner pocket," Samson whispered as he thrust the stick forward and struck the other marble.

Asa let go of Hardon's legs.

Hardon rolled around on his bed, moaning in pain.

"Don't fuck with us this summer, Hardon, or else we'll inflict more pain on you," Asa chuckled. Samson jabbed the lit end of the cigarette into Hardon's chest. Hardon screamed. The two counselors walked out of the bunk, and I can still swear that I heard Hardon laughing the night away.

9

Reveille in the morning.
You grow tired of all the bugle calls. You'd think we were in the Army. First Call, Activity Call, Recall, Mess Call, .. Tattoo (the five minute warning till lights out), and finally Taps.

But in the morning it's Reveille.

The sound of the HCO loudspeaker being turned on, the shuffling of feet, the screen door to the shack squealing open and slamming shut as someone else enters. Every noise amplified.

A fly buzzing around my head, waking me before I needed to be up. Then that insipid bugle call, and nobody but Harris and The Mayor moving out of bed. Harris made sure he was the first one up. He dressed, and quickly made his bed before anyone else even pulled back a blanket. He didn't want to see anyone. As Harris walked out onto the porch Chick entered and surveyed the scene. He quickly walked over to Hardon's bed, and lifted it off the ground. He let it fall with a thud that had everyone jumping up. How strong was this old man?

"What the fuck?" Hardon shouted.

"What are you all doing in bed?" Chick whined. "Reveille blew, get your asses out of bed. You got five minutes before first call for breakfast. If you didn't stay up all night fooling around you'd be out of bed. Now let's get moving. Don't let me catch you in bed when I come back. And make sure you make your beds before breakfast!"

"We don't want to get up," The Brain moaned from under his pillow.

Chick walked over to The Brains bed and lifted the bed to a 45

---

degree angle. Then he let it fall to the floor with such force that The Brain tumbled out of bed.

He then walked over to my double decker. I was up, feet on the floor, yawning when I saw Chick grab the broom and start swatting Stocum, who still hadn't gotten out of bed.

"What's the matter with you, you lazy no good fart! You're the counselor, set an example. You have to be the first one up," Chick shouted.

He swatted Stocum until he jumped out of bed. Stocum was dressed in just his underwear and he couldn't stop yawning as he tried to wipe the sleep from his eyes.

"Old man, what's the rush," Stocum stuttered.

"I'll show you an old man, you squishy fart. It's your job. Get these kids ready for breakfast, or I'll clobber ya," Chick demanded. He tried to slap Stocum on the back of his head, but could only reach his shoulders. "Eh, you're not worth it!"

Chick threw his arms up in disgust and left the bunk. You could hear the screen door to Bunk 17 open and the same routine begin again. More beds were rocked and dumped with Chick screaming for everyone to "move!" If Chick wanted to set an example of what our morning routine was to be like, he was doing a damn good job.

After breakfast ended I found myself racing Harris back to the bunk, and was surprised to see we were the only ones heading in that direction. I was also surprised to find that Harris was a pretty speedy little thing.

"Don't eat the pancakes," Jericho had warned at breakfast.

"Why not?" Harris asked.

"Because they put EX-LAX in the batter. You'll be shitting your brains out all day."

"Bull shit," Harris said as he stuffed a pancake into his mouth, syrup dripping down his chin.

"They also put salt peter in the food."

"What's that?" I asked Jericho.

"I don't know. Something that prevents us from becoming a

group of raging horny hormones. There's nothing worse than young boys with horniness and perpetual hard ons."

I had no clue what he was talking about, but I did avoid the pancakes. I didn't think Harris was racing me back to the bunk because he had to take a dump, so I quickly surmised he was on the same mission as I was. We needed to listen to the five most important minutes of the day.

"It's 8:24" Harris shouted as we leaped onto the porch, and threw the screen door open with such force it almost came off its hinges. We both lunged at the transistor radio that sat on the edge of Harris' cubby. Harris turned on the radio and played with the knobs, looking for the exact station while I played with the single antennae, aiming it in every direction, hoping to hit that magical spot that would dissolve the static into beautiful clarity.

"This is Howard Cosell."

It was the voice we waited for in the summer. He spoke the truth, he informed us of what was happening in the outside world. There was no T.V. and we rarely saw any newspapers.

This morning Howard Cosell was praising my favorite baseball team, the New York Mets. The Yankees were pathetic, but the once abysmal Mets were suddenly playing with a never-before-seen spark and Howard Cosell was talking about them after another win.

"The Cubs are coming to town," Harris said after Cosell signed off. "If we sweep them we can inch closer to first place. We've never been this close before."

"Ha, the only thing we have to sweep is this floor,," I said picking up the broom. "Where is everyone? We have to clean the bunk before inspection."

"They're at the infirmary, pretending to be sick so they can look at girls' side coming out of breakfast. They're hoping to talk to them," Jericho announced as he walked into the bunk and plopped down on his bed.

"How do you know? And why aren't you there?" I asked. You have a girlfriend."

"Mine's real. The losers in this bunk all think or dream they have one, or will have one. My brother always told me to make women wait for things, makes them want it more, so I'm waiting for the first social. The only two who really need to be there are Oliver and Hardon."

"Why Hardon?" I asked.

"He needs his special medicine."

"So we're stuck sweeping?" I was furious.

"Well, our numb nuts counselor hasn't created one of those pie chart schedules that instructs us as to what chore we have to perform every day. So I guess if we want to pass inspection we better start sweeping," Jericho said as he took charge of the second broom.

There was a method to cleaning a bunk and when I saw Jericho start sweeping under The Brain's bed on the left side of the bunk, I knew I had to start under Bugsy's bed on the right. Dust was everywhere and some dustballs were as large and fluffy as dirty cotton balls. Dust floated up from the floor, awakened from its winter hibernation. We instructed Harris to get a paper cup, and fill it with water. We showed him how if he sprinkled a little water on the floor it made it easier to sweep up the dust.

When the pile of dirt was swept and accumulated near the front door we swept it up into the dustpan that Harris manned.

"That's all we have to do inside. They don't really care about the backroom, and I'll take care of the porch,," Jericho told us.

"You know what the problem is?" I said boldly. "The problem is everyone here has a sense of entitlement."

"What do you mean?" asked Harris as he dumped the dust into the waste basket.

"Wake up! Everyone here has a maid who does everything for them," I shouted.

"I don't," Jericho said as he carefully sat on his bed, hoping not to wrinkle the blankets.

"I don't either. I help clean the house every other week. Wait,... you have a maid?" Harris asked me. There was a look of shock, revulsion, and amusement all rolled up into his tiny little face.

"What, I have a choice? My mother hires a maid, and she cleans the house but I won't let her into my room. It's just that you get to some of these camps and kids have a sense of entitlement that drives me crazy. What gives them the right to think they're better than others just because their daddy makes more money? And the mothers! My God, the mothers, prancing around in tiny tennis dresses, showing off their bodies, and getting into teasing all the boys in my grade. They don't lift a finger for their own child all week, and then finally do so when the maid leaves just so they can present themselves in some false light as wonderful and loving mothers. Meanwhile all week long they think you've missed the obvious signs that they're screwing the tennis pro at the club while their fathers are so oblivious to the obvious."

My rant ended just as quickly as it started. I had been sweeping the floor so hard that there was now a shine to it. I looked at Jericho and Harris and realized their mouths were agape.

"I agree with your assessment of these spoiled kids, but do you really know mothers like that?" Harris asked.

"Yes. My mother."

Jericho and Harris looked at each other and not another word was exchanged. Jordan swept the porch and I picked up the dirty towels in the back room. The rest of the bunk returned from infirmary call. Not even a nod that their bunk was cleaned, nor a thank you for doing it. Stocum slid into the bunk, hopped up to his bed and just sat there with a stupid smile.

10

S tocum didn't last two days.

By the end of the second day it was obvious that I had emerged as the best athlete in the bunk. This might sound infantile, to talk about how many hits I had in a softball game, or how many points I scored in a basketball game, but in a lot of ways it's how boys measure their worth. You compare and rate yourself in three basic categories. Are you a jock, a good athlete who can hold his own on all the fields of play? Are you cool and suave with the girls? Or maybe you are brilliant and you can impress your peers and outwit them. I wasn't sure where I ranked yet, but I knew I was at least a jock and a good one. If you were lucky you qualified for at least one of the three categories. Oliver maybe had brains. Harris didn't possess any of the necessary qualities, but Jericho had all three. And this drove Hardon crazy.

Mickey Hardon began pacing back and forth in front of my bed, daring me to say something about his dancing spit, which he kept flicking out of his mouth in anger. All this because I scored more than he did in the basketball game. To add insult to injury I then knocked him to the ground while trying to grab a rebound.

What really upset Hardon was that after the game a skinny dude, who was obviously a teacher during the winter but spent his summers at this camp, had pulled me aside. This dude was all the color of fall foliage, blazing red, from his curly bush of hair, to his matching Fu Manchu mustache and muttonchop sideburns.

I guess I was supposed to feel honored by his interest in me because as it turned out the redhead was part of the camp's monarchy. He was the head of the waiters, and he also coached the waiter's basketball team. I think he was perplexed that I wasn't impressed with his interest in me, but I also thought he admired that. Unlike Hardon, I wasn't pissing in my pants for this guy's attention.

Hardon continued giving me the dancing spit eye all afternoon, and it lasted through dinner. It had started to bother me. I was going to say something to him during free play, but he bolted to the basketball courts once the needle started to scratch the record and the call for Free Play blared over the loudspeaker.

Hooky and the Mayor were heading down to the lake with their fishing poles. Asa and Samson were in a foul mood as they were assigned waterfront duty for free play. I deduced that this was not a favored assignment as they groaned and protested when it was announced at the flag pole at the dinner lineup. Asa kept kicking Hooky in the ass. He was blaming Hooky for such a lousy assignment.

I took my usual position sitting on the boot box with book in hand, sandwiched between Harris and Oliver. Then Jericho bolted from the bunk, skipped off the porch and looked around. When he was sure no one was watching he slowly inched to the edge of the bunk and then turned and headed towards the woods.

I decided to follow him.

Jericho had approached the woods behind the bunk, and looked around to make sure nobody was watching. Then he hopped into the greenery and disappeared. I waited a minute or two until I entered the same keyhole, and brushing aside a bush or two, followed a short path down to the lake. I came upon a small patch of beach at the edge of the woods, and there squatted Jericho

"I've been waiting for you," he said as he exhaled a billow of smoke.

"Was wondering where you disappeared to. Two nights in a row," I squatted next to Jericho.

"You smoke?" he asked, offering a joint. "It doesn't mean anything to me if you do or you don't, just offering."

"I haven't yet... I mean I've never gotten high before."

"Sounds like you're open to it," Jericho whispered as he took a long toke, and held it deep into his lungs for what seemed like an eternity. He tilted his neck, exhaled and smiled. He offered the joint again.This time i took it.

"Will this get me kicked out of camp if we're caught?"

"Most certainly."

"Good."

I put the joint to my lips and sucked in. I just sucked on that joint like it was a straw, and the smoke filled my mouth and made me cough. My hacking was so violent that I was lucky I was still able to hold onto the joint. I gave it another try. This time I took a more controlled toke, and felt a mellow stream of smoke enter my lungs.

"Like this, you don't just suck it, but you have to gently surround the paper with your lips, and breathe in, not suck in, breathe in," Jericho told me, as he lit a new joint.

I watched and understood his demonstration. It seemed I was willing to do anything Jericho asked. The feeling of having someone to confide in for the first time, someone who I sensed understood all my feelings and anger, was enlightening.

We squatted on the sandy path watching the sun slowly set on a clear summer evening. I could feel my toes starting to tingle, and then my nose and ears. I started to laugh.

"Good, ... it's good stuff isn't it?" Jericho asked.

"How would I know? I have nothing to compare it to."

"Trust me it's good. My brother taught me about getting high. We would get high all the time. My parents never caught on. I mean.... I know they get high, but they never got high with us until the day he was drafted. When he left he gave me his stash and told me to enjoy. Like I said, my parents sent me back to camp. I didn't want to come to this place. That was their way of getting me to stop worrying about my brother. Smoking a doobie is another way. It also helps me cope with the morons here every summer."

"I'm sorry about that," I said, not really knowing why I said such a stupid statement.

"Yeah, so I spent the entire spring rolling joints to take up here. Then my brother started sending me shit from "Nam" and I was swimming in the stuff, so I started to sell some shit, and had this real good thing going until my parents forced me here. So I have my shit which I'm gladly going to share with you because it sucks getting high by oneself. But you have to promise me you won't act stupid when you're high."

"I promise."

"Then get that shit-eating grin off your face, and let's head back," he said as he patted me on the back and led me out of the woods.

A warm wave of loneliness seemed to exit my body and an aura of mirth bathed me. I couldn't stop laughing. I felt grounded to the earth next to Jericho. It felt like my feet sprouted roots. Every step was a struggle.

Jericho suggested that if I had sunglasses I should put them on as soon as I got back to the bunk. He told me to drink a lot of water and to stay away from Hardon, but I really wasn't listening. I was drinking in the sweet-natured country air, tinged with cow dung. I was listening to the sound of kids having fun, which at this moment seemed more intoxicating than sitting all day inside my home, alone, back in Westchester where the only sound I would be listening to would be the buzz of air conditioning. We sidled up the side of the bunk, where the bathing suit line was littered with wet trunks from the afternoon swim, and before we turned the corner Jericho looked me in the eye, straightened my shirt and reminded me to act cool.

Just as Recall blew to return from Free Play we walked around the edge of the bunk to see Lenny pushing Stocum straight through the screen door of Bunk 18. The screen door cracked off its hinges. Stocum's height was no match for the flabby flesh of Lenny and Lenny was pushing him forward like a sumo wrestler on the attack. He didn't stop at the porch banister but continued on, pushing Stocum over the railing catapulting him to the ground.

Stocum gained his footing but Lenny bounced down the stairs as fast as he could, which was really very slow. This allowed Stocum to gather his wits. Chick intervened before Lenny could make another charge at Stocum. Chick stood between the two counselors. Lenny kept stomping his foot like a bull ready to charge, but Chick kept his ground.

"Ehhhhh... now what's going on here?" Chick wailed.

"That kid... that skinny little kid took a SHIT ON MY PILLOW," Stocum shouted.

"WHA???" Chick screamed.

"That little shit they call Hardon. He threw my shirt on the floor for no reason and I told him to pick it up... and he told me to go fuck myself.. I walked out of the bunk to keep my cool, and then that little shit took a shit on my BED. I walked back into the bunk to find three dark turds on my pillow."

"How do you know it was even him?" Chick asked.

"WHAT DIFFERENCE DOES IT MAKE? SOME KID TOOK A SHIT ON MY PILLOW!!! YOU'RE ALL FUCKING CRAZY JEWS.".

"THAT'S IT!" Lenny screamed and he charged Stocum.

Stocum suddenly had such a look of fear in his eyes I thought he was going to shit himself in his pants. Chick tripped Lenny, and he fell to the ground with a thud that shook pine needles off the trees.

"What?" Chick demanded as he gave a hand to Lenny and helped him up.

"I came into the bunk because I heard the screaming. He was holding Hardon against the wall by his neck. He was choking Hardon. He had lifted him off the floor and was choking him against the wall. Mickey Hardon was turning blue, and then I heard this piece of shit shout, .. "I Hate you fucking HYMIES".. HYMIES?? I'll show you a Hymie you stupid hick." Lenny screamed. He stood there sucking in air, obviously running out of steam from all the exertion.

"You said that?" Chick asked Stocum who suddenly feared Chick more than Lenny.

"The Kid took a shit on my pillow. What's the matter with you? He took a shit..." Stocum kept babbling, pleading for his life.

Chick looked up at Hardon who was looking down at us from the porch. He had a smirk on his face, the type of smirk that screams of an entitled kid who knows he can get away with anything. The type of a smirk that you know rich kids wear all day. The type of smirk that makes you want to slap the shit out of that kid.

"Mickey Hardon isn't going anywhere," Chick said. "But what we have here is a difference of opinion. I think trying to choke the living shit out of a kid, and I can see the marks on his neck from here, certainly is grounds to call the law. How does a kid shitting on your pillow even come close to you attempting to choke him to death."

Stocum knew he was a goner. He just stood there shaking his head and muttering to himself.

"You people are all fucking crazy!"

Stocum stormed into the bunk to pack. It took only a minute for Stocum to bolt out of the bunk with his belongings stuffed into his bags. Hardon stepped aside, and waved.

"Have a nice summer, Slow Scum."

Suddenly Bugsy came running up the hill from the waterfront. "You got to come and see this–you have to see this," he screamed.

He tried to catch his breath. He wanted to say something but he couldn't produce anything but a wheezing sound. Besides, all attention was being paid to Stocum chugging toward the pit and his car. He never looked back, but his final word was the middle finger thrust high in the sky.

"You got to come to the boys' waterfront," Bugsy screamed. "Hooky cast his rod and hooked the Mayor. The Mayor has a huge hook in his head, and Samson fainted and Asa doesn't know what to do.. you got to see this... Asa's too sick to help and the Mayor has a hook in his head."

Jordan looked at me, and wanted to warn me not to lose it, but I was already on the ground hysterically laughing .

11

The only other person I had ever seen fired was our maid. My mother caught the maid red-handed with some of her jewelry and she was gone the next day. The exit of Stocum was greatly appreciated, because with the vacancy came the realization that I had more room to breathe in my little corner at the bottom of the bunk bed.

The Mayor was brought to the infirmary, where he sat for a while. Finally the doctor, a retired old fart, sauntered in. He looked at the hook, and wondered what to do. He decided on a scissor and proceeded to cut off one half of the hook, leaving the other half embedded in the Mayor's scalp. The Mayor was then whisked to the local hospital in Honesdale, which was about half an hour away. He had to have minor surgery... after all you can't walk around with half a hook embedded in your scalp. Samson had the night off, and Asa walked around like nothing had happened, refusing to admit he was a pussy around blood and couldn't help.

Hardon was going nowhere, just as Chick had predicted. He had a sister and a brother in camp, along with four cousins. Joe Geisinger was not going to send him home. Joe Geisinger would rather lose one counselor than face the threat of losing the other six related Hardons. Problem was that Hardon now walked around like he was invincible.

Chick moved into the bunk at nights, as we were without a counselor. Chick went to bed early, before curfew, and he slept soundly, and snored. This was perfect cover for the Jewish Mafia, and they made their move once again.

With Harris finally falling asleep the Mafia arose again like ghouls emerging from the dark. The Mayor and Hooky tiptoed over to where Harris slept and pinned him to his bed. Mickey Hardon straddled Harris, sitting on his chest. Bugsy clamped his hand over Harris' mouth, silencing him.

Harris struggled. He tried kicking but Hardon rode him like a bucking bronco. Harris was a prisoner, unable to fight back. He was pinned to his bed.

"Know what we're going to do now, Harris? We're going to initiate you to the bunk. We're going to give you another circumcision," Hardon whispered.

Harris tried to cry out. His desperate plea was muffled. From the back room The Brain emerged with a Boy Scout knife. The blade was open, and the Brain was honing it against a rock. The click swish of metal against rock drowned out the terrified muffled cries from Harris.

"The Brain's uncle is mohel. After he carves another inch off your dick he's going to suck the blood from the incision," Bugsy added.

"Usually we like to get our new bunkmates drunk before we do this, but there's no alcohol to be found anywhere," The Brain whispered as he knelt next to Harris' head.

Harris stopped struggling, and just stared at The Brain. He stared at the tiny blade that The Brain brandished at eye level. The Brain took out a Bic lighter, and sterilized the blade. Harris started to struggle again, fighting for every inch of freedom.

"Pull his pajamas off, it's time to cut him," Hardon instructed.

The knife inched closer to the exposed shmeckel, but before any incision could be made Harris bit Bugsy in the hand, who then cried out in pain. Harris was able to break free and he ran out on the porch.

"GET BACK INTO BED!" Chick screamed, finally awakening from his deep slumber. But he didn't move, he didn't even turn over in his sleep to see who was out of bed. The Jewish Mafia laughed their way back into bed while Chick kept muttering for them to shut up.

Jericho got out of bed, put on his sneakers and walked out of the bunk. He made sure that the screen door closed softly so Chick didn't wake up. I followed him out into the warm night. We saw Harris slumped to the ground under a copse of trees a few yards from our porch. He was crying. Some of the ODs on the other porches looked on. They didn't want to get involved, or else they had their girlfriends sitting with them on the porch. They didn't care about a singular camper crying in his pajamas in the darkness of a July night.

"Harris, they weren't going to do anything to you. They were fucking with you," Jericho told him.

"How do you know? How do you know he wasn't... he had a knife."

"Because they're crazy, but not that crazy. They do this every summer. I should have warned you."

We helped Harris up, and he brought his breathing under control. His sniffling receded to nothing as we walked back into the bunk and sort of tucked Harris into bed. Harris fell asleep immediately.

Near midnight, as curfew approached, I heard the screen door squeal open, and again I saw the familiar sneakers of Asa. He was alone tonight and reeking of beer, with another freshly opened bottle in his hand. He walked to the backroom in order to pee in our toilet. When he was done he flushed, and as he was walking out of the bunk he decided to stop and think. He turned and walked over to where Harris was sleeping. He took out his shmeckle and started to stroke it. Then, as if he really had a decent thought in his brain, he thought better of the situation and tucked it away. Instead he sprinkled drops of beer all over Harris, massaging it gently into his scalp. Harris never woke up, and Asa sneaked out of the bunk as he once again commenced stroking his cock.

In the morning when Harris awoke, he could feel something sticky in his hair. He took out his comb and tried to brush it out, only to find a snowstorm of flakes fly off his scalp. Harris complained to Chick that someone did something to him overnight. He didn't know who, he didn't know what it was, but he knew someone did something to him the night before.

"What's that I smell?" Chick asked.

"I don't know... what is it?" Harris asked.

"It almost smells like beer?" Chick said as he sniffed Harris from shoulder to scalp.

"I told you, somebody did something to me."

"Eh.. you know what a wet dream is, kid? Maybe you had a wet dream, and that's what all the sticky stuff is. Maybe you had a wet dream in a bar? Were you drinking last night?"

"NO! Of course not."

"Then go in and wash up, get rid of that stench. You smell like a college frat house."

Harris wanted to cry. He was defeated. He walked into the back room to wash up. Nobody said a word. I was the nobody. I felt like a nobody. I didn't have the guts to get involved... I didn't say anything.

"What is wrong with those two? " I asked Jericho at breakfast.

"Nobody ever disciplines them or stands up to them. They know they can get away with anything. They're bored. Ever notice Hardon? He can't sit still. He's all over the place. Here's a secret that I didn't tell you before. You know he goes to the infirmary every morning. He needs his medications. He takes something. Helps him focus," Jericho said, stuffing a soft onion roll into his mouth.

The onion rolls were soft, warm, and so very tasty.

Chick told us we would be getting a new counselor in a day or two.

Harris sat there playing with his onion roll. He didn't feel like eating. He took a shower before breakfast so at least he felt clean. I didn't have the guts to tell him what I had witnessed.

Later that morning another game of basketball proved that Mickey Hardon had it out for me. He never looked my way, never passed the ball. I decided to grab as many rebounds as I could, and dribble up the court without an inkling of giving up the ball. I was going to make as many uncontested layups as I could. Or I would just continually pop and swish from the outside. This infuriated Hardon and he got Hooky to rough me up a bit. Stupidity! We were on the same team, and I was being mugged by my own teammate.

The shocking moment of the day came after lunch, when during rest hour, I was summoned onto the porch. Waiting for me was Heshie Greenberg, the man in charge of the waiters.

Heshie was the same redhead who had earlier talked basketball with me. In the sun, his red hair, Fu Manchu mustache and crimson muttonchops glowed, almost blinding me. His mustache surrounded his lips tightly like the bush around a woman's vagina, or at least like the ones I saw in the porn magazines my father tried to bury in his closet. That's all I could think of as he started to talk to me, a talking vagina, and I had to do everything in my will power not to laugh.

Heshie wore cut off jean shorts, and was rarely seen in a t shirt, only a button down work shirt that he never tucked in. And what kind of basketball coach could he be? He never wore sneakers, only hiking boots.

He had one crazy habit. He carried a whiffle ball bat around and he twirled it like a baton. He would spin the solid plastic bat between his fingers, and sometimes use it as a cane to lean on.

When he wanted one of his waiters to do something, and they didn't comply in an expedient manner, Heshie would give them a few whacks with the whiffle ball bat. He aimed for the back of the thighs where the red welts would eventually blossom. Waiters screamed out in pain. Then they would giggle. Then they would beg for more. Turns out that if Heshie liked you, he would hit you with his whiffle ball bat, or pull your hair back and then kick you in the shins.

"Do you know who this is?" Heshie asked, rubbing the shoulders of a waiter who stood by his side.

"Scott. He's our waiter."

"Good. I watched you play basketball this morning. You have potential. I want you to spend free play with Scott. He's going to work with you on your basketball skills." Heshie started to rub Scott's ass, and then whacked it with an open palm and told him to get back to the Waiters' bunk.

"What if I don't want to?" I asked. I was thinking about getting high with Jericho. "Can we do it during rest hour?" I was hoping he would say yes as I wanted any excuse to get out of the bunk.

Heshie was not a tall man. I was almost able to look him directly in the eyes. He had the potential to look insanely evil, but today a mischievous and thoughtful grin spread across his face. The softest smile whispered the softest laugh, like it was squeezed out of his body as he pondered my response. I could see that his face was growing as red as his facial hair.

"Son, do you know who I am?"

"Yes, the head of the waiters. We already discussed this."

"Well, yes.. but I'm also the basketball coach at a high school which has one of the finest basketball programs in all of New York City. I've sent many of my kids off to college, to play in major programs. And one or two have even made it to the pros. I've taught these kids how to play basketball. Now why would you want to reject my offer to help make you a better basketball player?"

Heshie reached out and started to massage my shoulders with the hand that was not holding the Whiffle ball bat. He smelled of some cheap after shave, but his touch was very soft.

"Because I never thought of myself as being very good at basketball."

"Well, I'm telling you you're special. Now Scott will come and get you when he has a chance, and if you want to make it during rest hour we can arrange that on the days Scott is not playing ball,"

Heshie then whacked me on the ass with the Whiffle ball bat.

I entered the bunk and Hardon rushed up to me, and poked his bony fingers into my chest.

"What did Heshie tell you?" he demanded.

I ignored him. I pushed him away and sat down on my bed, and reached for some comic books but Hardon wasn't backing down.

"You think you're special? That's it. You're the new Sunshine this summer. You can't fuck with me. Screw Harris, we're going to Sunshine you. You're going to be crying all summer and you're going to wish you were never here. "

12

"Who's Sunshine? What's Mickey Hardon talking about?"

I took the joint that Jericho thrust at me. We sat on the sand in our hidden alcove during Free Play. I took a long toke that made me float off the ground for a second. Already into our sixth day at camp, and I was feeling more comfortable than ever before. Was it the pot or the friendship with Jericho?

I had already proven my athletic prowess in softball, basketball and volleyball and was selected to the A team for inter-camp games. Amazing how young boys measure their worth. It creates a caste system that was hard to break.

Again, we were promised that a new counselor would arrive any day. Hardon and his friends constantly attacked Harris yet I found myself taking some pride in knowing that I wasn't softening up and caring about someone else. I suddenly wondered if I would remain silent if Jericho was the one being picked on.

Then I thought about Hardon's threat and I knew this would portend a change in events.

The loudspeaker woke up and Recall was sounded. The end of an extra long Free Play because we were promised a fireworks display this night. It was July 4th, and we were going to celebrate. We were told that first we would gather in the Social Hall and sing patriotic songs, and when darkness had fallen we would be led outside to the massive hill that fell into the second lake. From above the water ski lake we would watch the fireworks.

"The Night of Sunshine is camp lore. I don't know if it's true or not, but it's a story that every camper knows. Has to do with the two counselors in our group, Asa and Samson. They met when they were six years old and in Bunk Two."

Jericho settled in and knew he was going to tell the story. He took the joint back.

"Camp Tonkawa? Right here?"

"Yup. Asshole buddies and bunkmates all those years. Then they were waiters under Heshie. Now they're in college, and rooming together. Go figure. So this one year, when they were like ten years old, they picked mercilessly on this kid named Sunshine. I mean every year they would learn a new trick or two and just tear into kids, but this year they just wailed on Sunshine. They would do things to him that bordered on crazy. Finally Sunshine lost it. They came back from swim one day and Sunshine just started pounding his head against the wall. When the counselor tried to stop him, Sunshine kicked him in the balls and ran out of the bunk. Took the entire camp three days to find him. He was hiding in a tree stump out in the woods on the golf course."

"You're kidding?"

"Nope. Have you seen the golf course yet? Pretty nice for a camp. I mean it's only eight holes but it's still pretty cool. Anyway, they took Sunshine away in a straitjacket. We're told he had this look in his eyes that scared everyone, but it never stopped Asa and Samson. They relished the hunt and cherished the fear it created. Every summer they pick someone to 'Sunshine'."

"What, you mean as counselors they're still doing it?"

"Oh yeah... and it's even worse now. They feel they can't really get into trouble because who's going to stop them?"

"So how did Hardon and The Brain fall into this?"

"Asa and Samson have been their counselors for the last two years. Hardon and The Brain beg for attention, and every year they pick a 'Sunshine' and terrorize the kid. They're lauded and praised for their actions. It's like Hardon and The Brain are disciples in a cult."

Jericho took another long hit, and looked out on the calm lake. Out on the water a rowboat inched by.

"My first year in camp we had a kid just like Oliver, except not sickly. Nice kid, but such a loser. Made it easier for me because they just tormented this kid till he left after the third week. He cried all the time. When he left, Hardon and The Brain felt like they accomplished something because Asa and Samson bragged about their escapade. Last year the kid they picked to 'Sunshine' lasted two weeks."

"And? Now they've picked me?"

"You know, every summer I've been here I've watched those bastards just destroy someone. I mean it never really bothered me, and I don't know why." Jericho's smile betrayed the fact that he knew something I didn't. "And I'm sure Mickey Hardon wanted Harris because he's so damn easy to pick on."

Jericho took a deep toke, and held it in for what seemed forever before he exhaled. He took another toke and gazed out at the lake for what seemed a really long time before he blew out a puff of smoke that melted into the peaceful orange glow of a setting sun.

"But you… , you got under that asshole's skin, and he wants you bad. He picked you and you know what? I think you'll be the only one I've seen who can stand up to the bunk. This should be very interesting."

We heard the loudspeaker flash on, the sound of a needle scratching through worn grooves, and Recall being blown and echoing through the desolate countryside. So we both took one last long drag, and then flicked the joint into the lake. We watched it float off between the water lilies.

Harris and Oliver were still sitting on the boot box when Jericho and I walked onto the porch. Harris kept giving me this look, the type that basically meant he knew what I was doing. Or was I just paranoid from being high?

I walked into the bunk and grabbed the broom, returning to the porch with the broom handle sticking out between my legs, riding it like a witch. I was very, very high.

"What's that for?" Jericho asked.

"For the bats."

"What bats? There are no bats."

"My last camp. There were always bats hanging out in the rafters of the Social Hall. We had to bring brooms with us. When the bats decided to attack we swatted them away with the brooms."

"This camp has no bats. Joe Geisinger doesn't allow them. It's not a bat zone. Get my drift yet?"

"No bats, no brooms?"

"Not recommended," Jericho said as he took the broom away from me and returned it to its rightful corner slot behind the door.

We felt bathed in the warmth of a sweet, sanitary summer evening in the hills of eastern Pennsylvania. Sanitary because we were separated from reality, cleansed from the ills of everyday society.

The hills and vast farmland encapsulated our summer home in a subtle hush. A car approaching the front gate of the camp broke the silence. It was a soft swoosh, like the wind before a storm.

It was really the first time that we sat as an entire camp in the Social Hall. The south end of the Hall opened with two large barn doors to the back porch. This wrapped around the sides of the back of the hall. To the north end was the stage where I assumed plays were performed, but tonight a piano sat majestically in front of the stage. The camp music director (some semi-retired music teacher at a Brooklyn high school) started to play a Sousa march as we entered. The large barn doors were open , and for the night were kept open to aid in air circulation.

Sheets of paper were handed out with the lyrics from patriotic songs. We started singing "When Johnny Comes Marching Home." Harris and Oliver got into the spirit quickly, but Jericho and I just sat quietly mouthing the words and giggling between ourselves.

"These songs are bullshit," Jericho whispered. "We should be singing songs by Phil Ochs."

"Who?"

"Phil Ochs... you know... 'I Ain't Marching Anymore,' 'Outside of a Small Circle of Friends'..."

I shrugged my shoulders.

"Anti-war protest songs.., and just plain old brilliance."

An hour later we were sitting on the hillside watching the fireworks. It was a simple display, but it seemed more majestic as we lay back on the grass and watched the night sky bursting into flames right above us. Chick stood in front of our group, and every time a rocket was shot into the air, he would swoop his hand skyward in a sweeping motion like Pete Townsend playing his guitar. We would all shout "OOOOOOOOOOOOOOO"

Chick, with his baggy yellow shorts, and v neck white t shirt, was a child at heart. When the rocket exploded overhead in a mosaic blaze of light, Chick would raise both hands, open his fist, and we would all scream "Ahhhhhhhhhhhh."

"OOOOOOOOOOO"

"AHHHHHHHHHH"

This was something I would never experience at home. This was something that we never had at any other camp I went to. I did not partake in the "oooing and ahhhing" even though I enjoyed watching Chick dance in front of us.

Harris and Oliver sat in front of our group, following Chick's lead. Hardon stood off to the side, whispering to Asa and Samson. I could have sworn he was pointing at me. When the fireworks display ended, I didn't want to move. There was a half moon that blinked brightly between the wafting smoke from the exploded shells.

The grass felt serenely soft, like a bed of feathers. I could see a multitude of stars, something never seen at home. Jericho had to pull me up off the ground as the mob of campers walked back toward their bunks. It was a silly amateurish evening, but I ... loved it.

13

It was the morning of July 9th. We hurried through a boring breakfast. The small cereal boxes were stacked neatly on the tables with a basket of onion rolls stationed at each end. It was an "egg" morning. Sometimes we had French toast or pancakes, but today was an "egg" morning. Scrambled eggs flew off platters that the waiter brought, but then orders were taken for those who wanted hard or soft boiled eggs. I kid you not.

The breakfast I loved the most was the Sunday morning fare. Bagels and lox. As much lox as you'd like, tons of it spread across plates on every freaking table. The bagels weren't New York bagels, but they weren't bad. Especially after you added the cream cheese, onions, and tomatoes. It was the best breakfast ever served at any camp I had ever been to.

I'd wolf down two bagels with a "schmear" of everything before Jericho even finished one. I thought I was being piggish, but then I sat back and watched the two counselors who were football players. They were wolfing down four jam-packed bagels. They had never tasted such a delicacy and were now addicted. By the end of the summer they would be close to twenty pounds overweight. Eventually you would see panic set in as they realized that two-a-day practices were only days away and they were so out of shape.

After breakfast on the morning of July 9th Harris and I tore out of the Mess Hall and raced up to the bunk. We had to listen to Howard Cosell because we knew he was going to sing the praises of the New York Mets with the brilliant Tom Seaver on the mound. It turns out that Harris and I were the only Met fans in the bunk, everyone else being Yankee fans. Yet, for once, we were no longer the laughingstock and brunt of teasing comments about how abysmal our Metsies were. They were surging.

We flew into the bunk only to be grounded by the sight of a stranger half naked, wrapped in a towel. He had emerged from the back room after taking a shower. He was about my height with wavy brown hair, and the most amazing six pack abs I had ever seen. He was pure muscle which seemed to make up for his lack of height. He had close set blue eyes that made his face seem to pinch in above his nose. Yet he had this warm and welcoming smile that sort of disarmed us. I looked at the top of the double decker and saw that it was no longer bare. It was now bedded with a quilt. This must be our new counselor.

"Breakfast over so soon?" he asked as he continued drying off with a second towel.

"Yeah, we ran all the way back here to listen to Howard Cosell," Harris told him as he scrambled past me to get to his transistor radio.

Things had quieted down for Harris, as Hardon and The Brain had stopped their incessant attacks. For now, they were concentrating on what they were going to do to me.

Harris fumbled with the radio and tilted the antenna until the crackle of static finally gave way to that nasal voice that electrified the airwaves of the Pennsylvania countryside. Howard Cosell was our link to civilization.

"Met fans? So am I," our counselor said as he turned his back to us and slipped on some underwear and a pair of shorts.

He dressed in silence as we listened to the five minute report from the distant city. We listened to Howard Cosell sing the praises of Tom Seaver. In his voice we heard the excitement that was building all over New York. Something special was happening with the Mets. This was so monumental for us. It gave anyone who felt like they were losers in life a glimmer of hope that one day we might head into a winning streak and be wildly successful.

Harris turned off the radio just as Jericho sauntered in, and the three of us began the bunk cleaning process. Harris had dustpan duty, and watched as Jericho and I swept the dirt from each side of the bunk into the middle aisle.

"So you're our new counselor?" I asked, finally breaking the silence

"Guess so. Just drove up here this morning from Long Island. My name's Ben Solomon. Anyone want a bagel and lox?" he asked as he pulled three plump bagels out of a bag. These were the real bagels, you could just sniff the difference in this delicacy. They were fully loaded bagels--with tomato, onion, lox and a thick schmear of cream cheese.

"We just had breakfast," Jericho said. "But thank you anyway."

"You have bagels and lox on Sundays? Try this Lox! Go ahead... try it. Nosh a bit... "

He kept at us, almost shoveling the bagels into our mouths. Finally, we each took one, and stopped our sweeping for a few seconds while we munched on our bagels.

"Holy shit... this is real lox... we've been eating phony lox," Harris blurted out.

"No... you're eating belly lox in camp... real salty... cheaper than the Nova. And now you're munching on real New York bagels, not phony ones baked by local yokels," Ben said.

"Freaking good," Harris said as the cream cheese oozed out of the corners of his mouth.

"Figured it was a long drive, and I might get hungry. I left at five thirty, but just didn't have the appetite. Glad you're enjoying it. So what's the story, where's the rest of the bunk?"

"Oliver has a reason to be at the Infirmary," I told him. "He has to take pills and he has to have the doctor listen to his chest."

"And The Mayor has to get the stitches taken out of his head today, as a result of a fishing accident. He's going into Honesdale to the hospital," Jericho said. "The rest of the bunk just goes over there to sit on girls' side in hopes of seeing their girlfriends. Hardon takes some medication."

"Hardon? What kind of name is Hardon?"

"You'll see… anyway, they're always complaining about something and they get out of cleanup. I can't finish this. Mind if I throw it out?" Harris asked as he licked the cream cheese off his fingers.

"Sure, be my guest. No refrigerators to preserve it. So you're saying the rest of the bunk just assumes you're going to clean up for them?"

"In a sense. I mean if we don't do it, then it will never get done and we won't pass inspection. Not worth the fight," Jericho told Ben.

Ben pondered this fact for a minute and then took the brooms out of our hands, and rested them in the garbage pail next to the door of the bunk. He told us to sit on our beds and then proceeded to tell us about himself.

"I'm pre-med at Yale. Or at least my desire is to go to medical school. The last couple of summers I've been volunteering at hospitals, and research labs. I guess you can say I'm a bit burned out. Just took my MCAT'S, and I know I did well on them, but I just needed a break. So I'm sitting at home wondering what job I can find where I could be outdoors all day and make a little money? And then it hits me…I could be a counselor at a summer camp. Right? I have a family friend who knows Joe Geisinger so he called him on my behalf and here I am."

"Have you ever been a counselor before?" I asked.

"Nope. Was a camper once, but that was many, many years ago."

The screen door flew open and the rest of the bunk marched in. Maybe it was more like a march of the moronic braggarts. They completely missed Ben, who was standing next to Jericho.

"Have fun at the infirmary?" Ben asked, stepping forward.

"Who the fuck are you?" Mickey Hardon asked.

Ben laughed. "This must be Hardon?"

We nodded our confirmation.

"I'm Ben Solomon, your new counselor."

"Who the fuck cares?" Bugsy said, trying to sound like he was a tough motherfucker. The rest of the bunk laughed.

"I care," Hardon said as he walked up to Ben, dropped a dancing spit that almost hit the floor. Then he sucked it up in an act of defiance.

Ben softly pushed Mickey Hardon aside and strode over to his bed.

"I'm assuming this is your cubby as everyone else is already sitting on their beds." Then with one swiping motion he threw everything in the cubby onto the floor. There was a moment of stunned silence.

"You fucking bastard," Hardon shouted as he charged Ben.

Ben simply put out his hand like a cop stopping traffic, and clamped it on Hardon's head. It stopped him in his tracks. With his other hand he flipped over Mickey Hardon's bed, dumping it on the floor. Hardon went wild, screaming and flailing his arms. Ben finally released him and watched as Hardon's momentum caused him to fall to the floor.

Ben then turned to The Brain and dumped his cubby. He then went around the room, and began to upend the beds of everyone who went to the infirmary. The Brain just stood there, his mouth open in shock.

"The Brain is angry! The Brain is mad. The Brain needs to control his temper or else he'll be tossed from this contest!" Beckett announced into his phantom microphone.

"Oh, you're dead meat," The Brain finally muttered as he started picking up his clothing.

Ben then attacked one cubby after another. Clothing was flung onto the floor like confetti fluttering to the ground. Nobody moved for a second, nobody knew how to react. Harris and I found our way to Jericho's bed, where the three of us sat and watched in amazement. Oliver walked in to see the bunk in a state of disarray, and he looked at us for an explanation, but we could only shrug our shoulders.

"Now hear this," Ben said loudly. "I don't know who you think you are, but you will no longer go to the infirmary after breakfast and allow three of your bunkmates to do all of the cleaning. I don't know what entitled lives you've lived, but this is camp, and you're not going to get away with this anymore. Now I'm going to make a chart and each and every one of you will have an assignment every morning. Beds will be made before you go to breakfast. Your cubbies will be neat, and you will learn to respect each and every member of this bunk."

"Go fuck yourself," Hardon muttered.

Ben slowly walked over to Hardon and glowered at him. They almost stood eye to eye.

"Oh, you little twit... that may be physically impossible. But I'll tell you what... I'll help you contort your body into any position possible which will enable you to be the first to do such an act."

"Are you a homo? What's the matter with you?" Mickey Hardon screamed as he tried to jab Ben in the chest.

The counselor grabbed Hardon's hand and twisted it in an ungodly manner. Mickey fell to his knees as Ben continued to twist his hand, causing more pain. Mickey Hardon squealed like a baby.

"No, I'm not a homo. But from now on you're going to respect me and everyone else in this bunk. You've got five minutes to get your cubbies in order or else you'll be sitting here during first period making your beds and cubbies again."

Ben let go of Hardon's hand, and eyed each and every camper who had spent clean up at the infirmary. He then jumped up onto the top of the double decker and laid down, just staring at the ceiling.

"Oooo, I like this," Harris whispered, giggling with excitement.

Today was the day that our group was finally divided into four teams. Each team was named after different Ivy League schools. I was on Dartmouth, and Hardon was on Harvard, and we were to play each other in basketball that morning. Mickey didn't want to miss the game. Basketball was his passion, so he didn't argue with Ben and proceeded to clean up the mess.

When everything was put away, Ben jumped down from the top of the double decker and threw the brooms at Hardon and the Brain, and told them to finish sweeping the bunk. Hooky was given the dustpan and we watched as the three of them finished their duties just as inspection was blown over the loudspeaker. A few minutes later Chick walked through the bunk and without much thought said the bunk was in good order.

Out at lineup I watched as Ben stood off to the side, not part of the clique of counselors. Chick introduced him to the group. Nobody seemed impressed. He was shorter than all the other counselors and looked out of place. Mickey got up and whispered something to Asa. Bugle calls sounded and we started walking out to our morning activity as if nothing happened.

.

Mickey Hardon tried to intimidate me during our basketball game, but I brushed it aside. What infuriated me was that I fouled out of the game before the fourth quarter even started.

Jericho was on my team and he kept shaking his head every time a phantom foul was called. I had scored ten points before I fouled out of the game. Then Hardon took over and led his team to victory.

"It's not fair what they did to you today," Jericho said as we walked back to the bunk.

"No shit."

"Asa and Samson called everything against you. You had no chance out there. None of those fouls were fouls. It was like they were picking on you."

"Of course they were. I don't care anymore."

But I did care. What right did Asa and Samson have to pick on me, to cheat me out of any enjoyment? I didn't know if I should complain to Chick, or just let it go till the next basketball game and see if I was treated in a similar fashion.

"What should I do?" I asked Ben when I got back to the bunk. "Let it slide or fight back? What do you think?"

"That's your decision to make."

So here's the scoop about being sent to summer camp. You grow up fast. You're on your own. You ask a counselor something, they'll probably tell you that they're not your 'MOMMY OR DADDY' and at camp there is no mommy or daddy to come to your aid. Counselors don't give a damn about bunk "politics." You're flying solo, having to navigate every little issue that confronts you. If you're bullied, ridiculed, ganged up on, well... you have to find it in yourself to resolve every issue. You learn to communicate, to fight, to negotiate... basically it's preparing you for life.

You're measured by your athletic skills, or how cool you are with the girls. Sometimes you're sized up by how much money you come from, or whether your father is someone famous or important. Sometimes you could even become the King of the Bunk. This was not a particular honor at times, as I would find out after visiting day. I was always the King of the Bunk, crowned every summer, seconds after visiting day ended.

This is the way summer camp really is. Many kids have a great summer but there are those of us who will only have a few good memories buried amongst the tortured moments in which one is trying desperately to cling to their self esteem. Camp is not the squeaky clean, fun loving time many people seem to conjure up in old age. There's a dark side that will always come back to haunt you.

I recall 1968 was askew with assassinations, riots, and the escalating Vietnam War. Style was everything in the world.... who had long hair... who was cool... who had the biggest bell bottoms that would swish as you walked. Now 1969 was turning out to be as monumental as the year before.

This is the way of the world, and this would eventually drive Joe Geisinger into some pretty weird behavior.

The rest of the day turned into a glorious coming out party. Ben was turning out to be our savior. At lunch he slapped away The

Brain as he lunged for the lunch tray. When the Mayor, newly bandaged after his trip to the hospital, reached for the platter Ben gently stabbed him in the hand with his fork. The Mayor sat back down, venom pouring from his eyes. He rubbed the spot where one could see puncture wounds.

Then Ben handed the tray to Oliver, who then passed it around to Harris, who then gave it to Jericho and when I finally got the tray I took my lunch. I then offered it to Ben. He shook his head no. He refused to take anything before the entire table had lunch. He even helped Harris stack.

At rest hour Ben jumped onto his bed and closed his eyes. With a counselor in the bunk, Mickey, The Mayor and The Brain were afraid to do anything. It was the first peaceful rest hour since the beginning of camp. We were supposed to write letters home every day at this time. The Mayor was sent to the Canteen with our candy orders. We took fifty cents out of our canteen books, and waited for our candy bars.

During rest hour we were supposed to write home. Everyone had to have a letter, addressed and stamped before dinner. Mine was easy to compose.

Dear Mom and Dad,

Today is July 9th. Remember me? I haven't heard from you all summer, so I don't know if you're alive or not. Obviously I am. Having a decent time here, been getting high every day with a new friend, but I know you won't read this letter so what difference does it make?

Well, it's official. They've cooled on picking on Harris. But now they are working on me. I fouled out of a basketball game and I never touched anyone because these two asshole counselors have it out for me. They make me clean up all the wet dirty bathing suits that have fallen off the line on the side of the bunks. It's a disgusting job. And if I don't do it, the counselors punch me in my arm.

We have some stupid talent show to watch tonight, and Tom Seaver is pitching for the Mets.

Those two counselors keep waking me up at night, and our new counselor has told them to stop it. So far that has worked. Please write to just let me know you're alive.

Jason

Rest hour was also mail call time, and Ben had Jericho and Harris pick up the mail from the HCO shack. This time they returned with two big care packages, one for Bugsy, and one for Hardon. When Bugsy tore apart his package he let out a scream of delight. His uncle sent him a dozen Playboy magazines, and Bugsy was descended upon by the Jewish Mafia, who tore into the magazines like pirañhas savaging human flesh.

Hardon opened his care package from his parents and immediately started dividing up the stash with the Jewish Mafia. Most of it was candy, and bubble gum, but there was a box of homemade sugar cookies which smelled so enticing that I was almost tempted to ask for one.

The afternoon was spent playing softball. Ben was umping our softball game and he was enthusiastic in his approach. Actually he may have been overly enthusiastic with his ball and strike calls, but he was also kind and considerate. He took his time to instruct Harris on the proper technique of swinging a bat. He seemed to care about us and this drove the other counselors in the group nuts. The other counselors in the group despised him.

After the game we had an afternoon swim, and upon our return from the lake we found Oliver sitting on his bed. On his lap he had a shoe box with holes punctured along the top. He had a smile on his face that we had rarely seen this summer. Most of his daytime activities were limited to Arts and Crafts and Nature. We barely saw him. He wasn't allowed to participate in sports, and had to stay out of the lake. I had no clue why his parents didn't allow him to swim. Swimming in a lake is one of the little delights in life not many people experience. I wasn't even sure if he could swim. Then again I certainly couldn't understand how his parents even thought that sending him to camp was a good idea.

"What ya got there, numb nuts?" the Mayor asked.

"They're letting me keep this. I found it under the nature shack."

Oliver lifted the top of the shoe box to reveal a turtle that was almost the same size as the shoe box itself. Oliver had to use two hands to hold the turtle. He gently petted the turtle's head as it emerged from its shell to look around at its new surroundings. "I mean, you can't play ball, and you can't swim because of a fear of allergies, but they let you keep a turtle?" Ben asked as hopped up on his bed.

"Yeah,... why? He's not going to hurt anyone," Oliver said to Ben, as he cleared a space in his cubby for the shoe box.

"Well, you are a bit paranoid about germs and you know turtles aren't particularly clean animals... "

"I don't care. I'll be careful," Oliver said, as he sat on his bed with a far-off gaze, and a sheepish smile of innocence. He finally seemed to find his contentment.

After dinner and free play we were herded back up to the Social Hall for the campers' talent show. This is always excruciating no matter what camp you go to. Entitled kids who think they have talent will try to perform on stage, yet ultimately the camp will discover that their peers have no talent at all. Maybe, just maybe we'll all be surprised by an occasional ray of sunshine--a camper who really does have talent.

The Met game had started at 7:00 pm, and we were heading into the Social Hall by 7:30. Harris had his small transistor radio by his side. A single white earpiece kept falling out of his ear, his only link to the game. Through the static and weak signal, Harris was able to pick up Ralph Kiner, Lindsay Nelson, and Bob Murphy, the broadcast voices of the Mets. Harris had a hard time listening to the game. What we knew was that by the bottom of the second inning the Mets were up 3-0 thanks to two Chicago Cub errors. A Tom Seaver single, followed by a Tommie Agee double rounded out the scoring.

We marched into the Social Hall, and took our seats on the hard wooden benches, awaiting the start of this insufferable evening. There already was a lot of muffled cheering from the rest of the camp as word spread of the 3-0 Met's lead. A silent wave of excitement surfed around boys' side.

Mickey Hardon and his cohorts were sitting on the aisle near girls' side. Asa and Samson sat like bookends on that side of the aisle, pretending to be counselors but instead found themselves in prime position for gawking at the female counselors.

We sat on the opposite side of the bench, huddled together as Harris listened to the game. He whispered every pitch and every out the Cubs registered. I glanced over at Ben who was trying to keep Chick distracted by having a conversation with him. As the top of the seventh inning ended, and the Mets still held a 3-0 lead, it became apparent that Tom Seaver was throwing a perfect game. Two girls, who were around eleven years old, were doing a tap dance on stage. It was brutal.

"No hits, no walks, nobody reaching first," Harris whispered

"What does that mean?" Oliver whispered back.

"Perfect game!" I blurted out.

It was between acts, and I didn't disrupt anything on stage. A number of campers in front of us started whispering the news to their friends and suddenly it was like the game of 'telephone.' The wave of excitement was a flood. Most of the boys' side kept looking back at Harris. Ben sat down next to Harris in an attempt to deflect attention.

"Keep it down," Ben whispered as he saw the commotion we were causing.

"Okay," Harris whispered.

"What's happening now?" Ben asked

Harris looked up at him with a quizzical look on his face. "You just told me to keep it down!"

"I know... but a perfect game? Fuck, this has never happened before for the Mets, only against the Mets," Ben told him.

In the bottom of the seventh Cleon Jones hit a home run and there was an eruption of excitement as Harris whispered the news. The buzz grew louder as we had to bite our tongues to keep from screaming.

Joe Geisinger looked over in our direction and pointed an angry finger at Ben, the type of pointed finger that's supposed to strike fear into the hearts of campers and counselors. The excitement could not be denied. It soon became apparent that two other campers from the older group had brought in their transistor radios, and now all interest lay not on the performances on the stage, but on those who had radios relaying information.

Top of the eighth inning and Harris was doing his Howard Cosell imitation as he softly whispered the exploits of batter after batter. Three outs away from the perfect game. And then Joe Geisinger started walking toward us, his eyebrows raised in anticipation of catching us doing something illegal.

Ben quickly took the radio out of Harris' hands and slid it, earpiece and all, into his shorts.

"I just hope you're wearing underwear," Harris gasped.

"Nope."

Harris started to retch. I poked him in the side and pointed at the owner of the camp who was a few rows away. Harris held his breath. We all looked toward the stage as Joe stared at us, studied us, and then moved on. He ended up confiscating the two radios from the campers in the oldest group, banishing the culprits to sit outside on the back porch.

Joe walked back up to the front of the stage and the next act was introduced. Ben slid the radio out of his gym shorts. Harris refused to touch it.

"What's the matter? Take it!"

"What are you, crazy? That was in your shorts, next to your junk."

"Okay, then I'll listen for you."

Ben put in the earpiece and became our play by play announcer.

"Top of the ninth and … Randy Hundley grounds out," Ben whispers.

The news travels through boys' camp from one row of benches to the next row of benches. A young girl with a guitar had taken the stage and was singing a Joni Mitchell song, and she wasn't that bad. Suddenly Ben groaned loudly, followed by a whisper. "Jimmy Qualls gets on base with a single."

There was no filter this time. The entire boys camp moaned in anguish, bringing an end to the talent show as the girl on stage faltered, sobbed and then ran off into the wings.

Boys camp was apoplectic while girls camp had no clue what was going on. Ed Barnett placed his pinkies into his mouth and blew a shrill whistle that brought the Social Hall to attention. He then lectured boys side for the next five minutes about 'respect'.

Once more Ben hid the transistor radio in his shorts as Ed Barnett strolled down the center aisle. He was giving us his infamous 'Death Stare', the one where you know he's looking through your soul directly at your hidden guilt. I was surprised that Asa or Samson didn't turn us in, but they were too busy chatting with their female counterparts across the aisle. They never knew what was going on.

Now I really regretted being up at camp, having missed this incredible once in a lifetime game. The Mets were surging, and I was in isolation. I was going to have to smoke more joints with Jericho in hopes of either getting kicked out or numbing my summer experience.

14

Social Night.

This was it, the evening most of the bunk was waiting for. Jericho and I disappeared during Free Play and smoked a joint, while the rest of the bunk lined up to shower. We knew there wouldn't be any hot water when we returned to the bunk, but our ritual was now a cherished one, and I really had no dreams of meeting someone over the summer. I never did.

Jericho was in a melancholy mood, having just received a package and a letter from his brother over in "Nam." The package contained some more pot hidden in a t shirt.

"He's not seen any combat lately, but he thinks his company is going to be sent out in to the jungle any day. He's not looking forward to it, and... I think he's scared," Jericho told me.

"He can't run away, can he?" At thirteen years of age there was very little we could comprehend about combat.

"No, he's stuck there. He says that the only thing getting him through the days is that he's completely whacked out of his mind. Says the weed is phenomenal over there and it keeps him sane."

"Sucks."

"One more toke, and then let's get back to shower."

Jericho was in a far off different world as he contemplated what his brother was going through.

"I hate socials," I told him

"I'm dying to see Beth. You're going to like her, Jason. She's beautiful and smart and sweet. Not like the other bitchy princesses in this camp. Only problem is there's never any privacy so we can't make out. Counselors are always watching."

"Have you ever made out before?" I grounded the joint into a lifeless pulp on the rocks at the edge of the lake.

Jericho laughed.

"You crack me up... I shouldn't say this, cause I don't brag, but I trust you. We've been to third base already and I think this winter I'll go all the way. Don't say anything to anyone though, promise?"

I was obviously in awe of this news. He was truly the coolest dude I'd ever come across, and I just stood there with a stupid smile spread across my face. I mean, after all, just to have a girlfriend was a big thing, but to actually kiss her and ... well..

"Jason, do you promise?" Jericho asked again, and I could only nod yes as we made our way out of the woods and back to the bunk.

"Yeah, I promise, but Jericho... what do you actually mean by 'getting to third base'?"

"You're killing me. I have put my hands down her pants Jason... that's third base."

"And what do you do then?" I asked.

Jericho laughed and shook his head in amazement. "Didn't you ever have that talk about sex with your parents?"

"You're kidding, right? I'm lucky my parents acknowledge me, much less talk to me. It's as if I don't exist. My mother has like a 40-foot extension cord on her Princess phone so she can walk around the house in a perpetual conversation with her friends, or her lover.... either one... always on the phone.... and my father? Ha! He's so uptight. You have this older brother... I'm alone. Because of my mother I'm treated like a leper in school..."

"Wow... when I was like ten years old my mom and dad came into my room and sat down on my bed... My mom asked me if I had any questions about sex... not the birds and bees bullshit about how babies are born... about sex! So I asked my mother... because I heard some counselors talking about it... 'Mom, is it true that you suck on Daddy's dick?"

"And???"

I could sense that my eyes were popping out of my head because Jericho looked at me with a sense of fear, horror, and empathy.

"And my mother gave the scripted answer."

"Which was?"

Jericho thought about whether to continue, but when he smiled I knew he would tell me the truth.

"My mother told me that if you really love the man you're with you would do so."

"Really?"

"That's what she said. I've never seen my father jump up and run away as fast as he did that night."

"That's so cool." I meant it. To have parents who would and could talk to you about anything was such a dream.

And that's how I learned about sex in my most formative years. Fact, fiction, lore... all this knowledge was funneled to me by listening to bunkmates and counselors.

Ben was sitting on the boot box reading an Anatomy textbook, using a pink highlighter and writing notes in the column. He didn't even look up when we approached.

"You know, there'll probably be no hot water when you shower."

There was chaos in the bunk. A river of water flowed down the center aisle from the steady use of the small metal stall shower in the back room. Towels were strewn across the floor as most of the bunk continued to dress for the social. Harris finally scurried out of the back room, a towel wrapped around his minuscule waist. His wet skeletal body displayed the bruises from punches thrown by Hardon and the counselors. He dodged the rat-tails that were snapped at his legs, and he only howled when Hooky connected. You could hear his skin being ripped. A perfect rat-tail is a towel that is wrapped so tight that it resembles a whip, and when the tip is saturated it becomes a dangerous weapon.

Mickey Hardon and The Brain were already dressed, and were dousing themselves with aftershave lotion. They believed the scent gave them superhuman erotic powers. They were dressed in tight bell bottom jeans, which flowed like elephant ears and hid their lustrous black boots. They wore identical dress shirts. A ghastly purple color decorated in multi pastel circles. They probably thought this made them look so groovy. They kept the top two buttons of their shirt open, exposing nothing, not even a whisper of chest hair.

Bugsy wore his preppie outfit, Chinos and a pink Izod shirt with its black alligator hanging over his left nipple. Penny loafers with no socks. Hair immaculately combed with a part on the side.

Harris was busy sliding on dungarees that were a bit baggy. I watched as he pulled on a white Izod shirt, but unlike Bugsy, he left it untucked. Black socks and white bucks... He caught me shaking my head and started searching his cubby for white socks.

By the time Jericho and I finished showering, the rest of the bunk was on the porch waiting for First Call for our social. This evening we would be down at the waterfront. This was a big disappointment to the Mayor because he was having a chocolate fit. He needed chocolate, and when the socials were at the canteen he could order as much candy and burgers as his heart desired.

I watched Oliver dress for the night, and it was obvious his mother never understood that this was not a business meeting, but a social. Jericho came over and removed Oliver's clip-on bowtie, and threw it into the garbage.

"This is a no-no. And open your top button, man, you just don't look cool," Jericho told him as he undid the top buttons of Oliver's oxford button down shirt.

"My mother... " he started to say.

"Your mother has no clue what to dress you in. The girls will be running from you, and our counselors will tear you apart. You're supposed to look like a kid, not a little businessman. And dude... white socks with black shoes just doesn't cut it. Don't you have black socks anywhere?"

Oliver shook his head no, so Jericho went back to his bunk and threw him a pair of his own black socks. Then Jericho looked at me, shook his head and laughed., "But man, what the hell am I going to do with you?"

Jericho was wearing a pair of bell bottom jeans with two or three patches sewn on the pants where the fabric had worn down to nothing. He wore a tie-dyed t shirt with a huge peace symbol on the back and sandals instead of sneakers or shoes. He looked at me, dressed in my dungaree shorts, and Izod white tennis shirt which I refused to tuck in. "You're going to chase women away. Don't you own a pair of bell bottoms?"

"No, I don't."

"How come, man?"

"Cause... my mother only bought me one pair of bell bottoms and they were ugly, and when I wore them to school everyone made fun of me because I wore them with penny loafers. The bell bottoms were lime green with kelly green stripes... ugly."

"Yeah, I would have burned that too. Look, I have an extra pair. Just don't come in them when you meet Beth. I don't know what you'll do about shoes though. Maybe have your mom send you up some new ones?"

Jericho looked into a small mirror above his bed, and made precision swipes in combing back his hair. "Can't let my friend look like a loser in my presence."

If he only knew my mom.

One of my two favorite moments in a camp day were the minutes before reveille, when it always seemed I was awakened by a strafing fly. I would walk out of the bunk and sit on the boot box and look out at the lawn with its thousand glistening dew diamonds. I could feel the silence, and taste the purity of the morning.

The other moment is at dusk, when Free Play is at its end and the sun, so mellow and soft, an orange ball of tenderness, is kissing the tree-tops before it sets for the day. A quiet befalls camp, a peaceful meandering of laughter from campers who are free to do what they desire until evening activity call. Later in life I would remember these moments while sitting in traffic, watching maniacs navigate the highways, all the while stressing out about work, and making a living. At times I would just zone out and wish I could have traveled back in time for those two moments of serenity.

It was in this peaceful moment, while standing around waiting for the evening activity call, that Jericho caught me looking at him.

"What's up?"

"How do you get to be as cool as you?"

"What are you talking about?" Jericho asked. He pulled me off to the side of the bunk, away from everyone.

"I'm just looking at you, and you're so fucking cool... how do you do it?

"I don't do anything."

"So you're born with it? You're born with this incredible gift of brains and the looks that all the girls want?"

"Are you okay?" Jericho asked.

"Yes," I told him. I started to laugh as I felt like I was coming out of a trance.

"Look, I have an older brother who is cool. He teaches me, guides me, and I try to emulate him in every manner. He's living through these times, it affects him, eats at him, but it makes him stronger, sharper. You're an only child, you have no one to guide you. I have close friends and we talk all the time about music, fashion, politics, sex,...I mean, you just need to talk to people, and to listen carefully to what is being said. I don't see myself as cool. I just think I'm more aware of the world than my peers."

This was the first social of the summer. There would be about five others, but for now the entire boys' side gathered outside of their bunks waiting for the needle to hit the grooves of the record that would play the bugle call for Evening Activity. Every group was going to a different venue for their social; the Canteen, the Social Hall, the Mess Hall..... If I was a romantic at heart I would say that the waterfront was an enticing setting for meeting girls, but I didn't know what romance was.

Jericho had not only given me a pair of bell bottom jeans, but also one of his cooler t shirts. I was told to put away my sneakers and wear my rubber flip flops in lieu of sandals. If I had longer hair, and a peace symbol chain I might have looked like Jericho's cousin, but I was still a neophyte when it came to dressing in cool attire.

Chick was nowhere to be found, so Asa took it upon himself to act as the group- leader. Samson stood next to Asa, wearing a button down oxford neatly tucked into his shorts. A pair of white bucks without socks touched off his attire. He had a cigarette dangling from his mouth, and he was prancing back and forth in front of us like a chicken clucking and digging at the dirt. He stopped, took a deep drag from his cigarette and blew out perfect smoke rings, reminding me of the Marlboro Man in the heart of Times Square.

Lenny was wearing a pair of painters' pants that were baggy on him, and his white t-shirt made him look like a Good Humor man.

"Now boys... now boys... listen up," Samson was saying while blowing more smoke rings, "This is your first social and we want you to be prepared for anything. So we're going to show you something. See what this is? Anyone know what this is?" Samson took a small plastic square out of his pocket.

"A piece of candy," Harris shouted.

The counselors all laughed and Samson called Harris to come to the front of the group. I tried to pull Harris back down but he thought by being picked he was going to do something special.

"No, this isn't candy. This is what is known as a scumbag. Anyone know what a scumbag is for?" Samson asked.

"Keep girls from getting pregnant," The Brain shouted. The group giggled like little girls.

"Not bad, Brain. Now the important thing is that you might get lucky tonight... "

"Oh please... this is ridiculous," Ben suddenly muttered from the side. He refused to stand up front with the other counselors.

"No no... they might get lucky," Samson continued. "Now, just because you have a scumbag on you, doesn't mean you know how to use them so we're going to show you how to apply it. Gentlemen, with your assistance."

The other counselors approached Harris. Lenny and Spanky each took an arm, and they lifted Harris off the ground. He tried to struggle, kicking wildly. He tried to bite his captors, but he was trapped. Samson ripped off Harris' belt and pulled down his pants. Harris struggled like a fly in a spiders web, but was getting nowhere. I looked at Jericho, but he only looked away. The two of us wanted to help, but knew that this was not a battle we could win.

"Now boys, you have to make sure the rubber, or scumbag, fits properly. And with the help of Harris here, we're going to show you how it should fit," Samson shouted.

With his teeth, Samson ripped open the plastic pouch and pulled out the rubber.

Ben suddenly took action, and tried to get around the two football players who kept pushing him back. Ben didn't want to fight , so he kept trying to reason his way around them.

"Now, it comes all rolled up, and the idea is to put the tip of this on your erect penis and then roll it down, almost like the jelly roll blankets on the edge of your beds," Samson shouted.

"Cut it out!" Ben shouted. He continued to fight, trying frantically to get around the human blockade.

"Cool it," Asa warned Ben.

Asa grabbed Harris by the ankles, and spread his legs wider like he was about to break the wishbone at Thanksgiving.

"Now, with the help of Harris we'll demonstrate," Samson said as he pulled down Harris' underwear. Harris struggled harder than ever, and I glanced over at Ben. I didn't see how it happened but the two football players were suddenly lying on the ground. It finally filtered through the commotion that everyone was laughing.

"OH MY GOD... He's dickless..." Asa shouted. "It's so small... it's like he's got no dick at all."

Harris stopped struggling, went limp. He started to cry. The entire group started to laugh at him. In a sense Asa was correct. Harris had the smallest penis I had ever seen. It was the same small penis that my newborn cousin displayed at his Bris. I always wondered why Harris disappeared when we were showering or changing for swim.

"We can't demonstrate this on dickless here," Samson shouted as the laughter grew into a tidal wave of humiliation.

"Then demonstrate on me, you asshole," Ben shouted as he pulled Lenny and Spanky off of Harris. Without being supported at all ends Harris fell to the ground. He quickly pulled up his under-wear and pants, and ran into the bunk.

"What's the matter? Why don't you want to pull down my shorts?' Ben shouted as the counselors fell onto each other laugh-ing hysterically.

"What's your problem? We're only having some fun and trying to educate these thirteen year old boys" Asa said. He was bare-ly able to get out a word between gasping for breath through his laughter.

"Why pick on him?" Ben asked

"We didn't know he had such a small dick. Did you?" Lenny shouted.

"What difference does it make? You humiliated him in front of everyone," Ben said.

Ben was furious. He stared down the counselors and then start-ed to walk back into the bunk to talk to Harris.

"Oh come on, he's just a Sunshine for the summer. Fuck him if he can't take a joke," Samson shouted.

"What did you just say?" Ben asked before disappearing into the bunk. You could see the anger spread over his face, his hands clenched into two fists.

"He's our Sunshine for the summer, and if you're not careful, we'll make you one too," Asa threatened.

Samson towered over Ben by what seemed a full body length. Yet, at this moment, as Ben stared down both tormentors, he stood taller than any other counselor in the camp.

"Go screw yourselves," Ben shouted, spit flying out of his mouth.

Chick walked up from the HCO shack and asked what was going

on, but nobody said anything. Chick then led us to our first social. I kept looking back at the bunk, wondering what was going to happen to Harris.

"It's not right," I said to Jericho

"I know it's not. Asshole counselors think they can get away with anything they want, and they usually do." Jericho replied. "At least there's a counselor this year who seems to care."

The boys' waterfront was a cement deck, maybe fifty yards in length. A wooden pavilion, highlighted by blood red shingles across the top, bisected the deck. This was the only shelter the staff had in case it rained. The girls' waterfront stood side by side with the boys' waterfront almost naked in comparison. There was no pavilion, no shelter from the rainy days, and it was half the size.

The dock on both waterfronts were of a wooden build. It was squared and formed the crib area where the younger campers and weaker swimmers could still touch bottom. Beyond the crib was a roped off quadrant for the deep water section. I had easily passed my deep water test on my first attempt, and now I loved swimming out to the two floating rafts that marked the outer boundary of the swimming area. Jericho and I were always swim buddies.

A small stereo was placed under the pavilion, and Spanky manned the music for the evening, deftly picking one 45 after another. The boys arrived first, and we immediately gravitated toward the left side of the cement deck. Wooden benches etched the railings, and the few of us who weren't waiting under the pavilion for their girlfriends to arrive, sat quietly as if we were praying. The placid lake began to sooth my fragmented state.

"What's on your mind?" Jericho asked, as he sat down next to me with Oliver by his side.

"Well first ... why are you here?"

"What does that mean?"

"Why are you sitting with us... you have a girlfriend."

"Yeah, so?"

"So look under the pavilion. Seems like it's the meeting place for anyone who already has a girlfriend."

"Don't want to hang out with those wannabe boyfriends... I don't need to prove anything."

I just nodded in agreement.

"What else? I know there's something else.."

"I'm confused. Why was I so upset back there. I was angry about how Harris was being treated. And yet I just sat there... I didn't do anything.. So... I'm wondering why I would even care about him?"

"Dude, you live in solitary confinement. From what you tell me you're the lone survivor on a desert island... dude... you're socially inept."

"You're right. My parents are always out, and I never have any friends come over... "I'm living in a bubble."

"And if you didn't care about someone I'd worry about you because in times like these, we need all the love we can get."

"Why aren't those asshole counselors in the war?" I asked.

"My brother chose to fight. I don't know why. I have a feeling he was flunking out of school, was doing too many drugs, not enough studying. Those two assholes will have to face the music once they get out of college, but that ends this year unless they go on to become teachers or doctors. I do hope they're shipped off to Nam and get their asses blown off."

"I never picked on anyone in my entire life. I just don't get it."

Before Jericho could answer me the girls arrived.

Where the boys veered to the left, the girls bolted to the right side of the pavilion. The couples seemed to congregate in the middle. Mickey Hardon and The Brain sauntered over to their girlfriends and held hands The Mayor, Hooky, Bugsy and Altman just seemed to glom on and stood around like they belonged. Jericho had immediately left us when the girls appeared, but now he emerged from the group with Beth.

She was more beautiful than one could imagine. Beth had long wavy blond hair that fell to the middle of her back. She was one of those natural beauties with a great smile and sky blue eyes that just made you melt. She was about the same height as Jericho and she had dimples when she smiled. Beth seemed to have developed perfectly round little breasts over the last few months because Jericho was in shock and couldn't take his eyes off them.

She dressed like Jericho. Bell bottom jeans, with a myriad of patchwork. Her v neck white t shirt made her tan even more glorious. Jericho introduced us, and for once in my life I wasn't tongue tied.

"Jericho told us you were beautiful, but ...you're beautiful," I gushed. "I mean, the two of you are like the perfect couple."

"You should see her play softball and tennis.. she's the best.," Jericho bragged.

"No, really, you could be a model," Oliver chimed in, his voice suddenly two octaves higher.

"Thank you," Beth said softly.

She was shy. How could this be? Someone as beautiful as she was should have so much confidence in herself. Yet she was so soft spoken and so understated that I immediately fell in love with her. It was like the setting sun only shone upon her, illuminating her flaxen hair. She had such a sweet scent..... maybe from some shampoo or soap she was using.. The aroma of fireplaces burning on a cool winter's day has always remained with me. The scent that accompanied Beth will now forever be my summer memory.

We chatted a bit, and then she excused herself and walked over to the other side of the dock to be with her friends.

"You are so lucky," Oliver shouted.

We all laughed because Oliver was right.

"She was always cute but she grew over the winter, and where did those breasts come from? They weren't that obvious the last time I saw her. They just like .... Boing.. popped up. But you should see her on the softball field. She's fantastic. Grew up in a family of boys and they taught her how to play baseball. I just wish I had some privacy so I could kiss her for a long time."

Suddenly Harris appeared. He was walking toward us with Ben.

Ben had his arm around Harris, sort of supporting him. Harris' eyes were red, but he seemed to have overcome what had just occurred.

Or maybe he hadn't and never would.

Looking back on this evening I would finally come to the realization that Harris had lost his dignity, and self esteem at the hands of Asa and Samson. He was probably never the same. I would never understand the feeling of disgrace, and the utter humiliation he faced in those few moments, and the damage that was done. But I would always remember the courage it took for Harris to show up to the Social, and I admired him for that.

Ben didn't say anything. He left Harris with us and then went to speak to Chick. We stood there dumbfounded. It reminded me of the time my uncle died, and I had no clue what to say to my cousin. We just stood there looking out at the water hoping Harris would say something first. But he didn't. So I did.

"Why don't you go to Joe and tell him what the counselors are doing to you?"

"I can't," Harris mumbled.

"You can't? Or you don't want to?" Jericho asked.

"I can't and I don't want to," Harris told us. He barely looked up.

"Then why doesn't Ben tell Joe what's happening?" I asked.

"He can't."

"What are you saying?" Jericho asked.

"He can't. I won't let him."

"Joe could stop all this. Chick can stop it too. Just say something to either of them," I begged.

Harris said nothing. He just stood there shaking his head, never looking up at us. Thank goodness for Beth, as she returned with two other girls. Beth introduced us to her friends who, like me, were new to camp. Rachel was tall and thin. She was my height and gangly. Her arms looked like long string beans. She had short red hair, wore small wire-framed glasses and had freckles all over her face. She was the chatty type and immediately took off on a rift of conversation that had me mesmerized. She wore a t shirt under a pair of white overalls, capping it off with white tennis sneakers. I loved the look. It was a natural look, one that hid any observance of her willowy body. She looked so comfortable within herself, and I immediately took a liking to her.

Ellen was a tiny sprite. She too wore glasses, but they were sized too big for her tiny face. It seemed the only thing keeping her glasses from sliding off her face was the small bump in the middle of her nose. She had thick brown curly hair and like Rachel, she was far from seeing the first bud of development. When she smiled, her braces reflected the setting sun. She was slightly taller than Harris, but such a waif that you thought the slightest breeze would blow her away. Harris took an immediate affinity to her.

Harris turned slightly red as he sputtered anguished, incomplete sentences of complimentary phrases in an effort to impress Ellen. It was amazing he could even conduct a conversation after what he went through. I don't know what Ben had said to him, but it did seem like an immediate recovery.

Carrying on a conversation with Rachel was difficult. I kept sneaking glances at Jericho and Beth. When they thought nobody was watching they would sneak a quick kiss, and then sigh and hold hands. It really was very cute, but you knew they were hoping that all this innocence would evolve into something heavier.

"Well, what do we have here? The losers?"

It was Mickey Hardon. His mouth was a gash, spewing sarcasm. He looked like an octopus with his arms slithering all over what must have been his girlfriend.

They emerged from the throng of bored and shy boys--the ones who had no interest in girls or did not know how to talk to the opposite sex. They appeared like mosquitoes in a swarm ready to attack us. They were all here, The Brain, Hardon, The Mayor, Hooky, Bugsy and Altman. The Jewish Mafia and their molls.

Mickey Hardon's girlfriend was... so homely. Yet she carried herself with an air of confidence that forced the blind to believe she was beautiful.

I guess this was the first lesson I ever learned about girls. It's a simple lesson. If you believed you were pretty, you could force your belief onto others. You could bully other girls into seeing you as being attractive. A girl could brainwash her chorus of sycophants', the weak-minded and cerebrally stunted, into thinking you were beautiful. Mickey Hardon was one of the weak-minded.

"What do we have here? Two surfboards without tits? Or should I say two spears without tits, judging by the size of their noses," Hardon shouted and everyone laughed.

Rachel looked away, and almost buried her face into my chest in shame. Just having her breathe against me caused a rush that started to give me a boner. Ellen pushed her glasses back on her nose and was about to say something but Beth jumped in.

"Hey Bonnie! Why don't you take your moron ape parade back to the other side and leave us alone? Why do you have to bother us?"

"Stay out of this, Beth. Bonnie has nothing to do with this. I wanted to come over here and see what losers would be interested in those two lowlifes."

Hardon nodded toward me. I knew he also meant Harris.

Hardon pointed at Ellen.

"I hear the little one over there still uses a training bra, and she doesn't even need that because she has nothing growing. So what could she possibly be training? And what could she possibly want with dickless? Don't you know Harris has no dick? Hey, maybe that's perfect...no dick with no tits.... And the one you're with, Jason, now that's a real dog. Look how she dresses... she's like a farmer."

"Shut up, Hardon," Jericho warned.

"Seriously... dickless with titless..."

Ellen tried to hide her tears but she couldn't hold back. I thought Harris might run and hide but I was shocked by his resiliency. Or maybe I was in awe of Harris as I watched his anger grow. Jericho had to hold Harris back from attacking Hardon.

Then they were gone, like a foggy morning burned off by the sun. It was surreal; did it really happen? If the girls weren't sniffling and trying to hide their hurt I would say it was a dream, but the tears that rolled down Rachel's cheeks made it all too real.

"It's so hard to be here with those mean jerks. They take my bras and put them on the flag pole. Then they pin a tail on the back of Rachel's overalls and make fun of her, " Ellen told us, her voice quivering. "I'm called Schnoz, and Rachel is 'Flatso' and I just want to kill them."

"Seriously, and tell me the truth," Rachel asked, She was staring straight into my eyes. I've never had such contact like this before. I felt myself starting to shiver from such an intense stare. I had never been this close to a girl before, and she was beseeching me for the truth.

"Okay..."

"Did you see Bonnie? I mean she has a bigger nose than I do, and her thighs are so flabby. And how big is her ass? All she has are bigger tits, and that's because she developed before anyone else, and they're so flabby and ugly, but she walks around the bunk naked thinking that she's beautiful and all of her friends just fawn over her. And that awful boy, Hardon, just keeps calling her beautiful, but what does everyone see in her?"

I was suddenly in love with Rachel. She was brutally honest and sensitive, and truly beautiful. I was melting into her, wanting to hold her close but was afraid to do so.

"I think she's pretty grotesque if you were to ask me. You're so much more beautiful," I told her.

"She threatens everyone in the bunk into thinking she's pretty. Breasts are a powerful weapon in seducing little boys," Beth whispered.

"You have very nice breasts, almost perfect ones," Harris stuttered.

There was a stunned silence. One, it was a bold statement, and two, it came from Harris who we thought would be traumatized beyond conversation for the rest of his life. We all started laughing. It was a wonderful feeling because it felt like we suddenly belonged together.

"Truthfully, Jericho liked me from the moment he saw me. He saw me for who I was, and until a few months ago I had nothing to show too." Beth kissed Jericho on the lips, making everyone blush.

Jericho's breath was stolen away by the kiss. When he finally was able to breathe all he could muster was, "I wish we had some privacy."

It was at that moment I crossed the line. It was something building up inside of me, an anger and a desire to bond even closer with Jericho. There was also a sense of decency to be reclaimed. Or maybe I just wanted to protect a girl's honor. These were new feelings that I had never felt before.

I boldly took Rachel by the hand and told Harris to follow me. He clasped his hand into Ellen's and they fell in line as I led them across the deck to the side where the girls congregated. We passed Ben and he looked at me with a warped smile, and I wondered if he knew what had just occurred.

I really had no clue as to what had gotten into me as I marched across the pavilion. I passed all these girls who had spent hours blow drying and curling their hair, doing their nails and picking out just the right outfit for this big night.

I knew that Beth, Wendy and Ellen were not like those girls. They were probably out on the tennis courts all day instead of preparing for this stupid social.

Hardon was sitting atop the railing, his hands on the abundant fleshy hips of Bonnie. I took Rachel in my arms and kissed her. Just like that! I pressed my closed lips against hers. I didn't close my eyes, so I knew that she was as stunned as I was. Then I pretended to lose my breath and my balance. I choreographed being faint, dizzy, and stumbled backward right into Bonnie, and my momentum created a wave of energy that eventually pushed Hardon over the railing and into the lake.

The loud splash had everyone running over to see Hardon floundering in the water. That's all I wanted. I wanted to create a diversion so that Beth and Jericho had a few moments alone. Rachel stood there stunned, and Harris was agog between reveling in seeing Hardon falling into the lake, and my having enough nerve to kiss Rachel. Harris took it upon himself to make a quick dive onto Ellen's lips, a quick kiss, which was more like a peck, but the result was an instantaneous high for the little man. The courage he displayed in kissing Ellen, who was just as flustered as Rachel, seemed to inflate his ego. It seemed to be camouflaging the hurt from earlier in the evening.

The counselors helped Hardon climb out of the water. I moved to the outside of the crowd and peeked over to see Jericho and Beth. They had their moment of privacy.

That night as we undressed for bed Hardon kept trying to blame me for pushing him into the lake, but Ben refused to listen to his complaint. The more Hardon complained, the more Ben ignored him. Flustered, Hardon bolted from the bunk and we saw him run next door to complain to Asa and Samson. No one saw what precipitated Hardon's accident, except maybe Ben, so I knew I was in the clear.

Mickey Hardon was devastated when he realized that nobody really cared about him falling into the lake. There was a slow realization that maybe he wasn't the center of the universe anymore, and that his power over the bunk was beginning to wane.

We could see Hardon gesticulating to Asa and Samson, pointing at us, and then the two counselors turned their backs on him. We watched as Mickey Hardon slowly made his way back to the bunk. He walked like a delicate child, one who can't accept defeat.

"I know you did that on purpose, and I know why, so thank you," Jericho whispered as he passed me on his trip from the back room.

"Do you think she likes me?" I asked Jericho

"Of course she does."

"How do you know?"

"Beth told me."

And I was in heaven. I would look back on this summer and forever realize how important a summer romance was. It was innocence with the blessing of a dream of deeper and more meaningful romances to come. Hardon was sitting up in his bed, just eyeing us.

He took his pointer finger and mocked slitting his throat in a direct threat to me.

Bugsy pointed his finger at me, and cocked his thumb like a gun, pretending to shoot me. Then he strapped on his night braces. He adjusted the strap around his head and attached the thin curved rod to his braces.

"You look like a stupid chipmunk," Jericho told him

"Whlat whew thay?" Bugsy shouted. With the wire attached to his braces he mostly spit and slurred his words.

"You're fucking ugly."

Bugsy flipped Jericho the bird, but before Jericho could retaliate Taps sounded, and Ben turned off the lights and left the bunk. Chick came in and warned us to behave, telling us that he was going to be down at the HCO shack all night and could hear everything. Our OD, was Spanky. We knew he wasn't going to stand for any noise because he was hoping that his girlfriend would sneak onto boys' campus and keep him warm in the cool night air.

Jericho went right to sleep, probably with thoughts of Beth dancing in his dreams. Harris tried reading for a few minutes, but ended up writing a letter, and Oliver and I commenced reading by flashlight.

"Okay, now that we're all horny from tonight who wants to see what I learned over the winter?" The Brain announced. "I learned how to jerk off."

"Shut up in there," Spanky shouted. "If I hear anymore noise you'll be out here doing pushups all night."

We knew that would never happen because Spanky was more concerned about when his girlfriend would arrive and wanted us asleep.

"I learned how to jerk off," The Brain whispered.

"What's that?" Altman asked.

"It's what you do when you get a boner. Here, I'll show you. Everyone get your flashlights and come here."

Harris and I remained on our beds. Jericho didn't budge and I didn't know if he was faking sleep or not. The rest of the bunk, including Oliver, gravitated over to The Brain.

"What's the matter, you guys don't want to learn something?" The Brain asked.

"I know what you're going to do, and I already know how."

I wasn't lying either. I learned how to jerk off by reading Gore Vidal's novel, "Myra Breckenridge" the year before. I stole the novel off my father's bookshelf and delved into it a winter ago and lo and behold... there was an explicit scene where someone masturbates. I could never ask my parents about this, and I had no older sibling who could enlighten me. I ate by myself during school lunch, and maybe that's what all the other guys were whispering about at their lunch tables. Maybe they were sharing stories about masturbating, where to do it, how to do it, the different techniques, and most important of all, how to hide the evidence from your mother that you're jerking off. No, I learned how to use my nimble fingers from "Myra Breckenridge."

"Now, when you get a boner, or want to get one, you have to take your thumb and pointer fingers from both hands, grip your cock and slowly massage it up and down. Even if you don't have a boner you can do this and it will still make you hard."

I peeked over and saw that The Brain had pulled down his pajama bottoms and had begun to knead his cock with his fingers, just as he instructed.

"Well, what happens?" Mandelbaum the Mayor asked.

"It starts to feel good. Real good, and you start to get really hard," The Brain told the bunk as his breathing slowed, and his voice got deeper.

"Know what I learned?" Mickey Hardon said out loud, his eyes never leaving The Brain's cock. "I learned that when a girl is about to have sex, her pussy starts to vibrate."

"Vibrate? What do you mean vibrate? Like back and forth and up and down?" Hooky asked, his curiosity piqued.

"I don't know. I was told it moves, goes all crazy. And I was also told that a girl's tits get rock hard when they're having sex."

Before anyone could question Hardon's statements The Brain interjected with a moan.

"What's the matter?" Mandelbaum the Mayor asked. "Should I get the OD?"

"I can feel it coming. I can feel it rising."

Everyone leaned in, their flashlights, shining brightly on The Brain's cock.

"DON'T GET TOO CLOSE. BACK AWAY," The Brain shouted. "You don't want to get any in your eyes."

All those around his bed jumped back a few inches, while The Brain continued to stroke himself.

"Oh yes, I can feel it, I can feel it, " The Brain shouted. "Watch out," and a second later The Brain was moaning and clutching his cock and stroking it furiously.

"Here it comes!" he screamed.

Everyone jumped back another foot, expecting a major explosion. I watched Hardon and the Mayor shield their eyes. The only one who didn't move was Oliver who had kept a flashlight and his focus on The Brain.

There was silence as The Brain tried to catch his breath.

"Nothing happened," Oliver finally stated.

"Of course something happened. You saw cum. Everyone saw it. You're just blind, Oliver,"

"No, I didn't see anything..What's supposed to come out?"

"White scum... white scum, you moron. Sperm, like you."

The Brain wiped his hands all over his pajama bottom. He pushed Oliver back toward his bed, and began to rub his hands together as if he was washing them in the sink.

"Now everyone get on their beds and do as I taught you and I'll come around and check. Of course, Dickless can't do this because he can't find his pecker."

The bunk laughed at the Brain's joke. They looked over toward my corner. Harris never looked up. Instead he slowly gave him the middle finger, and continued to write his letter.

Oliver had made his way back to his bed and mouthed to me

that he saw nothing. In the meantime a symphony of creaking bed springs swelled to a crescendo as labored breathing and furious stroking took over. One by one, each member of The Brain's School of Masturbation, reached climax. The sound of bed springs squealing at night would haunt me for a long time.

15

The most feared activity in camp, outside of arts and crafts, was Swim Instruction.

This was an hour and a half activity period at the waterfront. Usually it was the first period of the day. During this period we learned how to sail or canoe around the lake. Those who were lazy would man the decrepit rowboats and just paddle out into the middle of the lake and catch some rays. Then there were those mornings when we were forced into the freezing water.

Now, don't get me wrong, because I believe there's nothing as refreshing as swimming in a lake on a hot day. And don't even try to compare it to swimming in a pool. Who enjoys chlorine stinging their eyes, and sticking to you like glue so you smell like a pool all day? So sometimes you didn't mind that the lake water was chilled beyond comprehension from the cool night air.

Walking down to the lake we passed an old man painting an intricate design on a war canoe. Wooden war canoes were long and sat eight paddlers instead of the usual two.The old man had the deepest tan I'd ever seen, and the years in the sun had turned his skin into a shiny leather. Sitting next to him on a folding chair, was an equally wrinkled, tanned, silver-haired woman. She had more lines on her face than a New York City Subway map, and she looked to be the same age as the man painting the canoes. She was withered, and she was smoking a pipe. It was a corn cob pipe, and you could smell the cherry aroma from the smoldering tobacco.

"Why is she smoking a pipe?" I asked.

"Oh, that's Hal Goodkind's wife. She smokes that thing all day long," Jericho told me.

"She's squinting her eye like Popeye. And who's Hal?"

"He's the older guy painting the canoe."

"Why's he painting the canoe?"

"I don't know," Jericho said. A quizzical smile spread across his face. "Hal is one of Joe Geisinger's oldest friends. Joe just hires Hal to paint the war canoes every summer. The only time we use the war canoe is in a race during color war. I still can't figure out why she smokes the pipe, she just does."

I couldn't stop staring at the woman smoking the pipe. She finally noticed me, and smiled. She took the pipe out of her mouth, wiped her lips with the back of her hand. She then winked at me, and closed her eyes. She leaned back, slid the pipe back into her mouth and reveled in the morning sun. She revealed a moment of contentment so profound that I have never forgotten it.

Our canoe trip down the Delaware River was a week away, and we had to learn the proper techniques of paddling, and how to right a canoe on the river in case we tipped. Jericho and I were partners, and I was glad to relinquish the stern seat and sit in the bow because Jericho had experienced the Delaware River.

"I'm afraid of Skinners Falls," I confided as we paddled out to the middle of the lake with the rest of the group.

"Nothing to be scared of, just as long as you don't fall out of the canoe," Jericho teased.

Seemed like the entire bunk loved this canoe trip. It consisted of two days on the river and one night camping. The Brain talked reverently about the different falls we would hit. In order they were Skinners, Barryville, Colang, Crazy X, and finally little Mongap and Big Mongap. However, the conversation always returned to the fact that people die at Skinners Falls.

"And if we tip, and I fall out?" I asked.

"You're wearing a life preserver, and you just float down the falls."

"Float down the falls? I mean we're going over falls and the only floating we're going to do is through the air and we're going to get crushed at the bottom of the falls. How high are the falls anyway?"

Jericho took his paddle and smacked it against the water. The splash of cold made me cringe.

"Don't be such a pussy. What are you talking about?"

"How high are the falls?"

"You moron. These aren't waterfalls like Niagara Falls. They call it 'Falls' because there's a slight drop in the riverbed, and we're going over rocks, which cause haystacks, and they are so cool to ride."

Once again Jericho splashed me with water.

"What's going on?" Ben asked as he paddled his canoe over. Ben made sure that Harris would be his partner for this trip. Harris sat in the bow of the canoe like a mogul in his limousine. The contrast in weight between Harris and Ben caused the bow of the canoe to tip out of the water. Harris was barely able to reach over and get his paddle into the water.

"Jason thinks Skinners Falls is like Niagara Falls, and he's scared about going over them," Jericho told Ben.

"What are you, an idiot?" Ben laughed, and he too scooped the lake water with his paddle and splashed me. This turned into a full-fledged water fight between all the canoes.

Sy Schwartz, the head of the waterfront, kept blowing his whistle in an effort to get us under control, but we were beyond control. Ben jumped out of his canoe and swam over to our canoe. He then rocked us till we tipped over and fell into the water. It was so cold that it was hard to gasp a second breath.

Then Ben helped us right the canoe and held it steady as we climbed back in. My fears were quelled by Ben's assurances that nothing would happen on the river and if Harris wasn't scared, then I surely couldn't show any fear. We spent the morning canoeing across the lake, jumping in and out of our canoes, and learning how to rendezvous by pontooning the canoes together.

When we got back to shore it was obvious that Ben was going

to be the only counselor from the group joining us on the trip. Asa, Samson, Spanky and Lenny were not going down the river and didn't partake in this morning's exercise.

"What's the matter, Asa? Can't swim?" Ben chided him as we walked back to the bunk after the end of the period.

"Shut up, you dry hump. My knees can't take a canoe trip, and I can't jeopardize my senior season."

"What did you call me?" Ben asked as he approached Asa.

"Dry hump. What? You think we don't see you at night walking back from the fields before evening check -in with that wad of cum staining your pants? What's the matter with your girlfriend? She doesn't put out?"

"At least I'm not cavorting with..."

"Say another word and I'll kill you."

"All I'm saying is that you're just a bit too friendly with..."

Asa went berserk. He charged Ben, and Ben didn't back down. This scared Asa. He stopped inches from Ben, and tried to intimidate him with his ugly death stare. Then he started jabbing his fingers into Ben's chest. Samson and Lenny had joined the fray.

"Watch what you say, Dry Hump. I'll kill you if you ever say that again!" Asa shouted.

Ben calmly slapped Asa's hand away. Asa had to be restrained by Lenny and Samson.

"I'm going to rip your head off and shit down your neck."

Asa was frothing at the mouth as Lenny and Samson wrestled him to the ground. Ben just stood there with a shit-eating grin on his face, expressing no fear.

"I guess you know something that he doesn't want anyone to know?" Jericho said in passing as we continued our trek to the bunk.

"I don't know anything. I just see what I see. He's too friendly with some of the older campers on girls side."

To Ben it was as if the altercation had never taken place, but to Asa and Samson this hit home.

Rest hour found Harris writing home. He was burning through

the letter, his tongue wagging with every word he penned. There were one or two quick peeks at the rest of the bunk, wanting to make sure that no one was paying attention. He knew if Mickey Hardon and The Brain stole the letter they would rip it up.

Hardon was sent to the canteen this day to pick up our snacks and the Brain was busy doing the 'I gotta shit' dance. Hooky and The Mayor had occupied the toilets and The Brain was begging them to get off the pot. He kept running into the back room, checking on their progress when suddenly he saw something that made him stop dancing.

"Guys... you got to see this."

The toilet doors flew open as Hooky and The Mayor bolted out of the stalls like horses at the starting gate. They joined The Brain at the back window and they too started to laugh.

"Guys, you've gotta see this," The Brain shouted.

Bugsy, Beckett and Cahn ran into the back room and joined the chorus of laughter. I needed to know what was making them laugh so I flew out of the bunk and jumped over the railings. I ran to the back of the bunk where I saw what everyone was looking at. Ben was doing what looked like ballet. A slow high kick of his leg, bringing it down to earth in a deliberate motion. Turning and twisting side to side. I had never seen anything like it. Harris was suddenly by my side, smartly holding the envelope with his rest hour letter to his parents.

"What are you doing?" Oliver asked.

Oliver and Jericho finally caught up to us. The laughter from the bunk had grown louder, and we could see their ugly faces pressed against the screen windows of the back room.

"Tai Chi, some Karate, etc. etc."

'But what is it?" Oliver pleaded.

Ben continued his precise motions.

"I'm sure you know all about Karate. Well, Tai Chi is another form of Oriental self defense. But I also do it for relaxation and exercise."

"Homo... " The Brain shouted from the back window.

I shot him the middle finger without even looking back.

"Don't bother listening to him. I haven't had a chance to practice but now I'm going to work out every rest hour. Want to join me?"

Jericho begged off, but Harris and I agreed to join him. Oliver was a bit wishy washy on it, and told us he would decide later.

"Oh shit!"

It was the Brain, but this time he wasn't standing in the window. There was a commotion out in front of the bunk, and we ran around to see what was happening. Ben stayed behind and continued his Tai Chi.

Mickey Hardon, candy from the canteen in hand, stood next to Samson and they were staring at something on the ground.

"I swear I didn't mean to do it," Hardon pleaded.

"But you did throw the rock?" Samson asked.

"Yeah, but I didn't expect to hit it. It was a long shot. The sucker was crawling out of the garbage can and I wanted to scare it. I didn't mean to hit it."

On the ground there was a squirrel, obviously struck between his eyes. Drops of blood rolled down the face, and the squirrel was twitching, trying to desperately crawl away, but barely able to move.

"Get me a large cup and fill it to the top with water," Samson commanded.

Mickey Hardon stood there motionless, until Samson shouted "MOVE!" Mickey Hardon dropped the bag of candy and ran into the bunk and returned with his large plastic cup. It looked like the one he used to keep his toothbrush in. Water was sloshing over the sides.

Samson took the cup, and with his other hand lifted the squirrel by its tail. He dangled the spasming squirrel in the air and slowly lowered its head into the cup of water. The squirrel seemed to know what was happening and started to thrash violently, seeking a way to claw itself out of the cup.

"What are you doing?" Oliver screamed, his face a radiant red. He was hyperventilating. "Stop it! You're killing it. You're killing it. Please stop," he wailed, tears streaming down his face.

Oliver suddenly charged Samson in a valiant effort. He wanted to knock him over and cause him to drop the cup. Instead he bounced off the counselor like a tennis ball off a racquet.

"It's got to be done."

"No, it doesn't!" Oliver screamed as he charged Samson again.

Samson just stepped aside and tripped Oliver, who actually flew through the air before he crashed to the ground.

"Sometime's it's the best thing to do. Put someone out of their misery and pain," Samson told us. He was cool and authoritative.

Harris made a mad dash around the back of the bunk in search of Ben. Slowly, one by one, the other counselors in the group emerged from their bunks. Mickey Hardon and the rest of the group stood silent, watching Samson murder the squirrel. Oliver was on the ground, crying, pounding his fists into the grass. The dirt flew up into his face and after mixing with his tears it caked into muddy streaks.

The squirrel died. The thrashing and twitching had subsided by the time Ben came charging around the corner of the bunk with Harris far behind. He body slammed Samson to the ground, knocking the cup over. The squirrel lay limp on the ground. Samson got up and tried to punch Ben in the face, but Ben just knocked away his flying fist like it was crepe paper.

"What the hell is the matter with you? Are you an idiot?" Ben screamed.

He turned his back on Samson as he kneeled down to come to the aid of an inconsolable Oliver.

"What were you going to do, save the squirrel?" Samson asked. Asa and Lenny helped Samson off the ground, where he brushed himself off and then charged Ben.

Ben was blindsided. He was busy comforting Oliver, when Samson jumped on top of him. Ben was almost successful in breaking free, but he was pushed back down on the ground by Lenny, who had joined the fray.

"Who the hell do you think you are? You don't touch any of us, do you understand?" Lenny said as he pushed Ben's face into the ground.

Samson spoke loudly, "I was just teaching the kids a fact of life. You don't save people or animals who are beyond help. It was the humane thing to do. You don't want to prolong their agony."

Somehow Ben wriggled free from Lenny. He struggled to get up, and was a bit woozy. He stood toe to toe with Samson who towered over Ben.

"You don't do this in front of everyone. You do it in the woods away from these kids. You don't act like an executioner. What are you teaching them? That's it's okay to kill a living creature?"

Ben was hurt. His ribs ached, but then who wouldn't have been injured when gang-tackled. Ben helped Oliver off the ground. Oliver couldn't stop sobbing and Ben led him back to the bunk.

"What's all this commotion? Get back to your bunks and change for afternoon activity."

Chick had finally made it onto the scene and surveyed the situation. He didn't realize what had taken place, or maybe he did and didn't care.

We entered our bunk and found Ben sitting on Oliver's bed.

"Sometimes it's for the best. I don't think anyone could have helped that squirrel."

"Ben, he killed the squirrel..." Oliver cried.

"Yeah, and it was great, wasn't it?" Mickey Hardon shouted. "I threw that rock and hit that sucker, and..."

Before Mickey Hardon could say another word Ben had exploded off the bed. He sprinted across the room, surprising Mickey Hardon, who froze like a deer in the headlights. Ben wrapped his hand around Hardon's neck like a vise, lifted him off the ground, and pinned him against the back wall. Ben was squeezing Mickey Hardon's neck tightly, and either out of fear or lack of oxygen Hardon's eyes bulged out like ping pong balls.

"You little shit. You tried to hit that fucking squirrel."

Ben opened his grip and Mickey Hardon slid to the floor, gasping for breath.

Ben walked back to his bed, and reached into his cubby and pulled out a hardball. He twirled around and in one swift motion

126

threw a perfect strike at Mickey Hardon's head. It missed by inches as it exploded against the wall and bounced back down the center aisle of the bunk.

"You're fucking crazy," Mickey Hardon screamed.

"Maybe. Maybe I missed you by accident. Or maybe I have an incredibly accurate arm and missed you on purpose. That's for you to decide, but remember this… If I ever catch you tossing anything but a ball again I will take aim with whatever I have in my hand at the time… a stone.. a ball… a knife…. and you better pray that I didn't miss you by accident today because who knows what my aim will be like the next time."

There was utter silence in the bunk. The Mayor quietly gave out the rest of the canteen as Ben tried to let his anger simmer down from a boil. I wasn't interested in my candy anymore, and neither was Harris. We told Mandelbaum to keep our order and we sat on my bed and listened to Ben.

"Sometimes in life we have to make decisions. Now you shouldn't have seen that. That was wrong. That was sadistic to do it in front of everyone. Maybe I would have done the same thing myself, but not in front of everyone."

"I felt so helpless. There was nobody there to help the squirrel. I HATE EVERYONE IN THIS BUNK," Oliver shouted, as snot oozed out of his nose. Mickey Hardon just gave him the finger.

"Listen to me," Ben said softly. "You have to move on from this. Nobody could have stitched up the squirrel, right? Sometimes you just play the hand you're dealt."

"NO, you don't. Don't say that!" Harris screamed and he bolted off his bed and ran out of the bunk crying.

"You could have saved it. You're going to be a doctor," Oliver answered

"Oliver, listen to me. That squirrel was going to die anyway. I wasn't going to try and stitch up a squirrel…"

"But you didn't even try."

Oliver pushed away from Ben and walked into the back room where he was obviously going to cry while sitting on the toilet.

Ben then turned his attention toward Harris and headed onto the porch where Harris was sitting, bawling like a baby. Jericho and I looked at each other and wondered what triggered this. I was sure Ben was thinking the same thing.

"There's just so much violence in this world," Harris was whispering, but we could still hear him from my bed. "I'm tired of so much violence. The war... the assassinations, the.... this.. the that... death.. I don't want to see death anymore!"

Bugsy started imitating the squirrel squirming in the cup for his last breath of life. The bunk laughed with Bugsy. Oliver emerged from the back room, saw Bugsy twitching and returned to the confines of the toilet where he started to cry all over again.

Ben sat on the boot box with Harris and just let Harris cry. I had never seen so much crying in all my life, and it was so baffling. There were times I wanted to cry, like when I felt isolated, and picked on, but I always held it in. Harris and Oliver were so sensitive that they cried on a whisper. I wondered how these two innocent creatures would ever survive high school, much less the rest of life.

During Free Play that evening Harris and Oliver went to the Nature Shack. Everyone made fun of them as they left, calling them "sissies" and "pansies," but Oliver wanted to show Harris a snake that was just caught.

"Why aren't you guys playing basketball?" I asked Hardon as Jericho and I got up to leave. It was weird to not see the bunk run out to the basketball court

"What do you care? We're just hanging today," The Brain told us.

We took a more circuitous route to our spot that early evening because we wanted to make sure Bugsy or Mandelbaum weren't spying on us.

Ben was in a foul mood because he was assigned waterfront duty and the memory of The Mayor and Hooky tossing their rod and hooks so carelessly was giving him nightmares. Even though they were both docked from fishing for the rest of the summer Ben knew there were other crazy kids who wanted to fish, and who swished their tackle haphazardly. There was another accident-in-waiting for sure.

"I didn't know Ben has a girlfriend," Jericho said, as he lit another joint. It was getting harder and harder for him to find privacy to roll the joints. Everyone wanted to know why Jericho was on the toilet for so long. It was his private chamber where he could roll joints, but everyone in the bunk thought he was masturbating, so they taunted him with insults.

"Do you know who she is? And why do they call him Dry Hump?"

Jericho laughed, and took two more tokes before he handed me the joint. "You really don't know anything, do you? Do you even know what a dry hump is?" he asked.

I shook my head no, indicating I had no idea.

"I guess Ben and his girlfriend haven't fucked yet. Instead, they just rub and hump on top of each other fully clothed. All that friction causes an orgasm."

I still had a perplexed look. "He comes in his pants. All that jism just wetting his pants. But then again... wow..." and Jericho wandered off in thought.

It was a serene moment, the silence.

I heard the soft click, swish, of rowboat paddles entering the lake and propelling the flat bottomed tubs. The sound of kids laughing and having fun filtered gently into the panorama,...basketballs ping ponging off the cement courts, girls laughing, counselors blowing whistles, and even Ben yelling for someone to put their rod and reel down...... but what didn't you hear? .... No airplanes. Not one. Never!

"Wow..." Jericho again said as we were both pretty high. "She must be very shy because if she gave him a blowjob then there would be no stains... unless she didn't swallow and she spit it out, because then she could get it all over his jeans anyway, and maybe she does that on purpose to get even for making her suck on his cock..."

"What the fuck are you talking about?" It was all gibberish to me, this sucking and swallowing. Jericho saw the look on my face and knew I still wasn't getting it.

I stared at the perfectly round orange ball of warmth that was setting at its own pace. The softness of the evening was debilitating. Who wanted to leave this moment?

"What's it like to have a brother?"

"What? What the fuck?"

"What's it like to have a brother? Remember, I'm an only child."

Jericho with a pensive look, tumbled into deep concentration.

"It's like never being alone or afraid. To know someone's always watching your back. It's like having the coolest teacher as your best friend."

That stung a bit. Best friend. I never had one and I'm sure Jericho has a few of them. I was always alone, sitting at home, and I had grown to enjoy it. Those summer months at camp… those were the insufferable times when I had to coexist with strangers.

"What's he taught you so far?"

"You know…. music… cool music. And drugs.. .lot's of drugs… cool drugs. And about the world, what's right and wrong…. and how so many things are wrong…."

Jericho had a faraway look, like he was seeing the future reflected off the lake.

"And of course,… Sex."

Jericho smiled.

"He's my teacher man. … but then again, who would have ever taught you what a dry hump was…. You really have a lot to learn, don't you?"

I laughed and looked at Jericho. Was there pity in his eyes? And then he smiled and smacked me in the head.

"Then I guess I'll have to educate you."

We squatted staring at each other, passing the joint back and forth when we heard the boys' loudspeaker switch on, and the sound of Ed and Irv storming back and forth. We knew it was too early for Free Play to be over, so it had to be something else.

"Attention, Boys' Camp, Attention, Boys' Camp.. Will all turtle burners come to the boys HCO shack immediately. All turtle burners come to the boys HCO shack immediately."

Then we heard the loudspeaker swivel around toward the lake. This time it was Chick speaking, "Eh.. Ben... please send all campers back to their bunks and report to the HCO shack."

"Turtle burners?" I looked at Jericho and he just shrugged.

The loudspeaker squealed again as it turned toward our bunk.

"Dammit Hardon, you know I'm talking to you. Now get all your accomplices and get down here now," the Head Counselor shouted over the loudspeaker, his voice echoing into the countryside.

"Turtle burners?" I said again, and I looked at Jericho and we realized at the same moment just what everyone was so angry about.

Jericho flicked the joint into the water and we ran back to the bunk. Bounding up the steps we flung open the screen door, nearly tearing it off its hinges. It was an eerie feeling to enter a bunk that seemed to be vacated in a hurry. Clothing, baseball mitts, sneakers were haphazardly strewn throughout the bunk, signifying that everyone left in a hurry.

"It's gone," Jericho said as he searched Oliver's cubby.

"What is?"

"The box. The box with Oliver's turtle. It's gone.

"You don't think they really burned the turtle?" I asked.

We walked back onto the porch and looked down at the HCO where the Jewish Mafia sat like hostages, heads bowed in shame as they awaited their fate. Ed Barnett paced back and forth like an animal enraged, his anger building to a crescendo. Oliver and Harris stood off to the side where Ben and Chick were trying to console a grieving Oliver. Beckett and Cahn were heading back to the bunk when Ed Barnett suddenly exploded in a tirade that sent the birds that were perched on the HCO roof screaming into the sky.

"What's going on?" Jericho asked as Beckett and Cahn joined us on the porch.

"I just wanted to hear the story first hand," Beckett told us.

"What's the story?" I asked.

"This is big, and you'll find out soon," Beckett told us as he ran inside the bunk to get his tape recorder.

"It's bad, it's really bad." Cahn said.

Ed Barnett's fiery sermon culminated in his walking away in disgust. He dismissed the 'turtle burners' who plodded back towards the bunk. They walked past us without saying a word. The Mayor and Hooky pouted and jumped on their beds in disgust. Beckett was immediately in their face with the tape recorder.

"What was your punishment?" Beckett asked The Mayor.

"Docked from canteen for two weeks, and no intercamp games," The Mayor told him.

"Why did you do it?" Beckett asked Hooky.

"We didn't. We just stood there. It was Hardon's idea. Hardon did it." Hooky told him.

"Why didn't you stop him?" Beckett asked.

There was silence. Hooky looked up at the intrepid reporter and just shrugged his shoulders. "I don't know. It seemed funny at the time. Hardon told me to do something so I did it. The same with the Mayor."

The Brain was strangely silent, laying on his bed as he turned his back to the bunk and stared at the wall. Mickey Hardon was livid. He paced back and forth, cursing, and dropping his dancing spit in staccato spasms. When he realized that he was being ignored he flopped down on his bed and smothered his face with his pillow.

Both Hardon and The Brain were docked from intercamp games, canteen, and socials for the next two weeks. Bugsy was docked from one canteen because of his participation as the lookout.

Ben finally headed back to the bunk with Oliver and Harris. All the counselors had tried to console the grieving Oliver, but he was still a sobbing mess as he entered the bunk. The eerie silence of the guilty campers served to only punctuate the pain Oliver was feeling.

"What did they do?" Jericho asked Ben.

"They took Oliver's turtle, sprayed it with their arm pit aerosol, and then lit the turtle on fire. The Brain bet Mickey Hardon that he wouldn't do it, so while Hooky and the Mayor doused the turtle, it was Mickey Hardon who set it ablaze."

"Is the turtle okay?" I asked.

Ben just stared at me and shook his head in disgust… "No, you idiot… the turtle is dead." And then he looked over at the other bunk to see Asa and Samson sitting on their bootbox, laughing.

"Those two shmucks have lowered the bar for human decency."

We would later find out that Joe Geisinger was finally contemplating sending Hardon and The Brain home, but this never happened. Jericho knew that would never happen. Too many siblings and relatives in camp. If shitting on a counselors' pillow doesn't get you thrown out, then nothing will. Not even cooking a live turtle. Not even that will get the privileged thrown out of camp.

16

A lesson learned.

With the turtle burners being docked from inter-camp games it was now my chance to (do i dare say) shine. We were heading to Camp Equinox, supposedly our fierce rival and Hardon and the rest of the "turtle burners" were furious that they had to stay behind.

Tuesdays in camp were known as trip days. Some groups went hiking, others into a small town called Honesdale which was about twenty or so miles west of camp. There we would go to the bowling alley or the movies. Sometimes we'd go northeast into Caldwell, which was even smaller. In Caldwell the movie theater was at the end of the only street in town. It was antiquated, and it looked more like a barn than a theater.

We had been to Caldwell the week before and it was there that I heard another word that shook my world. It made me feel uneasy, and it sent Ben, who was in camp for only a day or two at that time, into a fit of rage.

We had arrived in Caldwell early and had too much time to just sit around before the start of the movie. Instead of sitting inside the decrepit movie theater (It should have been condemned), Chick had allowed us to walk the town for fifteen minutes.

This was not a good idea. Young Jewish boys with money in their pockets descended on this sleeping town like locusts invading a field. Even though it was only the $2.50 we took out of the canteen allowance, we still felt rich. Some kids were richer than others, as is always the case. They were the ones who had extra money in their pockets that mommy and daddy had sent up in the mail. Harris and Oliver had a few extra dollars in their pockets, but I bet nobody had more than I. I still had the bill my father gave me at the busses on our first day of camp. I could have treated everyone, but I wasn't into sharing.

I was immediately drawn to the only candy store on the only street in town. The owner of the candy store was an old woman whose face had many sagging layers of skin. Each layer seemed to capture the smoke from the worn out cigarette butt that never seemed to leave her mouth. She watched us with accusatory eyes as we entered. Jericho, Harris and Oliver, we were all polite. We nodded hello, and answered "Yes ma'am" when questions were asked. Then the rest of the group crashed into the store and all hell broke loose.

The Mayor was grabbing as much candy as he could find, and Bugsy knocked over a glass container, spilling gumballs all over the floor. Others descended on the old lady like a horde of starved peasants begging for food and she looked scared. She suddenly stood up, and reached for a baseball bat under the counter and smashed it against the wall. The sound of the bat breaking tile acted as a switch that shocked us all into silence. At the same time Ben slipped in through the door.

"You damn Kykes…. get the hell out of here. Now!!! I don't want your filthy money, you nasty kykes. And if you take one more step toward me I'm going to bean you with this bat."

We were scared. The Brain and Hardon stood still with their mouths open. We were all afraid to move an inch. Total silence. I didn't know what a Kyke was. I had never heard that word before, but obviously Ben had because he slowly moved to the front of the store. He was not intimidated by this woman. He was angry. He clenched his fists, and I could see him grinding his teeth.

"How dare you!" he whispered. His voice stayed under control even though you could hear it waver with anger.

"You get these kykes out of here, mister!" the store owner shouted.

"Don't ever use that word again. DO YOU UNDERSTAND ME?" Ben shouted, his rage rising.

I think he scared the old lady because she sat down with the bat resting across her lap. She looked stunned. There was dead silence in the store.

"It's okay, Ben," I said, but he was ignoring me.

"Show some decency, you old anti-semite. You don't want us, you won't get us. You need us to survive. Look at this stinking deplorable town. The only time you make money is when we send our kids to the movies. We won't come back here anymore. In the meantime you owe every kid in this store an apology for being so nasty."

"I will not. NOW YOU GET OUT OF MY STORE BEFORE I CALL THE POLICE," she screamed as she stood up and patted the head of the bat into her open palm, a threatening move that didn't register with Ben.

"Anyone who has candy, and hasn't paid for it yet, come forward and gently drop the candy on the counter and then leave," Ben ordered.

It was a quick procession as the few who had taken candy moved to the front and then quickly exited the store. I remained frozen in the back with Harris, Jericho and Oliver.

"We will never come back here again, and no one from the camp will. You can keep your lousy candy and remain a bitter, blind, and stupid woman. Never use that word again!"

"What's a kyke?" I whispered to Oliver.

"Nasty name for Jew," he whispered back.

"Oh yeah, and what are you going to do about it?" she taunted.

"I'm not going to do anything. We're leaving and you're going to remain in this beat up old town for the rest of your life, you miserable human being."

Ben whirled, pushed us out of the store, and never looked back. All the kids were waiting outside and Ben calmly moved us all over the train tracks toward the movie theater. Chick came up to Ben, asked about the confrontation and was satisfied with his explanation. The old man herded us back into a semblance of a group and we marched into the theater where we knew they appreciated our summer business.

As Reveille broke on this Tuesday's trip day it had become obvious that something was up with The Mayor. He was always the first one out of bed on Tuesdays. Tuesday was also laundry day, a pain in the ass for each and every bunk. Yet, how many camps actually had towel and linen service? Beds had to be stripped before breakfast, and all the sheets were thrown into the middle of the floor where The Mayor seemed to always volunteer to stuff them in a large canvas bag. The Mayor stood in the middle of the bunk holding the bag for the sheets and pillow cases but everyone still remained in bed.

"Everybody up. Let's go," Chick shouted, "it's laundry day, let's get this done before breakfast."

He went from bed to bed and lifted one end off the ground, sometimes shaking the beds like a roller coaster making a turn. Where did the old man get the strength? The good thing about double decker beds is that he couldn't mess with them, so when he approached our bed he went straight to Ben and smacked him in the head.

"Ehhh... what's going on with you? You should be the first one out of bed, setting an example. You should be the first one out of bed forcing everyone else out of bed," Chick shouted.

"I can't," Ben said, sleep still in his voice.

"And why not?"

"Cause," and he motioned for Chick to step closer. "Cause I've got this huge erection and I don't want to scare the kids. I don't know what it is about this mountain air but I wake up hard every morning."

"You have to be shitting me. Get the fuck out of bed. You don't think they've seen boners before?" Chick shouted. "Get your ass out of bed."

"Okay... okay," Ben said as he fell out of the bed. From my vantage point, underneath him, all I could see was his boner. I mean, for a little guy it was huge, and sticking up straight in his white underwear, almost forming a little pup tent.

"Nice boner," Harris commented, and somehow this did the trick because suddenly everyone was out of bed hoping to see Ben with his erection.

"You must have been having some dream," Chick said, trying to suppress laughter.

"I'm telling you, it's the cold mornings up here. The cold air just does something to you," Ben said as he ignored all the comments from the bunk and slid on some shorts. Then he stripped his bed, and threw the sheets to The Mayor. He then walked around the bunk and pulled the blankets back on anyone who was trying to fall back asleep. The Mayor kept collecting sheets and stuffing them into the large bag.

I dressed quickly and walked into the back room, dragging out a dirty, heavy canvas bag of the wet towels we had collected during the week. I had to count the towels and present a count to Ben. Every week each of us were supposed to get seven laundered and fresh towels, so there should be 77 wet towels returned. The Mayor and Ben each dragged the bag with our laundry. It always freaked me out that my underwear was mixed in with everyone else's because you never knew who had shit stains.

We began our trek across boys' camp, our footprints leaving tracks on the grass which was morning dew moist. Now I realized why we had to wear hard shoes and not sneakers to breakfast. All the dew would dampen our sneakers for the day. However, there was still the mystery of why we still had to wear shoes and not sneakers to dinner.

A small dirt path passed in front of the younger bunks, and this was where the laundry truck stood. All the laundry was done by a company in Honesdale. A young man, obviously home from college, manned the truck where we checked in. He had a clipboard, and wrote down what our numbers were from Bunk 18.

"How many towels?" the young kid asked.

"Ninety" I told him.

"Bullshit! How's that possible? You're only supposed to have 77. Dump the bag and count them," I was ordered.

Ben was smiling with satisfaction because he knew I had counted the towels the night before so the count was going to be correct. Ben always had us casing loose towels down at the waterfront after our General Swims. We would steal them.

"Why are we doing this?" Harris had asked him.

"So we get extra towels every week. I bring them to school with me. This way I don't have to do a weekly wash. I have enough of a stash of towels to last me two weeks."

The count was confirmed to the disgust of the kids from the linen service, and the process was continued. The Mayor was handed a stack of neatly piled pillow cases and started back to the bunk. They were draped between both outstretched arms. He looked like Frankenstein walking. He was half way back to the bunk before the laundry men loaded Jericho up with sheets, two sheets for a bed, and then handed Harris and I the ninety towels which were tied into bundles of ten.

"Anyone else notice that The Mayor is always the first one out of bed Tuesday mornings? How he's always the first to strip his bed," Ben asked as we watched the Mayor skip ahead of us and into the bunk.

"Yeah, so?"Jericho asked.

"Mayor, you better not drop those pillow cases," Ben shouted as he saw The Mayor have trouble opening the bunk door.

"What about the Mayor?" I asked again.

"He's a bed-wetter. I saw the stains. He must wet his bed every night. Don't tell anyone else in the bunk. Maybe save this info for when you really need it, but for sure, The Mayor is a bed-wetter."

"Why can't we say anything? I mean he's nasty to us?" I said.

"You don't fight nasty with nasty... at least not yet. Besides, that's not something to make fun of. Interesting fact though,... I studied this in psych... Almost all serial killers share three traits... bed wetting, and torturing animals..."

"And the third?" Jericho asked as we approached the bunk.

"If you see The Mayor trying to start any fires let me know..."

After breakfast we'd pick up our laundry from the previous week from the same service who delivered our linen and towels. Jericho and I always joined Ben at the truck, and we would carry two bags of clothing back to the bunk. We then dumped the clean laundry on someone's bed where Harris and Oliver checked the name tag sewn on the back of every piece of clothing. This is how they would sort out the laundry for the week. Read the tag, and toss it to the person. Fold the laundry and put it away. It was a neat system, but there were so many mistakes made, and so many missing socks.

Our beds were cleanly made and our fresh laundry put away and now it was time to board the buses and head to Camp Equinox. As we lined up in front of the bunks it was with great satisfaction that I saw the Jewish Mafia, aka the 'turtle burners', sitting on the porch looking forlorn. Asa and Samson were standing right next to the 'turtle burners'. Chick decided that Asa and Samson needed to stay back in camp as a soft punishment for killing the squirrel in front of everyone. This bothered Asa because he loved coaching basketball, but for me it was a reprieve. Ben would be coaching the A team and maybe I had a chance to play.

Two buses left camp this morning as a girls group was heading to White Mountain Camp, the sister camp of Equinox. I saw Beth, Ellen, and Rachel being herded on board the second bus, by two of their counselors, a pair of friends named Fawn and Doe. They were Russian, and nobody could pronounce their last names so they were just called Fawn and Doe, the girls side version of Asa and Samson.

Fawn was a tiny little thing, with the cutest face you ever saw. She hid her beauty behind long wavy red hair, her bangs constantly dipping over her eyes. She could have been mistaken for a small boy.

Doe, on the other hand was a big boned girl. She stood about six feet tall with stupendous breasts that begged to flow free from the constraints of her massive bra. Her manly hands and short cropped jet black hair highlighted her angular cheeks. Doe's 'Carolina' blue eyes and her pouty mouth were the only femininely gifts bestowed upon her.

And then there were her thighs, which were stupendously muscular. It was known that the male counselors all had a desire to be caught between them and crushed like a walnut in a nutcracker.

Fawn and Doe were dynamos. They were perpetually vivacious, and were constantly seen wrestling each other to the ground. The two women were Phys. Ed. majors at a State University in New York. Joe loved them. Girls camp loved them. Their enthusiasm was contagious as they tried to inject some life onto girls camp.

"Now, those are two special women," Ben told me as we boarded the buses.

"What? How do you know?" I asked. With the Jewish Mafia in exile, Jericho and I commandeered the back seats. Ben sat in front of us.

"Come on, we all know. The only one who doesn't realize this is Joe Geisinger. He loves those two girls so much that he allowed them to bring up all their friends. There are about ten of these Physical Education majors on girls' side. They're all playing on the same team."

"What does that mean?" Harris asked.

"They like each other. I mean you can be sort of attracted to them, you know... they have cute faces and athletic bodies... Ha... look at Fawn and Doe... I'd be afraid to get in a fight with them. I mean Fawn is cute, hot cute...but she never hangs out with us. It's like she doesn't know how to talk to men."

"So, they prefer the company of women?" Jericho asked.

"Well, everyone else trusts them, and they were here last year, at least that's what Jen told me,"

"Who's Jen?" I asked.

"The girl I'm seeing this summer."

"The dry hump girl?" Harris asked.
Ben just smiled.

We arrived at Camp Equinox around 10:00 a.m., and the girls' bus passed us on the way to Camp White Mountain. It was a warm morning, and we were all wearing our blue Camp Tonkawa shirts. Just normal T shirts with CT inside a circle which was emblazoned over our right breasts. Lenny would call these our Cock Tease shirts. It was an inside joke which the owner never seemed to discover.

Compared to Camp Tonkawa, Camp Equinox was more rustic. Their bunks were a single structure, not two separate rooms under one roof. There was physical beauty to the camp, but not like the manicured lawns and potted flowers of Camp Tonkawa.

I was placed on the A softball team, and we followed a counselor from Equinox to their best field. We found our opponents throwing around softballs, dressed in button down baseball shirts that read "Equinox" on the front.

"Who do they think they are in that uniform... the Mets?" Jericho asked.

At first they looked intimidating in their uniforms. They reminded me of my little league uniform, except the shirts were left untucked and splayed over their shorts. Jericho came over, put his arm around me, and pointed to the field.

"See left field? Hit it over the outfielder's head and you're in trouble. There's a hill there that brings the ball back into play. The idea is to hit it to right field, because as you can see, there's a huge hill that just drops to nowhere. Get it past the right fielder and it rolls downhill forever and you have a home run."

He was right, and with Ben putting me up fifth in the order I responded with two home runs to right field. I circled the bases hiding a smug look of satisfaction, knowing that Asa would never have put me on the A team. We were victorious, even though we had to put up with their "home rule." I mean, who plays softball where bunting is allowed.

For lunch we had our usual baloney, turkey and salami sandwiches which were packed and bagged for us by the waiters earlier that morning. However, as was the way of the camp, the counselors took most of the turkey sandwiches, and all of the salami sandwiches. This left only the baloney for the campers. And there was no mustard. And it was on white bread, not rye. Then as we were sitting around awaiting the afternoon basketball game, the Equinox waiters brought us some juice and cookies for dessert.

"See, this is the only thing good about this camp. It's juice and cookies. We have milk call , and only get chocolate milk or regular milk with our cookies. Who wants to drink milk on a hot day? And you know when we throw away those stupid little boxes the milk spoils and that's why our garbage cans smell so bad... Why can't we get juice?" Jericho lamented.

The afternoon basketball game taught me the lesson of a true "home job," or as Chick would later refer to it as "Union Temple" rules. We were getting fucked and it was denigrating. With Ben as the coach I suddenly felt free to express myself on the court. Without Asa directing every move I found myself so liberated that I was hoisting shots from thirty feet out. I made half of them, and even though we would end up losing the game I was happy with my performance. Especially since with five minutes left I was called for my second technical foul and was thrown out of the game.

I had lost my composure for the first time in my life. I cared enough about a "team" for the first time that my actions were not only wild, but they were uncalled for and unexpected. Ben wanted to know if I was high, and for a moment I wondered if he knew about Free Play.

I probably would have fouled out anyway, since the Equinox ref, some counselor named Matt, was calling every little touch a foul. I was being butchered under the boards. It was like Asa and Samson refereeing our games back home. I complained every time I was hacked, but it was nothing out of the ordinary. I really didn't say much for most of the time I was in the game. I was trying to let Ben do most of the complaining. Unfortunately, Ben acted more like the polite outsider, questioning each bogus call against our team in a soft and mild tone.

But you see, in this old barn which was converted into an indoor basketball court, there was a dead spot. Home field advantage. Equinox never took the ball up this one side of the court, and we never caught on. I would dribble the ball into this one spot and suddenly the ball made a dull thud sound, and never came back up into my hands. It lay on the wooden floor like a cracked egg, while my hand kept oscillating phantom dribbles.

The Equinox players, knowing this would happen, would guard us close and when we dribbled near the spot they would swoop in and steal the ball.

"What the hell is the matter with this shitty camp? Can't you find a good court?" I screamed after this theft took place for the fourth time. Whistle, and my first technical.

"We need you in the game, you need to keep your cool," Ben told me as he pulled me out and sat me on the bench to cool off.

"Ben, they're cheating. They're calling walks, when we don't move our pivot foot," I complained. "They're setting picks and charging into us, and we're getting all the fouls."

"Listen, if you don't want to go back into the game, then let me know," he said.

I hated counselors who used reverse psychology on me. He knew how much I wanted to play so I kept my mouth shut, but Jericho was about to lose it on the floor. Jericho was getting as beaten up as I was, and no matter how hard we tried we couldn't overcome a six point deficit. Chick was watching from the stands and he would shout something out at the ref every now and then, but seriously, who listens to a sixty something-year-old man wearing baggy shorts that can't seem to hold his balls in place.

Finally, with about five minutes left in the game, and down by four points I was put back in.

A shot was taken, and I crashed the boards along with Jericho.

The ball bounced once on the floor and Jericho fought for it. Jericho caught an elbow in the eye and went down. That was it for me. I flew through the air and tackled the kid who gave Jericho the elbow.

Both benches emptied and a pretty good fight ensued. Jericho was on the ground with Ben checking out his eye. I was taking on most of the Equinox team, while my teammates seemed to disappear. Suddenly I saw Chick flash by. I thought I was dreaming but there he was, the old bow-legged man throwing people to the ground like they were stuffed dolls.

That was it for the basketball game. Chick felt it was wiser to end it, hand the victory to Equinox, and head home before any more fights took place. Equinox was kind enough to get some ice from the infirmary, but Jericho's eye was swelling faster than one could imagine.

"You're going to have a nice shiner, that's for sure," I laughed as we sat together on the way back to camp.

"They are such sore losers! They didn't like that we trounced them in softball so they made sure we would lose basketball. You played well. You know Asa would never have let you in the game," Jericho said.

I sat in a quiet glow of satisfaction.

Chick walked toward the back of the bus to check on Jericho. Jericho pulled back the ice pack and Chick took a close look

"Ehhh. that's nothing. You'll be okay. And you, Jason," he said, turning toward me. "It's about time. I didn't think you had it in you. It's about time you showed some passion about something."

Chick was right. Living in a cocoon sucks, and I shouldn't accept that life. I was beginning to realize that one day in life I would probably have to deal with assholes like The Brain and Hardon. I started wondering what life would be like if I took chances and put myself out on a limb. Maybe something would happen that would make me feel fulfilled.

17

The next two days we'd be on the river.

I couldn't sleep at all, wondering if I was going to make it back alive. I needed to experience the moon landing. There was still no word on whether we were going to be able to watch this. I was hoping that they would bring in four or five TV sets and we could all sit around and watch. In reality that probably wouldn't have sufficed since I truly doubted we would be able to get any decent reception up in the mountains.

Harris was very antsy the morning we were to leave, and I thought it had to do with nerves before hitting Skinners Falls.

"I haven't heard from my mother or father," he confided in me. "I wrote about all the horrible things they've done to me here, and I haven't heard a word. I keep begging Chick to allow me to call home, but they're not letting me do that. It's been four days since I wrote that letter. They should have called by now."

"You fool," Hardon shouted across the bunk. "Your parents are never getting that letter. You think Asa and Samson would ever allow that to leave this camp? They open your letters at night and if there's any bad news in it they rip it up."

"That's Illegal!" Harris shouted.

"What's illegal? Nobody gives a shit in camp," The Brain told him.

Harris was apoplectic. I tried desperately to calm him down, but he started to hyperventilate. We were dressed in our canoeing uniform; bathing suit, sneakers and baseball caps. Some of us had canteens by our side, filled with cold water that would be warm by midday. Ben walked into the bunk and Harris ran into his arms. Ben took him outside where Harris again broke down. I could see him beating Ben on the chest and crying. After a few minutes he calmed down, but already the bunk was making fun of his dramatic flair. Finally Harris walked back to his bed and lay down on it where he remained well past first call for morning activity.

It took Ben a few minutes to get Harris to finally emerge from the bunk. Only two bunks were going on this trip, so Asa and Samson had shit-eating grins spread across their faces as the waterfront counselors handed out our paddles.

"Be thankful for small things, Harris," Ben told him.

"Like what?"

"Like Asa and Samson won't be on the trip with us."

"Is that why they look so happy?"

"That's the reason. But don't worry, I'll take care of everything when we get back."

Chick got up in front of the group, and held up his hands for silence.

"We wish Bunks seventeen and eighteen a safe voyage, and the counselors have picked....... Harris to be our Honey Roll king. Come up here, Harris," Chick announced.

Ben had a disappointed smirk on his face but Harris who was ever so in need of attention, walked up to the front of the group. He stood in front of everyone trying to hide the remnants of his tears, and forced a weak smile.

"Harris, you have been elected the Honey Roll King for this trip. It's a very important task. Are you up to it?" Chick asked.

"I guess so."

"Gentlemen, the Honey Roll please," Chick shouted, and Lenny emerged from his bunk with what looked like a canvas belt. The belt looped through five or six rolls of toilet paper.

"What is that?" Harris asked.

"It's the Honey Roll. You're in charge of the toilet paper, and you better make sure it doesn't get wet!" Chick told him.

Harris bowed his head and then Chick placed the belt around his neck. "Now go, and conquer the river!"

Sy Schwartz, the head of the waterfront, was going to lead us down the river. Like most of the older specialty counselors, Sy was a teacher. He taught at an inner city school in Brooklyn and rumor was he once took a major beating from one of his students and had to have a metal plate inserted in his skull. The two months in camp were a reprieve from the toxicity of teaching, and he relished the freedom and sweetness of spending his days down by the lake. Then there were the interludes of canoeing down the Delaware that always seemed to liberate him even more.

We took a school bus down to the bridge we crossed over on the first day of camp. There was a small dock area where the canoes had already been delivered and were resting like ten fingers reaching out to touch the river. A pickup truck sat by the canoes, and two large figures sat silently in the cab, almost like sentries guarding a castle.

"Who are those guys?" Harris asked.

"That's Bramo and Cisco.... they're the strong men, the security in the camp. When Joe goes to bed at night, they patrol camp. They also do all the heavy lifting, like bringing the canoes to the river," Jericho told him.

Ben grabbed the two large black garbage bags from the back of the pickup truck, and dumped one of them in his canoe, while handing off the other to the Brits. "What's that? Our lunches?" Jericho asked. Ben nodded.

"Harris, you have nothing to worry about, because you know we can't tip," Ben told him as they dragged their canoe to the edge of the water.

"Why's that?" Harris asked, as he bathed in sun tan lotion.

"Because we're carrying lunch. We're not allowed to tip."

Summer camps employed many counselors from Europe. It was a great deal for the adventurous European teens as summer camps would pay for their airfare to the States, and employ them for two months. They were paid a pittance but it wasn't the salary that consumed their thoughts, but the promise of traveling across America after camp ended. After all, the camp paid their round trip airfare, and there was a return date that gave them at least a month of travel time.

We had two of the more popular waterfront counselors serving as guides, Gary and Eric. Both were from Great Britain, and both had shoulder length hair, which was driving Joe Geisinger crazy. Every morning when they walked into the Mess Hall Joe would pull them over, smack them in the head and tell them to get a haircut.

Gary was one of those good looking Brits who made all the girls in camp swoon with his accent. The "Beatles", thing. This morning he was carrying the bag with the cans of soda, and he tied it to the gunnels of their canoe, alongside the other bag of lunch.

"Everyone gather around," Sy Schwartz announced.

Sy had his shirt off and he was busy applying lotion all over his body. He was another old man with huge nipples.

"Who do you think has the bigger nipples, Chick or Sy." I asked.

"What? Really... you're interested in ..." Jericho started to say.

"Whose is bigger? Longer?"

"What's with the obsession with those nipples?"

"They're huge! Is that what happens to men when they get older... their nipples get long and hard?"

"Have you been smoking behind my back?"

"Look at the difference. All of us, we have small nipples... the counselors have small nipples... but the two oldest men in camp have those long, hard nipples. Is that what happens to them when you get old?"

"Yeah, and some of us lose our hair, and most of us won't be able to get boners when we get that old... and oh... maybe we'll also have gray hair on our balls, and just maybe our nipples do grow longer," Jericho said.

He saw the horror spread across my face, and started to laugh.

"What?" I asked.

"I'm fucking with you. I don't know why they're that big and I don't care, and neither should you."

Sy called us to attention and we gathered around him, life vests tied snuggly to our bodies and paddles at our side.

"To some of you, this will be your first time down the Delaware. You will face Skinners Falls, Barryville Falls, and so many other Falls you won't know what hit you. So we must make an offering to the river gods for a safe trip."

"Give them Harris," The Brain shouted. Harris gave him the finger back.

Sy reached into his canoe, and pulled out a knife. When he drew it out of its sheath we were stunned by the huge blade that dazzled us in the morning sunlight. I wondered where he found a knife that big, and 'what does he need a knife that big for? What is out on the river?'

Sy slid his finger over the sharp edge, and opened a slight jag on his thumb. He licked off the blood.

"I'm not going to drink his blood," Harris said loud enough that everyone turned to face us.

"No, you're not going to drink my blood. What world are you in?"

At least Sy was laughing as he called Harris forward. Harris gave me the Honey Roll to hold as he reluctantly walked over to Sy. Sy smiled, and wrapped his left arm around Harris' shoulders, and with his right hand he reached into his canoe and pulled out...what looked like...

"Boys, look at this beautiful twelve-inch Kosher Salami. Isn't it a beauty?" Sy shouted.

Then he stuffed that 12" salami between his legs so it looked like a 12" red penis. He turned left, he swiveled right, and with his 12" salami he knocked Harris over. I couldn't stop laughing, ... none of us could. Sy helped Harris up, the salami still sticking monumentally upright between his legs.

"So kid, I need to give this salami a little trim. Need you to cut off a slice from the tip."

"With what?" Harris asked.

Sy handed the long blade to Harris without a qualm of hesitation.

He placed his hands on his hips, and looked to the heavens. Harris approached the salami but jumped back when Sy wiggled his ass and made the salami dance. Sy assured Harris he wouldn't play anymore tricks on him so Harris again approached, but this time with way more trepidation.

"Cut away son... I won't flinch."

Harris did as instructed and started to saw a slice off the tip of the salami. Sy stood confidently still, knowing the salami was securely held between his legs. If Sy twitched, or that meat slipped an inch, Harris might flinch and slice a vein in his leg.... or worse.

"Hey boys, this is what we should do to you," Sy said to the Brits, and laughed at his own joke. "It's called a Bris."

"Cheers mate, but ya see...British women only like ten percent off on a sale, not on their men. Isn't that true in America?" Gary asked.

"Nah... American women want fifty percent off."

Harris kept both hands on the knife as he finished sawing off the tip of the salami. The piece of meat fell into the sand of the riverbank. Sy carefully took the knife out of Harris' hand and congratulated him on a job well done. He pushed Harris back toward me where I gave him back his "Honey Roll.' Sy picked up the end piece of the salami, and cleaned it off, even as he still clenched the remaining ten inches stiffly between his legs.

"So we ask the river gods for a safe trip and we make this sacrifice to you," he shouted as he flung the cut piece of meat out into the middle of the river. "To the river gods," Sy shouted.

"To the river gods," we all shouted.

Sy cut up the rest of the salami, and passed it around. From that moment on, summer mornings that were oven bake warm, sweet, and tranquil, would always have me salivating for a taste of salami.

"Now, one other thing before we head out on the river. Who's the "HONEYROLL KID?" Sy asked.

Everyone pointed to Harris.

"You again? First you cut my shmeckle and now I have to come to you to wipe my ass? You have too much power in those little hands of yours."

Sy asked him to step forward and slipped one roll of toilet paper off the belt, and handed the remaining rolls back to Harris.

"Now son," Sy said to Harris, "you are in charge of probably one of the most important condiments we need for this trip. If you tip your canoe, by all means save the toilet paper. I am going to keep this one roll just for an emergency and, just in case we only have one roll to share amongst all of us, I am going to demonstrate the proper technique to wipe your ass."

"We already know how to wipe our ass," The Brain shouted.

"Oh Sherlock? Can you do it with one small square? I want you to get up here and show us how to use this one little square piece of toilet paper to wipe your ass."

The Brain stood there, silent, and with a stupid look on his face.

"I thought so, so step back," Sy demanded and the Brain complied. "Now, with just one small square in your measly little hands I will teach you how to wipe your ass."

Sy carefully unraveled a stretch of toilet paper and then ripped off one small square. He folded the square in half two times so that it was an even smaller square.

"Now, watch carefully, because this may save your sanity. I have folded it into this little square. Now from the middle of the square just rip off a small pinch, but never throw away this little half moon of toilet paper. Keep it in a safe place. Then you open the paper to its full length."

Sy demonstrated and revealed the square of paper now with a hole in the middle.

"What's that hole for?" The Mayor asked.

"Ah... that's the secret. See.. if you're down to this one little square of toilet paper you will fold it as I showed you. Now you take your middle finger and stick it through the hole." His finger now looked like it was wearing a skirt of white toilet paper.

"...And you take your middle finger and you stick it up your ass, and clean out the shit. Once you do that you just pull the rest of the paper up over your finger so you're wiping the shit off. Now that little piece of paper that you clipped off before? The one that I told you to save... well you use that to clean the shit out from under your fingernails."

This was another lesson that would stay with me for the rest of my life, not that I ever had to use the technique. It just made sense that day in a perverted sort of way.

"Female canoeists approaching," Sy shouted as we continued to munch on the salami that Sy had cut up and handed out.

Floating down the river, laughing and giggling, were twelve canoes filled with girls who looked like they were fifteen or sixteen. From their T shirts we could only surmise that they were from another camp. The counselors in the group, four stunning blondes dressed in bikinis, waved hello.

"Howdy ladies... do you see the moon out this morning?" Sy shouted.

"Saw it last night, but not this morning," came a reply from one of the female counselors

"Could have sworn I saw the moon just a moment ago. Let me look in our canoes for a pair of binoculars.

Sy and the two Brits, bent over as if to look into their canoe, but they quickly pulled down their shorts, exposing their bare ass essentials.

"Can't seem to find my binoculars. How can I see the moon without my binoculars?" Sy said as he shook his naked ass in the direction of the girls. The two Brits did the same.

"You're disgusting," the girls screamed in unison as they all paddled harder than they ever paddled before just to get past us.

Sy straightened up and realized that none of us were looking at the girls in their canoes, but rather at a sight we had never seen.

"Boys...I told you... they're not cut! That's the same shmeckle that you have, but without the benefits of a Bris. It's the same one-. eyed monster you have, but with a hood."

Sy motioned for Gary and Eric to pull up their swim trunks so we wouldn't be further traumatized.

Blue skies, not even a feathery cloud on the horizon, found the sun beating down on us, and the reflection off the aluminum canoes only intensified the heat. Jericho and I would paddle for about five minutes and then we'd stop and float to the back of the pack where Harris and Ben made sure nobody lingered. That was a shame because Jericho had rolled a nice fat joint and we were dying to smoke it.

I had never experienced canoeing on a river before and I immediately fell head over heels with the seductive power of slowly flowing water. At all of my other camps the canoeing was relegated to a lake. But now... listening to the water kiss the banks, the silence of isolation that floated down the hills which the river cut through, and the reflection off the canoes of the palest blue sky I had ever seen had my head spinning.

"I never want to leave the river," I told Jericho as we continued to slide behind Ben, only to have him turn around and tell us to catch up.

"Same here," Jericho answered as he lay back against the gunnels and just took in the sun. "Sometimes I can't stand the world. I'm thinking of my brother at war. He writes about the bugs and leeches he encounters on patrol."

"Leeches, what are leeches?"

"Blood sucking worms. We got them in the mud at camp. They don't hurt, they just gross you out and you got to burn them off because if you rip them off then they can make you bleed and you'll get an infection. I guess the only thing grosser would be....."

"Be what?"....

Jericho stood in the canoe, and I did everything I could to keep it steady.

"What's going on?

"Hard left...Hard left...", he shouted as he fell into his seat and started to frantically paddle. I followed his command and when I looked up I thought I saw the water parting ways.

"It's an eel trap, and it looks like a live one. The locals make a trap. They set rocks in the middle of the river forming a V. The water runs faster into the V and at the end of the V they build a wooden trap with wire mesh in the basket to capture the eels. Look at those assholes."

Jericho pointed at a canoe that was stuck at the end of the V, sitting high on the rocks with the tip of the canoe resting on the wooden trap.

"The Brain and Hardon are stuck. They're always fucking around, but maybe this is our chance," Jericho said as we paddled around the V.

We turned around to watch Ben and Harris slide into the crux of the eel trap and dock their boat on the rocks. Ben got out of the canoe and began to help The Brain pull the canoe off the wooden slope. Hardon was using his paddle to slap away the slithering eels.

"Stop that, you idiot. The locals might kill you for this," Ben shouted.

We were a safe enough distance from Ben, who was concentrating on rescuing that canoe, and far enough behind the rest of the group. Jericho lit the joint, and suddenly I relaxed. I listened to the glistening water rushing over the rocks that formed the eel trap. However, this moment of serenity was shattered by Ben screaming at The Brain and Mickey Hardon, who were giggling like innocent little children on a playground.

By the time we reached Skinners Falls I was floating over the water. I could feel nothing and yet everything.... I could feel the current intensifying and sucking us into the unknown vortex. Jericho stood up in the canoe to survey the Falls.

"Again, what are you doing?"

"Plotting a course. I want to hit every haystack. So when I tell you which side to paddle on just do so and do it as hard as you can."

Jericho sat back down and started to paddle furiously. I kept looking for the precipice and horizon, the place where the water ends and all you see is sky. I was looking for the edge we paddle over. I was wrong, and Jericho was right. What lay in front of us was pure river, with a lot of swirling whitewater and no precipitous edge for me to fear. The pot had calmed my nerves but now I felt emboldened. I wanted this challenge, and I was accepting of it.

"We're going to start left and then head right," Jericho shouted as we started to paddle.

"Okay, let's fucking do this. I'm ready...!" I shouted.

I stood up in the canoe and felt it quiver as if it were begging me to sit down before we tipped. It was Jericho rocking the canoe.

"Well then, sit down already, you moron," Jericho laughed as we were sucked into the rapids known as Skinners Falls.

The first haystack I hit took my breath away. The front of the canoe dipped down severely and I felt like I had slipped under the river. A white mist was splashing my face. Then suddenly the bow of the boat, like a seesaw heading skyward, bolted upright. I was drenched as we came up through a wave. Over and over Jericho charged into the fray, one haystack after another. It was exhilarating. We skidded through one rapid and searched for the next, one haystack after another, followed by a swirling eddy.

I'd call out a rock and Jericho knew what to do.

"Rock on the left," and Jericho would steer us as close to the rock as possible so we could slide down a chute of churning water.

I was a saturated sponge. The front of the canoe continually fell under the waves created by the rushing water cascading over rocks. The Delaware tried to throw me from my canoe but I knew I was conquering it. The ride only lasted maybe twenty seconds. I had survived.

"Let's do it again!"

I shocked myself. I never thought those words would ever leave my lips on the Delaware River. I realized that if I could conquer all my fears by facing them head on, then I could make my life a simple place to live in. I was suddenly in love with rivers. From that moment on I knew I would never be satiated by just looking at a river. No, from now on I had to be one with a river... paddling or rowing on it, swimming down it... I had to be a part of a flowing water.

We pontooned the canoes out in the middle of the river, securing the armada by clipping our life preserves together in a chain. Time for lunch. Sy Schwartz stood in his canoe and started singing a ditty with which only he was familiar,

"It's snack time,
let's rendezvous,
It's snack time, let's rendezvous...."

We never heard how it ended because he started tossing plums to everyone. I suddenly realized how hungry I was, and I desired the fruit. Sy kept tossing the plums, but if you fumbled the offering it plummeted to the bottom of the Delaware.

Ben started to hand out sandwiches and they were passed from one canoe to another like an old time bucket brigade. The Brits tossed the soda to everyone, making sure they shook the cans so that when we popped the tab we would get spritzed. A baloney sandwich never tasted so elegant.

We pulled off the river later that afternoon without seeing anymore rapids. We had floated down the river in a state of euphoria, a mixture of smoking the joint and a sense of surrender. This led to a peaceful intercourse between the sun, which was baking our bodies, the chilled water which we dipped our hats into in an effort to cool off, and the sound of a hawk talking to us as it circled in the blueness of a cloudless day.

Waiting for us on the beach of the campgrounds were "Bramo" and "Cisco". They were the two gentlemen who delivered the canoes in the morning. Both played football in college and were now high school football coaches. It was even rumored that Maxie "Bramo" Abramowitz played one year in the AFL.

"I still say Joe hired them as protection," Jericho said.

"Protect us from what?"

"I don't know... things. I mean the "townies" hate Jews, and maybe there are some bad counselors. Whatever it is, it's nice to have those two guys on our side."

Bramo and Cisco each pulled two canoes out of the water and carried them up the beach. They simply tucked a canoe under each arm, making it look as simple as carrying loaves of bread. Our clothing and sleeping bags were tagged and waiting for us on the back of the pickup truck. Asa and Samson were tossing them down to us.

"Thought you guys were free from this," Ben said, showing a sign of disappointment.

"Chick forced us to sleep out overnight. He said just you and the Brits weren't enough coverage, so we're here and we fucking hate it," Samson told him.

After we changed out of our wet bathing suits and donned the dry clothing we had packed, we watched as Bramo started the fire. I've been told that most other camps carry their own dinner with them for an overnight canoe trip, but not this camp. While Cisco unloaded the coolers of hamburger patties, frankfurters and buns, Bramo threw the wood they had transported from camp into a pit that was enveloped by rocks. Then he took a plastic gallon jug filled with gasoline, poured it over the wood, and lit a match.

"Stand back," was all he said. "Bramo" was a behmoth, close to six and a half feet tall, and his bald pate, and round face almost reminded you of 'Charlie Brown'. For no matter how humongous Bramo was, there was a softness to his personality that radiated in his quiet mannerisms. He was a paradox, a man who lived most of his life in the violent world of football, but was actually a gentle giant.

Bramo was guzzling cold beer from one of the metal pitchers that we usually found on our tables in the Mess Hall, while keeping an eye on the lit match. His legs were muscular and as thick as redwoods and his chest as massive as two beer kegs standing side by side.

Cisco walked over to Bramo and the two of them watched the match burn down to nothing, Bramo never flinched as the flame was extinguished in his finger. Cisco had his own pitcher of cold brew and they both took large swigs before Cisco handed him a thick branch with a gasoline saturated rag wrapped on the end. This time Bramo took a lighter out of his pocket and lit the branch, creating an ancient torch.

"Stand back," he mumbled again.

And then he smiled. You could barely see his eyes, as his cheeks were so flush and round that they almost devoured his sockets. Yet his smile turned into a warm childish grin and for a second you weren't scared of him. Then he threw the torch on the pile of wood. The combustion itself caused a shock wave that almost knocked us over. The pile of wood turned into a raging fire. Cisco and Bramo clinked their pitchers in a toast, downed the remaining beer and went back to the truck to replenish their brew.

The warmth of the fire felt toasty as everyone looked for a place to bunk out for the night. I found a flat piece of ground between the river and the fire and proceeded to unroll the sleeping bag. Jericho, Harris and Ben joined us while the rest of the group spread out around the fire. We then took our soaking wet sneakers and lay them on rocks at the edge of the fire. We were hoping the heat would dry them out for the next day's paddling.

Bramo and Cisco waited till the pyre died down, and then threw a grill across the rock stanchion of the cooking pit. Then they proceeded to throw hamburger patties and frankfurters on top of the grill. The Brits had laid out the condiments on a picnic table along with some jugs of fruit flavored powder water we all called Bug Juice.

"It's really Kool Aid," Harris once told us, believing that he knew a secret. "So why do they call it Bug Juice?"

"Because eventually bugs get into the pitcher and die. It may not happen every time, but it happens often enough that we call it bug juice," Jericho told him.

Harris only drank water from then on. As a matter of fact Harris had earlier found a small spigot on the upper landing of the camp grounds. There was nothing more refreshing than cold water from a hose on a hot day. We had a place to fill our canteens for the next day's trip.

"You know those girls who paddled past us this morning, the

ones Sy chucked moons at? Well, they're camping out up there," Harris reported.

At the mention of young girls, Asa's eyes lit up, and he whispered something to Samson, who only laughed and shook his head with thoughts of debauchery dancing through his childish mind.

"Line up, and slip and slide," Bramo announced. When a fire is as hot and roaring as they made it, it took no time to cook the meat.

Everyone took buns, stood in line, and waited till Bramo called us up to the fire. Bramo slid a hamburger onto his spatula and slipped it onto our buns. It was perfection.

"Hey… you're dripping sweat all over the burgers!" Harris complained.

Bramo just growled, pointed the glowing spatula at Harris, and motioned for him to move on.

When Hardon took his turn, he just stared at the burger that Bramo had placed on his bun.

"What's the matter?" Bramo growled.

"I'd like mine rare," Hardon said.

Bramo tossed the burger over his shoulder, and never took his eye off of Hardon. He scraped a new pattie off the grill and handed the raw meat to Hardon.

"Could it be cooked a bit more?" Hardon asked.

Bramo just stared at Hardon. Bramo was like a superhero, his hidden power being an icy stare that withered your soul. We saw Hardon succumb to the "stare," his knees started to buckle, and his arms quivered into jelly, causing the barely cooked pattie to fall to the ground.

"That's yours, kid," Bramo said, pointing at the sullied pattie. "But I'd suggest you only eat the hot dogs. You understand?"

Hardon got the hint, and had two hot dogs for dinner.

After dinner the marshmallows came out of the truck, we went in search of long thin sticks, and proceeded to bake s'mores. Everything was laid out for us on the picnic tables and after we roasted our marshmallows we grabbed the graham crackers and pieces of chocolate and made our sandwiches.

Asa and Samson took most of the group to the upper camp-grounds where there was an open field. They tried to organize a game of football, which quickly morphed into a game of S-P-U-D. Samson pulled a flask out from his ankle high socks, and took a swig. He shared the drink with Asa.

I decided to sit by the edge of the river with Harris and Jericho. Ben helped the Brits pack everything up. The sun was starting to dip below the hills that bordered the river, and with a belly full of burgers and hot dogs I didn't feel like moving.

"The sound of the river is so soothing," Harris said, but we were all thinking that. "You really can't see it flowing but you can hear it. Makes me want to forget about what those assholes did to my letters home."

"Ben will take care of it when we get back," I said.

"Do you think there's something about Ben that he's hiding? I mean, he shows no fear around Asa and the rest of them. I think that's pretty cool," said Jericho.

He started to skim rocks off the surface of the river.

"I like what he's been teaching us," Harris said as we all got up to search for the flattest rocks we could find to skim off the water.

"You do? Well, here's one more tip," Ben said as he walked up to us and started searching the ground for rocks.

"Shit , you scared me," Harris said. I could sense that there was an affinity between the two, that they'd bonded in the canoe.

"Now watch this. Open the palm of your hands," Ben said, and we did just that. "The base of the palm, that's the strongest part of your hand. If you're ever being attacked all you have to do is shoot your hand out, keeping your hand open and aim that base of the palm at the nose of your attacker. One quick thrust and bam.... you'll break the assailant's nose. Now try it."

So we put down our rocks and took a stance that Ben directed us to take. Then we practiced shooting our hands out, open palms, with a thrust at the end. We were aiming the base of the palm into an imaginary nose.

"I spent last summer in Israel, spent a lot of time with the soldiers out there. They're animals. They taught me so much self defense, besides what I practice here. You have to go for the eyes, so take your thumbs and gouge out the eyes of your attacker. Kick them in the balls, and then the shins," Ben told us, as he demonstrated some moves.

"So basically fight dirty," I said.

"As dirty as you have to, to survive."

As darkness slid over the campsite, Bramo and Cisco prepared to leave. They threw some more lumber off the back of the pickup truck so we could have a fire through most of the night. They packed up the cooler and told us that they would be back early in the morning to cook us breakfast. Nothing like room service.

Asa and Samson returned with the rest of the group, and immediately took off on a hike, flashlights leading the way. However, this was a decoy for their real mission. They wanted to scope out the girls who were on the upper campgrounds.

Ben and the Brits were sitting around the fire, while Jericho and I meandered down to the river to smoke another joint. Jericho had hidden a few more joints in his overnight bag, which was such a brilliant move. There was a magnificence to the night sky. It was this summer that allowed me to appreciate the magnitude of the stars. Was it the pot altering my mind, allowing it to expand and see the beauty in the world? Or was I finally at ease and able to accept and see what was around me?

"Do you think Oliver is right when he thinks there are UFOs?" Jericho suddenly asked, bringing me back to reality.

"Why do you even ask that question?"

"Just looking at all those stars. Hard to believe that there's not another world out there. Hard to believe we're the only other beings who are looking at the stars."

"Too many questions to answer."

After a moment of silence Jericho turned to me and said, "This is about the only thing I like about camp."

"What is?"

"Think about how lucky we are... we get to do things every second of the day. Sure we have to put up with a lot of crap, but would you have ever canoed down the Delaware? Would your parents take you camping? Or what about learning how to use a sailboat? That's not readily available to us at home. And we get to play ball every second of the day, or learn how to play golf. I mean we get to do things... like you... you're taking the Junior Life Saving course with Sy during swim instruction."

"Yeah,... that was a mistake.. I have to study for a written test and then they're going to test me in the water on the last day of camp."

"But it's an accomplishment, man... it's good."

And for once I felt good about myself.

Maybe it was a bad move to smoke before falling asleep on a sleepout. After all, we now had to sit through the obligatory 'horror story' told in front of a campfire. Horror stories told in a bunk just don't carry the same feeling of fear as when they're told in the wilderness. The sound of animals howling in the distance, insects biting you, and the trickle of a river running by, makes you feel more vulnerable.

Asa and Samson had finished off a bottle of Jack Daniels. I saw them drinking behind the pickup truck while Bramo was cooking us dinner. They were fried. And they were now in charge of evening activities.

First, we were treated to Samson demonstrating how to light farts. He had brought a can of baked beans for himself and had eaten the entire can at dinner. It was fuel for this epic centerpiece of art. He sat on the picnic table and pulled down his sweatpants, and then brought his feet over his head as he laid back on the table. He spread his cheeks and Asa asked if he was ready, and Samson told him to light it up. All Asa had in his hand was a book of matches. He ripped off about four matches and struck them on the matchbook.

"Ready?" Asa asked.

"Let her rip," Samson shouted.

Samson produced a loud, noxious stream of gas. It sounded like the shofar being blown on the High Holidays. Asa inched the matches towards Samson's ass producing a flamethrower. This was followed by a few staccato farts that sounded like a machine gun, and ended with one silent but brilliant gush of gas that when lit, created a torpedo of flame.

We all gave him a standing ovation.

"Now don't try this at home, boys. You've got to be big enough with a belly full of gas or else you might burn your little asses," Samson joked.

Then Asa started in on the Cropsey Maniac story. I was hoping for an original horror story but this was the same one I'd heard every summer at every different camp I had occupied. And for some reason, it was always called the Cropsey maniac.

"Why Cropsey?"

I finally had to know so I asked Jericho.

"I don't know."

"Cropsey is an avenue in Brooklyn," Ben told us. "I bet some counselor from Brooklyn made up this story and it just stuck. But it is an evil-sounding name, isn't it?"

CROPSEY MANIAC
The obligatory horror story for campouts

1) *It always has to take place in the same exact location you're in at the moment the story is being told*
2) *Has to relate to kids close to our age.*
3) *It was always the exact anniversary of the original murder. Same story...someone escapes from a mental institution, someone who killed members of his own family... same character, ...same chopped off hands, replaced by hooks, and now the crazed man is back for revenge.*
4) *Oh, and did we see all the WANTED POSTERS tacked around the campgrounds?*

Redundancy... young couple out for a night on the town, and they go and park at the river... (no shit!!! at the exact same place we're in now)... and the guy is trying to get into the girl's pants when he hears scratching on the roof of his car... and the scratching isn't going away... and the girl knows that the escapee has hooks for hands and .. not that she thinks much of it... but this scraping sound keeps getting louder... and the girl panics and insists the boy drive her home... and OOPS!!!! When the boy gets out of the car and walks around to open the girl's door he finds a hook stuck in the door handle.

And then the storyteller ALWAYS pulls his hand out from under his sweatshirt and bares what looks like a hook, but is really a metal hangar bent in half. Panic. Some kids gasp... others laugh nervously. Asa paused again for effect. He had almost everyone gripping their sleeping bags tightly.

Asa had succeeded in scaring some of us that night, but not me. The only thing that scared me was if someone ever discovered how lonely my life really was.

The campfire had died down by midnight, some smoldering embers glowing faintly in the darkness. It offered enough light to make things sketchy. Harris had to go to the bathroom, and he awakened Ben.

"You're the honey roll king, take a roll and go crap near the river," Ben told him drowsily.

"I can't. I need a toilet," Harris whispered.

"Crap near the river," Ben reiterated.

"Need a toilet. There's one on the upper campgrounds. Please take me, I'm scared. The Cropsey Maniac might be out there."

"No such thing."

"Pleeeeease."

Ben grudgingly climbed out of his sleeping bag, and slipped on his sweatpants and a hooded sweatshirt. He wasn't angry or frustrated--he just wanted to get back to sleep. As Ben led Harris through the maze of sleeping bags I crawled out of mine and followed them.

"I have to shit too," was all I mumbled.

We headed up the small hill and hit the dirt road which would lead to the bathroom. Suddenly off to the right we heard a rustling, and a high pitched voice that shrieked "NO!" Ben twirled and flooded the area with his flashlight, and there standing before us was a goddess in blond hair. She couldn't have been more than fifteen years old. She was wearing a thermal t shirt, that fit tightly over her perfectly pert little breasts. She was crying, but you could tell she had just thrown up. There were smidgeons of puke still dripping from her chin.

"You okay?" Ben asked.

"No..." she sniffled, and then she threw up again, just gobs of puke into the tall grass.

"I'm not going to hurt you," Ben told her, as he slowly approached the trembling girl. He carefully pulled off his sweatshirt and offered it to her in an attempt to make her stop shivering. He turned his back to her as she started to pull her puke stained shirt off, and he made Harris and me do the same. Every time Harris tried to catch a peek Ben would slap him in the head.

"Thank you," she said quietly after she slipped the sweat shirt on. She was trying to control her emotions between dry heaves.

Suddenly there was a small commotion off to the right. We didn't see anything, even after Ben flooded the area with his flashlight.

"Sssshh, listen," Harris said.

"Listen for what?" I asked.

"Ssssh... just listen," Harris said again, but this time punctuating the moment with a finger of warning.

And there it was. You could hear sneakers sliding down the dirt road toward our campsite.

The blond girl was trembling and trying to clean the puke from her lips. She was clumsy, and a bit out of it. She looked spastic as she tried to walk a few steps. She kept laughing.

"Were you drinking?" Ben asked.

"Maybe?" her giggle a telltale sign that she was drunk out of her mind.

"Where did you get the alcohol?" Ben asked.

"Some guy from another camp...." and then she puked again.

Ben slowly led her down the road until we came upon another campsite. We followed him and watched as he woke one of the female counselors and explained what happened. The counselor was visibly upset. Ben pointed to us and explained that he was just taking us to the bathroom and this seemed to neutralize the situation. The counselor took the girl back to her tent, and emerged with Ben's sweatshirt. They talked for a bit longer and then Ben turned and led us to the bathroom.

"We'll see if they remember anything in the morning. Nobody had a pen or paper to write down anything, so we'll wait to see if their camp calls Joe Geisinger," Ben explained.

We returned to the campsite to find Asa and Samson reeking of alcohol, snoring and lost to the world like nothing happened.

Just as the sun was coming up the next morning Bramo and Cisco drove their truck onto our campsite at full speed. The sound of gravel and twigs crunching under the tires woke us, and we heard them unloading the wood for a new fire.

We crawled out of our sleeping bags, chilled by the evening, our hair damp from the morning dew. It was a luxury to just pee into the woods, and then we quickly pulled on our second bathing suit that we had packed away. Bramo created a campfire and we stood around praying that the intense heat would toast our sneakers in a last ditch effort to dry them. It didn't work, and that feeling of putting on cold wet sneakers filled with sand and dirt would be an irritating sensation I'd always remember.

We were handed a piece of bread, and Bramo instructed us to take the bread, fold it in half, and to take a small bite out of the folded end.

When we opened up the bread there was a nice sized hole.

'This is just like the toilet paper trick Sy taught us," I said to Jericho.

"We're having rocky mountain spotted egg," Bramo told us,

and in groups of five we laid our bread on a skillet. We watched as Bramo let the bread toast a bit and then he cracked an egg, dropping the yoke into the center hole. He let the egg fry. When cooked, it was delicious.

There were nasty looks exchanged between Asa and Ben.

I kept looking up the hill, hoping that the counselor from the girls' camp would come down and complain to Bramo and Cisco, but she was nowhere to be found . We rolled up our sleeping bags, threw the dirty bathing suits and our sweats back into the appropriately tagged plastic bags, and then threw everything into the back of the truck.

"If they're old enough to bleed, they're old enough to be butchered," Asa whispered to Samson, but it was a whisper that was meant to be heard.

Ben heard it.

He turned and charged Asa, only to bounce off Bramo who had moved with the grace of a pro football player and cleanly placed himself between the two counselors in an effort to avoid a conflict. Ben fell to the ground like he hit a brick wall, which in a sense he did. Asa made his escape. He jumped into the cab of the pickup and waited for Bramo and Cisco to take him back to camp. Samson had thrown the extra bags into the back of the pickup, and settled down amongst them. He fell asleep before the pickup even left the campsite.

"Something happened last night at the camp site," Ben told Bramo.

"Okay,.. what?"

"Seriously, Joe Geisinger may receive a phone call..."

"Don't worry about it," Bramo said. He stepped on the gas and zipped out of the parking lot, leaving behind a cloud of dust.

Ben realized that this was a losing fight so he turned and doused the fire. Sy Schwartz cut the new salami that Cisco had brought from camp. Offering a prayer to the river gods for a second time, he threw another slice into the Delaware. We were off on the second leg of our trip.

We hit the Barryville Falls, and the Colang Rapids, and finished up with the Mongaup Falls near Port Jervis. It was five hours of paddling.

Ben fumed in his canoe, paddling with determination and leaving the rear of the pack unguarded, so Jericho fired up another joint he had packed away in his overnight bag. We proceeded to get high for the entire day.

Sitting in a canoe on a sunny day becomes a task. You try to prevent sunburn, but you can't. The sun beats down and burns the skin off your back. The sun reflects off the river and then off the aluminum canoe. We felt like we were baking in an oven. But I was at peace.

And I had conquered a fear. It was a first for me, but maybe it portended a future path of handling obstacles. There was more to life than sitting at home. One had to take chances in life if one were to succeed.

18

July 20th, 1969. Man is going to walk on the moon tonight. Most of us visited the infirmary when we returned from the canoe trip, seeking a remedy for our severe sunburn. We were handed Sucrets to suck on, and the nurse rubbed cream on our backs.

Dear Mom and Dad,

The canoe trip was incredible. I was in the same canoe as my counselor, Ben.

I wasn't scared with him in the canoe. We made S'mores at night and slept outside. It was just nice not to be picked on all day and night.

And all I can think of is coming home. Why did you do this to me? Why did you send me away? I'm going to do anything I can to be kicked out. I just found out you haven't received any of my letters because the counselors read them and tear them up. But not anymore. I have to go

Love, Harris.

That morning Asa and Samson were called down to the HCO shack, and you could hear Ed Barnett screaming at them. The loudspeaker wasn't even turned on. Ben had taken Harris to Grayson Hall to make a phone call home. There was no doubt Ben had confronted Joe Geisinger with the allegations that Asa and Samson had been tearing up the letters that Harris had written.

You could hear Asa and Samson denying those allegations to Ed Barnett.

I thought maybe Ben would have said something about the night at the campout. He didn't say a word.

"It's against the law to tear up a letter," Asa pleaded.

"You better be telling me the truth. You can piss on my head, but don't tell me it's raining!" Ed Barnett finally screamed.

Asa and Samson returned to the group and their first stop was our bunk. They looked around and wanted to know where Ben was. Hardon told them he had taken Harris to Grayson Hall to call home. The counselors slithered back to the bunk, any confrontation diverted for the day.

Harris finally returned, and you could tell he was crying again. The tears were bleaching riverbeds down his cheeks.

Ben returned toward the end of cleanup, and sat on his bed. He put in a cassette tape and started listening to Blood Sweat and Tears. He loved the song, "Spinning Wheel" and would sing along with it, but today he just listened.

"Can't you put something good on like Led Zeppelin?" Jericho asked.

"Too strong."

"Then Beatles, or The Who? Please, anything but this," Jericho begged.

"Get me a cassette and I'll play it for you.... in the meantime I'm listening to this."

"Led Zeppelin is the greatest band of all time. "

"Are you crazy?" Hardon screamed. "Dylan is God!"

"Who's the God,... Dylan. Dylan is no God He's good, but his music just doesn't compare to Led Zep," Jericho said.

"The words, man. Listen to Dylan's words. He's a poet," The Brain added.

"I'm more impressed by Paul Simon." I just wanted to throw something into the conversation.

"Paul Simon? You nuts? Listen to me. The songs, ... Blowin in the Wind, The Times, They are a Changin', Highway 61 Revisited... songs that mean something."

"I Am a Rock, The Sounds of Silence,... I'll agree with Jason that Paul Simon ranks up there... but there's no better band than Led Zep," Jericho told Hardon.

"Blood Sweat and Tears, not the greatest but good enough," Ben said from under his pillow. His voice was muffled as he clutched it over his head trying to bury himself in darkness.

"The Doors. Now that's a band!"

Jericho was so secure in his knowledge of music that he sort of intimidated everyone with his fervent opinions. I didn't want to mention that I also loved the Archies, and their hit 'Sugar Sugar.' And was I crazy to love Neil Diamond and Sweet Caroline?

"You know, I heard that 'Light my Fire' is about getting a blow job," I said.

"Not quite, but close enough."

Jericho walked over to Ben's cubby, and ejected the Blood Sweat and Tears tape. He popped in another tape and "Touch Me" by the Doors resounded throughout the bunk. Ben didn't even flinch from under his pillow. He was either dead or in deep thought, and troubled by something.

"Now that's a love song!" Jericho said as he lay down on his bed, plopped the pillow over his head and started to mellow out.

That night was Boys Sing. It was a summer tradition, probably brought up to camp from the city schools. Brooklyn, The Bronx, the breeding grounds for the generation that first sent their children off to summer camp. A place for their offspring to experience summer outside of the city. Most of the camps were traditional Jewish camps. It was like a belt that looped through the Berkshires, the Adirondacks and the Poconos. We were in Wayne County, Pennsylvania. We were Kosher style, meaning no milk with meat. We had Sabbath services on Friday nights, sang a couple of songs, ...recited a few prayers... and then off to bed.

Summer after summer, counselors would bring their school traditions up with them to camp. The legends and rituals grew through
the years.

For example, Mickey Hardon was the "Ah Bay" man for the summer. Chick would always pick one camper who had the charisma
to stand on tables and lead the cheer. At his signal he'd point at
Hardon, who would jump proudly onto the dining room table. Chick
would shout "Quiet" with all the volume his tiny old aged body
could muster. It turned out that he could muster quite a shout as
there was now silence throughout boys' side of the mess hall. Then
he would point at Hardon again and give the "nod".

"Ahhhh Bay" Mickey Hardon would scream.
Our group would shout back "HEY"
"AHHHH BAY" Hardon would scream even louder
And we would respond with Hey
"Ugga sawa sawa" Hardon would croon
"Heeeeeeyyyyyyyyyy" we'd respond in a soft sweeping
response.

Jericho didn't have to play ball all day, but he definitely didn't
want to memorize a song and perform it in front of the whole
camp. It was a contest, and we were going to be judged on how we
performed.

We ended up winning sing that night. Big Fucking Deal! I
couldn't understand why the group went crazy when we were
awarded first place. Our March was sung to the tune 'Yellow
Submarine' by the Beatles. Chick stole the show, a camper at
heart, a youthful soul. We had marched up on stage, and took
our assigned places between two rows of benches. We staggered
our spacing with the back row standing on the benches. The row
in front of them simply stood in a straight line, while the next row
sat on the benches. Finally the rest of the group sat on the edge
of the stage. The entire group of forty-eight boys was ready to
perform.

The music director manned the piano and another counselor sat at the drums. After our group was introduced, a spotlight from the back of the social hall flashed on Chick. He made a grand entrance, surfing down the main aisle on top of a large wooden plank that was being carried by four of the waterfront counselors. He was gyrating to "I Want to Hold Your Hand" and yet he never lost his balance. He was dressed not in his signature yellow shorts, but in bell bottom jeans. His white t shirt was replaced with …. Jericho's peace t shirt?

"He asked me for it and I gave it to him," Jericho said.

Chick had secured a wig with shoulder length brown hair that kept swishing around with each jump and kick he made. A pair of small round framed sunglasses pinched his face. Chick surfed and danced the entire way to the stage, and the camp exploded in laughter. How he never fell off that platform will always remain a mystery to me.

We flew into 'Yellow Submarine' with the new lyrics by Asa and Samson. Jericho had something else in mind, and he talked me into substituting our own lyrics when we hit the chorus;

"We all live in a dirty scummy camp,
A dirty scummy camp...
A dirty scummy camp..."

A few other campers, including Harris, caught on and joined in singing our revision.

We knew what we were singing, but we were so bad that most of the camp couldn't decipher our lyrics. Yet, it didn't matter what the lyrics were because Chick was out front gyrating to the music. The entire camp was standing and clapping and Chick was basking in the adulation which, of course, distracted from the song I didn't want to sing. It was childish, immature, written by two warped minds, and I thought it was stupid. But Asa and Samson penned it and they forced it on us.

Our alma mater, with its sappy lyrics was sung to "Old Friends" by Simon and Garfunkle. We even had a slide show to go along with that. Maybe everyone got excited because Chick took the sing seriously, and he loved the tradition.

Harris and Oliver were caught up in the revelry that the rest of the group seemed to soak in. Maybe it was because we earned an extra canteen as our reward for winning. Jericho and I couldn't have cared less.

Ben had OD that night. The rest of the counselor staff fled camp and headed to the local bar in Cochecton in hopes of seeing the broadcast of the moon walk on the tiny black and white t.v. that sat behind the bar. Joe added an extra half hour to their curfew to allow them the opportunity to view it, if all went according to schedule.

Ben offered the opportunity to sit on the porch and look at the moon, so a few of us put on sweatpants and sweatshirts and carried our jelly rolls outside. We wrapped ourselves into cocoons. We just stared in awe into the night sky.

"You know...they're up there now, just sitting on the moon waiting to walk on its surface," Oliver told us, his eyes like a radar tracking the night sky.

'Wonder what they're thinking?" I asked

"Probably praying they don't have to take a shit," Ben answered and we all broke into laughter.

"NO seriously," Oliver cried out softly. We all looked at Oliver who was staring right back at us, and we realized it was the first time in a while we had made eye contact with him without there being tears fogging his sight.

"I'm upset that we're not watching this. I wanted to be home this summer just so I wouldn't miss it. Instead I'm in this hell hole where we're cut off from the outside world, and can't get any TV signals. And the only radio reception we can get is from WABC radio. Just once I wish my mother would have listened to me."

He looked at each of us, silently begging for our approval. We were a bit stunned to say anything.

Then Ben chimed in, "My mom never listens to me either," and then we all repeated the same response about our mothers never listening to anything we ever said. Except I went a step further... "My mother doesn't even know I exist."

"Of course she does, she gave birth to you," Ben chided.

"She was knocked out. She told me. She didn't want to feel the pain and wanted it over as soon as possible."

We sat in silence as everyone digested what I just said.

"Do you think we'll ever see this event again?" Oliver asked, once again breaking the quiet that had befallen us.

"I'm positive," Ben told him.

"Hey Ben, did you ever go to sleepaway camp?" Jericho asked.

"I was at a sleepaway camp for one summer and that was enough for me. I was like seven. After that summer I stayed home and always did science day camps. Then when I got into high school I just kept volunteering at hospitals, hoping it would look good on my college applications."

"And now you're here with us," Harris said.

"Yup... I'm here, and ... I'm missing the man walking on the moon." Ben laughed at the absurdity of it all.

"So let's just sit out here and look at the nighttime sky and imagine Aldrin and Armstrong frolicking in the heavens. I mean, it's visiting day in less than a week. Man walks on the moon, you'll see your parents...."

"Nothing great about that," I said, only to find Harris and Oliver in agreement.

"Why, what's the matter with your parents?" Ben asked.

Neither Harris nor Oliver said anything. Harris pulled his knees up to his chest and rocked back and forth to comfort himself. Oliver rested his head in the palms of his hands and looked away. It was obvious, they weren't going to say anything so I spoke up.

"Oh... you'll see. My parents are a trip, and just wait till you see what my mother wears. I'm sure she's shopping for the outfit right now."

"It can't be that bad," Ben said.

"Oh it is. You weren't at the buses on the first day. Harris was there. You saw my mom, didn't you?"

"It's that bad," he said meekly to Ben. And then he started laughing, and he continued laughing until it turned into crying and Ben helped pull Harris up off the floor and led him to his bed where he sat with Harris until he fell asleep.

Man walked on the moon that night. We all missed it.

19

I didn't get high during free play.

I was called up to the basketball court by Heshie.

Scott was already there, and I watched our waiter take numerous jump shots while Heshie shouted suggestions. Heshie called me onto the court. He had Scott demonstrate the proper technique for shooting jump shots, and then Heshie ran me through drills to refine my stroke. Heshie then arranged for a small three on three game with a number of waiters and allowed me to participate. He coached me from the sidelines, on how to set a pick, how to play a pick and roll, screaming at me to box out and to be more aggressive.

Beckett Studberg was sitting on the bleachers with a small cassette tape deck by his side. I caught him speaking into the minuscule microphone that was wired to the tape deck.

"Heshie has them primed for the game tonight. He's especially counting on the newcomer, the unknown, the number one prospect by the name of Jason. Heshie is being particularly hard on Jason, expecting him to show his best."

When we were done, Heshie put his arm around me and told me I had potential. Beckett Studberg tried to interview me, but I pushed him away. Then Heshie slapped my ass and told me to wash up as the loudspeaker blew Recall.

Mickey Hardon was watching from the other side of the basketball court and you could feel the contempt blowing icicle darts on a warm summer's evening. He just stood there, staring at me, dribbling his basketball, and playing with his dancing spit. The Brain kept asking him questions, but Hardon kept slapping him away like he was a buzzing fly.

Scott told me I could visit him anytime in one of the annexes behind the waiters' bunk. This was where some of the second year waiters lived. An annex was a glorified shack, a step above a large outhouse except there were two double deckers and one single bed squeezed inside. And living in this shithole was supposed to be something magnificent. Thus, I felt special because no camper was ever allowed to even walk near the annexes, and I got an invite.

Things were heating up between Jericho and Beth, well, in a sort of gradual way. They were always trying to steal kisses at each social. They were always hugging and holding each other under the watchful eyes of the counselors. In other words, they were celibate, so the young sexual frustration kept building.

Rachel and I were practicing on just reaching first base, a quick glance here and there followed by an aborted peck on the cheek. Harris and Ellen seemed to have a very deep meaningful relationship that was slowly developing. They would walk off to a corner and hold hands and just look into each other's eyes and talk all evening.

Jericho was already on the porch, showered and ready, dressed in his white bell bottom pants and white boots. He wore a tight fitting white t shirt with a peace symbol on the front and a raised "power to the people" fist on the back.

"It's easy to take a shower tonight," Jericho reminded me. The Jewish Mafia, the turtle burners, were still docked from socials.

"Are they in the bunk now?"

"Yes... sad sight, isn't it? Lenny is staying behind with them. I had to hide..." he leaned in close to me and whispered "... the weed. I don't trust those mothers. I think they'll rummage through my stuff. And I think they'll go into Harris' stuff so tell Harris to hide anything personal."

Walking back to the shower I had to dodge a maze of angry stares, and a couple of bump and runs with Hooky and The Mayor. Harris was just walking out of the shower so I whispered to him what Jericho had told me. I quickly showered, and then threw on whatever Jericho had laid out for me to wear. In a matter of seconds I was out the door and on the porch sitting on the boot box next to Jericho.

"It's tough to leave us behind alone tonight, isn't it?" Hardon whispered through the screen door. "Who knows what we'll be doing?"

Just then Asa and Samson emerged from their bunk with two large oak tag poster boards. They tried to sneak past us, obviously hiding something.

"What's that?" Hardon asked through the screen door.

"It's a chart. We're going to post it at the Boys HCO," Asa told him.

"What's it say?" Hardon wanted to know.

Asa and Samson turned to look at each other, and without saying a word they decided that it was appropriate to show us the oak-tag. The screen door opened and Hardon stepped onto the porch followed by Harris who was again dressed in a white Lacoste tennis shirt and khaki pants.

They turned the chart toward us to show us two columns. In the first column were the names of some of the counselors on girls' side. The second column had tennis balls, ranging from an empty slot to four balls.

"We call this Love/Tennis," Samson told us. "Every tennis ball represents a set of tennis played. This chart is a representation of how many sets of tennis one of these girls plays, and how badly we would still want to go down on them and eat them out. Thus the number of tennis balls represents the number of sets of tennis played. I mean, after four sets of tennis, it's got to be pretty raunchy down there, so if there are four tennis balls being shown, you know the girl has to be pretty hot."

With that explanation the two counselors turned to walk toward the HCO and tape up their chart.

Mickey Hardon loved the poster and ran inside to tell the rest of the bunk what he had just seen. Harris sat down next to me, making me squeeze closer to Jericho who was almost pushed off the boot box.

"What does he mean by ' going down'?" Harris asked.

I sat silent. I wasn't sure myself, so I didn't want to say anything, but Jericho leaned forward, and spoke up.

"I mean, you know what a blowjob is, right?" Jericho asked.

"Every boy knows what a blowjob is," Harris told him.

"Well, going down on a girl is the same thing. A man puts his face between a woman's legs and licks and kisses and..."

"And girls like this?" Harris was mesmerized.

"My brother says it drives them crazy. They crave it."

"Does it taste good?" I asked.

"Yeah.. my brother says it does."

"But does it smell?" Harris asked.

"My brother says sometimes it smells like tuna fish."

"Ugh.. I'm never going to have that sandwich again."

"All I know is that girls side won't be happy about that chart," I said.

"They're putting it on the boys HCO shack. How are the girls going to see it?" Harris asked.

Jericho looked at Harris, and started to laugh at his naivety.

"Trust me, they'll find out. Girls always find out everything. And I'm sure they won't like what's posted. Maybe I'll rip it down at night."

I looked at Jericho and I knew just what he meant.

Evening Call was sounded, and we lined up in front of our bunks. The Brain and the gang of turtle burners all sat on the porch staring out on the campus. Lenny sat on the top step, acting as a blockade. He was happy he didn't have to walk up to the Social Hall.

Spanky sat down next to Lenny. He had picked up sodas on his day off, and kept them cold by hiding them in the tanks of the toilet bowls. We had to improvise without refrigerators so, to keep the chill, the toilet bowl tank was the only solution to keeping sodas cold. Spanky gave Lenny one his sodas and the two of them guzzled it at the same time. Then they belched out the theme song from Bonanza.

Jericho was looking forward to this social as the Social Hall was more spacious than the canteen. The back porch had many dark corners that he and Beth were hoping to slip into.

Suddenly Joe Geisinger appeared. He had walked around the back of the bunks, probably coming from the waiters' annexes. He had a big smile on his face, but you knew he was tired. There was a lot of pressure in preparing for visiting day, which was now only a day away, You could tell it hung over him like a hundred pound weight.

"What's tonight's activity?" he asked Chick.

"We're playing hockey. Are you kidding me? Look how they're dressed. It's a social."

"What's this? You, over there," Joe shouted, pointing at Jericho. "What's that you're wearing?"

"Bell bottoms."

"You know I don't allow bell bottoms in this camp. It's hippie wear. I sent a note home before camp that bell bottoms were explicitly prohibited. Now go and change."

"I don't have any other pants, so I'm not changing," Jericho told him.

"Then you're not going to the social." He turned to face Chick. "He's not going to the social until he changes."

"Come on Joe, let the kid be. The summer's half over," Chick pleaded.

"NO BELL BOTTOMS! AND WHEN THE BARBER IS HERE YOU BETTER GET YOUR HAIR CUT!"

"I don't have to."

"Yes, you do. I am going to make sure you look good for your parents."

"Ha, my father has hair longer than me. What are you going to do, make him get a haircut too? You can't tell me what to do."

"Oh YES I CAN, MISTER. I OWN THIS CAMP. IT'S MY RULES. YOU

WILL DO WHAT I SAY. ALL OF YOU WILL DO WHAT I SAY. THERE'LL BE NO LONG HAIR ANYMORE IN THIS CAMP AND NO BELL BOTTOMS. NOW GO BACK IN THERE AND CHANGE. THIS IS MY WORLD AND I MAKE THE RULES!"

Nobody moved.

"I SAID TO MOVE, MISTER!"

It wasn't fair. Almost everyone else was wearing bell bottoms, but Joe zeroed in on Jericho. Jericho, for his part, stood there in defiance, never once ratting out the rest of the group. Joe targeted Jericho for his hair, and the bell bottoms were secondary.

Chick had to finally approach Jericho who wasn't backing down an inch. I was scared out of my mind, but Jericho stood firm, not even a flinch of intimidation. He stood there so calmly, with so much self resolve that I started to question my own manhood. I didn't know if I would be able to stand up to Joe Geisinger.

"Just listen to me... go inside and pretend that you're putting on pants. I'll take care of everything," Chick whispered. "Jason, take him inside and look for a pair of pants. You look about the same size. If I can get rid of Joe, you'll sneak up to the social. Now go."

I took Jericho by the arm, and I started to walk him back to the bunk, but he refused to dissolve eye contact with Joe. The owner didn't blink either, and stood like a boulder as he continued staring down Jericho. We walked into the bunk past the giggling Hardon, and I looked for a pair of jeans.

"I'm not wearing your pants," Jericho told me.

"You just have to wear it out of here. Bring your pants with you, and change on the way to the social. You don't want Hardon ratting you out. Just put these on and we'll sneak your pants out."

For once, Jericho listened to what I had to say, and surprisingly my pants did fit him. I folded his bell bottoms neatly into my backpack and when we looked outside and saw Joe marching away we walked back out and joined the group heading up to the Social Hall. Once we were out of view of our bunk Jericho pulled my dungarees off and slid on his bell bottoms. It was as simple as that.

"But I'm not getting a haircut," he told me. It was more of a warning than a statement.

Each venue for a social afforded a different aura, and thus different behavior from the girls and the boys' side of camp. Everyone preferred the social in the canteen. Though confined, it was an evening when you could buy a hamburger from the grill, and eat as much candy as you wanted.

In comparison, the waterfront was expansive and, even though it was the most boring locale, it kindled romantic feelings for those of us who are losers and can only dream of having even half a chance of getting a kiss.

Yet the Social Hall provided a new twist. If there was a sympathetic counselor manning the back doors one could slip out onto the porch, disappear into a dark corner and maybe suck some face.

When we got up to the Social Hall Asa and Samson took their position and sat on the stage, their legs dangling over the edge. They chatted with their counterparts on girls' side and two of the cuter female campers were sitting on their laps. One big happy family. Rachel and Beth hated their counselors as much as we hated Asa and Samson.

Ben had dragged one of the benches toward the back door and he was the guardian of the porch. I already knew that Jordan had slipped onto the porch with Beth. I'd looked all over the Social Hall but couldn't find him.

I had gotten up enough nerve to hold Rachel's hand, which was a huge step for me. Just the contact with her soft skin made me sprout a boner that I tried to hide. I noticed Ben spying on me. He tried to hide a smirk at my pathetic lack of chutzpah.

Harris had his arm around Ellen's back and he kept trying to slowly move his fingers closer to her tiny budding breasts, but Ellen was sly, and kept adjusting her body. Each twist of a finger was infinitesimal and resulted in Harris's fingers never reaching their goal.

I figured it was time to make my move so I stood up and hoped that Rachel didn't see my erection. Harris saw it and couldn't stop laughing. I tried to sneak towards the back porch. I turned around to check on Asa and Samson and was glad to see that they were preoccupied. As usual the boys were too shy to talk to the girls and they congregated on one side of the hall while the girls on the other side of the hall tittered and made fun of their immaturity.

We took our time inching towards the back, pausing to look at the pictures from summers past that hung like a museum display. We knew if we made any sudden move Asa and Samson would grab us, and then they would embarrass us in front of everyone. Fortunately they were surrounded by their girlfriends and fawning young girls, and we were invisible to them. We approached Ben, and he smiled knowingly. It was like knowing a rock star, and receiving backstage passes.

"Just stay to the left. Jericho's on the right," Ben whispered, acknowledging that he was given strict instructions by Jericho to help maintain his privacy.

I walked to the darkest corner and leaned against the railing. Rachel kept her distance, but she held my hand and just this emotional moment of innocence had me reeling.

I could detect a slight scent of perfume, something her counselor must have given her. My legs were growing weak, or was it that I had an urge to pee... or was that just a tingle of excitement? I had no clue how to make a move, how to get her to kiss me. I was hoping that she would just lean in. I looked over to my side and suddenly saw Harris and Ellen locking lips and I just felt so incompetent that I threw all inhibitions to the wind and drew Rachel close to me.

She smiled. I closed my eyes and slowly moved my face closer to her and prayed that somehow our lips would dock and we would kiss, and this is basically how it happened. My first kiss... all luck. I drew her closer with my hands but suddenly realized that she was feeling my newly developed boner pressing against her and she jumped back giggling.

"OH MY God!" screamed Ellen. "I can't believe you stuck that thing in me... you put that thing in me." She was hysterical and

Rachel turned her attention to her friend. Harris stood there, bewildered . Ellen raced into the Social Hall to find her counselors. Rachel followed her.

"HE PUT THAT THING IN ME, HE PUT IT IN."

Ellen's hysterics started to fade away as she ran into the front of the Social Hall. She either stopped crying or was muffling her whimpers in the arms of a counselor. Ben walked out onto the porch and saw Harris cowering in the corner. I could tell Ben was trying to hide laughter, but he was also trying to be an understanding parent in training.

"Ah, Harris…. what just happened?" Ben asked, doing his best to swallow the laughter that crawled up his throat.

"I don't know," and you could hear Harris' voice crack…"I was just kissing her."

Before he could say another word, Asa and Samson stormed onto the porch. They surprised Ben, knocking him to the ground, then rushed toward Harris who was a quivering mass of Jello.

Samson lifted Harris skyward, rocketing him off the floor of the porch. His powerful hands clenched Harris by the shirt lifting him high till they were facing each other eye to eye. Harris' turned blue from pure terror. It seemed like the entire group had flooded onto the back porch of the Social Hall, with some of the campers starting to scream 'Fight… Fight…Fight..'.

"What did you stick in her, you little pervert." Samson screamed.

"It can't be your prick, you little shit. That's too small to even be seen!" Asa screamed.

"What did you do? Are you a pervert?" Samson barked.

I thought Harris was going to shit in his pants out of fear, but just at that moment Ben picked himself off the floor, and did a sideways kick into the back of Samson's right leg, making his knee buckle. Harris dropped to the floor. Samson rolled around in pain, screaming like a little baby as Harris gasped for air. Ben turned to face Asa who was charging him. Instead of panicking, Ben simply stepped aside and used Asa's momentum to push him over the railing and down into the bushes. I wanted to clap, I wanted to scream, but I just stood there in awe.

"You fucking asshole, if you fucked up my knees and ruined my basketball career I will sue you.. you fucking asshole," Samson moaned as he tried to stand up. The pain kept causing him to fall back to the floor.

"Everyone back inside. Now! Move!"

It was Chick walking out onto the porch that finally broke up the crowd. He physically pushed the boys back into the social hall, and screamed at the girls to follow suit. "Now what's going on here?"

"This little pervert molested a girl," Samson whined as he slowly picked himself off the floor.

"It was my tongue. I stuck my tongue in her mouth. Everyone keeps talking about a French kiss so I tried it," Harris whispered, as he rubbed his neck and attempted to clear his airway. "It was just my tongue."

It was a delayed laugh, but Ben and Chick couldn't hold it back anymore. It was a moment of innocence that caught everyone by surprise.

"I guess she wasn't ready for that," Chick chuckled.

"I guess not," Harris croaked.

The two counselors helped Harris to his feet and slowly led him back into the Social Hall. I followed them wondering how Harris had the courage to do what he did, and how I didn't have the guts to do the same. I looked over at Jericho who was standing off to the side with his hand around Beth's shoulders. Everyone had the nerve to really kiss their girl but me. All I could muster was a blind lip docking. For a moment I felt so pathetic. I slipped into the Social Hall and watched Ellen and Harris talk to each other. It was obvious Ellen was apologizing for overreacting, and Harris was soaking in the compassion from all the counselors and campers.

Jericho and Beth were forced back into the Social Hall and the back door of the Social Hall was now closed. We were stuck inside. Asa and Samson were both now limping. They took their seats on the edge of the stage, pointed at Ben, and flashed their middle fingers at him.

We lingered in limbo, just staring at each other. Inside the Social Hall we weren't allowed to touch, and whatever conversation was left to muster concerned the aborted attempt at a French kiss. Harris was showing off the deep bruises on his neck where Samson attempted to choke him. He was in surprisingly good spirits. I think he gained some respect back that night.

A few minutes later the girls were lined up and sent back to their bunks, and then Chick announced it was time for us to head back to ours. I was talking to Jericho and Harris when Ben approached us with Oliver by his side.

"I have a nickname for you," Ben said as he put his hand around my shoulders and led me out of the Social Hall.

"This I have to hear," Jericho said as a grin spread across his face.

"From now on, you're Flanken. That's what I'm going to call you."

"Flanken? What the hell is Flanken?" I screamed in protest.

"Flanken is a soft piece of meat, one's that on a bone—one found in mushroom and barley soup. At least in my grandmother's mush-room and barley soup. It's actually delicious. Very soft, very tasty... but it's the softness of the meat... it falls right off the bone. And that's you, Jason. You have no backbone. You're soft... you're a great kid, and have so much to offer, but you're just too damn soft. Harris even tried kissing his girlfriend...a bit awkward and ballsy, I must say..."

And this caused Harris to blush, even though he was cheered on by Jericho who hugged him.

"... but you... I was watching, ... you didn't even have the nerve to kiss your girlfriend until you saw Harris doing it with his girlfriend. You're soft, Jason. On the basketball court you're one of the biggest kids out there and you're intimidated by Mickey Hardon at times. Stop being so quiet, reach out to people. Stand up for yourself. Be a man, and not some piece of Flanken... that soft piece of meat that simply pulls away from the bone. Until I see some backbone from you, I'm going to call you Flanken. Hell, maybe I'll always call you Flanken. That way you'll always remember this day and never back down from anyone again."

20

O h, they heard about the social. The Jewish Mafia was awaiting our return with all of their barbed comments. I don't
know who related the evening's events to them, but they
were waiting for us.

We had lingered at the Social Hall, talking to Ben and now Harris
and Jericho were calling me Flanken. We walked back to the bunk listening to Ben ramble on about all the failures he had with women. The
sound of the pine trees swaying ever so slight tickled my eardrums. I've
found that a clear and starry night made me a bit light-headed. It felt
good and for a moment I didn't t have a care in the world. I kept sniffing
my fingers for the lingering scent of Rachel's perfume.

The second we walked into the bunk they were upon us, calling
Harris "dickless" and a "loser." They circled around Harris, pushing
and poking him as he tried to make his way to his bed. They tried to
pull his pants down just so they could embarrass him. Harris tried
to push everyone away, but he was being overwhelmed.

"Flanken, are you going to stand there or are you going to try to
help him?" Ben whispered in my ear as he entered the bunk.

I just stood there.

Ben pushed past me, and started to throw everyone off of
Harris. The Brain went flying across the room. Mickey Hardon was
tossed over one bed and landed on Bugsy's bed. Hooky and the
Mayor were pushed to the floor where they landed on top of each
other.

"I have OD tonight, boys... there will be no more acting out," announced Ben. "If I see any one of you even leave your bed for a second you will be standing outside with me all night. And I do mean standing! And you'll be holding your sneakers in your hands and if your hands drop I'm going to whip your legs with my belt." .

The Jewish Mafia, bruised from being manhandled, made their way back to their beds.

I was in the back room washing up with Harris when Ben turned out the lights in the bunk. Jericho joined us and as he started to brush his teeth he nudged me.

"I'm going over to girls' side tonight... are you going to join me?"

"What? You're crazy."

"No. I told Beth that I was coming over and I told her to tell Rachel that you might come too. I need you. I can't do this myself. I could use your company." Jericho spit out a mouth of water.

"I want to go too," Harris suddenly said. It was a fire burning bright in his head that now seemed to be roaring. From the moment he'd walked into the bunk tonight Harris had slid into his shell, but now he was animated. "I'm going with you. Fuck these guys, I'm going."

"Okay then, Harris is going. …. What about you, Flanken?" Jericho asked. A huge smile spread across his face. He knew how to push my buttons.

"Will it get me kicked out of camp if I'm caught?"

"Absolutely."

"I'm in."

I had no idea what time it was when Jericho woke me. He put his hand over my mouth, just like in the movies, and whispered in my ear to get up. I stretched and then focused on Harris standing at the foot of my bed, dressed in navy blue sweat pants and a blue sweatshirt. Jericho just nodded for me to follow him, and when at first I didn't roll out of bed, he angrily pointed his finger to the ground, ordering me to stand and get dressed, which I finally did. Silence. Ben let out a snore and none of our bunkmates even rolled over.

We carefully opened the screen door in a major effort to avoid any noise. Softly tiptoeing onto the porch, we gently closed the screen door until it kissed the jamb.

Now we ran across the Great Lawn. Was this planned all along? It was a new moon, and a cloudy evening. No stars and no moonlight. Total darkness…. except for the two white stripes crossing in front of us.

We turned into statues and held our collective breath as two skunks walked past us without a care in the world. When we felt they were out of the way Jericho still signaled for us to wait. He ran to the boys HCO shack and ripped down the poster Samson and Asa had stapled to the screen door. Then he shredded it into little pieces and sprinkled it into the barrel that was used as a garbage can. He ran back to get us, and we followed him in a mad dash toward girls' side. Then we hit the road. And we stopped.

We were near Bunk One on boys side, deep in its umbra, protected from who… Joe? We tried to quell the nervous gasps we were expelling. Harris approached the road first, and after looking both ways he finally dipped his toe onto the road like an old man testing the temperature of his bath. Then he jumped back and hugged himself. Now it was my turn. I inched toward the road and touched my toe to the dirt and gravel. I jumped back like it was electrified. In all honesty, Harris and I were too scared to cross.

I felt a tingling in my balls again, like I had to pee. I started to shake, one strong convulsion, and then I succumbed to the calm of the moment. Was I about to commit my first act of nastiness? Lawlessness? Breaking the rules? Just being a bad kid?

"You pussies, just follow me!" Jericho said as he bounded across the dirt road and hid in the shadows of the Girls Arts and Crafts shack. Harris was next.

"See you on the other side," Harris whispered as he tiptoed across the road… dainty little steps.

I held my breath and in two leaps I found myself in the arms of Harris and Jericho who were congratulating me. We tiptoed onto girls campus and hid in the shadows of the Girls HCO shack. We surveyed the campus.

Silence. No sound up the road of Joe approaching.

Jericho led the way. Swiftly we crossed the smaller girls' campus and approached the bunk where our dates supposedly lay waiting. Harris looked at his watch, and whispered to us that it was 2:00 am. I'm sure this was his effort to calm my fears. Who would be up at 2:00 a.m.?

"Wait," I whispered, "what makes you even think they want to get up now and see us?"

"Just wait here, and don't worry. They want to see us!" Jericho told us. He had that broad, sweet smile that melted all the girls.

Jericho slipped into the bunk, and we slid against the side of the bunk, into the deeper shadows of night.

"This is crazy... we're going to get caught... I mean what are we supposed to even do with the girls when we get inside?" I babbled.

Just then the screen door opened with the slightest squeak, and Jericho waved us inside.

"Just kiss your girlfriend," Harris giggled as he darted toward the girls' bunk. Not wanting to stay behind, I followed suit.

Slipping inside the girls' bunk was... just as good as I pictured sex. I felt like my whole body was in an orgasm of excitement. The counselors were asleep and some of the girls were even snoring, which was a revelation. Jericho slid into Beth's bed, and under her blanket. They started kissing immediately.

Ellen lay in bed, but she was propped up on her elbows. She waved Harris over, and he sat down on the edge of the bed and they too started kissing. I looked around and Rachel was the dark shadowy figure standing alone in the back room. I approached her slowly, trying to be light and feathery. I was balancing myself on the tips of my toes so that I wouldn't wake anyone up in the bunk. She was wearing pink sweatpants with a white crew neck sweatshirt.

"Hi," was all she said, but I knew she was glad that I had come.

I didn't know what to do. My feet suddenly grew roots, but then again, Rachel didn't seem to know what to do either. We stood staring at each other for a few seconds, and then I took a baby step toward her. She copied me. After what seemed like an infinite number of baby steps we stood face to face. I could smell the sweetness of bubble gum toothpaste.

"Hi,.. I don't.."

Before I could say another word I found myself leaning in to give her a peck on her lips. This time she didn't move away, and our lips remained glued for at least a full minute. When lip contact was finally broken, she hugged me.

And I trembled like a minor earthquake.

"What's the matter?" she asked.

I didn't know what to tell her. It wasn't an orgasm, even though holding her so close was driving me crazy. I couldn't bring myself to tell her that it was her touch, her softness that made me tremble. I had forgotten what a soothing lotion a hug from a female could be. I had forgotten the gentleness of a female's skin.... and I truly couldn't remember the last time my mother hugged me. I hadn't been held for such a long time, and this felt so wondrous.

"It's just that..."

"I'm sorry," she said, even though I don't think she knew why she even said it. Rachel's scent was driving me crazy. All I wanted was to feel her cheek against mine, to swallow the sweetness of her scent. When we finally pulled away from each other Rachel smiled and giggled and looked at me with impish embarrassment. I knew she had felt my boner which had rocketed into orbit. I kissed her lips again, and I felt her mouth opening and the tip of her tongue flicking against my lips when....

Suddenly there was the sound in the distance of a screen door screaming open , and then slamming shut with impudence. A car door opened, and exploded shut. Then the sound of a Cadillac engine turning over and a car backing up in haste. I just knew they were coming for us, not really knowing who the "they" were, but knowing that we were the prey.

Jericho jumped out of bed and Harris and I met him at the front door. We could see the car headlights approaching girls' camp.

"What do we do?" Harris was scared shitless.

"I don't know," Jericho answered.

"Get out of here NOW!" Beth hissed as she actually started to push us out of the bunk.

The second we were on the porch they closed and locked the door on us. We were screwed. The Cadillac's approach never slowed. It was as if someone knew we were here. We were the proverbial scared deer in the head lights. Then the car stopped short, the door opened, and someone stepped out. His flashlight beam floated off the ground signifying his approach on foot.

"What are we going to do?" Harris danced around like he had to take a shit.

"I'm going to run toward the lake," I told them. "I'll make sure the driver of the car sees me and chases me. You do an end around and get back to the bunk." This was it. This was my moment to get kicked out of camp.

Before Jericho or Harris could protest I was off and running. I darted out of the shadows of girls' camp and cut across the gravel road in front of the Mess Hall. The flashlight beam caught me the second my first step crunched onto the gravel. As I ran I felt the strange sensation that my pursuer was cool and controlled. There was no mad dash to get back into the car. Instead I heard a heavy sigh and the slow retreat of footsteps. Then the sound of the Cadillac moving forward.

I ran as hard as I could down along the gravel road behind the boys' HCO shack. I passed the two waterfronts. I wanted to be as close to the lake as I could get so Jericho and Harris could sneak back through the darkness at the top of the hill. The Cadillac quickly caught up to me, and I slowed to a trot, and then stopped completely. I was winded. I was waiting for the anger.

Instead, a rumble of a laugh whisked through the night air as the car door opened again. It wasn't Joe, it was Bramo. HIs mammoth size seemed to blot out the car headlights as he approached me.

"Now, what are you doing out of your bunk? HUH?" He chuckled.

"Nothing... "

"I like that. You didn't answer with a wise remark. I like that.... Are you with anyone? Did you leave anyone behind? "

I shook my head no.

"Get into the car."

Bramo put his hand on my shoulder, and I never felt such force in my life. He wasn't hurting me in any manner, but on the contrary, he was gentle. And yet I felt an omnipotent surge of power and strength course through my body as he led me back to the car. I remember not being scared, as a feeling of calm sedated me.

Bramo drove me back to the bunk, opened the back door of the car and let me out. He didn't have to say anything. He just tilted his head toward the bunk, and the shifting of his eyes commanded me to move.

I walked into the bunk to see Harris and Jericho lying under their blankets, while the rest of the bunk snored in a deep sleep. When the car pulled away Jericho and Harris jumped out of bed and sat down beside me. I was concerned that their extra weight would make my bed sag and wake Ben, but he was dead to the world.

"Who was that? Joe?" Jericho asked. He was wide-eyed with excitement.

"Nope. It was Bramo."

"What did he say? Did he see us?" Harris wanted to know.

"He didn't see you. At least I don't think he saw you. And he didn't say anything to me. It was kind of strange, because I felt like he was quietly laughing at me under his breath."

Jericho and Harris climbed back under their respective blankets and the silence of the night followed. Until Jericho lifted his head off his pillow.

"Hey, thanks for what you did," he whispered .

The next morning Chick asked me to stay back as the group walked toward the HCO for the morning flag raising ceremony. I was prepared to be told to start packing, as I was being sent home. Jericho and Harris lagged behind, but Ben prodded them forward.

They wanted to see what Chick was going to do to me. We sat on the boot box on the porch.

"Ehhhh.... you crossed the road last night? You're lucky it was Bramo who caught you,"

"How did he even know it was me?" I asked, knowing that Bramo had no clue who I was.

"Well, don't kid yourself. Bramo may not know everyone by name, but he knows everyone. All he had to say to me this morning was that it wasn't one of those morons in your bunk, and I narrowed it down to you. I mean I know you went over there with someone, but you were the one who wanted to get caught. You're not going to be sent home."

I was a bit disappointed.

"Why not?"

"Why not? Because you're going to end up loving this summer. I'm going to see to it. Besides, I told Bramo that you were a really good kid, but you know what, Jason?"

I sat there, almost paralyzed. I really wanted to be sent home, but for just a milli- second I had doubts. Maybe I was glad that I was going to remain. I looked at Chick, and had to bite my tongue. His right testicle, like a shy little turtle head, was now drooping out from the corner of his shorts.

"Jason, you're a good kid, but sometimes in life you just need to get into trouble. I'm proud of you. You can't be good for your entire life. You have to get into trouble, get caught, do something out of the norm sometimes. You crossed the road. It's about time you did. There are many roads in life you're going to have to cross, literally and figuratively. Just be prepared for the consequences of your actions. Oh, and I know who went with you, but I'm glad you didn't rat them out. You're a real mensch."

Chick laughed and patted me on my knee. That one testicle that kept slipping out of his shorts was driving me crazy. Chick wasn't wearing any underwear.

"One other lesson in life," Chick said as he stopped and turned towards me. "Always remember, never marry a beautiful woman.

They're headaches. Marry a plain-looking woman. You're a mensch, so look for someone just as nice as you."

"I hate being called a mensch. It's like the kiss of death."

"It's a compliment."

"Too many old and smelly relatives have pinched my cheeks and called me a mensch. You get pummeled for being a mensch, and girls run from a mensch."

"Only the right girls won't run. They know a mensch is golden. But always remember, marry an ugly girl!"

21

O n the day before Visiting Day you could sense the excitement in those who wanted to see their parents. Giddiness seemed to reign. Counselors were even seen kissing the ass of the kids they had punched and noogied all summer. Did they think we were stupid? Did they really think we'd fall for the "nice" behavior after they'd been nasty toward us for the entire summer?

Earlier in the day Lenny wailed on the Brain. One... Two... Three roundhouse punches. Two to The Brains left arm, and one to his right arm. Huge welts quickly developed and you just knew they would turn black and blue in time for a parental interrogation.

Samson and Asa were seen favoring other kids, the ones they'd tormented with their words. They showered love and affection on their targets. But really, did they think we're idiots? Did the counselors really believe 24 hours of abnormal sweetness would erode campers' minor traumas? I had a feeling that this visiting day would turn out to be a life-changing event.

Every camp has its cast of characters, but Camp Tonkawa was awash in them. Suddenly every character was on display, parading around camp like preening peacocks. It was quite a show that lasted for two full days.

Chick started the festivities by suddenly transforming into his alias, his super hero character known as the HAWK. Jericho mentioned that this was the ritual that was performed every year on the morning before visiting day. A rope was jerry-rigged into a zip line that ran from the top of a bunk down to the boys HCO. Chick was dressed in black pajamas, with a black cape, and he wore a mask that was similar to the one Batman wore, except for the huge hawk nose.

Fanfare blared over the loudspeaker as all attention turned towards the bunk closest to the HCO shack. Chick suddenly appeared on the roof. He took what looked like a bicycle handle bar and slid down to the HCO.

When he landed on his feet, a black motorcycle roared out from behind the HCO, the rider also dressed in black. Chick jumped onto the back of the motorcycle and off they roared to the cheers from boys side.

The parade continued on through the day. The corn-cob-pipe-smoking woman sat on a rocking chair down by the waterfront watching her mate put another coat of paint on the war canoes. She watched with satisfaction as her husband made sure those war canoes glistened.

Heshie trimmed his Fu Manchu mustache, and walked around with a glistening new whiffle ball bat. He suddenly became an army drill instructor, making sure the waiters bunks were spotless. Fail to comply with his demands resulted in a couple of whacks from the whiffle ball bat.

Marsh Goutman, the golf counselor, walked into breakfast dressed in purple Plus Fours, with a matching golf shirt. There was even a purple tam o'shanter adorning his head.

Cara, the Camp Mama, was seen scurrying around, tending to the youngest campers. She was busy cutting fingernails, brushing teeth that weren't brushed all summer, giving shampoos where necessary, and making sure cubbies were neat. She was their Jewish grandmother. Everything had to be proper for the parents.

Dani Jordan, the dramatics counselor, pranced across camp, practicing her magic tricks. She wore a director's hat, the old style floppy ones seen in silent movies and also dressed in Plus Fours. A white t-shirt with an argyle vest completed her outfit. She carried around a director's chair and talked to everyone through a large megaphone.

Morris, the Canuck, walked out of the kitchen for the first time all summer. On visiting day the kitchen staff was told to disappear, but Morris was different. Morris was a legend. Everyone loved Morris and he was there to greet the parents when the waiters delivered bottles of soda during their lunch time.

Morris, the Canuck's fame rode the wind of tales spoken by the waiters. They would speak reverently of the stunts Morris pulled in the kitchen. This morning he was walking down the aisle pulling cream puffs out of a burlap bag that was slung over one shoulder. With his left hand he balanced a tray containing two platters of pancakes. With his right hand he threw the cream puffs at campers, many who were sitting with their mouths open, looking like tiny baby birds in a nest waiting for their mother to return with a worm. The cream puffs exploded in pastry bombs, as Morris wasn't really trying to toss them into open mouths. The tray of pancakes remained steady on his left hand while he scurried down the aisle, still tossing cream puffs and chasing our waiter.

'Scc—Scc—Scc—oottt," he shouted.

Morris had a horrible stutter which was exacerbated when he became nervous. Sometimes we could hear him screaming at the kitchen staff, in English, in French, and even throwing in some Yiddish. Morris loved to bake. He barely came out of the kitchen, but now he was trying to grab Scott's attention. Scott had just handed Ben the tray of pancakes when Morris reached our table.

"D..d...d...d...d."

"Morris, calm down," Ben told him.

"D..d..don't.... eeeat the p...pp....ppp..pancakes. Take these instead," Morris said as he handed a new tray of pancakes to Ben and took back the original stack.

"Why?" Ben asked.

Morris looked at Scott and then at Ben. His face grew tense but then it suddenly relaxed, and you could see the muscles around his jaw dissolve their tension.

"These we...wer...were...supposed to be for Joe. I mixed with a touch of Ex Lax. Just a sm...sm...smidge to make him poop and calm down."

Morris made the exchange and then ran back into the kitchen.

Joshie, the Canteen manager, wore one of those old soda jerk outfits,... white shorts with a white button shirt and a small triangular soda jerk hat. The polka dot bowtie completed the costume. Jake, the head tennis counselor, had his staff dress in all whites, and made them carry their tennis racquets everywhere. Ari, the counselor who led us in Friday Evening services, was forced to wear a yarmulke all day so that he looked more like a religious leader instead of a regular counselor. Joe even gave him an extra bonus to grow a beard for the week so that he would look even more pious. Everyone had to play their part for visiting day.

Joe Geisinger knew the little things that would make a difference. He knew how to create great public relations with the visiting parents. A professional cleaning team entered our bunks right after breakfast and swabbed the floors and toilets with Pinesol. It was so concentrated that our eyes burned all morning. Hamburgers and fries for lunch. Need I say more about brown-nosing the parents.

There would be no MILK CALL the day before Visiting Day. Milk Call was the horrible ten minutes after our selective period where the waiters delivered small pint sized milk cartons, along with a couple of bags of cookies. Most of us never drank the milk. We would toss the cartons into the large metal garbage cans in front of our bunk. Here they would stew in the afternoon heat and turn sour, finally emitting a foul stench. This was something Joe would not tolerate, his camp smelling like a garbage dump, thus no Milk Call.

Friday night services ended in a blur. Ari did his best to speed along the service, especially with his one paragraph sermon.

"Let's all remember how fortunate we are this visiting day. We're all up in the mountains, this beautiful land, and amongst friends. How lucky can you be? Make sure you thank your parents for such splendor. There will be no Oneg Shabbat fruit tonight."

Every Friday night after we returned from services, the waiters would bring around fruit for the Sabbath, but for the same reason we skipped milk call, we were skipping fruit. Instead of the putrid smell of soured milk, having fruit at night meant that we would be greeted in the morning by the eye tearing odor of skunks. Anything that was thrown out in the garbage cans would attract the skunks at night. Even if they don't spray, skunks still smell, leaving a distasteful odor wherever they go. It was like a deadly fart wafting casually in the air for at least 24 hours, well into visiting day. Thus, no fruit was waiting for us when we walked into the bunk.

Jericho flew backwards onto his bed like he was doing the Fosbury Flop. He crossed his arms and held himself so tight that he looked like he was wearing a straitjacket. There was no smile. Not even a glimmer of a smirk.

"You're that disappointed about not getting fruit?"

"Fuck the fruit...you know that's not it."

"Okay... but I can't tell which emotion your pout is trying to convey? Are you angry, sad, or pissed?"

Long pause. One bang of the head against the wall. Jericho didn't even wince.

The barber had set up shop in the Social Hall early Friday morning and with his three assistants, started to buzz the hair of the younger campers. They then fought with the older campers about how much was to be taken off. Jericho refused to sit if the razor was still in the barber's hands so Chick forced the barber to take out his scissors and snip off just a small amount of hair from the back of Jericho's head.

Jericho trusted Chick. Chick looked at the barber and pinched his forefinger and thumb to a sliver of an opening.

"Cut more than this, and I cut your balls off. One snip, and that's it. More than one snip and I will stab you ten times that amount. Understood?" Chick threatened.

The barber nodded, then snipped off the tiniest amount of hair.

He handed it to Chick, who produced a small envelope that was hidden somewhere inside of his shorts. He dropped the snippet of hair inside. With a flourish he licked the envelope and sealed it.

"This way if Joe questions you, I have proof that they cut your hair. I hate lying to Joe... he's an old friend, but this way I can tell him that yes, definitely, you got a haircut and I wouldn't be lying. "

"Then what is it? Are you angry, sad, or pissed?" I asked again.
"All three!"
"Why? It couldn't be the haircut?"
"Yes... that's exactly the reason."
"Look at me," I told him, pointing at my butchered scalp. "I asked for the same cut as you had, but did I GET IT? NO!... but you get special treatment. Your haircut is one small lock and you're sitting here like a pouting baby. I had the Last of the Mohican's scalping me. Look at me... one side of my hair is long and the other looks like a jagged cliff. I wasn't going to let him use that buzzer on me, so I made him use the scissors. I was taking my life into my hands when I bolted out of that chair. He could have stabbed me."

Jericho just stared ahead. It was a long pause and I was about to turn my back on him when...

"You're right. Your haircut really does suck."

Saturday morning the sun rose. Never take that momentous fact for granted on Visiting Day, because there's nothing more painful than a rainy Visiting Day. All these somewhat normal parents cooped up in the bunk with their kids with nothing to do and nothing to say for six hours. That was the true definition of insanity.

Reveille sounded, echoing over the hills, officially heralding the milestone known as Visiting Day. For the first time, I witnessed everyone in our bunk jumping out of bed at the first sound of the needle hitting the vinyl. Beds were made, cubbies tightened up, and everyone was in the backroom brushing their teeth only minutes after Reveille.

Counselors were told to make sure everyone still had their toothbrushes and Ben even asked where he could find toothpaste tube caps. We had all lost our caps in the first days and toothpaste could be seen oozing out of everyone's tubes.

Breakfast was thrown at us, and we wolfed down the eggs, the onion rolls, and then ran back to our bunks to clean up. We were threatened with not being allowed to leave our bunks unless we passed inspection. All this was an eye game to appease our parents.

It was only 8:00 a.m., but we knew some parents had arrived already. Bramo and Cisco and Jake, the Tennis counselor, desperately tried to keep parents behind a roped off area. They were lining up like racehorses being pushed into their chutes. Ben walked up and down the bunk, looking under everyone's bed and finding unused boots and rubbers lying like dead fish.

"Get your boots and prophylactics off the floor and into the boot box NOW!" he shouted in a poor attempt at humor.

When Ben was pleased with our efforts he told us we could go and sit on the porch, but Harris didn't budge from his bed. Neither did Oliver and Jericho. So I sat inside with them. Jericho had already smoked a doobie and was lying on his bed with a soft buzz.

Harris was rocking back and forth in a panicked mantra, obviously with a lot on his mind, and nothing pleasant. Oliver just sat on his bed sighing, long deep sobs punctuated with a hit from his inhaler.

We heard a helicopter hovering overhead.

"That's my mom and dad. Joe's letting them land across the way in Abner's backyard," Bugsy told us. "My mother can't walk. She lost one of her legs... so they're letting my parents fly in on our helicopter."

"What do you mean, lost her leg?" Ben asked.

"She had a problem with one, so they had to remove it. She'll never be the same."

"And you own a helicopter?" Oliver asked.

"No, you moron, we don't own a helicopter... we rent one when we need it."

Finally, and exactly at 9:00 a.m. the turntable flicked on, and the bugle call, the Cavalry Charge, resounded through the campus. Cisco and Bramo dropped their ropes, and they were off to the races. Jake was almost trampled to death. The horses were out of the gate, a mad charge commenced down all the little dirt roads that meandered through the camp. Every parent carried shopping bags, coolers, and backpacks filled with soda, candy, pastrami sandwiches, comic books, magazines, toys, and everything else you could imagine. There was no etiquette. Grandparents were in danger of being trampled. Some parents even thought it was a race to see who could reach their child first.

Most parents were dressed in garish outfits. Fathers were wearing white shoes, and white pants with white belts that were partially hidden by sagging bellies. The mothers splattered their faces with broad, oversized sunglasses. They wore matching capri pants and blouses. They were on a desperate march to see their children. Mothers, fathers, grandparents, ugly varicose-veined legs peeking out of baggy shorts from all sizes of humanity. It was a swarm of Jewish army ants, boldly marching forward and eating anything in its way.

Chick walked up to our bunk, and pulled Ben aside to whisper something into his ear. Then he turned toward the flood of parents that started to leak out between the bunks. At first their sound was akin to the crickets we hear at night.... off in the distance, gathering en masse. When the ropes fell it morphed into the crescendo of a wave approaching the shoreline...the tinkling of a swell followed by the crashing WOOSH of the water exploding onto the shore. BAM... the parents were here, spilling out of every crevice.

"Ehhh.. I don't mind seeing parents swarm in like they do now.... much better than in the fiftys..." Chick said.

"That was only ten years ago," Oliver reminded him

"Well, a bit earlier than 1959. Back in the mid-'50s Joe had to construct rope barriers to keep the parents away from the kids. He had two long rope lines, parallel to each other, running from the outfield grass on the softball field, all the way down to the lake."

"Why?" Harris asked.

"Polio. A cursed word. He was so scared that someone could infect everyone with polio. Every camp was like that, though. It was a disease so contagious it could wipe out an entire camp. If a polio outbreak was announced in the city then the ropes would come out. That's what happened to the camp across the water ski lake. It was never the same after it was decimated by polio. Nobody came back after that summer in the mid-1950s. So if the parents are storming the camp like they do, well.... I really don't mind. It's healthy."

The counselors were warned to keep their campers on the porch, but once that Cavalry call sounded there was no holding back the mass escape. Campers cascaded off their porches, running up the back roads to meet Mom and Dad and Grandpa and Grandma. It was like a cold front meeting a warm front and the collision caused a thunder of cries like "Look how much you've grown!" It's only been four weeks so why do parents always say this?

We finally emerged from the bunk, and joined Ben on the porch. Jericho stepped off the porch and looked toward the wave of parents, trying desperately not to look excited. Ben slowly walked over to Harris and put his arm around the gnome's shoulder in a very protective way, and I had a feeling that they were sharing a deep secret. The wave of parents rolled onto the campus, engulfing every child, Somehow parents found their children and swept them up in their arms. Through the crowd walked Bugsy's mother... two legs and all.

Then suddenly, all this commotion, this jubilation, this outpouring of emotion died. Completely stopped. Samson and Asa walked away from their porch, their mouths dropping open. Lenny, who was already sweating a river of precipitation in his blue Banlon Camp Tonkawa shirt, had to clean off his foggy glasses three times. Ben looked where everyone had started to stare. Magically the masses parted and out spewed my parents.

All Ben could utter was, "Holy shit."

Dad was dressed in his lime green Bermuda shorts, white Izod Lacoste shirt and white bucks. He carried a putter, pitching wedge, and a seven iron in his hand. Three golf balls could be seen bulging inside his pockets.

But it was mom, my lovely mom, who again stole the show. She slinked through the crowd in a tight-fitting, finely laced one piece body suit. It wasn't see through, but fit so tight to her body that the lace was like a second skin. It was as good as see through. No lines could be seen bulging underneath that thin layer of clothing, which meant she wasn't wearing any underwear. No panties, no bra. Her breasts, so perfect and perky, shimmied ever so slightly. Her nipples burst through the lace. Her blonde hair glowed in the sun, blinding those too close to her. She walked like her shit didn't stink, (which it probably didn't), and she knew that she was sucking the breath out of every male. "She's shaved," Samson gasped. "Oh my god, she shaved her pussy."

"Look at those nipples.. she's got silver dollar nipples," Asa cried out as he bit Samson's shoulder.

"That your mom?" Ben asked.

My weak, embarrassed smile was his confirmation. My mother bounded up the steps, gave me a quick peck on the cheek and headed into the back room, and only I knew why. My father shook my hand, and asked where the golf course was. I just pointed and watched him twirl on his toes and head off to shoot a quick eight holes on our quirky little course.

The rest of the parents followed my mother, parading into the bunk to lay down their bags of food and candy. The Brain's father was tall and thin and had the same Brillo curly hair, but with spots of baldness creeping in. Mickey Hardon's parents were as conservative as they come, with his father sporting a button down shirt and khakis, and his mother wearing a summer dress that was so loose fitting that the slightest breeze might make it billow and turn her into a kite.

Oliver's mother was a chubby little thing. I wouldn't call her heavy or fat, just chubby, and she was very shy. She wore her hair in bangs and covered her eyes with thick sunglasses. Oliver ran to her and hugged her so tightly that she almost tripped over him.

Then Jericho spotted his parents, ran into their arms, and the day was saved. His mother was very young and sexy. She was the opposite sexy of my mother. She seemed warm and gentle, and had a smile that made me feel like I was her own child. She wore bell bottom jeans that swished as she walked, and they were ripped and patched with peace symbols. Her T shirt clung tightly to her body and ended just above her belly button, revealing a slim waist. A brown vest with beaded fringes lay on top of her t shirt. I was in love with the tinted granny glasses that adorned her face. OH... and that face, it was pure sweetness, hidden under the floppy hat she wore.

His dad was just as Jericho described him. Tall, athletic, and with hair down to his shoulders. He was a lawyer, his own firm, and he could be whom he wanted to be and nobody could tell him to change. I admired that. He too wore bell bottoms and a leather vest, but no shirt, revealing well developed pecs. He wore a leather braided head band to keep his hair out of his eyes, which also were covered by the tinted granny glasses that were so popular that summer. They were both barefoot, so Jericho immediately shucked his sneakers. Then he led them over to the porch.

"This is my counselor, Ben, and my friends, Harris and Flanken."

The hair on the back of my neck stood at attention because for the first time ever I was introduced as somebody's friend. It was an alien feeling to be someone's friend, and I relished the moment. I didn't even care if he called me Flanken.

Jericho took his parents by the hand and headed toward the

woods. He told me the first thing he was going to do with his parents was to get high, and read the letters from his brother that they brought from home.

And then my mother made another grand entrance.

The screen door flew open and my mother exited the bunk like she was a movie star. What an entrance! She stood on the porch for a second to make sure that everyone could see her. She was dressed in the tightest fitting bikini one could imagine. Something she picked up in France. Her breasts were oozing out of the top, barely constrained. For her bikini bottom there was only a small triangular patch of cloth covering her front and a flimsy piece of material up the crack of her ass so that her two perfect melon shaped buns were visible for all to see. She stretched so that every six pack popped into place and then she pretended to yawn just so she could take her hands and run them over her body.

The mothers in the bunk were already gossiping as my mother passed them. The group of counselors that had gathered in front of Bunks 19 and 20 gave my mother a standing ovation as she stepped off the porch.

With act one now behind her, my mother began her carefully orchestrated play. With a blanket in her hand, she found the perfect patch of grass to sunbathe in. She carefully laid the blanket on the ground, not in some corner, but out on the lawn in front of Bunk 18, my bunk... in the middle of the campus. She lay down on her back, facing the sun, and then like she has done every summer, started to do her ab exercises. She placed her hands under her ass, lifting it slightly off the ground, and slowly opening and spreading her legs in a scissor motion. The silhouette of her "pussy," as Asa kept sighing ,was clearly on display.

Ben saw what was happening, and he motioned me to follow him as he led Harris up to Grayson Hall.

"That's some mother you have," was all Ben could come up with.

"Trust me, there is one more act to follow, and it's majestic. By the time this day is over I will be banned from another camp and I will be crowned 'King of the Bunk'."

We approached Grayson Hall, and Ben put a hand on my shoulder and held me back. He looked at Harris and nodded for him to continue on. Harris tucked his chin to his chest, held back a sob, and continued on. Sitting in front of Grayson Hall was a woman in a wheelchair.

It was the same woman I had seen at the buses when we departed for camp. The same woman who came running up to the bus as we pulled out. The one who reached for Harris. Now she was confined to a wheelchair, looking paler and thinner than before. Her eyes were deep black sockets, almost lifeless. A bandana was wrapped around her head making her look like a pirate. She could barely sit up in the wheelchair. She had no energy, but she perked up when Harris approached her and she opened her arms for a hug. Harris looked at his dad, who was standing behind the wheelchair, and then melted into his mother's lap. Harris cried uncontrollably.

Ben motioned me to follow him toward the Social Hall. I kept looking back to see what was truly transpiring, but Ben kept telling me to just look ahead.

"What...?"

"She's dying, Jason. Cancer. I have no idea why Harris was sent to camp, but that was his mother's decision. Life's not fair. She's so young. Can you imagine the burden Harris has to live with this summer, wondering every day if he's going to hear his mother's voice again. Wondering if his mother has died. I understand it's a very aggressive cancer, and they didn't want Harris home to witness her deterioration. Personally I would never do that to my child, but to each his own."

"But he never said anything to anyone," I said, still trying to peek at what was happening in front of Grayson Hall. We sat down on the steps of the Social Hall.

"Who's he going to tell? The idiots in the bunk who have been picking on him mercilessly? You think he's going to tell you, Flanken? You barely show any emotion and you don't seem to care about anyone except Jericho. I think Harris has been look-ing to you for friendship and you've abandoned him. When he's needed you the most you turned your back on him, and he's not the type of kid who will beg for attention. He's stronger than you think."

"I didn't know," I whispered. I was shaken.

"Can you imagine what he must be feeling? I'm sure his parents are thinking that this was for the better. And what does he encoun-ter in camp? Nastiness? Cruelty?"

"Why doesn't he tell Joe? Why don't you say something to Joe and stop all this crap?" I asked.

"Because he won't let me. He won't let Chick talk to Joe either. We're not allowed to talk to Joe, and Harris won't approach Joe either."

"Why not?"

"Because he doesn't want his mother to know. He doesn't want his mother to worry about anything. He's keeping it all to himself so his mother won't worry about him and his father can concentrate on caring for her."

"I feel like shit now."

"He's a tough kid. He's stronger than you could ever imagine. I can't be around him all the time so he's had to take a lot of crap."

"I should tell the bunk that..."

"No! You can't mention this to the bunk. This is just between you and me... and, yes, you can tell Jericho. He's mature enough. Besides, maybe the two of you can keep an eye on him when I'm not around."

"This really sucks," I said.

"But then again, seeing your predicament with your parents, I don't know who has it worse. Harris, who has the love of a mother, or you. Harris is going to lose that love soon, but you... I bet you've never felt love from your mother..."

"I don't know if she knows how. So what's better? To have love and lose it, or to never have it, and never feel the pain of losing it?" I asked.

"That's something I can't answer."

"Neither can I."

"I don't know how much longer she has, but all I can ask is if you can show some empathy. Care for him. You don't have to be his best friend, but be a bit more understanding."

"I mean, I really don't have friends at home. I've never had anyone over to my house because I'm so embarrassed by my mom. Besides, most mothers don't want their kid in the presence of my mom."

"If they can't come to your house, why don't you go to their homes?"

"Other parents shun me.... they don't want their kids to be friends with me because they think I'll corrupt them. Then, other times I think about my dad and wonder if he even knows I exist. I have all the comforts you can think of and all I want is...."

"All those years in camp you never made any friends?"

"Nope. I always have to fight for respect in the first few weeks, and then my parents show up on visiting day and it's guaranteed that I will not be allowed to return. It's hard to be the new kid in a bunk every year. Why are my parents so fucked up? The only love I ever felt was from my grandparents and they all died when I was really young. My parents never wanted me, so I'm ignored."

"I see that. I do feel sorry for you," Ben said.

I hung out with Ben for most of the morning. We just sat on the cement steps talking. We continued to talk about Harris. We talked about my mother and father and how I've survived by myself for most of my life. And we laughed about how cool Jericho's parents seem to be.

"What do you think about Oliver's mom?" Ben asked.

"I don't know... she's just a mom. I wonder where his father is?"
"I'm sure we'll find out," Ben said.

We returned to our bunk when Recall sounded and I discovered my mother hadn't moved an inch. She was now pouring baby oil all over her body, and rubbing it in. Spanky, Lenny, Asa and Samson were sitting on the porch of Bunks 19 and 20, just staring at my mother, hoping she would ask one of them to... and oh shit, she did. She crooked her pointer finger at Lenny and motioned for him to approach. Lenny got up slowly, somewhat shyly, and walked toward my mother. He kept looking back at the other counselors with a goofy grin on his face like he had just won a prize. Sweat poured off his brow, and he was chewing furiously on his cheesy mustache. He could barely see out of his glasses they were so badly fogged. I don't know if it was from the humidity, or his rising body heat that was stewing inside his Banlon camp shirt. The thick material acted like a sauna. He approached my mother and she handed him the bottle of baby oil and asked him to rub it onto her shoulders, which he did with a sense of relish that drove me crazy. Ben just placed his hand on my shoulder and whispered for me to ignore it.

All campers returned to their bunks, as the parents were directed up to the basketball court. The camp provided box lunches for the parents. I saw my father for a second as he walked into the bunk to wash his hands.

"Cute course. I think I'll play it longer this afternoon, you know, instead of aiming at one green, go for the green in the distance. I mean, it's easy to sink putts when using coffee cans to line the holes, and the greens aren't bad, but son... there are no challenges here. No sand traps, no water, and everything is flat. "

"Dad, it's a summer camp, not a country club,"

"For what I'm paying it should be a country club," he snorted as he turned and joined my mother for their lunch. They brought up a picnic basket complete with a couple bottles of wine.

Mess call sounded and boys camp and girls camp headed

towards lunch at the same time. All the counselors in our group kept looking back at my mother, who finally put on an oversized t-shirt and a pair of cut off jean shorts that were so tight they seemed to be painted on. Jericho whispered that his parents brought up a substantial amount of weed, so we were set for the summer.

"They also told me that in two weeks there's going to be this amazing music festival just twenty miles down the road in the town of Bethel. We passed through it on our way up here. It's supposed to be fantastic. The Who, Ten Years After, and Jefferson Airplane are some of the bands playing. They're going to get tickets, and I told them I want you to come with me."

"But we're in camp. How are we going to get out?"

"We're going to break out of here," Jericho said, laughing . "Who cares about camp. I'm working out a plan with them now to pick us up. We'll sneak away during swim or something and wait for them on the side of the road. If we're caught we're caught. You know that this will get us kicked out of camp, but I'm ready to go home already."

"Okay,... I'm with you.. I guess this will be pretty cool."

"Beyond cool. I bet we remember this concert for the rest of our lives."

Lunch was a manic event, with waiters rushing to get the food on the tables. But who wanted to eat? Almost everyone wanted to get out of the Mess Hall and back to their parents. One seat was empty at our table, as Harris was given permission to have lunch with his parents. Oliver sat silently picking at a platter of cold cuts that were presented to us as our meal. The rest of the bunk was abuzz over the amount of candy their parents brought up. Hooky was planning on how to slice up the salami that was now in his possession.

Once all the dishes were removed, the camp was dismissed and there was an explosion of joy. The younger children were allowed to leave first so they wouldn't be trampled by the stampede. There was no rest hour that day. Instead there was a mass exodus and a tidal wave of children heading up to the basketball courts to find their parents.

"Meet me at the bunk at two o'clock to hang with my parents. We can smoke a joint with them," Jericho told me as he ran off.

Ben walked with me back toward the bunk. Oliver was with us, quieter than I had ever seen him. Ben put his arm around Oliver's shoulder and he started to cry. Ben stopped and hugged Oliver in a full embrace, and just let Oliver sob until he was able to talk.

"My parents are getting divorced. I knew it might happen. They fight all the time. I didn't want to go to camp, but my mother insisted. She didn't want me home to see what was going on. My dad just goes off on her. Sometimes he hits her. Sometimes he hits me when I'm trying to protect her, but I'm so scared he's going to really hurt her. She didn't want me around this summer because it was getting really violent and all I want to do is protect her."

"She's lucky to have you. You're a great kid, Oliver," Ben said. "You're sensitive and yet strong. There's nothing you can do about this so it makes her feel better that you're not around to see it."

"Yeah,.. if she understood how I'm treated here she would freak out. I won't tell her. I don't want her to worry about me too."

I was confused by the fact that Harris and Oliver were both more concerned about protecting their mothers. They preferred to suffer the humiliation and the pain that the bunk set upon them than to cry to their mommies for help. I couldn't grasp this act of bravery, especially upon reaching the bunk, where I saw my mother standing in the middle of a group of counselors. I would toss my mother to the wolves in an instant.

She was back in her tiny bikini, teasing the shit out of them. They all towered over her and they were just staring down at her cleavage. Lenny, who seemed to have succumbed to the heat, was sitting on the top step of the porch, just staring straight at my mother's crotch.

"Oliver, is it possible that I might have it worse than all of you?" I finally asked.

"I don't know—do they think you're invisible or what?," Oliver asked as he left to join his mother.

My father had already departed to play his second round of golf, while my mother excused herself from the gaggle of counselors and took her position back on her blanket where she started to practice her yoga stretches. I couldn't take it anymore. She was in her tease mode. She was an exhibitionist. She loved to display her body, making my asshole counselors drool till it was running down their chins.

Then there were more nasty looks from other mothers, their caustic disdain burning through me. I also had to live with the leering grins from Asa and Samson knowing that they were thinking, 'Man, I'd love to fuck your mother.' It all came crashing down on me. I left Ben and just ran away. I ran toward the waiters' annexes looking for Scott, but he hadn't returned from cleaning up after lunch.

I ran to the basketball courts, because I couldn't stand seeing all these happy families, couldn't stand seeing all the campers smiling and laughing. I sat on one of the benches by the basketball court and buried my head in my hands, trying to breathe deeply to find some composure. Then I heard my name called. I looked up and saw Rachel approaching me with her parents.

"Jason, I want you to meet my parents," she said in her soft, singsong voice and I desperately attempted to wipe away any remaining tears. Her smile cut through me, and I felt a warmth spread through my body that helped to evaporate my feelings of self pity.

"So nice to meet you," her mother said as Rachel held my hand. Her father stood away from her mother, which was kind of weird. I tried to shake hands with her dad, but he wouldn't touch me, and just looked away.

"Phillip, stop being so nasty, and be nice to Rachel's friend."

"Stop telling me what to do all the time," her father hissed.

"You're such a jerk," her mother said.

I thought Rachel was a byproduct of normal parents, but I was wrong. Her parents hated each other. Her mother tried to be super nice to me, but her father ignored everyone. There was something seriously off between the two of them. Rachel's mom asked the obligatory questions about where I lived, what school I went to, what I liked about camp (nothing much except meeting your daughter), and finally where my parents were?

"My dad's on the golf course and my mother is somewhere sunbathing," I told them.

She was pretty much taken aback by this and didn't know how to respond. I felt bad that I had put her in such an uneasy situation, but I didn't know what else to say. I told the truth. I could have lied, but why do so?

"What time is it?" I suddenly asked.

"It's almost two," her father told me. He hadn't stopped looking at his wristwatch from the moment I met him. He was dying to get out of camp.

I apologized for leaving so suddenly but I realized I had to meet Jericho. I couldn't be late for that, so I made up some story about having to meet my mother and politely excused myself. I gave Rachel a quick peck on the cheek and then ran back to the bunk praying I hadn't missed Jericho.

I was lucky; they had waited for me. Jericho waved to me. What I thought was really cool was that his parents weren't even staring at my mother. I mean everyone else in camp couldn't take their eyes off her. She was in the middle of her yoga exercises. Samson and Asa gave her a standing ovation.

Act Three was soon to commence. This was where she would sit up, untie the top of her bikini, and hold it scantily against her breasts. Then she would tease her hair, flinging it in all different directions. It was a ballet. She swished and gyrated till it all flowed so rhythmically that she was able to perform a silky smooth flip. Now she was lying on her stomach. My mother then started humping the ground. Every freaking summer, the same thing. My mother would slowly start to grind against one hand that she had slid under her body and between her legs. She was a pro at this. It was such a slow, calculated act of grinding that it was barely visible to the naked eye. Of course, my four shmucky counselors were born with those naked eyes. A year or so later I would come to realize that my mother was masturbating for the crowd.

Jericho led us off the porch and we went to our favorite spot behind the bunk down by the lake.

We saw Joe Geisinger flitting about camp, his red shirt ablaze. He was talking to parents while laughing and playing with the campers. It was quite a show by the owner, but it was cool for us because we knew he would never come down to where we were hiding. Actually, I knew Ben was looking for Joe because he had to meet with Harris and his parents. I knew for a fact that we were safe.

"So Jericho tells us you live up in Westchester. You'll have to come down to Long Island and visit us," his father said as he pulled a nice-sized joint out from the little satchel that he draped over his right shoulder.

"I would like that," I said as I watched him light the joint and pass it to Jericho.

Actually I was looking at Jericho's mother who grew more beautiful in a very down-to-earth way. Her skin sparkled, and she wore a jasmine perfume that was driving me crazy. I swear I wasn't trying to look at her because I know how it kills me the way everyone stares at my mother, but she was really a stunning woman. Jericho passed me the joint and then sat down on the ground between his mother's legs. His mother was sitting on a tree stump, and she immediately started to run her fingers through Jericho's hair. He sighed in delight. It was tender.

She caught me staring at them, and I really couldn't turn away anymore.

"I gather that's your mother out on the lawn putting on that show?" she asked.

"Yes, that's her. She does it every summer, no matter what camp I go to."

"Oh you poor child–that's so sad," she said as she kissed Jericho on the cheek and messed up his hair.

I was jealous of Jericho. I envied him. I wanted to push him away and sit between his mother's legs and have her run her fingers through my hair. I wanted to hold her and feel warmth and affection. I wanted to be held and coddled. I wanted to cry. I wanted to be touched. It was a void in my life.

"Jericho told you about this Woodstock Festival in a couple of weeks. We would really love to take you," his father told me, shaking me from my thoughts. "But you do realize we could get into trouble and you will certainly get into trouble."

"I'm willing to take that chance if you are," I said as I took another toke. "Honestly, you've seen my mother. She doesn't care what I do. She's oblivious to what my life is all about."

"Good, then it's settled. We'll work something out and send you a letter within the next week."

"Why did your son go to fight in Vietnam?"

There was silence. My God, why did I blurt that out? I should never have opened my mouth, but I just had to ask. Jericho rarely talked about it, and I just felt so attached to his family already. I realized that I was even worried about his brother fighting over there.

"We didn't want him to go. There is going to be a draft at the end of the year, fifty-fifty chance he'd get picked anyway," his mother explained. "He was graduating college... wasn't going to be a doctor or a teacher, so he volunteered because he heard if he did so there might be a better chance of him not going overseas."

"He could have gone to Canada. He could have gone up there and stayed out of the war," added his dad. "But he thought it would be an adventure. And who knew it would escalate so fast? We still can't figure out why. We just pray God looks over him every day."

It was such a downer.

We finished the joint, and headed back up to the bunk. The shit that we smoked was so potent that my feet weren't touching the ground. It was a good feeling because it was pretty obvious that Act

Three was over, and the cadre of counselors who were watching were stunned into silence. Their mouths hung open like bear traps that hadn't been sprung. My mother was getting up to go back into the bunk to wash off. She smiled at the counselors, knowing that she would never be forgotten. No... my mother was now forever a legend. As a matter of fact, she's a legend at every other camp I've been to.

Jericho's parents left before the announcement that Visiting Day was over. It wasn't tearful like so many other departures would be, maybe because they knew they would be back in two weeks. My mother left without saying goodbye. She changed in the back of the bunk and walked to the car. My father returned from the golf course, slipped me a hundred dollar bill and told me he would see me in four weeks.

As my parents walked away Asa, Samson, Spanky and Lenny gave me a standing ovation.

"You're not only the King of the Bunk Jason, you're the King of the Camp!" Asa shouted.

I had to get away from those morons so I walked over to Grayson Hall with Jericho and told him about Harris. He was shocked, and that feeling of despair intensified. From a distance we watched Harris saying goodbye to his mother. Ben was standing off to the side, and when he saw us he left Harris and joined us. He wanted to give them more privacy, knowing that Joe wasn't going to make them leave with the other parents.

We walked back to the bunk to find most of the other parents lingering inside, packing up to go home. Oliver was sitting on his bed, his head buried in his mother's chest, trying not to cry. Ben had already talked to most of the parents when he met them earlier in the morning. Suddenly the relative silence of departure was interrupted by a thunderous clap that jolted everyone.

"DON'T TALK BACK TO ME, YOU LITTLE BASTARD!" and this was followed by another loud smack across the face.

The Mayor's dad just slapped him silly. It was an open palm slap, but it was so hard that it almost made The Mayor's head spin around. It definitely left a welt.

"I'll beat you so hard if you disrespect your sister ever again. Do YOU UNDERSTAND ME?" he hissed.

The Mayor looked defiantly at his father and never flinched even when his father slapped him a third time.

The Mayor looked around to make sure we all knew he wasn't crying. We watched his father push him out onto the porch where he proceeded to spew a tornado of spit and venom. He was lip to lip with The Mayor, and yet The Mayor never budged nor blinked.

Ben walked out to say a few words to Mr. Mandelbaum, who turned and threatened Ben with physical dismemberment if he took another step. Mandelbaum's mom was on the girls' side, packing up for their daughter, so no one was there to protect Mandelbaum except for Ben.

"This is between me and my son, so just turn around!"

"Not if you're going to hit him again."

"Hit him? Who hit him? That was a slap, not a hit. Besides, I want to know where he got all of these black and blue marks from."

"That I don't know."

"Then you're no good to me, so just turn around and walk back to the bunk," Mandelbaum's dad commanded.

Ben gave it a thought to stay and fight the fight, but he thought better of it and backed away. He kept his eyes on Mandelbaum, making sure his dad didn't hit him again.

Oliver's mom started to sob; she frantically kissed Oliver good-bye and told him to be brave. She made sure Oliver had all his new magazines, and then ran outside in a panic, smack into Ben.

I looked out the window from my bed, and watched as she and Ben walked off the porch. She was thanking him for looking after Oliver and then she whispered "Don't let that man get away with treating his son like that."

She then pulled off her sunglasses revealing two shiners that were deep, dark and purple. "I walked into someone's elbows at home. It's been so rough on Oliver. My husband... I don't know if he has a drinking problem, but there's so much rage. I couldn't take a chance for Oliver to be home this summer. There's only so much dignity I can maintain and I didn't want him to witness his father beating me."

"You really need to call the cops," Ben told her.

"I will, I will, "she promised. "I'm doing the right thing, aren't I? You wouldn't want your own child living in an environment like that, seeing his mother...." and she choked up and couldn't finish the sentence.

Ben hugged her and told her that he would look after Oliver.

Suddenly I realized that I had a lot in common with certain bunkmates. We were all victims, abused by life in some way. We were an army of the wayward, a battalion of the empty child. Harris was losing his mother. Oliver not only was losing his father but had to watch his mother being beaten and abused. It was obvious that the Mayor's dad was physically abusing him at home. Jericho was being scarred and abused by war, as he constantly worried about his brother. Me? I was the victim of emotional abuse. And I now considered myself luckier than all those in my new found family.

22

With Visiting Day over, we were officially into the back end of the summer.

As the parents made their way back to their cars, dissipating like morning dew in a day's rising sun, one could hear a bit of whimpering emanating from the beds of Oliver and Harris. I truly expected Hardon and The Brain to attack Harris, but they were subdued. Mandelbaum the Mayor was silent, still shaken from the earlier confrontation with his father. I remained on guard, wondering if Hardon was going to pick on Harris, and wondering if I would really come to the aid of Harris as I had promised Ben.

Visiting Day also took its toll on the counselors and on Joe Geisinger. There was a little confrontation between Mickey Hardon's mom and Ben. You could sense it coming at the end of the day when Hardon whispered something to his mother, who gasped in shock. She pulled Ben out of the bunk, onto the porch, but you could hear every word she said, and Hardon sat on his bed with a sneer of delight.

"My son tells me that you used the word prophylactic," she hissed.

"I did," Ben confirmed with the utmost confidence.

"How dare you use that word around my child."

"Nothing wrong with the word."

"It's sexual. You wear that when you're having sex with someone."

"Wow, I didn't know that," Ben answered, trying not to laugh.

"The kids know what it's used for. I'm sure you do too."

"See that little box next to you?" Ben asked, pointing to the boot box. "We put our boots and rubbers in there, saving them for a rainy day. Now rubbers are also in the sexual lexicon, but I didn't use that word. That's more slang. I used the word prophylactic because it's also a medical term. What your son didn't tell you was that I used the word in a sentence that had nothing to do with sex, and might be heard all the time in a hospital. But the real reason I used that word was to expand your son's vocabulary so that maybe he could learn something that might be useful on his SAT test in the future."

Hardon's mom was totally bewildered by the response.

"You're lying! You're fucking lying," Mickey Hardon screamed.

"No... I do understand... quite interesting," she told Ben, shaking his hand to end any conflict.

Joe had fielded so many complaints that it seemed to dim his once-sparkling eyes. The smile from the first day was now gone, and I'm sure he was thinking that he only had to make it through four more weeks without a major incident. But the world was changing, and Joe was going to do everything in his power to keep the outside forces away from his beloved camp. No talk of protest marches, no rock concerts, and an increase in tension between the owner and the campers concerning their attire. He was on the warpath, trying to keep us from wearing "hippie clothing" and threatened to throw out any of that type of clothing we received on visiting day.

Oh, and there were a number of complaints about my mother.

Joe questioned Asa and Samson about all the black and blue marks that parents found on their children. What were the two counselors going to say? This was their method to keep campers in line, the quick jab to a bicep or tricep. A hard punch to force a camper to behave left a mark. Joe warned the two college roommates that they had better keep their hands by their side for the rest of the summer. Asa and Samson nodded that they understood, then went back to their bunk and started pounding the shit out of the campers who complained. They knew that the black and blue marks would disappear in four more weeks.

Harris kept sliding into deeper despair. Every rest hour he was allowed to walk around the camp with Ben, and on canteen days he would come back and find his requested Hershey and O'Henry bars a melted goo as they were thrown under his pillow. It was the passive aggressive behavior of The Brain that masterminded this attack. He took the warnings given by Ben to a level that would antagonize Harris and yet always have a plausible explanation.

"You told us to leave his candy on his bed, so I did," The Brain told Ben without admitting that he knew he shouldn't have put it under the pillow where the midday heat would ruin the treat.

"Flanken, did you see him put it under his pillow?" Ben asked.

"I was taking a dump when the candy got back. I didn't see anything," I told him, which was the truth though I'm sure he found it hard to believe.

"Yeah, right. I was hoping you'd keep an eye on Harris' stuff."

"I had to take a shit. What, you don't believe me?"

"You've given me no reason to believe in you yet."

The Monday after visiting day Ben was assigned fishing for Free Play, and Oliver scampered over to the nature shack where he was in charge of feeding the baby goat. That left Harris sitting alone on his bed, reading letters from his mother. I looked at Jericho, and even though he silently begged me not to do so, I asked Harris if he wanted to take a walk with us. It was a gamble, but I couldn't stand seeing him so sad. I just felt he couldn't be alone anymore.

The three of us walked out of the bunk only to be confronted by Chick, who was sitting on the boot box.

"Where you boys heading?" he asked.

A bag of red pistachio nuts sat by Chick's side. He looked like he was in a trance as he shoved one nut into his mouth at a time. He would crack the shell, suck out the nut, and then drop the empty shell on the floor. There was a red stain, long and winding like a creek, that ran under his feet. His fingers were now crimson. Chick was dressed in his usual garb. He was wearing those loose fitting yellow shorts and the v neck white t shirt. His nipples were as hard and erect as they ever were, and his two gray-haired and withered testicles were drooping in plain sight.

"I asked where you boys were headed,"

"Um.." I tried to speak, but couldn't take my eyes off his eggs. Harris guffawed, his first happy emotion since visiting day, and Jericho kept giggling. We weren't even high yet. "We're just going to go for a walk," I told him.

"Okay, .. don't go far," he said without taking his eyes off Harris. He never missed a beat breaking apart a nut with his teeth.

"Want some?' he asked. When we shook our heads no he sighed, spread his legs and allowed his aged balls to droop even lower. "Just do me a favor and sweep all this off the porch later."

We told Chick we would, and then we bounded off the porch.

"That was so disgusting," Harris finally said. He was the first to gain some self control. "Where are we going?"

"Man, Chick is old. How old do you think he is?" I asked.

"Mid sixties? Look at him, that's what happens to a man when he gets old. His nipples get longer, his scraggly gray-haired balls droop lower and lower," Jericho told us.

"And you know this... how?" I asked

"Hell, I go to the gym with my dad once a week and all these old guys just walk around the locker room naked. I mean what the hell? They don't even bother covering up and all I know is that it's time to retire when my balls droop low and grow gray pubic hair."

I was going to explain to Harris what our custom during Free Play was, when I heard my name being called. It was Scott. He was waving for us to come to his annex. He'd just finished cleaning up the Mess Hall and had returned at the end of the day. I looked at Harris and Jericho and motioned them to follow me.

Scott brought us into his Annex. It was a glorified outhouse. We expected that the annex would be a disaster area. The waiters were 17-year-old boys, and they did not have the 24-hour supervision we campers had. I expected the annex to look like a tornado hit it, but instead it was immaculate. Clothing neatly folded, and not a dust mite on the floor.

We entered with much trepidation because the waiters were like gods in the camp, and the annexes were definitely off limits. Yet there was Scott ushering us inside.

We sat on the one single bed, which was sandwiched between two double deckers. Scott and his fellow annex mates stripped out of their waiter uniforms. Gone were the white t shirts and khakis, and quickly into gym shorts and tank tops.

"Got something for you boys," Scott said as he reached into his cubby and pulled out a bottle of wine.

"Manischewitz. My favorite," Harris squealed.

It was the choice of young Jewish boys. A red grape wine that was so sweet that your lips puckered and the taste would stay with you forever. It was the wine that was soaked in gauze and dabbed into our mouths when we were only eight days old, and the beverage we imbibed during Passover. Scott was pouring a glass for his friends. He then offered it to us, and we gladly took the paper cup and downed the sugary sweet wine.

"I love this stuff," Harris said as he asked for another glass. Then he suddenly fell quiet like a blanket was thrown over him. "Reminds me so much of my mother, the holidays, the seders,... "

"I know I shouldn't share this with you, but hey, who hasn't had Manischewitz?" Scott said as he poured a second cup for everyone. "There's a reason I called you here."

"What's that?" I asked.

Suddenly Scott pulled out a joint and fired it up. He started to pass it around to the other waiters, and then he looked at the three of us. Harris was a bit taken aback, but Jericho and I smiled and took the offering.

"What? You think I don't know where you go every free play?"

Scott said. "I see the two of you sneak into the bushes near the lake. I know what you're doing."

Harris looked at us, knowing that we had kept a secret from him, and I felt guilty.

"Do you know what tonight is?" Scott asked.

We looked at each other and shook our heads. He knew we didn't know so he kept us in suspense as he finished off the joint.

"What the fuck? Are you going to tell us?" Harris finally blurted out.

"Tonight, my little friends, is the night we're going to the Wayne County Fair. Tonight is the night we're going to the Hootchie Kootch."

"The Hootchie what?" Harris asked.

"The Hootchie Kootch. Oh man, we wait for this night. See, the Wayne County Fair is just outside of Honesdale and Heshie takes us every year."

Jericho tapped me on the knee and I nodded that he should. He pulled out a nice big fat joint from his pocket and lit it up. The first joint was already dispatched.

"I knew you had some good stuff," Scott laughed as he watched Jericho hand me the joint.

I took a deep drag and held it in as long as I could, and then I looked at Harris and offered him the joint. There was a moment where the world just paused, nobody seemed to be breathing. All eyes were on Harris.

"Will this get me kicked out of camp?"

"Absolutely," we all responded.

"How do you do this?" he asked, and everyone exhaled and laughed.

Jericho instructed Harris how to smoke the joint and we watched Harris turn blue as he coughed out his first toke. We waited for Harris to regain his breath and watched him take a smaller hit. He was a quick learner.

"The fair is typical of a country fair. It's shaped like a U, with everyone entering down Broadway. Upon entering, off on each side, you'll find the booths manned by the Carnies. Each one with a different game. You have the wooden milk bottles stacked like pyramids. You're supposed to throw a ball at them and knock them over, but it's impossible to do so. There's one game with squirt guns and you're supposed to shoot water into targets that blow up balloons. You only have a minute to make a balloon pop, but they never burst. All the games are rigged to take your money. I mean you never win at those games. We don't care about them, so we just laugh at the Carnies. We head right to the back. The back row is where all the action is. In the old days they had the Freak show and the Geek show."

"What's that?" Harris asked as he took another lungful of smoke. Harris was getting into smoking the joint. Scott gave him some more wine.

"Geek show? Used to be some guy who would bite the heads off live chickens. That's a Geek," Scott said. I thought Harris was going to puke on the spot.

"But don't worry. No more Geeks. Now the only thing back there is the Hootchie Kootch. It's in a tent. They get these women, most are pretty ugly, but then there may be one that's good looking, and they're all on a stage that's set up inside a tent. But first to get you inside the tent they have the girls out front. They dress them up like harem girls, prancing around on a stage... and then the barker comes out. The girls are gyrating into two poles, one on each side of the stage.

'Step right up boys... step right up.. .come and see the most amazing girls in the world. Step right up for in a second they will be as' ... and here the barker slaps the open palm of his hand.... 'as naked as the palm of my hand.' So we pay five bucks and charge inside and get right up to the front of the stage and the girls come out.."

"Naked?" Harris gulped.

"Naked as the palm of my hand." Scott laughed. "But that's not the cool thing... they'll dance for us, spread their legs..first time most of us saw a live pussy was last year."

"Live pussy?" I asked. "What? They're normally dead?"

It was a good feeling to say something that made everyone laugh, even though it was one of the dumbest things I've ever said.

"I mean they're on stage right in front of us, not in a magazine, and they're spreading their legs and then.. and then..."

I realized that we hadn't taken our eyes off of Scott. Jericho had pulled another joint out of his pocket and we were all passing it around and smoking and...waiting for...

"And then WHAT?" Harris shouted.

"And then we start giving them things to rub against their...you know...pussies. They took the Monkey's glasses last year and just kept rubbing it and rubbing it till it got wet and juicy."

Monkey, a meek looking waiter smiled at the memory.

"And Monkey didn't wash those glasses for the rest of the summer."

"I'm going to let her do it again," Monkey told Scott. "I'll just keep smelling my glasses all summer long," he said with a smile.

"Is Monkey your real name?" Harris asked.

"It's a nickname, my real name's Bailey."

"Who gave you such a stupid nickname?" Harris asked.

"Who else? Lenny! He saw me climb a tree to get a frisbee we were throwing around and called me The Monkey. It stuck. It's better than being called Bailey."

"So this year we're going prepared," Scott said as he pulled five large carrots out from under the clothing in his cubby.

"What's that?" Harris asked, squinting at what Scott was passing around to his friends.

"It's a carrot dildo. We found the largest carrots in the kitchen and we have been whittling them into dildos for days. We're going to have them use it on themselves..:

"So, do you want us to bring anything of yours to these women?" Monkey asked.

"Hell yeah," Harris screamed as he jumped up from the bed, and turned his back to us. He pulled down his shorts, and then took off his underwear. He slid his shorts back up and then turned, making sure we didn't see him naked. He handed his underwear to Scott, who held it aloft with one finger.

"There are no skid marks here, are there?" he asked.

"No... I changed right after supper."

"So what do you want us to do with your underwear?"

"Give it to the girls... I want to smell it when you come back to-night," Harris squeaked. And then he started giggling.

"I think he's higher than the moon right now," Jericho laughed as we watched Scott wrap up a couple of the seven-inch carrot dildos in Harris' underwear.

"I can't wait!" Harris screamed and then we all started to laugh as we watched Harris dance around the annex. We had never seen him so liberated and happy. We had fixed our gaze on Harris and didn't hear the screen door squeal open and then shut.

"What's going on? Why are there campers in here?"

We were slapped into silence. Harris stopped dancing, but he couldn't stop giggling. Scott didn't even try to hide the carved carrots, nor the joints.

"Just wanted to talk to Jason about some basketball moves, Heshie," Scott said.

It took a second for Heshie to recognize me and he nodded his approval that we were inside hallowed grounds.

. "And what's that I smell?" he asked.

I couldn't tell if he was angry or not, but Jericho decided to just be up front and handed the joint over to Heshie. He looked at it, and we awaited our fate. We waited for Heshie to march us to Joe Geisinger. We knew that our summer was sealed, and I could even detect a smile emanating from Harris, because he was thinking the same thing. Now we were all going to be expelled. Forced to go home.

Instead Heshie put the joint to his lips, and took a good, deep toke.

"Now this is good stuff. Scott, have you been hiding this from me all summer?"

"No Heshie, I wouldn't hide anything from you!"

'It's mine," Jericho chimed in.

Heshie sat down on the bed next to me, and put his arm around me and started to stroke my neck. "Now this is more like it. Why didn't you tell me you had a friend with some weed? You boys are welcome back here anytime, as long as you invite me."

Harris sat there, his mouth slack-jawed and open.

"What's the matter with you?" Heshie asked, finally realizing that Harris couldn't stop staring at him.

"You're smoking with us? You're not going to turn us in?" Harris said in wonder.

"Look son, you see these boys?" he said, pointing at Scott and the rest of the waiters. "They are seventeen years old. In a few months they'll all be eighteen years old and if they wanted to they could go and fight over in Vietnam. Lord knows why, but they could. They're also going off to college, and eighteen is the legal drinking age so I think they're mature enough to know that I don't give a damn what they do in their spare time as long as they don't run afoul of Joe Geisinger."

"But..."

"Your name's Harris, right?" Heshie asked. Harris was stunned. He was also high because he kept trying to pull his shirt around to see if Heshie had looked at his name tag. He would never realize that maybe word had gotten out about his situation. Seemed a lot of people were suddenly being nice to Harris.

"Harris, I work in the Public Schools of the City of New York. I would never ever do this in the school system. This is camp. Joe Geisinger needs me. He knows I can handle sixteen- and seventeen-year-old boys. Joe and I have an agreement. He won't interfere in my world, and my boys won't interfere in his. Now look at this annex. It's in perfect condition. Who knew hormonal seventeen-year-old boys could be this neat, but I keep them in shape. When Joe has parents come up for a visit to the camp on a sort of recruiting visit, do you think he brings the parents into the camper bunks? No, he brings them into the waiters' main bunk because he knows it will be immaculate. Besides, as my friend, Bob Dylan, would say, 'The times, they are a changing'. Nothing wrong with getting high, with smoking a joint with some good friends. Now is there?"

"We were just telling the boys about the Hootch," Monkey informed Heshie.

"What were you telling them?" Heshie asked as he handed me the joint which was now smoked halfway through.

"We'll always remember that it was you who took us to the hootch and allowed us to see our first totally naked woman," Scott told him.

"Now wait a minute. Just remember, I arranged for the bus to take you to the Wayne County Fair for the night, and it was all your idea to go to the Hootch. I had nothing to do with that," Heshie said as he squeezed my neck and stood up. "Now remember that. I may have facilitated the trip to the fair, but I never, ever, endorsed you going to the Hootch. I mean just because it's become a rite of passage for a waiter doesn't mean I approve of such a thing."

Scott, Monkey, and the other two waiters thought about this for a second and then started to laugh, because they saw right through this phony sanctimonious speech.

"Look, these women are denigrating themselves. But that's the way life is. Maybe you can't catch a break in life and you need to do in life what needs to be done. I once saw a woman on the boardwalk down in Atlantic City. She had no arms and no legs. She laid on a gurney and someone rolled an electric keyboard out in front of her and she played tunes with just her tongue. With just her tongue! And she made money. People kept dropping dollars, dimes... quarters into a bucket under her gurney. Finally some drunk approached her, and stood right in front of her and started to scream and shout... 'WHATS THE MATTER WITH YOU WOMAN! DON'T YOU HAVE NO PRIDE? DON'T YOU HAVE ANY DIGNITY?' And this woman looked up at him, I mean as best as she could look up cause you know, she was lying on her stomach... and she said...'Mister, I do what I gotta do. I have four mouths at home to feed, and I'm feeding dem." And I never forgot what that woman said. Sometimes you just have to do what you have to do, so never look down on anyone."

There was silence in the annex as we pondered what Heshie had just told us Suddenly Harris bolted out of the bunk and started barfing. The retching was dulled by the sound of campers enjoying Free Play, otherwise it would have echoed across the campus.

"I think he has a twenty-four hour virus," I told Heshie as Jericho and I got up to leave. We saw Monkey hiding the Manischewitz bottle as Scott talked to Heshie, and we knew that even though smoking a joint seemed to be on the approved list, drinking was frowned upon. Probably because you could end up barfing all over the place and ruining a few things.

"Okay then, go take care of your friend," Heshie said, offering our release. "Scott, the bus is leaving in ten minutes. If you're not on it, you're not going."

Harris stayed back from evening activity, puking his guts out. Ben stayed behind and tucked him into bed. We had to swear to Ben that we didn't give him the wine, and we weren't going to throw Scott under the bus. Ben laid on his bed and studied from his Med school books while we were at evening activity. He watched Harris fall asleep.

Ben had O.D. that night and barely left our bunk, keeping a close eye on Harris who was dead to the world. He had fallen asleep the moment his head hit the pillow. It was close to 11:30, and Ben was still on the porch studying, when Scott and Monkey walked into the bunk. I heard them walk in. They woke Harris up, and sat down on his bed. Scott pulled out a carrot and handed it to Harris. Harris was groggy from the wine and from being wakened in the middle of the night, a budding hangover blooming for the morning. He seemed to recognize what lay in his hands. Scott took the carrot and held it under Harris' nose. At first Harris gagged, his sense of smell dulled by the Manischewitz wine, but then some magic pixie dust seemed to have been sprinkled upon him and he began to relax. Then he realized what he was sniffing.

"Wow.. Oh wow...nice! " Harris cooed as the broadest smile of the summer swept across his face.

"Enjoy it," Scott told him.

Harris kept smelling the carrot as he slowly fell back asleep. He hugged the carrot like it was a stuffed animal he might have slept with when he was little. Scott laid Harris' underwear next to his head.

"Tell him we did nothing with his underwear," Scott said to me.

Scott got up to leave just as Ben walked into the bunk. Ben looked at Harris,, and he stifled a laugh. He patted Scott on the back.

"I'm sorry about getting him drunk. It was only Manischewitz. Everyone's had Manischewitz."

"Yes, from the moment they cut you till the day you die you'll always have a taste for Manischewitz... Listen it's okay, he needs a little release."

"I really feel bad about getting him sick."

"I'm square with you. Look at that smile on his face... haven't seen that all summer. It's a good look.... so thank you."

The next morning at the sound of Reveille Mickey Hardon got up and before he marched into the back room to go to the bathroom he saw the orange carrot cradled in the arms of Harris. Mickey Hardon walked over and grabbed the thick carrot, and took a bite of it. Actually he bit off a piece of the tip that was carved like a penis.

"Eh, what's up, doc," he mumbled, imitating Bugs Bunny, not realizing what he had just done.

"What the hell are you doing?" Harris screamed as he jumped out of his bed.

"Eating your carrot. What are you going to do about it?"

We watched as Mickey Hardon took another bite. Harris had to think long and hard about warning Hardon. We all thought Harris was going to freak out, but he remained calm.

"Nothing," Harris sputtered, now starting to gag.

"What's the matter with this carrot? It tastes funny," Hardon said as he took another bite from the top.

Harris bolted for the back room and you could hear him puking his guts out into one of the toilets. I couldn't resist, but Jericho beat me and finally got up and walked over to Hardon.

"Here's the story, Hardon," Jericho said as he pulled Hardon close and whispered in his ear.

Mickey Hardon ran into the back room, threw The Brain out of the second toilet and stuck his finger down his throat. The whole bunk stood in the back room listening to stereo puking, with Harris on the left bowl and Mickey Hardon on the right. I just hate the smell of puke. It would take days for this odor to pass away.

23

Everything changes on the first day of August. Doesn't make a difference what camp or what state, that first day of August was a game changer. A weird hex befalls us. Events were now going to be coming at us at an unusually fast pace. It's either the realization that there was only three to four weeks of camp left, or the fact that the nights suddenly were longer and cooler. A few were downright cold. The Jelly Roll always stood at attention at the end of our beds. The Jelly Roll, that extra blanket wrapped tight, ready to be unraveled into action by our drunken counselors upon their return from the night out.

The stars at night were brighter, the galaxies ablaze in a display that we couldn't see at home. Counselors refused to get out of bed in the mornings because the cold mountain air stirred in them erections so magnificent they would remember them for life.

Color War was approaching, and Asa and Samson were campaigning to be officers. This was the ultimate honor if one was a counselor. Especially those counselors who were "lifers"--those who started out as campers and grew up to be counselors. They named a pine tree, one of the hundreds of pines surrounding the camp, after a lifer. During Color War, for one week they would be leading and exhorting their teams in combat on and off the sporting fields. One week of high octane competition from the mundane bunk inspections after clean up, to the rehearsing and singing of songs that were crafted by the counselors into marches and alma maters for the final sing.

After being in camp for four weeks, with the albatross of visiting day now in the past, the campers were at the mercy of counselors. The counselors were now thinking about heading back to college, instead of supervising us. They were more relaxed, almost blasé in their attitude when officiating ball games, and they didn't give a shit about what was going on inside the bunk.

Everyone was mellow, everyone but Joe Geisinger. It was a race to the finish line, and Joe was riding shotgun, making sure that camp ended successfully and without injury.

We knew something was amiss on the morning of August 1st. The camp was assembled as usual before breakfast. The bugle call, "To The Colors" played over the loudspeaker as the flag squeaked up the rusty pole. Most of the campers held their right hand over their hearts as we were taught since first grade. However, Jericho began a movement and refused to salute the flag as it was raised. Some counselors, including Ben followed Jericho's lead. They stood there with their legs spread wide and their hands held respectively behind their backs. They were protesting the war.

Then Ed Barnett asked all the counselors to gather under the copse of trees at the side of the HCO shack, and there they stood for a good five minutes. Ed kept looking at his watch. The counselors started to twitch and whisper amongst themselves. We were impatient, our stomachs starting to rumble.

Ed Barnett stared up the hill, and all the campers followed his gaze. Charging down toward us, his red shirt ablaze in the early morning sun ,was Joe Geisinger. He looked like pictures of George Patton in battle, but there was insanity flaring from his nostrils. You could see the veins on the side of Joe's neck bulging in anger.

He didn't bother walking around the campers, but instead bulled right through them, knocking many children to the ground. He pushed his way through the counselors till he was standing in front of them, seething with anger.

"You SONS of Bitches! You Bastards!" he screamed.

He pointed his fingers at the counselors as if he were going to shoot them. You could tell the counselors were caught off guard.

"YOU SONS OF BITCHES, YOU BASTARDS," he screamed again.

"Joe?" Ed Barnett tried to step in, but Joe brushed him away.

"How dare you harm my camp? I'm going to find out which one of you bastards did this, and then I'm going to get my cripplers to cripple you. My cripplers are going to break your legs, they're going to rip out your arms. How dare you destroy my camp. My cripplers are going to cripple you!"

Joe turned and stormed off toward the Mess Hall. The counselors returned to their groups confused. We asked Ben what that was about but he had no idea. Every counselor was in the dark.

"Who are his Cripplers?" Oliver asked Ben.

"I have no idea, but would be willing to guess he was talking about Bramo and Cisco. I mean what other cripplers can he be talking about?"

"But what happened?" Harris asked.

"I don't know! Nobody knows," Ben said again.

We marched into the dining room, and our questions were somewhat answered. Joe stood behind a table with what was obviously his evidence. Eight large cucumbers lay on the table like lonely soldiers standing at attention. Joe stood like a statue, barely moving, staring into every counselors' eyes. He was looking for a clue.

"What's with the cucumbers?" I asked Jericho

"Have no idea."

We recited the Brachot's for bread and wine, as we did before every meal. For most of us in camp this would probably be the only time we would ever recite those prayers for the rest of our lives.

Scott was one of the first out with the scrambled eggs. Danish and rolls were already on the table, and they had already been scarfed down. Ben grabbed Scott, drew him near and wanted to know what his take was.

"I don't know for sure. I think it has to do with the freezer being broken into. Someone smashed the lock last night and took some food. Joe thought it was the waiters. That was who he blamed first. I was taking a shit right there because I thought he was talking about our carrot dildos. Heshie stood up for us and told him he was crazy, that we always had access to the freezer during the day so why would we have to break open the lock. Guess where they found those cucumbers?"

Ben looked at him, shrugged his shoulders, and waited for an answer. Jericho leaned in to listen too.

"On girls side!" Scott said.

"Really. Who would have guessed?" Ben said.

Scott waited for the empty pan of eggs to return to the front of the table and then wheeled around and returned to the kitchen.

"What's he talking about?" I asked.

Suddenly I realized that our table had fallen silent. Everyone had stopped eating and just stared at Ben for an explanation.

"Okay, look.. .there are women who prefer the company of women..." Ben started to say.

"Female homos," Hardon shouted out.

"Lesbians, they're called lesbians. There's a group of friends on girls side that... prefer to hang out with each other... but what's the big deal anyway? Joe Geisinger loves their vitality, their passion, their camp spirit, but he has no clue that they may also like each other a bit too much."

"But why cucumbers?" Harris asked.

"For the same reason why you slept with a carrot last night," Jericho whispered so the other end of the table couldn't hear.

"Ellen, Rachel and Beth have a counselor who's part of that group. Do you think...."

"Don't know and I don't care," Jericho told him. "They're no different than you and me. Don't make anything of it."

The social that night was in the Social Hall. We sat on benches watching the male and female counselors talking to each other. Samson and Asa were leading the conversation, One female counselor, her name was Dottie, was off to the side talking to a number of girls.

Oliver had finally found the nerve he needed to even sit on the edge of the bench with us, but he felt so out of place. I could tell. He kept fidgeting. The innocence of holding hands with our so-called girlfriends made him uneasy. So I gave him some credit for sitting with us.

We tried talking to the girls about Ben's theory, but they had no clue what we were talking about. Then again, we weren't even sure what we were talking about. We tried to tiptoe around the entire situation, but it was hard to ignore. Besides, Joe was on a rampage all day.

"I mean, it is weird. They're always hanging out with each other, never making friends with anyone else," Rachel said.

"And Dottie over there is super nice to Rachel. You've got to admit, Rachel, that she gives you extra attention. She even gives you back massages," Ellen started to say.

"Heshie sometimes smacks us on the ass.. so what? What's the big deal?"

"Whatever it is, Joe is crazed. He's all over the place. He follows us around, and he's keeping close tabs on the boy counselors. He keeps grabbing me by the hair and calling me a girl," Jericho told us. "He's preoccupied with so many other things."

Dottie looked over at us, and motioned for Rachel to come over to the group of girls she was talking to. Rachel excused herself and waltzed happily over to her counselor, who gave her a very strong and tender hug.

"You'd better not tell anyone... but Rachel told me last night that her parents are getting divorced," Beth said.

"Yeah, well, on visiting day her parents didn't look too friendly," I told them.

"Yeah, she's been crying every night, and Dottie is there to comfort her," Ellen said.

"Lately she's been holding Rachel all night while she cries herself to sleep," Beth added.

Suddenly Joe Geisinger walked in and slapped the needle off the record that was playing on the turntable. In a stern voice that was just a decibel under a scream, he chastised Samson and Asa for mingling with their counterparts on girls' side. Then he stormed toward us and prodded Beth and Ellen over to their counselors. He finally screamed that the social was over. Chick tried to calm him down, but saw that was useless, so he signaled for Ben and the other counselors to take us back to the bunk . No goodnight kiss tonight.

When the first day of August eventually melts into the first night, the full moon suddenly looks brighter than ever. The first shiver of cold sweeps through the bunk, and the stars seem closer to us than ever.

We felt the cold as we jumped into pajamas, or sweat pants, and buried ourselves under the blankets. You could hear the soft swaying of the pine trees as the wind made them dance. Something was wrong with Ben. He kept pacing and looking out the window. When taps blew he threw on a sweat shirt, turned out the lights and bolted from the bunk.

"It's the night of Sunshine," Hardon announced, and most of the bunk giggled in delight.

"You hear that, Harris? It's like our Halloween during the summer. The night of Sunshine is our open season," The Brain added.

"Big fucking deal," Harris replied, and then he popped his head up from his pillow and stared at me, hoping I knew what they were talking about. I only shrugged my shoulders.

Harris got out of his bed, walked over to the double decker, and stood in front of me as I read by flashlight. This was a first. He just looked at me until I put my book down, and then he asked, "Do you want to play cards?"

I thought about it for a minute, not knowing if I wanted to be intruded upon. Oliver shone his flashlight into my eyes, and said he wanted to play too, and suddenly Jericho was sitting on Oliver's bed. Harris sat on the floor and started to deal the cards.

"Poker?" Harris asked

"How do you know how to play?" I wanted to know.

"How do you know how to play?" he asked me.

"Easy, when you've been in camp as long as I have you learn to play poker. You grow up with poker. It's second nature."

"My father has a weekly game, and sometimes when I can't sleep I'll sneak down to the basement, stand by my father and rub his arms for good luck. I won't say a word, but I've picked up the game," Harris told us.

"I did a math paper on poker, so I had to learn how to play the game," Oliver added, and we all just assumed that Jericho's brother taught him how to play.

Harris dealt the cards and we played through the night. We were now a clique. We bonded. We formed a barrier around ourselves in one corner of the bunk, while the rest of the bunk sat in the back corner with The Brain and Hardon. They played their own game of poker and plotted some semblance of mischief.

We tried to stay up for Ben but by 10:00 p.m. we turned in. We were playing with an ante of Bazooka bubble gum. Oliver's mother brought up four boxes of the gum, and he dealt it out to us to use for betting purposes. It was hard not to keep unwrapping and chewing our winnings. The taste and smell of the sweet sugar melting in our mouths brought back memories of our first crew cuts when we were children. After the barber finished buzzing our heads, our reward for being "good" was that wad of Bazooka bubble gum. From then on whenever we smelled that tantalizing aroma of Bazooka bubblegum we'd remember the feel of short cropped hair, and talcum powder on the back of our necks. Those days were now long gone.

I awoke around 1:00 a.m. when I heard Samson, Asa, Lenny and Spanky walking back to their bunks. They were laughing their asses off. They couldn't stop laughing and I slammed my pillow over my head. I fell back asleep until I heard Ben walk into the bunk. He went directly to Jericho and shook him out of his sleep.

"I need one of your joints," Ben whispered.

"I don't have any," Jericho told him, still in sleep mode.

"Jericho, this is an emergency. I know you smoke. I know you and Jason have been smoking all summer, and I don't give a shit. But right now, I need a joint,"

Jericho kicked off his blanket and looked to make sure that the rest of the bunk was sleeping. Then he reached into his cubby and pulled out a joint from his secret hiding place. I looked at the radio alarm clock that Oliver kept on the stand between us, and it read 2:10 a.m. Then I heard the whimpering and the sobbing and thought it was Harris, but it was coming from the boot box on the porch. The one right under my window, and I saw a strange figure sitting there, his shoulders quivering with each deep sob that he was trying to hold back.

Ben walked back out to the porch, and fired up the joint. We knew this had to be serious, because Ben wasn't that stupid. You just don't smoke a joint out in the open unless it's an emergency. Jericho joined me on my bed and we sat quietly as we listened to Ben calming down this stranger.

"Here, smoke this," Ben said after he took a long hit and offered the joint to the stranger.

"I don't smoke," was the response.

"You need to do this... trust me.. it will calm you down."

"Why? Why.... did they... ? It's not true, is it?"

"None of it is. And I don't know why. They're a bunch of assholes and one day they'll get what they deserve."

The stranger took the joint, inhaled and tried to hold it down in his lungs but started to cough wickedly. He leaned over the porch railing and retched. Ben stood behind him, patting his back. He turned away and saw the two of us staring back at him through the window. I thought he would be mad that we were up, but he just looked at us and then went back to consoling the stranger.

Nothing else was said, but the retching stopped. Ben got him to smoke most of the joint, and it actually did calm the stranger down. He looked familiar, like someone I had seen in camp but never really noticed. About twenty minutes later Ben helped the stranger off the porch. He started walking him back to his bunk. From what Jericho and I could tell, he was a Rover counselor, his bunk all the way at the end of boys' camp. We pulled on sweatshirts, and took our jelly rolls and wrapped the blankets around us. Sitting on the boot box we waited for Ben to return.

When he saw us on the porch, he smiled. I think he was too exhausted to be angry. He slid down on the floor of the porch, right between us, resting his back against the boot box.

"I hope you don't mind, but I finished that joint you gave me," Ben said.

"No problem. Want to talk about tonight?" Jericho asked.

"It's late. You need to go to bed," Ben said. We started to get up but he threw out his hands and sort of forced us to sit down again. "Then again, ..."

"What happened. Who was that?" I asked.

"First August night. The night of Sunshine. They picked out their prey and executed it perfectly. I could have stopped it. I sort of knew it was going down, but wasn't sure who was going to be the victim. Those assholes... fucking with someone like that. It's cruel, but to them it's entertainment."

Ben took a deep breath, and let out sort of a whimper. Or was it a sign of disgust and surrender?

"At check-in, down at the HCO, all the counselors were hanging out. Bullshitting. And this Rover counselor, a nobody, a nice kid, comes in and suddenly gets sucked up into the conversation. Did you know the Rover and Ranger counselors, they have the younger kids, aren't even considered part of the camp by most of their peers? They put the weakest counselors down there because there are less problems. So anyway, this Rover counselor is suddenly enamored with the attention the big boys in camp are giving him. He's involved with their conversation and he just loses his perspective that he's a nobody here, and he's not a part of the inner circle. He starts talking about how he wants to get laid.... how he wants and needs a girl for the last month of the summer, but right now he would like to get laid. And then Chick...., Chick of all people, he whines 'Hey, we've got to get this boy laid tonight,'.... and Lenny asks how that would even be possible.. and Chick lays it on thick by saying, 'Eh,.... why don't you just take him across the lake to the whorehouse?"

"There's no whorehouse across the lake," Jericho said.

"I know that, and you know that...it's absurd, but someone new to the camp who is in dire need of attention doesn't know this. The entire scenario starts to snowball. It's all improv....on the fly... Samson and Asa have now picked out their Sunshine."

"They didn't know this guy at all?" I asked.

"Not at all. They usually plan this during the winter through their lonely college nights."

"How do you know they're lonely?" I asked.

"You're right, I don't. Point is they have all winter to plan something but tonight was different. It was a spur of the moment thing. Samson and Asa start to bicker about taking a stranger to the whorehouse across the lake till they have this Rover counselor begging to go. So they tell him if he wants to come with them, he has to go to his bunk and wash his balls till their spotless. So he races up the hill from the HCO shack and everyone's following him. Samson and Asa are inside the bunk but the rest of the crew is outside the bunk looking through that large bathroom window. I'm standing in the shadows, on the fringes. I don't want this to happen... "

"Why not?"... I asked.

"It's not right! I told you that... they're all a bunch of assholes! ... Anyway, once he's washed his balls, they take off. They march to the pit and they jump into a huge station wagon, and settle this kid into the front seat between Samson, who's driving, and Asa. Three other counselors pop into the back seat and then Lenny and Spanky weigh down the car by jumping into the cargo area in the back. The car is barely able to drive out of the pit. It's scraping bottom with every single rock and pebble that's lying in its way. I don't have time to get to my car, so I start to run after it."

"You're going to catch a car?" I asked.

"It was only going around the lake, and the turnoff was only two

hundred yards up the road. Don't forget, that car held eight counselors and could barely move. Plus when they got into the woods
they would have to drive like five miles an hour. I could keep up
with them, and be invisible at the same time."

Ben gets up to stretch his legs. He looks around to make sure
that nobody else is awake, and then continues.

"So they pull out of the pit, and they make the first right where
the lake ends." He points to a far off corner of the lake where dirt
and water almost kiss. We could make out the opposite shore line
in the full moon.

"It's a road, a small one lane path, and I'm right behind them.
It's hard to see the road from the dying light of their car, but I make
my way. We get halfway around the lake and they stop. They all get
out of the station wagon and stretch. I sneak up on them and hide
behind a tree. I can hear them. I look down the darkened path and,
son of a bitch, there's a house down there about a hundred yards
into the darkness, and it has a fucking red light on the porch. A fucking red light. What are the odds on that?"

"Red light? What does that mean?" I asked.

"Red light district in Amsterdam. Legal whorehouses... the
whores of Amsterdam stand outside their little shops which have
red lights on the outside. When someone is interested they're led
inside and the whore turns off the light, meaning they're busy. So
this house has a red light, and even though this Rover counselor
wants to go first, they don't let him. They draw straws and Lenny
and Spanky are the first to head down the path. In the meantime
Samson and Asa are whispering into the counselor's ear that everyone has to be careful around Spanky because he's just gotten out
of Creedmore."

"The mental hospital in Queens?" Jericho asked.

"Yeah, that one. So they're feeding this kid a story about how
Spanky is nuts, how he had some shock treatments to try to right
him. They tell him that the shock treatment didn't work, but he's
still on medication so everyone has to tiptoe around Spanky because he might just get crazy again. Then Asa admits that they

shouldn't have sent Spanky down there first because anything can happen, and they're praying that Lenny can keep him in check."

Ben stared off into the distance, not wanting to go on. Jericho prodded him with one question after another until Ben broke down.

"In the meantime Asa has talked this kid into taking his pants off so he can just run down to the girls once Lenny and Spanky return. Now they got this kid standing there in the dark in just his underwear and he's shivering from the cold. About five minutes later Lenny and Spanky come back up the path. Spanky has his pants down around his ankles and Lenny is dragging him toward the car. It looks like Spanky is bleeding from the mouth, but I would later discover it was ketchup. Lenny's screaming that Spanky lost it, that he went nuts and beat his whore into a bloody pulp and the sheriff is coming for them. They have to get out of there. The Rover counselor is trying to get his pants on, but Asa has thrown them into the woods and everyone's panicking and forcing the Rover counselor into the car. They have to back out down the road because it's so narrow and they can't make a u-turn without crashing into a tree. I can hear them screaming at Spanky, who's now sitting in the back seat, and he starts to pretend that he's having a breakdown. He's crying, he's screaming in anguish. He starts to punch everyone in the front seat, especially this half naked Rover counselor."

"You can see all this?" I asked.

"I saw it. I heard it all. Samson is begging Spanky to calm down but he's gone full bore psychotic. It was quite a performance. I couldn't do anything but watch as the car passed slowly by. You could tell that Samson was having trouble driving backward on the dark road."

"You followed the car?" Jericho asked.

"From close up. First I ran and picked up the kids pants that they tossed into the woods. The car is inching down the road because they're driving backwards. So I jog along a parallel path in the woods till I catch up to the car. They don't even notice me. There was chaos in the car and I was invisible. Spanky is screaming and hitting and clawing at the Rover counselor, blaming him for all that happened. He's admitting to the counselor that he's crazy. Lenny keeps screaming that he left Spanky's medication back in camp and every-one's screaming for Spanky to calm down. Then you can hear Asa telling the Rover counselor that they can't control Spanky anymore."

Ben took a deep breath and leaned back to look at the stars. You could feel the pain he was in.

"Suddenly Spanky screams ' I'm going to kill him. It's all his fault. I'm going to kill him' and Samson stops the car and Spanky jumps out, just jumps right through the open window on the driv-er's side... crawls over Samson and out the window.., and runs around to the hood of the car, where he jumps on the hood and starts bouncing up and down, screaming that he's going to kill that "Rover motherfucker." Well the Rover counselor loses it, climbs out of the car right over Asa, and just runs screaming half naked into the woods. Everyone's stunned, and then those bastards just start laughing. Spanky gets back into the car and they proceed to back out of the woods, leaving this kid abandoned in the woods, not even caring about what happened to him."

"So what did you do?" I asked.

Ben's fingers kept twitching, moving rapidly, almost as if he was playing the piano. Then he started running his fingers through his hair like a comb. For a moment there was silence as Ben caught his breath. You could hear snoring from inside both Bunk 17 and 18, but then Ben pounded his fist into the porch floor.

"I waited till the car disappeared down the road. I knew the exact spot the kid ran into the woods. I found him hugging a tree, scared out of his mind. He was terrified. It took me another five minutes to calm him down. I tried explaining that none of what happened was true, that it was all an elaborate ruse, hoax, and that Spanky was just acting. I wasn't getting through to him, but at least he got dressed and we walked back to camp."

Ben vanished in front of our eyes. Physically he was there, but spiritually he was in a different world. Something was weighing on his mind. A small tear started to form in the corner of his eye, and he wiped it away, and choked back a breath. Suddenly he balled his right hand into a fist and smashed the porch floor again.

"Assholes! They're all a bunch of bastards. They think it's a sport. They think they rule the camp, that they have the right to pick on someone. What gives them the right to mock others? They can ruin someone's life."

Ben started pacing from one end of the porch to the other. He was in deep thought, and we almost disappeared in the moment.

"Anyway, I finally got him to smoke that joint you gave me and it calmed his nerves enough so we could walk across camp and I could put him to bed. They told him that Spanky sleepwalks and he'd better not fall asleep."

"How could he fall asleep? I'd be scared out of my mind," I said.

"That's why I wanted that joint. It took the edge off. I hate those pricks. I've hated them my entire life, my entire fucking life! I hate people like that!"

Ben stared out onto the campus. A gust of wind made the pine trees do the Twist. The sound of frogs discussing life amongst frogs rolled up from the lake. I looked at Jericho and he just shrugged his shoulders.

"What do you mean by 'you've hated them your entire life?'" I asked.

Ben looked like he was going to divulge a secret. Words were forming in his mouth, but they were never communicated.

"I'm just saying, I'm tired of people bullying innocent people. Where's the humanity in it? It's a sickness that needs to eradicated. I've been fighting that fight forever, and I'm just growing tired of being the white knight."

"So what are you going to do? Are you going to go to Joe Geisinger?" Jericho asked.

"No, that won't do any good. Joe already has too much on his mind. You heard him this morning. He's a bit high strung and if it doesn't involve the campers he won't give a shit. I'll think of something."

Ben stood, and motioned for us to follow him into the bunk.

"August--and it's only the first day. The shit is going to hit the fan," Ben said as he ushered us into the bunk for the night.

24

R eveille blew and last night only seemed to be a bad dream. "Good morning, boys' camp... it's another beautiful day here at Camp Tonkawa We have a little Pocono dew on the ground this morning so be careful how you walk down to breakfast. Counselors get your campers out of bed. Campers get your counselors out of bed. Let's go, Let's go, Let's go... it's a beautiful day here at camp. First call for breakfast is in fifteen minutes."

"Shut the fuck up," Jericho muttered, as we all pulled our pillows over our heads to deaden the HCO announcement.

Ben hit the ground first and he pulled back all the blankets from everyone's bed. The only one who had jumped out of bed before Ben was the Mayor, and we all knew why... but it was still our secret. The cold mornings of August were upon us, and there was a security in our warm beds that we didn't want to leave. Yet, there was an ominous aura in the morning sunrise that greeted us on the second day of August.

The counselors were gloating at the flagpole, laughing and boasting about the enormity of the "Sunshine Evening" as they were calling it.

"The greatest schtick ever," Samson kept spouting.

This seemed to excite and embolden the Jewish Mafia as they huddled together in what seemed to be logistical plotting of their version of "Sunshine."

Ben kept searching for the Rover counselor at the raising of the flag. He was not standing with the Rover boys. In the horseshoe formation around the flag, The Rover boys stood opposite our group. Ben knew full well that the counselor was missing.

The flag was raised to the bugle call of "To the Colors," and my skin started to crawl. I was so tired of the militaristic tone from all the bugle calls throughout the day. They traveled across the campus and echoed off the hills and trees that surrounded camp.

Jericho had started it but we were now joined by a number of other counselors who protested the insanity of the war, and the presidency of Richard Nixon. We did not put our hands over our hearts. We stood politely with our hands clasped behind our backs.

After breakfast Ben headed up to the Rover bunks to search for that counselor, and to see what the aftermath was. He returned before inspection, and surprisingly started throwing some clothing into a backpack.

"So what happened with "The Night of the Sunshine? How did it end?" I asked.

At first Ben didn't say anything. He finished packing his clothing, but then he sat down on the edge of Oliver's bed.

"Well, the counselor's gone. I tried to get him to stay, but he was adamant about not being around these assholes. He stayed back from breakfast and packed up. Then I walked with him to his car, all the way to the pit, trying to talk him out of it, but when we got to his car…. well, that was the breaking point. I don't know how they did it, or when they did it, but they broke into his car and filled it with newspapers. I don't know where they found so many newspapers, but they just crumpled up newspapers like package stuffing and filled his tiny Volkswagen Beetle with newspapers. He lost it right there. Started crying. Desperate to leave he just began flinging newspapers out of his car until he had enough room to fit in with a clear view to drive away."

"It's not fair," Jericho said. I knew what he meant. It wasn't fair that the scum of the earth seemed to be winning.

"Well, I'll see you guys tomorrow morning. Hold down the fort. And Flanken, don't let anyone take advantage of you," Ben said as he stood quickly, and grabbed his backpack.

"Wait! Where are you going?"

There was panic in my voice. If Harris hadn't swallowed his

tongue he would have been asking the same question, … instead, you could see the panic in his eyes.

"Got to go home for the night. I have a cousin's wedding. I'll be back before Reveille tomorrow. Just watch yourselves tonight. Take care of each other."

"You can't leave us alone! They'll kill us!" Oliver blurted out.

"We won't touch you!" The Brain purred.

Ben just pointed at the Jewish Mafia and said one word… "Don't," then he summoned me to follow him onto the porch.

"Look, Flanken…. sooner or later you're going to have defend yourself. You're going to face assholes your entire life, and one day you're going to have to protect your reputation and maybe your sanity. There's only so much shit a man can take. All I'm saying is that camp makes you face reality faster than usual, and your reality here is that it's…… it's time for you to stand on your own. Maybe punch some asshole in the nose. Anything, do anything to preserve your self-esteem…. Oh, …and please watch over Harris and Oliver. "

Ben walked out on us that morning. He knew we were afraid to be alone, to fend for ourselves, and yet he left. And within seconds of Ben driving out of camp we knew we were under attack.

Asa and Samson, both marched into the bunk for morning inspection. Samson carried with him a tennis racquet. Samson stood in the middle of the bunk and pointed his racquet, aiming at Jericho… then at me… then Harris… then Oliver… then Bugsy…. and then Hooky. But he stopped at Hooky, aimed the tennis racquet like a gun, and Hooky tried to bolt.

"It's time for WAFFLE ASS," Samson shouted.

Asa grabbed Hooky, threw him face down onto the floor of the bunk, and then sat on his back. Samson pulled back Hooky's shorts exposing the pinkest, whitest ass in the bunk. Samson placed the guts of the tennis racquet on top of Hooky's ass. Asa handed him a large, round, smooth rock. Samson pressed down on the racquet and with the rock started scrubbing the cat gut deep into Hooky's flesh.

Hooky was screaming. Samson used the tennis racquet like a washboard, just scrubbing vigorously till the first signs of blood. Only then did Samson stop, and only then did Asa finally stand up, freeing Hooky.

Hooky stood slowly, tears dripping from his eyes. You could see the waffle pattern etched into Hooky's ass. His bloody ass. He ran into the back room crying.

Then Asa grabbed Harris. I took a step forward but Samson pushed me back.

Asa reached into Harris' shorts and pulled the back end of his white underwear straight up into the air.

"Flying Wedgie time," Samson shouted.

Asa lifted Harris off the ground by pulling up on his underwear. You could hear his underwear ripping, and you just knew his balls were being squashed by the crush of cotton. Asa carried Harris over to the back wall, and knocked a baseball cap to the floor that was hanging off a nail. Asa lifted Harris off the ground and hooked his underwear onto the nail. Harris dangled like a marionette, his underwear wedged deep into his crack. Everyone laughed at him as he fought to free himself. Jericho and I rushed over to help him down.

Harris was crying. Hooky was crying. Oliver and Jericho stayed back with me as everyone left the bunk for morning activity. Even though Hooky was hurting, even though you could see the blood caking on his white shorts, he ran out of the bunk to join the others. He didn't want to be a part of our little clique.

In the morning basketball game The Mayor and Hardon took turns pummeling me. First it was with sucker punches to my back followed by elbows to the ribs. Asa and Samson never called a foul. I fouled out of the game at the beginning of the fourth quarter. Hardon, dressed in his high top black Converse sneakers, kept sneering at me and taunting me to hit him, but I never took the bait. Yet, after the last foul was called on me I lost my cool and told Asa he could go 'fuck himself'. Whistle. Technical foul. Out of the game.

"What's gotten into you?" Chick asked as he sat down next to me.

"Can't you see what's going on?" I screamed at him. I had to do everything to hold back the tears. "I'm being punished out there and they're not calling anything on the other team. It's so unfair."

"Ehhhh.... what do you care? It's only a game. Don't let them get to you, Jason. Be a man and don't let those punks get you down."

"You're not out there playing. Look at me," and I showed him the cuts and scrapes from being pushed to the court. "This isn't fun."

"No, but it's life. You'll see."

"I'll see what?"

"As you grow older you'll always come into contact with cheaters, and punks, and assholes like Samson and Asa. Then what are you going to do? Cry? You have to make up your mind that you're better than these morons and make your own destiny. This is one of the biggest lessons you'll learn in camp, one of your biggest life lessons... how will Jason overcome this?"

"Why aren't you calling me Flanken?" I asked.

"How can I call you something that I love to eat?"

"Then what should I do about how they're treating me?"

"Stand up to them. Even if they beat the shit out of you, make them see they'll never get the best of you."

"Ben told me the same thing this morning... you guys talk to each other?"

"No...I guess we just see things the same way."

"So, I should..."

"Hide your emotions. Don't let them see that they're getting to you, and you'll be a bigger man than they'll ever be."

Chick then smiled. He patted me on the back and then with his bowed legs he pushed himself up off the bench and started to walk down the edge of the court. When the ball rolled out of bounds he called Asa over, and started to whisper something to him. Asa bent down to hear him better. Chick suddenly grabbed the whistle dangling from the shoe lace that was hanging around Asa's neck, the lace that had the whistle that he never blew for me. Chick started twisting it. Asa started to choke, and the tighter the old man twisted, the lower Asa had to bend down. Soon he was eye to eye with Chick. Asa flailed his arms, gasping for air, but he would never hit the older man.

"I said, DON'T BE SUCH A SHMUCK," Chick shouted. He let go of the lace and Asa gasped to catch his breath. Chick walked away. Chick sent his message. I should have been the one to send the message.

We missed Ben during rest hour. We had gotten used to our self defense lessons. Just the day before, while practicing, we were surprised by a visitor. Oliver had joined us, even though he spent most of the time reading Ben's med school books. Harris would pair off with Ben while Jericho and I sparred with each other. We learned the simple things, like how to use our attacker's momentum to pull him off guard, and the continued practice of using the bottom palm of our hands as the ultimate battering ram.

"How long have you been doing this?" Oliver asked one day.

"Since I was ten years old," said Ben. "Came back home one summer and knew I needed to protect myself. It was great for my self confidence, and it's great exercise."

Ben asked Oliver if he saw anything interesting in his medical book.

"I'm looking at a picture of some guy with Elephantiasis of the balls. Pretty gross," Oliver told him.

"Who cares?" Harris asked as Jericho and I ran over to check out the pictures.

"Ha, maybe you can study that one day in med school instead of wondering about aliens," Ben told him.

"Nah... I'm going to stick with Aliens."

"Not medicine?"

"Nah, astronomy," Oliver told him.

"Well, stick to your guns, Oliver. You'll enjoy whatever you study," Ben told him.

Later in the day we returned from the afternoon swim. A nice respite from the dog days of August. As cold as the nights were, the days seemed to be getting hotter. There was even talk that if the temperature exceeded ninety degrees the next day we would have an all afternoon swim. Nobody ever minded being down by the lake for an entire afternoon of sunning and swimming because some days, and I hate to admit it, it was just too damn hot for kids to participate in athletic events.

An afternoon swim afforded us the opportunity to gaze upon the girls' dock, which was only separated from the boys' swimming area by about a hundred yards of water and beach. It was nice to peek over and see the girl counselors walking around in bikinis, and we all envied the girls' Head Waterfront counselor who was the only male allowed on the docks.

It was the first time we came back to the bunk without a handful of wet towels. We were a little rouge group, scooping up dirty towels when the younger campers turned their backs on us. We were now up to 100 towels exchanged for the week, and this made Ben happy.

We walked into the bunk that afternoon and there was a strange silence. Nobody was looking at us. For once, everyone had changed for dinner without lying around in their wet bathing suits.

We missed Ben marching up and down the bunk, pushing everyone to get ready for the next moment of the day. If it was after a swim he would walk around the bunk sharing his words of wisdom.

"My grandmother knows. My grandmother would always tell me that if you stay in your wet bathing suit too long you're going to get cramps in your penis. You don't want cramps in your shmeckle."

"That's all bullshit," The Brain would tell him.

"No, it's not. Girls don't sit in their wet suits because... "

"They'll get cramps in their penises?" Hardon interjected, causing the bunk to break out in laughter.

"No, they'll get yeast infections," Ben finished

"What the hell is a yeast infection?" The Mayor asked.

"They have bread growing in their twats?" asked The Brain with a touch of astonishment in his voice.

"It's an infection, you moron," Ben said. "It's more like cottage cheese."

"That's gross," Bugsy said.

"If it can happen to the girls, who knows... maybe my grand-mother was right!"

We missed him at dinner where the Jewish Mafia dominated the meal. We had no counselor at our table.

We missed him during free play,

We missed him while we undressed for bed. Then we heard the whispering.... "Bataan Death March tonight."

We missed him at midnight.

Ben's bed was empty when the counselors from our group marched in. You know the three campers they picked out. Like Ninjas they crept to our beds as everyone tossed and turned. First they went after Harris, and then Oliver. They gagged them with duct tape across the mouth and then bound their arms together with the tape. I prayed they weren't going to pick me, and slammed my eyes shut. Oliver had struggled at first, trying desperately to reach for but eventually knocking his inhaler to the floor.

Then the counselors stripped off their pajamas, leaving them barefoot and dressed only in their underpants, before they tied their feet together at the ankles. I should have kicked off my blanket, but I was stupid. What made me think that once they came for Harris and Oliver they wouldn't come for me. If I stepped up and started screaming maybe I could have stopped it, but by pretending that nothing was happening I allowed myself to become the next victim.

Lenny laid on top of me so I couldn't jump up, and then Samson and Asa swooped me out of bed. I fell to the floor, and grabbed Oliver's inhaler and clutched it in my hand. I knew what was next, and as much as I struggled they succeeded in stripping me, taping my arms behind my back with duct tape, binding my legs together, and finally gagging me. I held the inhaler like it was a million dollar diamond I was lifting out of a museum.

Next came the pillow cases, which they wrestled over our heads. We couldn't see, we couldn't scream. They lifted us over their shoulders like rugs being thrown into the garbage, and carried us out of the bunk.

We didn't know where we were going, but it seemed like the night was quickly turning into morning. My mind raced with thoughts of death...and anger. I tried not to freak out, but I couldn't stop thinking about how Harris and Oliver were handling this. I heard gravel crunching, and a minute or two later the sound of wood creaking. I heard the asshole counselors laughing and whispering to each other. I worried that Oliver might not be able to breathe. I wrapped my hands around the inhaler even tighter.

Suddenly I heard twigs cracking, skin being scraped, rocks being kicked aside. I knew where we were. We were finally dumped to the ground. Still bound and gagged we fought for our dignity.

I felt someone behind me, and then I heard Asa whispering in my ear… "Don't move."

Then I felt the knife against my wrists...the dull part. Asa cut halfway through the duct tape. I still couldn't free my hands but they were now loose enough that I knew I could eventually wriggle free. The sound of the counselors laughing receded into the night as I started to fight my way through the tape.

I sawed my hands back and forth as I heard the strands slowly ripping apart until I broke free in one violent spasm. Pulling my pillow case off my head I ripped the tape off my mouth. I didn't even wait to undo my ankles. I found myself crawling frantically on the dirt toward Oliver. I pulled the pillow case off of Oliver and saw he was turning blue. His eyeballs were popping out of their sockets as I tore the tape off his mouth, allowing him to gasp for every precious breath of air.

"Take deep breaths, Oliver. Relax."

"I can't … inhaler… can't breathe… going to die." He started crying.

I unraveled the tape around Oliver's hands and when he was free he grabbed the inhaler from my hand.

"You have to calm down."

I scrambled behind Oliver and hugged him while he took a hit from the Inhaler. I held Oliver against my chest, praying he would slow his breathing to a point where he wouldn't struggle any-more. It was the first time I ever hugged anyone. It was the first time I could ever remember being so close to another warm body. I could feel Oliver's blubber flapping against my skin as he heaved, spasmed, and gasped. I felt his sweat-soaked chubby body saturat-ing my chest as I loosened my hug.

"Do you need mouth to mouth?" I asked… praying that …

"No….I'll be okay," he gasped.

Harris had stopped struggling, because I knew he understood the dire situation we were in. He sat silently in the dark. Finally I watched the pink ebb back into Oliver's cheeks and his breathing started to return to a normal cadence. It was as much of a panic attack as an asthmatic situation.

I then crawled over to Harris and removed his pillow case and gag.

"I'm going to kill them. I'm going to kill them," Harris screamed.

Oliver hadn't moved. He just sat there sobbing. I struggled with the tape around my ankles, and then helped free Harris. He was seething, gulping like a fish out of water. I helped Oliver free himself and then picked him up off the ground. We were three boys stand-ing alone in the woods, in our underwear.

"Where are we?" Harris asked.

"I bet we're on the golf course," I said.

"How do you know?"

"I heard gravel from the road leading to the girls' side. Then it sounded like we were walking over a wooden bridge. The amount of time it took us to get here. I think we're in the woods behind the golf course."

"Battan Death March," Oliver whispered.

"What?" Harris asked as he started to pick twigs out between his barefoot toes.

"Battan Death March. You heard the whispers today. This is it. We're on our own. We're supposed to find our way back to the bunk."

"They want us to walk barefoot through the woods?" Harris asked.

"Forget the woods, we're going to have to walk across girls' campus half naked," I wailed.

"I'm not going to do that, Flanken. I don't want any girl to see me naked. I'm not going back to the bunk."

"Never Oliver?"

"Never."

Just then a bat flew past us, and Oliver started running through the woods. We chased him, and thankfully he was running in the right direction. Our feet were being cut by the twigs and rocks. We stumbled along until Oliver emerged from the woods and fell to his knees heaving and cleaving for oxygen. We stumbled down next to him. The grass was soft and cool, as the morning dew was being born. It was the perfect salve for the bloody soles of our feet.

"Why is it so soft?" Harris asked.

"Because we're on the first green of the golf course. I was right, they dumped us in the woods on the golf course."

I walked the perimeter of the green and felt the coolness of the August night starting to chill the beads of sweat that dripped down my body. I was angry. I was already plotting revenge. I heard Harris and Oliver whispering behind me.

"Fuck them. Fuck them. They're not going to get the best of us," Harris said as he walked past me on his way back to boys' camp. Oliver followed like a little puppy whimpering on his first night in a new home.

"Battan Death March, my ass. This is a piece of cake," Harris shouted as he marched boldly up the first fairway. I ran after them.

"What are you saying?" I asked.

"We're going back to bed. We're going to never mention this. We're going to pretend it never happened."

"But what about the cuts on the soles of our feet," Oliver asked.

"Put band aids on in the morning. Don't complain about it."

"I like it. It will drive them crazy to know they didn't get the best of us," I said.

"Exactly," Harris said defiantly.

And then we stood at the foot of the small wooden bridge that led to the girls camp.

We didn't take another step. Looking at each other, we realized just how afraid we were of scampering across girls' side in our underwear.

"I'm afraid someone will wake up and see me like this," Oliver said.

"This is a cinch. You just have to think of the most horrible thing that can happen to you and this will seem easy," Harris suggested. It made so much sense.

"Hearing my dad smack my mother every week when he's angry. I can tell the difference between an open hand slap and a closed fist. And I cry... and that's the most horrible thing to me. Hearing my father hit my mom, my mom crying, and I'm not able to help," Oliver said.

"Walking into the kitchen at night," I said, "watching my mother chatting on the phone with a glass of wine at her lips. She'll look right through me as if I wasn't there. Same with my dad. I don't exist in my own home. And then maybe one morning I'll walk into the kitchen and find them both dead on the floor from an overdose of drugs they ingested while having wild sex... and I won't even care. I won't shed a tear."

Harris nodded. " .... And I'm so scared that my mother is going to die, and I may not be there."

We looked at each other for a second, a link that was now forged by the night, and then took a leap of courage and started our mad dash back to the bunk as girls' camp slept in front of us.

We were giggling and laughing. The gravel road really hurt our feet but the pain was soothed the second we hit the cool grass of the great lawn on boys' side. We were like three blind mice racing across the pitch dark campus, with Oliver's pasty white body bringing up the rear like the light on the porch of a caboose. Oliver waddled and we slowed to keep him company.

We quietly crept into the bunk, waking no one. Ben wasn't back, but we survived the night without him, and we knew we were better for it.

25

Ben returned the next morning before Reveille blew. He placed a bagel with lox wedged between a ton of cream cheese on my pillow. I awoke with a smile. Ben also brought the same sandwich back for Jericho, Oliver and Harris.

"So did I miss anything last night?" Ben asked as the first notes of Reveille finally resounded across the campus.

"Nope, nothing," I told him as I licked an oozing wad of cream cheese off the side of the bagel.

"What do you mean nothing happened?" The Brain shouted.

"Nope, nothing happened last night," Harris told him matter-of-factly. He was sitting up on the edge of his bed, finishing off the bagel and lox.

"Then why are your feet all cut up?" Hooky asked.

Ben walked around to Harris and looked at the caked blood on the soles of his feet.

"Yeah, why are your feet all cut up?" Ben asked.

"Must have stepped on something in the back room."

Harris was right. It drove the bunk crazy when we put up the front that nothing happened the night before. I winked at Harris, and he grinned at Oliver, and Jericho suddenly felt like an outsider.

The counselors kept staring at us at lineup, wondering how we found our way back without falling apart. They kept looking at Ben to see if we had complained to him, but he just stood nonchalantly off to the side. As we walked down to the flag pole I pulled Jericho aside and told him about the "Death March."

"And you're not telling Ben?"

"We're not telling anyone. I'm only telling you,"

Jericho looked at me, and then nodded his approval to Harris and Oliver.

It was a Tuesday, and our last 'trip day' of the summer. We were headed to Ghost Town, a small amusement park about an hour and a half away in Scranton Pennsylvania. The girls were going to be there too. According to Jericho this was going to be our chance to roam freely with our girlfriends and not have counselors spying on us. At this age the freedom to be alone with a girl was both intoxicating and wondrous. A simple little thing like fumbled kissing was so exhilarating that the thought of it was driving me crazy.

"Besides, watch what happens," Jericho told me over breakfast. "They're going to be guilty of embezzlement."

"What's that?" I asked

"They're going to steal our canteen funds. They're going to give us our slips and tell us to sign our names at the bottom. They're going to tell us that we're going to get back five dollars for the day, but the counselors are going to actually request seven dollars."

"Even Ben?"

"No, not Ben. He won't be in on this."

"What are they going to do with the extra money?" I asked.

"After lunch they're going to disappear into the beer garden and get drunk. It happened last year and the year before. We're free for two hours. I can't wait. I've rolled like three joints, and I'm going to disappear with Beth. You should do the same with Rachel."

The ride to the amusement park was brutal. School buses in the summer should be illegal. Harris sat with Oliver, who was turning green. It was from a combination of the bumpy country roads, and the stale warm air that sifted through the bus. I sat with Jericho, and had to listen to his plans for the day in the park with Beth.

Personally I was nervous about being alone with Rachel. I really had no experience with dating, with being around a girl in a private setting. I was never invited to parties thrown by kids in school. I never shared in the experience of spin the bottle, or seven minutes in heaven. Just holding her hand gave me a an erection... what would happen if we started kissing for a long time?

The Brain sat in front of Harris, and every now and then he would take a swig of water from his canteen. The he would turn around and spit it into Harris' face. Ben was in the back of the bus, and when he saw The Brain spit water for the second time he grabbed the canteen and threw it out the window.

"You're fucking dead meat," The Brain screamed at Harris.

"Why are you blaming Harris? I'm the one who did it. What are you going to do to me?" Ben asked.

"You're dead meat too. Don't think I don't have plans for you. I've already written home about the night you rubbed my balls, you homo. Not only are you going to get fired, but I'm going to have you arrested."

"Now, you know that's not true," Ben said. There was a sly grin spreading across his face. "You're making it up, and I know you are."

"Who cares? I wrote home and my parents will care. They should have the letter by tomorrow."

"Oh, you mean this letter?"

Ben took an envelope out of his jean shorts. Everyone could see the shock that spread across The Brain's face. It was recognition. Ben proceeded to rip apart the letter and tossed the tiny little pieces out of the bus window.

"I know how to play the game too."

Ben turned his back on The Brain and returned to his seat.

There were always a few counselors who would abuse kids all the time. It was either physical or emotional abuse, and the physical abuse was obvious. They would either pummel you with punches to the arms or legs, leaving pock-marked purplish bruises. Other counselors whipped us on the legs with the lanyards that held their precious whistles. If you antagonized the OD, they would make you stand out on the porch in the cold of night. They made you hold your hands out and they would put a shoe in each dangling hand. If your arms started to droop, the OD would punch you in your thighs. You were at the mercy of the OD.

The difference between the physical abuse and the emotional abuse was the physical abuse faded. Not the emotional abuse. The counselors never seemed to realize how destructive the verbal assaults were. There was the constant mocking, the tearing down of our self esteem through the myriad of nicknames that every counselor seemed to dish out freely. Some were made to embarrass campers like "Shit-stain Stein", or "Cheton head." Why should someone be teased because he was born with a huge head?

Lenny, Samson and Asa were the name keepers. Once you had the name, it stuck with you for life. Oliver would always be known as Sperm, and Harris was Dickless. Or you could be called something like "Spanky" for the rest of your life.

I thought back to the previous hot afternoon, the type that made you light-headed and lazy, the type when you didn't want to be out on a softball field. The air was thick, not a breeze stirred, and the cicadas could be heard chirping all day long. Samson was umping our softball game. Then he had called for a Shmegma run.

Shmegma. The counselors had gotten into the habit of adding an "H" to almost every word that started with S. Thus, smut became "shmut" and smegma had become "shmegma." We never discovered till later on in life what 'smegma' meant, but our camp translation was a cool cold drink of instant iced tea.

There was just one water fountain in camp which had a chiller that worked. The water was always crisp and cool, and it was located in the corner of the boys Senior Hall. Asa had visited this fountain and appeared with two of the dented metal pitchers that were usually on our dining room tables. He gave one pitcher to Samson, who took a few big gulps, and then handed the pitcher to Mickey Hardon and Mandelbaum. Oliver, who was standing next to the Mayor, silently begged for a sip.

"You want some?"

"Sure," Oliver answered, licking his dry lips.

Oliver saw me twitch my head, begging him to refuse the drink. Nothing good could come of this.

"Then lie on the ground, and we'll see if you're worthy of a sip," Samson directed.

Oliver did as he was told, laid down on his back and The Mayor and Hardon each sat on an arm, pinning Oliver to the ground. Asa stood over him and told him to open his mouth. At first he teased Oliver by delivering an honest dribble into Oliver's mouth. But then Asa couldn't resist, or maybe that was his plan all along, and he dumped the rest of the contents all over Oliver's face. Oliver was still pinned to the ground by his two bunkmates.

"Bugs are crawling all over me," Oliver started to scream, as he struggled to get up.

"He wanted some shmegma, so let him sit in it for a little while longer," Asa ordered. Samson and Asa had retreated to the bleachers that rested under the shade of the pine trees, and finished off the second pitcher.

After a few minutes the counselors signaled to Hardon to get up. Oliver popped up screaming and slapping his face, knocking off the ants that had been attracted to a sugary substance. Oliver ran back to the bunk to shower, with mocking calls trailing his exit. To this day I could never understand why Oliver would even want to get involved with anything that Asa and Samson were involved with, except for the thought that he was desperately thirsty, and didn't expect to be the brunt of another cruel joke. From that day on Oliver was no longer known as "Sperm" but would forever be known as "Shmegma."

Ghost Town in the Glen was a second rate amusement park. We gathered under the rickety wooden roller coaster that trembled, threatening to collapse with each rumbling trip. The girls were gathered under a tree across from us, tantalizingly close, but still a million miles away. We had to eat lunch first, and the counselors rummaged through the three black garbage bags that carried our sandwiches. They were looking for the few salami sandwiches that were thrown in with the disgusting baloney and rancid turkey sandwiches.

"Don't eat the baloney. It's disgusting," Jericho whispered to me, and I passed that news onto Harris.

"But I'm hungry." Harris whimpered, a look of disappointment on his face.

"Can I have yours then?" Oliver asked.

Harris handed over his sandwich and settled on eating cookies. "I guess we can eat the crap they have in the park," he concluded.

"You're not in camp now," Chick lectured. "You're representing Camp Tonkawa in a public setting. Don't do anything foolish."

You couldn't miss us. We were dressed in our blue Camp Tonkawa T shirts. He was right. If we misbehaved we could be fingered in an instant.

Half the group raced down into the park, ready to hit all the rides. Oliver joined them. I stood off to the side of the road, along with Jericho, and Harris. Hardon, and the Brain and the rest of the Jewish Mafia stood off to the side, waiting for their girlfriends. The girls group leader was lecturing about the dangers of misbehaving. Then they were dismissed. Instead of the mass stampede that the boys exhibited, there was a festive parade. The girls liked to walk in packs of five or six, arms linked together, singing and dancing.

Samson, Asa, Lenny and Spanky all headed to the beer garden, just as Jericho predicted. Mickey Hardon, The Brain and The Mayor met their girls and headed into the park. Ben had stayed behind with us and watched as Beth, Rachel and Ellen approached.

The seven of us walked down the road and stopped in front of the first ride we came to. Twenty campers, dressed in their blue camp shirts, were strapped into shoulder harnesses' of a ride which was a massive wheel, ready to roll.

"That's the vomit wheel," Jericho told us.

"Why's it called that?" Beth asked.

"Just watch."

The wheel was parallel to the ground when it started to slowly spin. As the momentum of the wheel picked up speed, the angle of the wheel started to rise. As it spun the wheel tilted upward so that everyone was at a 45 degree angle to the ground. There was screaming. Some campers were crying to be released and others begged to 'keep the ride going'. It was too late, centrifugal force slammed everyone back into their harnesses. They were shrinking into tiny blurs. Suddenly a sticky orange liquid started to fly from the ride, pounding the dirt like the virgin raindrops from a thunderstorm.

"What is that?" Beth asked as we stepped back out of range.

'Vomit. Happens every year. Why the counselors give us food before these rides I'll never know," Jericho said as he headed down the road hand in hand with Beth, who was doing her best not to barf.

I looked at Rachel and she too was retching. I tried to hold her, but she pushed me away. The ride stopped and Ben saw that it was Oliver who did most of the puking, so he excused himself to give aid. Oliver wobbled off the ride, vomit splashed all over his shirt. Ben stood at arm's length and helped Oliver pull his shirt off, then he led him to a spigot to wash off.

I took Rachel by the hand, erotic fantasies of kissing her, and touching her tiny breasts were dancing in my mind. My heart beat faster than a drum roll, my palms were sweating and suddenly I needed a gallon of water to irrigate my arid mouth. My tongue was swollen in anticipation. We had taken a few steps down the path of sexual enlightenment when someone called out her name.

"Rachel, where are you going? You said you would spend the day with me."

It was Rachel's counselor, the one who was also friendly with Fawn and Doe. She was dressed in tight jean shorts with a white Camp Tonkawa polo shirt. What really made me stare at her were the work boots she wore. Every other counselor was wearing sandals or sneakers, but she wore thick wool socks that peeked out over her ankle high work boots.

"Well.. I was going to spend the day with Jason."

"Ohhh... now you know you promised me," she said as she

hugged Rachel and kissed her cheek. "Come on, spend the next hour with me. I have something to show you, and I promise you can spend the rest of the afternoon with your boyfriend."

The counselor tethered her fingers around Rachel's fingertips, and swung them like she was rocking a baby. She brushed back Rachel's hair and kissed her on the cheek again. "Please," she asked in a baby voice. "I'll spend all my money on you, and I promise I'll win you a big teddy bear,"

I pouted. "But I wanted to win her a teddy bear."

The counselor shot me a nasty glance, and then turned back to Rachel and flashed a big smile. Rachel relented and promised me we would spend time together. And off they went, leaving me standing alone feeling like a shmuck. This was not the last time in my life that I would feel like a shmuck, but you never forget the first time. Everyone had someone. I thought I had someone, but now I knew I had no one.

Ben approached with Oliver. He had finished cleaning him off, but Oliver still looked green. Luckily it was high noon on a hot August day, and Oliver could walk around without a shirt on.

But I couldn't take my eyes off Oliver's body, and I realized that I never noticed Oliver naked during the day. We saw Oliver topless at night when he was putting on his pajamas, but to see Oliver during the day immediately haunted me. Oliver never swam, he had a note. He just sat under the pavilion during every waterfront period. Come to think of it, nobody ever saw him shower. I mean, he had to have showered because he never reeked of body odor, so maybe he did it when nobody was in the bunk, or maybe again we just never noticed. And when we played shirts vs. skins in any sport, well.... of course, how could I have been so blind? He didn't play any sports! He had a note!

He had little boy man tits, little sacks of whatever that drooped. Every breath made his boy tits wiggle, and they were jiggling today because Oliver wasn't looking too good. He was obviously still dizzy from the ride, and his disgusting pasty whiter-than-white skin had a tinge of purple from puking so much. And he had stretch marks all around the sides of his body where his baby fat seemed to hang over the edge of his shorts... and how would I know what stretch marks were? Because my mother would walk around the house in her bra and panties and just look in a mirror and proclaim she was the only mother around without stretch marks. Then she would show me pictures of women with stretch marks. The thought of me hugging him the night of the Battan Death March almost made me puke. It also made me realize how traumatized we were... I mean, we didn't truly know how other people viewed us.

"Tough to lose a girl like that. I don't know what that was all about, but let's just walk. I think Oliver needs to get away from the sight of that ride," Ben said as he nudged me down the road, deeper into the park.

"She told me that she would spend the day with me today,"

"Flanken, the first lesson in life is that women will always break your heart. The second lesson is that women will drive a man to the brink of insanity. The third lesson is that you still need them. Let me guess. You and Jericho had something all planned out."

"Well, nothing in writing, but we were going to walk around together. I've never been on a double date... I've never been on a date."

"You're only thirteen years old. Think about it, Flanken. You've just entered your teen years so why worry about any of this. There will be many more girls, followed by women and they will enter your life and wreak havoc. You don't want to be beholden to any of them. Let it all come to you. You're a good-looking kid, things will work out."

"What about me?" Oliver asked, a question that was weak and punctuated by a burp. He was still tasting what he had spewed earlier.

"For you too. You're going to find someone, Oliver. Guys, remember this very important fact. There are more women than men in the world. And I want you to always remember the wise words of my college roommate, Larry Okusa, a very very smart man... you have to believe in the inverted triangle."

"What's that?" Oliver asked.

"Simple.. as a freshman in college…, you'll always find yourself at the base of a triangle. But at the apex, at the very top, is the girl. She controls the base. Broad spectrum. She can date either boys or men. She can date men older than her or she can date someone younger. However, as you both age, the man rises to the top of the triangle because now he has the choice of dating younger, or older women, or even women of the same age. A woman's options are now dimmed, as she has fewer men to choose from and she will start to panic because not many men want to date older women. I mean you can be fifty years old, and you may meet someone younger, like a woman who's thirty or you can meet a sixty-year-old woman who desires you because you're younger."

"I see, but if you're a fifty-year-old woman, how many men younger want to date you? You can only date someone older!" I added.

"Exactly. So don't let today get you down at all. You'll meet the right girl. It's not like your girlfriend is running off with her counselor. She wants you," Ben said.

We walked through the amusement park, with the sound of the roller coaster struggling up the creaking wooden planks, followed by the screams of its riders as the ride plummeted down. I wasn't sure if they were screaming because of the sensation of falling, or the fear that the entire complex would collapse.

Mickey Hardon and his gang were wasting their money at the venues, trying to win large stuffed toys for their girlfriends, who were standing behind them eating fluffy clouds of cotton candy.

"That should have been me," I sighed.

"Stop it," Ben said, as he smacked me on the back of my head. "Those games are rigged. They're not going to win anything. See Hardon trying to shoot that basketball? It's got to be a perfect shot, because they make the rims smaller. Why waste your money?"

We passed the beer garden where we could hear the counselors laughing at their own jokes, and probably laughing at the fact that they embezzled money from our canteen funds and they would never get caught.

"Don't you wish you were in there with them?" Oliver asked. He had finally put on his shirt. I think he was becoming aware of the stares that his pasty body elicited from passersby.

"Not at all. I hate those guys," Ben said. "I detest everything they stand for, everything they do. They're disgusting human beings."

We walked down to the center of the park. It was filled with a mixture of campers, the boys in their blue shirts and the girls in their white shirts. Everyone was running around having a good time, enjoying the freedom of not being on a schedule, not hearing bugle calls, and not having counselors always on their backs.

We sat down at a picnic table, and Ben jutted his chin off to the left where we spied Jericho and Beth in a deep clench, kissing passionately. Jericho finally came up for air, and spotted us smiling at him. He turned a deep red, whispered something in Beth's ear, took her hand and started to walk to a desolate section of the park. Suddenly he stopped, and turned toward us with a look of puzzlement on his face. He did a double take, as did Beth, and they moved on. They were obviously shaken by what they had seen.

It was as if a movie was being filmed, and the director and screenwriter knew exactly how to capture the plot twist in a slow point of view zoom in. As Jericho and Beth moved on, our vision was not deterred, and we saw what they had seen.

"What the fuck?" was all I could utter.

"I don't know, Jason, maybe your girlfriend is going to run away with her counselor," Oliver softly said, still in shock.

There, in the woods was Rachel tenderly kissing her counselor. Their hands were all over each other. I couldn't move. Ben jumped off the bench and swiftly made his way over to them, trying not to attract attention as he approached the couple. He jerked Rachel away from the counselor who then in turn, started to pummel Ben. I ran over to Rachel and helped her off the ground. Ben kept pushing the counselor away from her camper.

"Stop it!" Rachel cried. I don't know if she was scared, embarrassed or mortified.

"What's the matter with you?" her counselor shouted at Ben

"What's the matter with me? I'm not the one kissing my camper," Ben screamed.

"She wanted to learn how to kiss her boyfriend,... and that's you!" the counselor said, pointing her finger at me. She looked at me with such disdain because I was the preferred suitor.

"Oh please... don't throw that bullshit excuse at me." Ben told her.

"Go ahead and ask her," the counselor demanded, never backing down, going face to face with Ben.

All Ben could do was turn to Rachel, and he mouthed the question, "Did you ask her?"

"She... she's the one who suggested it," Rachel said meekly

"And you didn't say No!... so what does that tell you?" the counselor screamed.

Ben thought about that for a moment. He stepped back and studied Rachel, and then her counselor and you could just sense when he finally made a decision.

"Get away from her. I don't want to see you anywhere near her," Ben decreed, pointing toward the corner of Ghost Town. We watched as the counselor was banished from our presence and slunk away in defiance.

With one last gaze she mouthed, "I love you," to my thirteen-year-old girlfriend. Was she my girlfriend or was she not my girlfriend? I was so lost.

Ben put his arms around Rachel, and led her away as she sobbed quietly. He was going to find her group leader, and I couldn't help but wonder how he was going to explain what happened

"I won't tell anyone about this, but you have to promise me that you won't either," I said to Oliver.

"I'm still confused at what I saw. Why would two girls be kissing?" Oliver asked naively.

"That's just what I'm talking about, Oliver. Don't say a word about it. It never happened."

Oliver shook his head in agreement, even though I knew it would be years before he understood the magnitude of the moment.

26

The next morning, awakening to deep, ominous, black billowy clouds amidst a light charcoal sky, we discovered that Rachel's counselor was fired.

During breakfast, with Color War a week away, politics raised its ugly head. Every group, every camper took a side and campaigned for the counselor they wanted to serve as an officer during Color War. Every meal included a chant, accompanied by the banging of spoons and forks on the tables.

Mickey Hardon led a cheer for Asa and The Brain led a cheer for Samson. Of course there was always some smart ass who would always start a chant for a beloved past General named Ciccollo who hadn't been in camp for years. It amazed me at how tradition echoed so strongly at this camp. I later found out that Samson had slipped The Brain a twenty dollar bill to create some excitement for his run at being a General. Surprisingly, half the camp responded.

Color War always broke out two weeks before the end of camp, at the beginning of the seventh week. Color War was one of the high points of the summer. We're talking about one week of premeditated hatred and competition that was fed by the rabid furor of counselors who were harboring grandiose delusions of power. The camp would be split into two, usually the colors of the camp. At Camp Tonkawa there would be the White Team and the Blue Team.

However, the cheering stopped as the girls' camp walked in for breakfast. I noticed that the girl counselors were all whispering amongst themselves, giggling like little girls with a secret. In particular Asa and Samson studied this procession with more interest than usual.

After breakfast, Mickey Hardon returned from the infirmary. He bounded into the bunk, brimming with a secret he was about to scream to the world. Seems that the entire camp had discovered the supposed romantic interlude.

"I always knew your girlfriend was a Lesbo... no way any girl can dig you!" Mickey Hardon sneered in my face. "Did everyone hear that, this shmuck's girlfriend was caught kissing her counselor. She's a lesbian."

I turned red, I clenched my fists, but I didn't attack. Jericho kept shifting his eyes in Hardon's direction, silently begging me to hit him. But I couldn't. I didn't. Was it worth getting into a fight over a girl. Maybe I wasn't in love with Rachel. I was wondering what love was anyway.

However, I would forever remember that moment, as it would forever crush my illusion of love. Rachel was my first puppy love and it crumbled into a sweet memory with little emotion to follow.

First Call blew over the loudspeaker, and nobody in the bunk moved. We were like two gunfighters afraid to whip out our pistols, while the rest of the bunk stood on like silent townspeople. Ben entered the bunk, and the situation was diffused immediately. There was a deep exhale, like a silent but deadly fart. The bunk came alive and started to move about. Mickey Hardon made sure he bumped his shoulder into my chest, but I didn't take the bait.

Just as we took to the porch for the first period, the rains came. It started with a thunderclap that shook the bunk, and dimmed the lights for an instant. The heavens opened and what was the faint light of the day turned dingy. Rain pelted the camp like bullets from above, exploding on the ground and kicking up dirt. We threw our gloves back on our beds and plopped down for what looked like an extended morning off.

It was a deluge. Rain hammered the roof of our bunk. I sat on the porch, on the boot box, as water cascaded off the eaves. I felt like I was safely ensconced in a sheltered pool looking out through a waterfall.

I learned to love the evening thunderstorms, and the way you could see the storm approach the camp. First you saw a soft glow in the distance, a shadow of light flickering above the trees. Then the pine trees started to wiggle and shimmer with the sound of a cotton candy wind tickling their branches. Suddenly there would be a flash of lightning, followed by the tremor of thunder. The wind would pick up in intensity forcing the screen doors of every bunk to dance wildly if not secured. Storms during the day seemed to just explode upon you by surprise.

More lightning. I began to count, waiting for the next explosion of thunder. It was something my grandmother taught me. You could measure how far away the approaching storm was by counting after seeing the flash of lightning. The count ended when one heard the drum roll of thunder. If the count was to five, then the storm was calculated to be five miles away.

The rain was so heavy that the ground couldn't saturate the torrent. It pooled at first and then began to run off in rivers, heading down the hill toward the lake.

Harris joined me on the boot box. We saw a flash of lightning and then Harris was counting under his breath until we both jumped with the next eruption of thunder.

"The center of the storm is still four miles away," Harris told me.

"My grandmother taught me the same thing. She was more like a mother to me, but she died about five years ago."

"You know, you should have belted Hardon. I was waiting for that. Maybe Rachel was naive. Maybe she really wanted to learn how to kiss for your sake. I hear girls do that occasionally, practice kissing on each other."

"I just don't care."

"So what... what do you care about?" Harris suddenly asked. He was beyond angry. "What the fuck do you care about, Flanken? You don't care that those assholes in there have made assholes of you, me, and Oliver all summer? You don't care that they stripped us, and dropped us naked in the woods? You don't care that the counsel-ors are jerks and are making our lives miserable? You don't care that the bunk is making fun of a girl you like? What the fuck do you care about?"

"I don't care about anything."

"Why not?"

I paused for a moment to think about the question nobody had ever asked me before.

"Because nobody ever cared about me. My grandparents tried to spoil me, but my parents didn't allow it. Now they're dead. My parents ignore me. I'm like a ping pong ball. I ask my mother for help with homework and she says go ask my dad, and my dad won't take his face out of the paper and says for me to go ask my mom. I make my own breakfast, lunch and dinner. I'm not allowed to have friends over, and I live all the way out in the suburbs on an estate, isolated. Nobody ever wants to come over because their parents are jealous of my parents...and nobody wants their sons or daughters subjected to my mother who's always walking around in sexy, skimpy things. You know, my parents have a lot of friends, and not one of those couples have kids.... so maybe I was a mistake. I know they wish I was never born. You turn into a weed when no-body cares for you... you just grow, and do no good for anyone, and you're ignored until you're pulled out of the ground."

"I care. You've sort of been there for me," Harris said.

"The summer will be over soon, and we won't see each other anymore and we won't have to see the rest of the bunk anymore," I told him. "So why get into a fight?"

"Sometime's it's good to get into a fight. To express anger. Maybe you shouldn't be getting high so much. It dulls your senses."

"You seemed to enjoy it too..."

Harris flashed an angry look as he turned to me, his wart staring me straight in the face.

"My mother's dying and I'm not home to share her last days with her. Yeah, sometimes I can't take all this fucking craziness. I beg my father every day to bring me home, but he says I'm better off up here.

What does he know? Why does he make that decision for me? I'm never ever going to forgive him for this. So yeah... I appreciated getting high with you because I was having a really shitty day, and I can't stop thinking about my mother... and I can't handle these assholes anymore, and I wanted to get kicked out of camp, and I just wish you had given Hardon a punch to the fucking head and knocked him out."

Lightning flashed. We counted till three and then the thunder.

"Storm's moving fast," I whispered.

"I don't know if I ever thanked you for giving me your seat on the bus coming up here. I knew I just took it, but I wanted to see my mom before we pulled out."

"No problem," and then I began to laugh. Harris looked at me and shrugged his shoulders, wanting to know what was so funny.

"You're right. I was a bit pissed, but that's the way I am. I have created a life where things don't really mean much to me. I mean... what was the big deal? I'm like a toilet, Harris. I take shit and just flush it away."

"Well then, maybe there's a "who." Who do you care about?" he asked again.

"I don't know what caring means."

"You know what it means... think about who you have shared time with this summer."

"I guess I used to care about Rachel... but now I don't know. Jericho..." and then I paused and looked at Harris. "And I guess I sort of... somewhat... care about you."

"What about Oliver?"

We looked at each other for a second and then broke out laughing.

"I feel sorry for Oliver. Does that mean I care about him?" I asked.

"It sort of does."

"Then there's your answer."

Lightning, and a count to two followed by rolling thunder. The trees were swaying like a hula dancer's hips, and you couldn't see the HCO shack through the downpour. We were being sprayed with rain that was now falling horizontally, so we walked back inside.

The bunk was dark, all lights already turned off. Blankets were hung over the windows to deaden the lightning and thunder. Everyone was asleep. The rain, a heavy breakfast, six weeks of activity ... it drained us. It was a good morning for sleeping.

A 'rain day' in camp is spent sleeping and trying to rejuvenate ones soul. You may play cards, or read, but most just sleep. When it rains more than a day and a half you start to become stir-crazy, and that's when shit happens. Mickey Hardon and The Brain were sniping at each other, and The Mayor and Hooky were getting into constant fights. Finally the boredom was broken when Ben jumped down from his bed and made an announcement.

"Let's go! Get on your raincoats, rubbers or boots because we're heading up to the Social Hall".

We welcomed the opportunity to get out of the bunk, even though it meant we had to play Bingo.

On the third day of rain we went into town, a bus taking us to Honesdale. We spent the morning at a bowling alley. Some of us bowled, some just ate candy and burgers from the bar, and the rest of us played pinball games. In the afternoon they showed a movie in the Social Hall, but you could barely make out the images on the screen. It was so muggy and the air so stale that they had to keep the doors of the Social Hall open, which brought the roar of the rain in and that drowned out the dialogue.

By the end of the third day of rain the verbal abuse hurtled into toxic territory. Not that this was anything new for the summer, but it was sporadic up to now. Suddenly, like the rain, it was a torrent of insults hurtling toward Harris, Oliver, and yours truly. Ben had left the bunk to talk to Chick about something, so he was absent when it started. Bugsy, The Mayor, Hooky, The Brain and Mickey Hardon spewed the trash as if rehearsed.

"Hey Dickless, why don't you just become a girl."

"Hey Oliver, you got big tits for a boy....you sure you aren't a girl?"

"Look whose girlfriend prefers a girl over him? You sure you're a boy?"

"We're going to kill you tonight, Harris, don't go to sleep."

"Oliver, we're going to suffocate you slowly, sprinkle dust all over you."

"Jason probably doesn't even know who his true father is? Your mother looks like a whore."

"Three eyes... Harris has three eyes."

"Maybe we'll roast Oliver. He looks like a marshmallow, so let's roast him tonight. We already got his turtle."

"Boy, Jason, I'd love to fuck your mother."

And still nothing from me. I tried to ignore everything. And no defense for my mother... there was none... or I didn't care anymore.

The fourth day of rain, and Chick allowed us to wander onto the porches after breakfast. The counselors decided to play Jock football. This was our entertainment. The level of the lake was starting to rise, and would soon flow over the embankment. Samson and Asa didn't play, as they were afraid they would hurt themselves. The slippery grass was so saturated that every step created explosions of water, popping like pimples filled with pus.

Counselors from most of the bunks poured out onto the lawn dressed in only jock straps. It was funny to see so many bare-assed men. Ben showed amazing dexterity for a little man. Lenny, wore his shorts because he was embarrassed to be seen in only his jock. He was always trying to charge into Ben but Ben was too quick. Lenny would miss Ben, flying through the air in a belly flop and explode onto the grass. He looked like a beached whale.

We wanted to play. We wanted the freedom to run around in the rain naked except for a jock strap, but none of us really owned jock straps. We wanted to slide on the grass like seals. The entire boys' camp sat on their porches and cheered on their counselors. Then Heshie waddled out into the middle of the campus with Scott sheltering him under a colorful golf umbrella. He was the referee, and the game finally took on an organized look.

Twenty minutes into the game Joe came charging down from

Grayson Hall without an umbrella. He commanded everyone to get back into their respective bunks. The game was over. Heshie tried to reason with Joe, but lost the battle.

Heshie started to kick mud at Joe, like a baseball manager kicking dirt at an umpire. Suddenly Joe started kicking mud at Heshie, and they didn't stop until they were both caked with oozing dirt. Then they started laughing and hugged each other. Then Heshie took the umbrella from Scott and he and Joe walked back towards Grayson Hall as friends.

"Joe seems a bit more crazed these days," Ben said as he walked toward us, a huge smile spread across his face. His body was a messy cupcake of dirt.

"Why do you think so?" Jericho asked.

"Ha...you name it... from the cucumber incident to the realization that he might have a problem on girls side, and now the upcoming rock festival down the road."

Ben shook himself like a dog coming in from the rain and mud flew all over the porch. Jericho shot me a quick smile when he heard mention of the rock festival. We would soon break out of this camp and we could barely contain our excitement.

"Or... it could be that someone tipped him off on what people are calling his camp. You know that big CT emblazoned on our counselor shirts? The one's we're forced to wear to Friday night services?"

"Yes.. Camp Tonkawa,.." Harris said.

"Camp Cocktease... all the other camps refer to us as Camp Cocktease because of our CT initials. It's silly, it's not justified, and it's disgusting."

"What's a cocktease?" Harris asked, breaking the silence.

Ben just deflated in front of us, letting out a long sigh, and then a laugh.

And then he explained what a cock tease was, and I slowly realized how much I was learning this summer about girls and sex. Things I'd never learn at home from my parents.

"Well, .. anyway,... that was great! Where else but camp can you play jock football and not be arrested for lewdness," Ben said as he marched to the back of the bunk to shower.

On the afternoon of the fourth day of rain we were told to put on our raincoats, and to slip on rubbers or boots over our sneakers. We headed up to the Social Hall. This was the first time in all my years of camping when one really did need rain boots or rubbers. Heshie, Scott and a few other waiters were sitting on the stage awaiting our entrance. Their legs dangled over the edge of the stage. They had shit-eating grins on their faces.

"What are you smiling at?" I asked Scott after I discarded my raincoat.

"You'll see."

It turned into an afternoon of relay races, but not your typical ones. These were slightly askew. Heshie was the master of ceremonies, and he had a different outlook on these things.

In our first relay race we had to carry watermelons greased in Vaseline across the hall and hand them to our teammates. Not your normal beanbag race, and yet the next race found us picking partners and standing on opposite ends of the Social Hall. We had to stick a carrot between our legs and hop across the length of the Social Hall without letting the carrot drop. We had to exchange the carrot with the next man in line without using our hands then they had to hop back. I kid you not.

The final race was the "Dizzy Lizzy." We were split up by bunks, and half the bunk remained near the stage while the other half walked to the opposite side of the Social Hall. Each team was handed a baseball bat, and with one hand firmly holding the barrel of the bat to the floor, we were told to put our foreheads on the knob . When Heshie blew his whistle one team member at a time had to spin around the bat ten times, and then try to make it over to the other side of the Social Hall to tag his teammate. It was nearly impossible to make it in a straight line. The ten spins caused us to be dizzy beyond normal and everyone stumbled to the right or to the left till they got their bearings straight.

When this race was completed, Heshie blew his whistle and told us to form a circle. We all obeyed. We fell under his spell.

We watched as Scott took a long thick white rope out of a bag, and then he turned his back on us as Heshie helped him tie something to the end of the rope. When he turned around we saw an old, thickly padded, boxing glove dangling at the end of the line.

"What we have here is a little game about life. I play this with my basketball team in Brooklyn," Heshie announced. "You all see the boxing glove on the end of this rope. What I'm going to do is twirl this around, slowly at first. You will jump over the rope, and if it touches you, you're out. Last one standing is the winner."

Seemed simple at first but because there were so many of us in the circle there were a lot of poorly timed leaps and our ranks grew thin quickly. Within five minutes the circle of forty something boys was narrowed down to just ten of us. Mickey Hardon, The Brain and I were the only ones standing from our bunk. Jericho was in a different world now that he hadn't gotten high for four straight days, and he mistimed an earlier leap and tripped over the cord.

"Now it's going to get interesting," Heshie announced. He looked at Chick, who only smiled and gave him the thumbs up.

With the rest of the group surrounding us, cheering on their friends, Heshie started to twirl the rope faster than before. At first the boxing glove anchored the rope to the floor and it was easy to jump over it as it passed. However, as the last few standing started tripping over the rope the circle grew even smaller. With less people in the circle it became apparent that Heshie was now able to twirl the rope faster. The boxing glove began to rise off the floor.

Down went one camper after another. It was getting harder to jump high enough to get over the cord, and suddenly there were only three of us standing. I looked at The Brain and at Mickey Hardon and just knew I couldn't lose to them. I just couldn't.

I could hear Harris and Jericho cheering me on, but the rest of the group was clearly behind The Brain and Hardon. Of course they were egged on by Asa and Samson. I studied Heshie, and for just the briefest glimpse, I thought I saw him wink at me.

The three of us were spread out in a triangle, with Heshie in the middle. He started to slowly twirl the cord with the boxing glove scraping the floor. Then the rope started to pick up speed. The boxing glove rose about six inches off the ground and as it approached I knew I would be able to make the jump and I cleared the rope by inches. As it passed me, I realized that the velocity of the boxing glove increased, rising off the ground another five inches and caught The Brain squarely in the balls. He went down like a car smashing into a brick wall, screaming and clutching his nuts as the group went wild with laughter. Lenny and Spanky carried The Brain off to the side. They told him to breathe deep as he wailed in pain. He held onto his balls hoping they were still there.

"Now we have two," Scott announced as he tightened the glove to the end of the cord, and handed it back to Heshie.

Heshie started to twirl the rope and the glove skidded across the floor in a radius that made quick passes past the two of us. Mickey Hardon jumped, and then the glove came quickly toward me and I jumped. With no interference the glove now rose a few more inches off the floor and Hardon danced over the glove. As the glove flew higher into the air, I knew I wasn't going to be able to jump over it, and out of the corner of my eye I saw Hardon gloating. He felt he had this won. However, instead of jumping over the rapidly rising boxing glove, I ducked under it. Fell prone to the floor. It caught Mickey Hardon completely by surprise. He turned at the last second to see a boxing glove come flying out of the air. It landed a haymaker directly into the side of his face. Without exaggeration Mickey Hardon flew about ten feet off the ground and landed on his ass, completely knocked out.

"And we have a winner!" Heshie announced as he raised my hand in a victorious salute. Samson walked over to Hardon to check if he was breathing. He slapped Hardon's face lightly. Lenny dumped a canteen of water over Hardon's head, and this helped to bring him back to life. "Who kissed me?" was all Hardon could ask as he was assisted to his feet, and had to be carried back to the bunk.

Five days of rain. There was a short break of sunshine, and one game of softball was played in the morning but the clouds rolled in again with heavy thunderstorms. Swim was washed out, literally. It was impossible to get to the waterfront. The lake had swelled beyond its banks and crept up the hill of boys' camp. It almost engulfed the HCO shack.

"Been here ten years, and this has never happened before," Asa claimed.

The entire camp was waiting on the porches of their bunks, waiting for lunch call.

According to Oliver's watch we were five minutes late for first call. Lunch at least separated the boredom from the tedium.

"That lake has never risen above its bank, and look at it. If it rains anymore, the HCO shack will float away." Samson added.

Suddenly, through the haze of rain we saw a sight I would never forget. Slowly emerging through the fog there appeared the newly painted red war canoe. That old withered face of the woman who smoked the corn cob pipe sat stiffly in the bow of canoe like a wooden figurehead. You could barely see her face, as it was hidden under a broad-brimmed yellow rain hat. But you could see that pipe jutting out of her mouth, and she puffed clouds of smoke into the droplets that pinged off the swollen lake.

Then you saw our waiter, Scott, sitting behind her, stroking the canoe from the left side. He was dressed in an Indian headband with one feather, and his naked chest painted in gold stripes like a shield of bones.

In the middle of the war canoe stood Ed Barnett, sheltered from the rain by a rainbow colored golf umbrella. He looked like Washington crossing the Delaware.

The same man who painted the war canoes was paddling from the stern. The rising shoreline had separated and isolated the kitchen staff's headquarters from the Mess Hall. The war canoe was used to transport the chefs to the Mess Hall, and now it was slowly gliding toward the HCO Shack.

Ed Barnett jumped out of the canoe and sank into the supersaturated grounds. Each step sucked his feet deep into the mud, when finally on his last step his left sneaker succumbed to the murky grip of earth. Ed reached into the ground, pulling his sneaker out of the muck, and then jumped into the HCO. The canoe bobbed in the rain, waiting to take Ed Barnett back to Mess Hall. The old lady sat stoically in the rain, smoking her pipe.

"Okay, gentlemen, sorry for the delay. Let's walk to the Mess Hall. Do not walk across the campus. Make sure you're wearing your raincoats, rubbers or boots. Chick, take your group up the road in front of Senior Hall, and follow the road to the Mess Hall. No one is to cut across campus."

Ed Barnett turned off the loudspeaker, walked out of the HCO shack with both his sneakers in one hand and the umbrella in the other, and carefully made his way back to the canoe.

For the return trip Ed Barnett kneeled down in the middle, mindful of not rocking the canoe.

Ben had taken Harris to Grayson Hall for his weekly call home when suddenly Asa charged into the bunk. The rain ran off his perfect nose in a laminar flow. He was raging. Mickey Hardon had no chance as Asa charged across the bunk and threw him against the back wall, where he slid down onto The Brain's bed like a wet rag.

"What the fuck is the matter with you, you little shit?" Asa shouted, as he started to bang Hardon's head against the wall.

Mickey Hardon could only utter guttural nonsense as Asa continued to bang his head against the wall. When Hardon looked like he was going to pass out, Asa started to punch his arms. Ben didn't flinch. Nobody moved as Asa pummeled the camper's arms.

"Don't you know how to keep your stupid little trap shut?" the counselor screamed as he started to wail on Hardon's skinny thighs.

Mickey Hardon cried out in pain but never backed down as Asa threw him against the wall again.

"If I ever hear you utter another word on this I will come back and kill you," Asa screamed as he pounded Pinhead's chest, creating a hollow sound that reverberated around the bunk. "And if anyone else in this bunk says anything I'll rip your fucking nuts off ya, and stuff them down your mouth!"

Mickey Hardon sat on his bed whimpering as Asa turned and stormed out. He actually seemed paralyzed, both out of fear and from the pounding he took.

"What was that all about?" Bugsy asked.

The Brain only shook his head, signaling that the topic was buried and never to be brought up again.

"Do you know?" I whispered to Jericho. We were sitting on my bed and this incident didn't end our card game. I had hung a blanket from the top of the double decker to give us some privacy.

"Hardon saw Asa with a hot Super Senior girl sitting on his lap on the softball field bleachers and made up some story."

"The one with the nice tits?" I asked, because not all Super Senior girls had nice tits. They were just fifteen years old.

"No wonder that jerk is scared... I mean if it was true that would be big trouble. Would ruin his life for sure," Jericho said.

Mickey Hardon curled up in his bed, and put his pillow over his head to drown out reality.

The thunderstorms ended right before rest hour was over, but the heavy rains continued. I was on canteen duty, and had to wear a poncho over my raincoat. I covered my sneakers with two sets of rubbers. It was a liberated feeling walking in the rain, with no parent shouting out that I was crazy. Even though the August evenings were cold the rain brought on a warm front that made it seem as comfortable as a soaking bath. Heshie danced by, sheltered under his multi-colored golf umbrella. He couldn't recognize me as I was hidden under the poncho. I picked up the canteen order and danced back to the bunk, avoiding the ever growing community of pond-sized puddles.

Our mail was delivered to us at the end of rest hour, and my streak was not broken. No letters. No postcards. I hated this moment, and always envied everyone else who received a letter of some sort from home. Someone was thinking of them, but I was a void. I took out my Junior Life Saving booklet and studied it for a few minutes.

"Listen to this," Jericho said as he landed on my bed with a letter in his hand. There was so much excitement in his voice, and yet he had to lean in to me to whisper what he had read. "That rock concert is eight days away. Today is August 7th, and the first day of the festival is August 15th. They're calling it Woodstock. My parents will drive by the camp the morning of the 16th, the second day of Woodstock. We'll be waiting on the road and we'll just jump in."

"How are we going to get away from everyone?" I asked.

"It's easy. We'll be in the middle of Color War. Nobody will miss us, and when they do, we'll be long gone."

"You know they won't let us back into camp for this," I reminded Jericho

"So what...? We have only two weeks of camp left. Are you scared? Come on, this is supposed to be fantastic and I want you by my side to share it."

"I'm sure it will be fine."

Chick walked into the bunk, shaking water off his umbrella and getting everyone wet. He purposefully went over to my corner and he constantly flicked his umbrella open and closed so Oliver and I were sprayed with water.

"Hey, why are you doing that?" Oliver cried out.

"Ehhhh.... accept it. If I pick on you it's because I like you."

"Then maybe don't like me that much," Oliver told him. But he was laughing and in a good mood.

"Now listen to me. You have three minutes to get into your bathing suits, and to get on the porch. Wear a pair of sneakers. No shirts, just your bathing suits." Chick announced.

"What for?" The Brain asked.

"You'll see. Now move, move move," Chick shouted as he walked out of our bunk and into Bunk 17 to shout the same instructions.

Within minutes the entire group stood on our respective porches in just swimsuits and sneakers. We watched Chick parade out onto the campus, sheltered under his umbrella.

"Boys, I want you all out here in the rain, lined up in a single line across the grass."

We were bulls unleashed for a running. We nearly stampeded over each other as we scrambled to form a line behind Chick. It stretched from near our bunk and almost reached the HCO shack. The rain felt so refreshing, and just being out of the bunk revived our spirits. Chick waited till we were all primed. The entire boys' camp moved to their porches to watch.

"You've got fifteen minutes to make as many runs as you can. Charge!!!!!"

And when Chick pointed toward the body of water that used to be the bottom of the hill but now was part of the lake, we knew exactly what he was giving us permission to do. We broke out of our line in a mad dash like the start of the Le Mans race.

Trying to pick up speed on such wet ground was difficult, but we plowed down the hill and did belly flops and slides, skidding like hockey pucks down the slippery slope. We dissolved like Alka Seltzer into the swollen lake.

We were little children innocently splashing around in the rain. I'm sure there were some campers who heard the echo of our mothers, berating us to come in out of the rain. Sliding on the slick grass we would hydroplane like water bugs until we were submerged. Some decided not to make another run, but instead enjoyed the novelty of swimming in what was once the bottom of the hill, but was now a part of the lake.

It was exhilarating, wild, momentous. Five days spent pent up in a bunk were suddenly forgotten as we screamed wildly in one run after another. We moved even farther up the hill to get a better running start, and with the entire camp cheering us on, we made mad dashes down the hill. We were one with water. Water soaking us from the sky, and then cloaking us in a wet cocoon.

"One more run!" Chick shouted.

He made us all line up together, and we waited for the stragglers who had to swim back up the hill. When we were all together, panting and reveling in our lust of freedom from the confines of our bunks, he pointed to the lake and shouted "CHARGE."

And we did. Forty or so boys making one final dive onto the saturated grass, and sliding into the lake. We all knew that this would probably be the only time we would ever experience such reckless abandon with the knowledge that there would be no repercussions to follow.

Jericho and I plunged into the pregnant lake and swam underwater for a few yards. We surfaced at the same time. We looked at each other and couldn't stop laughing. I think that was the first time in my life that I ever felt such joy. We swam back up the hill, until the water's edge finally forced us to walk, and we all gathered around Chick. I glimpsed Oliver standing on our porch clapping and smiling and as giddy as we all felt at that moment.

"I feel sorry for Oliver, that he can't be a part of this," Harris said.

He had joined Jericho and me on the periphery of the group. I looked at Jericho and he looked at me, and we knew what we had to do. We broke away and ran toward the bunk, every step splashing mud onto our bodies. Oliver was standing there, with a strange look on his face, wondering why we were approaching him. We jumped onto the porch and grabbed him, and carried him off the porch.

"Come on Oliver, you have to try this," I screamed as Oliver protested.

"You know I can't."

"Stop saying you can't, and do something. Feel the rain. Feel the water. Be one with the water." Jericho had Oliver in a head lock and I had him by his feet. Harris joined me in carrying Oliver over to the group.

"It's time you started living a little," Jericho screamed.

"I can't, I may get sick," he whined as I let his feet drop to the ground. I ended up grabbing Oliver under one arm pit and Jericho had him by the other.

There was no traction on the wet ground for Oliver to plant his feet, so he slid along with us as we carried him toward the group. They parted ways, and we brought Oliver straight up to Chick.

"One more run for Oliver," Jericho begged.

"What do you say, Oliver? We can't force you," Chick told him.

"I'm scared."

There were some in the group who started calling him chicken, and other nonsensical derogatory remarks.

"Then I'll tell you what..." Chick answered, as he closed his umbrella, and let the rain beat down on him. "... You and I will do this together. What do you say?"

Chick took off his white t-shirt. His trademark nipples didn't wither in the rain, but stood stronger than ever. The group and then the entire camp started shouting "Chick, Chick, Chick..." and we looked on in wonder as this old man with the bowed legs that were covered in grotesque varicose veins, took Oliver by the hand.

Neither of them could run so it was a slow jog as they floated down the hill together, hand in hand. Chick jumped into the air, landing on his ass, and pulling Oliver down onto the wet ground with him. They slid into the rising lake, and disappeared for a few seconds.

Then Chick emerged, with his glasses still plastered to his face. He reached into the water and lifted a smiling and now confident Oliver up to his feet. They stood in waist high water, raising each other's hands like champions being saluted. Chick assisted Oliver in trudging through the water and up the hill where the entire group gave them a rousing cheer. It was just what we needed to defeat the boredom that had infiltrated our souls for the last five days.

27

The monsoon season seemed to disappear after our afternoon of mud sliding. Regular activity resumed for a few days, and then I was rocked by two explosions.

One would be the breaking of Color War, something I'd experienced before. Yet, on the afternoon of August 9th....

It was Free Play, and I was safely ensconced in our little cove with Jericho and Harris, who had now become a regular. All the rain had kept us from our nightly sessions for almost a week, so it felt good to be back on a regular schedule. I just passed the joint to Harris when we heard a twig crack from the weight of someone approaching. Harris panicked and threw the joint into the lake, much to the annoyance of Jericho who gave chasing the sinking joint a momentary thought.

We held our breaths collectively with thoughts of being caught. I'm sure Jericho and Harris had the same joyous dream of immediate expulsion and our being sent home. I must have been very high because I stood up and I offered my hands out to whomever was going to materialize through the bushes. Just slap the handcuffs on me and drag me away.

I almost took a shit when the Brain appeared.

He just stood there eyeing us. Then what looked like a smile slowly spread across his face. We weren't sure if he was smiling or not because his lips were tucked tightly against his teeth and it looked more like a demonic sneer.

"I knew I smelled it. Been smelling it for a long time. I just caught on to you disappearing during Free Play. So I studied you for about a week, of course not during all the rain... thought it was fun to see you crave this shit while we suffered cabin fever... so are you going to bogart that joint or may I have some?"

"What, you're not going to turn us in?" Harris asked, his mouth drooping to a gasped "O".

"Only if you don't share," said The Brain.

Jericho took another fat joint out of the pocket of his jean shorts, lit it and handed it to the Brain.

"I didn't know you smoked," Jericho said.

"Oh fuck man... why do you think I'm like I am during the summer? Look at me man... my mind races at the speed of light. I can't keep one thought in my head for a second.. yup, that's a good one.. Nobel prize thought, but on to the next one... You fucking guys make fun of my eyes... Yeah.. they twitch because I'm always thinking of things.. and I get mean when my mind races.. . so it was all so strange... One day I had to go to the bathroom in school... I was taking my life into my hands by going to the bathroom during school because everyone was always getting high in there... Suddenly I realized that I was able to concentrate when I returned to my classroom. I went again the next day during a different class and the same thing happened.. everything was lucid...I was getting a secondary high of sorts... So I started to smoke during the school year and yeah... everything slows down... and I can think like a normal person.. and I'm not a fucking creep....and my grades have gone through the roof!"

The Brain had taken enough tokes on the joint that he had smoked it halfway through before he offered it back to me.

"Yo, Flanken... you're not that bad of a guy... and I knew you were on to me when you saw Kafka on my bed hidden under my comic books."

"So why are you still friends with Mickey Hardon?" I asked.

"Hey, I'm not perfect. Give me a break. We've been friends forever and like I said if I can't get high, my brain is scrambled.... I'm really not that fucked up... or maybe I am but ... now this is good shit..."

The Brain had taken the joint back from me and finished it off. From that afternoon on he was a transformed Brain... using his wits for the good of mankind, and we found him to be brilliantly funny... and for one day Hardon was at a loss for words as he observed a new friend in a different light.

August 10th was a humid morning, the air thick with moisture that kept the grounds damp. The Brain greeted us with a smile and stood next to us at line up. He talked to us. This drove Hardon up a wall.

We returned from breakfast and Ben had what looked like a newspaper tucked under his arm.

"Grabbed it off of the owner's table when he wasn't looking," Ben told us.

While we cleaned the bunk he sat outside on the porch reading the paper, totally engrossed in the article. When he came back into the bunk he threw the newspaper into the garbage can, sighed, and went into the back room to take one of his famous triple "S's"...

"What's a triple S?" Jericho asked one morning.

"Shit, shower and shave. Nothing more holy, outside of sex in the morning, than for a man to sanitize his soul with a good morning dump, then physically clean himself off in the shower, followed by a hot shave. You're ready to face the world, and you feel like a new man."

So while Ben was in the back working on his "Triple S," Jericho grabbed the paper out of the garbage can and walked out onto the porch. I sat next to him on the boot box reading the story about the murder of an actress named Sharon Tate.

"One weird summer," was all Jericho mumbled.

Regular activity had melted tensions and the animosities that had grown to an explosive level during the five days of rain slid away. We were now officially into the last two weeks of camp, and the aftermath of the rains stayed with us. Every day we had to dry off the basketball courts that seemed to ooze water. When we played softball we watched ground balls burn holes through the infield as the ball hydroplaned across the grass, but by the end of every softball game, the Clinchers were so saturated with water that they felt more like balls of lead. Hits were hard to come by.

August 10th saw Abner Dingle ride up to our bunk on his tractor, the apparatus to cut the grass was attached to the rear. A wasp nest was growing in the corner of Bunk 17 and we had been complaining about it for a week. Abner was there to save the day. He jumped off his tractor, leaving the engine running to the tune of heavy duty put...put... put.. put...and he grabbed what looked like a large stick with a cloth wrapped around the end.

"Morning, boys," he said with that toothless grin. "You need all to step inside your bunks, or get off the porches and move far away."

I walked off the porch and stared in amazement as Abner doused the cloth at the end of the stick with gasoline, and lit it. He then took the blazing torch and approached the corner of the bunk, lunging at the wasp nest. The nest caught fire, but not before Abner was stung three or four times, and yet the man didn't even flinch. As the wasp nest burned, Abner knocked it to the floor of the porch. He continued to jab it with the torch. Within seconds the wasp nest was a simmering pulp, and Abner was stamping out the flame. He took a bandana out of his back pocket and wiped away the sweat from his forehead.

"Doesn't that hurt?" someone shouted from inside Bunk 17.

"For a little while... but nothing too bad," Abner answered. He hopped back onto his tractor and began to cut the grass.

"Chinese food for lunch," Jericho said as Abner drove away.

It was camp lore, but for some reason it was prescient. The lawns were mowed three times during the summer and the last two times we had Chicken Chow Mein for lunch. Kosher Chicken Chow Mein consisted of thin pieces of chicken immersed in a gooey green substance thrown on top of the provided sticky rice. It really sucked, but after six or seven weeks of a camp diet; you become immune to the taste of camp cuisine.

Jericho was on a different planet these last few days. He had received some letters from his brother telling him not to worry, that he wasn't seeing any action, and then there was the secretive countdown to the music festival. Every day he opened another letter from his parents with specific instructions, including the fact that he might as well carry with him all of his rolling papers and grass, and what other valuables he had since there was no way he was going to be allowed back into camp. Of course, this sort of left me hanging because I had nobody else to share this with, seeing as how my parents didn't give a shit. Besides... with only thirteen days of camp left I still hadn't received a letter.

We hadn't had a social in a week, and I hadn't seen Rachel since Ghost Town. In the glimpses we caught of each other she smiled and waved, and everything seemed to be okay. The murmurings of some forbidden love affair between a 13-year-old camper and her lesbian counselor were rumors that were fed by Asa and Samson. And the two asshole counselors continued to tease me with nasty comments.

"You are such a pussy,... what kind of a pussy are you? Get in there and get a rebound!" Words of wisdom from Samson as he refereed that morning's basketball game.

"Don't you know, he wants to be a pussy," Asa shouted from the other side of the basketball court... "after all that's all his girlfriend wants.. pussy."

No matter how hard I was hit when going up for a rebound, or how severely I was pummeled under the boards, the foul was always called on me. I was called a pussy every time. If I made a shot they would blow their whistles and wipe away the basket with some bogus foul. Finally I couldn't take it anymore, and as I dribbled up the court I threw the ball at Asa's head. He deflected it easily.

"And you throw like a pussy too," Asa shouted as he hit me with a technical foul.

I wanted to charge Asa, but Samson grabbed me by the back of my shirt and threw me to the ground. Then he kicked me out of the game. I stormed back to the bunk trying to hide my tears. It's hard enough to stand up to the bullying from your peers but when supposed adults start to pick on you... man that's when life falls apart.

Walking into the Mess Hall for lunch I realized I couldn't wait to get home, and I couldn't wait to sneak out to this Woodstock thing. Most of the counselors were talking about Woodstock, but Joe Geisinger held a meeting earlier that morning as we assembled to raise the flag. You could hear him screaming at the counselors that in "no uncertain terms" would anyone be allowed out of camp to attend the festival.

We said our usual prayer before eating, and instead of the waiters barging out of the kitchen we watched as girls' camp entered a bit earlier than usual. When the girls were seated, the waiters appeared on cue with…. Chicken Chow Mein. Scott was ahead of himself as he brought out the substitutes at the same time. Peanut butter and jelly or tuna fish sandwiches.

"Now, that's what I call a waiter. He's always prepared," Ben said as he passed along the gooey kosher Chinese meal. Ben opted for a peanut butter and jelly sandwich.

At the end of lunch, when all the dishes were piled up and the tables cleared, we sat there waiting for the waiters to return with dessert. In unison they all charged out of the kitchen, both boys' camp and girls' camp. They carried trays of fortune cookies. Scott threw the tray on the table and immediately returned to the kitchen. We opened the cookies as the murmurs of delight soon reached a crescendo of screams.

"COLOR WAR."

That was what was written inside of every fortune cookie. Suddenly the walls and windows of the Mess Hall rattled with the shock waves of cherry bombs exploding overhead.

Chaos ensued as there was a stampede of children trying to get out of the Mess Hall. Joe Geisinger stood in the middle of this rampage, realizing the mistake he had made. He tried to keep some semblance of order, but then air raid sirens started to wail, and the sound of a helicopter approaching ensured that this was the real deal. Color War 1969 was breaking.

Smoke bombs flared on the grounds of boys' side, blue smoke at the top of the hill, and white smoke at the bottom,where the lake had finally receded. The helicopter hovered overhead and dropped pamphlets that floated down like feathers in the wind. These were the rosters, announcing which team you would be on for a week.

"Blue Country Hicks and White City Slickers wow.. what shitty names." Jericho laughed as he grabbed a pamphlet and looked at it quickly. "You, me and Harris are on the Blue Country Hicks. Mandelbaum is also on Blue.

"Just the four of us? The rest of the bunk is White City Slickers?" I asked.

"Yeah, but who cares... the best news is that Beth, Ellen and Rachel are on the Blue team with us," Jericho announced.

"What difference does that make?" I asked as I grabbed a floating pamphlet.

All I had to do was look at the front cover and see that Asa was our General. Samson was the General on the White team, and about the only saving grace was that Ben was also on the Blue team. At least he could try to keep Asa off my back for the week.

"See, if the girls are on the same team we get to see them all the time. I mean, any free time we have when we're not competing in a sport is spent on sing rehearsal."

"Why so much time on sing rehearsal?" Harris asked.

"It's the last event of Color War. The outcome of Color War usually comes down to the sing. It's like a 50 point event, or something like that. We have to learn a march, an alma mater and a comic song. Lots of practicing, like during rest hour, and free play. And the girls are there right alongside of us. "

Whistles were being blown and team banners were being un-furled in front of the blue and white smoke bombs that were now slowly dissipating. As the helicopter flew off, we could hear Ed Barnett telling us to gather around our appropriate teams. For one instant I ran into Rachel and we jumped up and down like little children because we were together.

Asa emerged through the blue smoke dressed as a farmer, re-plete with a straw hat, overalls, and a pitchfork at his side. Two other counselors, his lieutenants were dressed in the same fashion and stood behind him. The girls on the Blue Team were all lining up behind Fawn while Doe stood under the White City Slicker banner as the White General.

"I don't get all the excitement?" Harris said as he approached us.

"I don't either. It's one week of intense athletic activity and si-lent meals... you're not allowed to talk. The judges deduct points if you're too noisy... how fucking stupid is that?" Jericho told us. "So no talking during meals, sabotage during clean up... "

"Sabotage?" Harris looked at Jericho for further explanation.

"Yeah... trying to make the opposing teams look messy, or dumping crap on the floor if the other team has sweep. You have to win everything, even clean up. Real blood and guts competition on and off the field."

The chatter was interrupted by a whistle and Asa called for si-lence. We listened to some rallying battle speeches (where Jericho stuck his finger in his mouth and pretended to puke), and then we were sent back to our bunks.

The only Color War activity on the first afternoon was the tug of war competition. The entire camp, both boys' side and girls' side, sat with their respective teams on the waterski hill. A set of tennis courts were below us.

A long tug of war rope sat across the tennis courts sans nets.

Tug of War. Put the chunkiest kid on each team at the end of the rope. Pull as hard as you can with counselors screaming and cursing at you. The counselors got right up close, so you could smell their rancid breath and feel their spit slither across your face.

Boys, Girls, didn't matter. Counselors became raving lunatics. Didn't make a difference what age was out on the court with the rope in their hands. Everyone's hands were cut and bleeding at the end because of the 2" thick burlap rope. If the counselors had whips they would have used them on us. As spectators we were instructed to scream "PULL" in unison. Jericho looked at me and put his finger to his head and cocked it and then mimicked pulling the trigger.

When the younger girls took to the court for their contest there was a wide range of emotions. Some were serious, and some ended up crying. As older girls took to the court the percentage of girls taking it seriously diminished in relation to those who cried.

Most of the girls worried that their nails would break and didn't give a shit about this event.

The August afternoon chill set upon us as it was finally our turn to take center stage. The "chunks" anchored the lines. The Mayor on our end and Hooky on the other side. The coarseness of the rope immediately began to tear our hands apart and it was difficult to get any footing on the slick surface of the tennis court.

"Damn it Jason, pull. Pull with your arms, anchor with your legs."

Asa was in my face. His breath was a foul odor. I lost it and started to laugh. My grip loosened for a second and the rope slid through my palms, cutting deeper into my skin. I grabbed the rope and again started to pull, leaning backwards with all my weight.

"You Pussy, Jason. You're a PUSSY... Pull you pussy, you can do this! PULLLLL."

Asa stayed glued to my face and this created a deep anger that suddenly dissolved into an inner strength. It felt like I was alone on the rope. My feet grew roots and penetrated the cement of the tennis courts. I felt like I was the strongest man alive. We gave one final tug and forced the White team over the center line.

It was a best of three competition and we found that the second contest was a bit easier as the White team was demoralized. We pulled them over the center line in a matter of seconds.

Asa offered no words of congratulations. Ben tended to my hands, applying some ointment that left a sharp sting, and then he wrapped gauze around my palms. Harris showed Ben his hands, skin ripped off his palm, and Ben dressed those wounds too.

Dinner was eerie. We were monks in a retreat. The code of silence.

The Mess Hall was divided with the entire Blue Team, both boys and girls, on the left side, and the White team on the other side. Rachel, Ellen, and Beth were only two tables away from us, but we couldn't say a word. Any desire to reach for something on the dinner table was pantomimed. All you heard was the sound of forks and knives scraping plates, and the squeaking of the waiters' sneakers as they ran back and forth from the kitchen.

The first evening of Color War ended up also being a silent one. At last we could go to bed without the fear of Mickey Hardon, The Mayor, Bugsy or Hooky fucking with us. I didn't have to worry about the Brain anymore. We smoked that afternoon during Free Play and he was mellow and tame. Nobody was going to get out of bed and risk being penalized for rowdiness.

Breakfast on the first full day was as silent as dinner was the night before.

How long would this insanity last? The officers of our Blue team, would walk around the Mess Hall, smacking the older kids in the head if they saw them whispering, and with the younger campers they would put their forefinger to their lips and "shush" them.

I understood why Jericho was excited that "our" girls were on the Blue Team. Two tables away meant we could stare at them, and just dream. It was exciting to see Beth and Rachel whispering to each other, and looking over at us. Jericho only blushed, but this was all new to me, and I started acting like a drunken mime, trying to pantomime my question of "What's so funny?"

The girls walked out first and Jericho and Beth clasped each other's hands for a second as she passed by.

"I really have to see her more often during the winter," Jericho whispered, only to be smacked in the back of the head by Asa who was walking by.

Clean up before inspection was as bizarre as I had ever seen. No other camp took Color War this serious. It was beyond militaristic in its rules and regulations. For the first time all summer everyone returned directly to the bunk, and immediately started to tighten their beds and clean their cubbies. Harris had sweep on our side of the bunk, The Brain had center aisle sweep and Hardon manned the dust pan. Everyone on sweep detail made sure they made two passes under every bed.

Jericho had outside line, where we would hang our wet bathing suits after a swim. No one, all summer, ever took this job seriously, but there was Jericho pulling all the wet, dirty bathing suits off the ground. He took care in stringing them up neatly on the line attached to the bunk.

I had back room sweep, and toilets, because Oliver was never allowed to get near the dirty bowls. He said he would puke if he had to clean the toilets.

"I hate the smell! I'm allergic to that smell," Oliver told us earlier in the summer.

"So how do you take a shit?" Jericho asked him. "How do you take a shit if you can't stand the smell of shit? I mean do you shit and puke at the same time?"

"I hold my breath. I wait till the last second when I can't hold it in any longer and I get dizzy, and then I breathe through my mouth and shit away," Oliver told us.

"So why can't you hold your breath and clean the toilets?" Harris asked him.

"Just the sight of a dirty toilet, someone else's shit makes me so sick that I can't stop puking. You can understand, can't you?"

NO Oliver! I don't understand. My response was screaming in my head but not leaving my lips.

"Just be a man for once," I finally shouted, breaking the silent clean up. Ben peeked into the back room to see who was breaking the code of silence. He just laughed when he saw it was me.

A group leader from one of the youngest groups, was doing our inspection that day. In turn, Chick was doing the Ranger bunks. We heard the Bunk seventeen screen door slam shut, and the porch creaking as the inspector approached. Suddenly Mickey Hardon broke across the center aisle, and just as the screen door opened he tossed a wad of candy wrappers under Harris' bed.

Harris started to protest as Hardon jumped back to his bed, but it was too late.

"ATTENTION!... EVERYONE TO THE FOOT OF THEIR BED!"

This was the fucking army. This was a joke. The inspector from the Ranger group entered with a clipboard fused to his left hand. An electric current ran through the bunk as we were jolted to stand at attention. Jericho took his time getting up and the inspector pointed at him and shouted, "That will cost your team ten gigs."

"Gig this," Jericho whispered. Luckily the inspector didn't catch the response. But I did, and I couldn't stop laughing.

"Another gig. What team are you on, son?"

"Blue, SIR."

Why not go full out schizoid military? Jericho caught on and suppressed a giggle.

The inspector took a quarter out of his pocket and threw it down on my bed where it rested in splendor. "Not tight enough, so that will be another ten gigs."

"Come on, not even a kangaroo can get a hop out of that mattress. You have to be kidding me,"

"Another ten gigs."

Harris was apoplectic as he waited for the inspector to pass. He kept trying to blurt out that Hardon had thrown something under his bed but the inspector kept taking gigs against him for opening his mouth. This silenced Harris but he was so uptight that his squirming was starting to look like a new rock dance. The inspector pulled Harris' bed away from the wall, and he saw the wrappers.

"Thirty Gigs. What team are you on?"

"Blue,.. But Hardon threw..."

"And who had sweep on this side of the bunk?" the inspector asked.

"I diiiiiiiiiid!" Harris screamed ".... but you don't understand. Hardon threw that junk under my bed."

"Another fifty gigs... you're doing real good, kid."

The inspector moved over to Hardon's bed. Mickey Hardon was staring at Harris with a knowing smirk when the Inspector pulled the blankets off his bed.

"What the hell is this?"

The bunk grew silent. Mickey Hardon turned to find the Inspector pointing at a melted Oh Henry bar sitting squarely in the middle of his bottom sheet.

"I.... I ... I don't know."

"I'll tell you what it is... you were eating in bed last night and fell asleep with the Oh Henry bar glued to your hand... and you thought it was a turd this morning and tried to hide it."

Mickey Hardon stared at the Inspector. His face turned red in anger as he clenched his fists. He started pacing.

"No, it's not me.. I hate Oh Henry bars... and I didn't..... "

"That's fifty gigs. When I come back tomorrow morning those sheets better be changed."

The Inspector continued checking beds and cubbies. He finished with Jericho.

Jericho at first stood at attention but then he slowly melted into a chuckle.

"I remember, Blue team?"

"Yup", Jericho answered, a snicker twirled onto the end of his one word answer.

"Thirty Gigs.... White team easily wins this morning."

The Brain remained silent while Hardon, and the rest of the White team, including Oliver, jumped around hugging each other in celebration. Harris stormed out of the bunk like a sore loser, his protest falling on deaf ears.

"They're cheating. They're cheating," he cried on his way out. Jericho had to go out and calm him down.

The Brain sauntered down the middle aisle and at the screen door he turned and handed me a candy wrapper. He had planted the Oh Henry bar.

Our first event on the first full day of the 1969 Color War, was the swim meet. The backstroke event led off the meet and Jericho easily took first place. When I edged out The Brain for first place in the breaststroke Mickey Hardon nearly had a coronary.

"What the hell happened? Nobody ever beats The Brain in the breaststroke." Mickey Hardon shouted.

"Hey... sometimes things happen," The Brain simply said.

Hardon barked at The Brain like a rabid dog. Then Hooky and Hardon both started screaming that I "cheated," and they took their false allegations to the judges.

"Did you let me win?" I asked The Brain as I walked by.

"That's for you to figure out,"

The Brain only smiled. I could not figure him out.

It really wasn't Color War. It was more like a civil war, bunk-mates fighting each other. Brothers and sisters were always on the same team, but sometimes cousins were on opposite teams. Anger and suspicion reigned as we dressed for lunch, and when first call sounded, everyone but Jericho and I ran out of the bunk. We sort of sauntered.

"Follow my lead. I haven't asked you for anything all summer, so please, just follow my lead," Jericho begged as we walked to the top of the hill where the blue team was massing.

"Sure, what's up?"

"I am so sick of this war shit. Silent meals, inspections, fighting... too much fighting. This isn't war...my brother's in the war, and I can't stand it anymore... I'm not cheering."

We joined the Blue team, and when lunch call blew over the loudspeaker we lined up in one long straight line. We were being judged every second of the day. It was sick. It felt like we were living in East Germany, behind the Berlin Wall, where we had to worry that every word and deed would be reported.

"One Line! Look Sharp!" shouted Asa, as the youngest campers started marching into the dining room.

"BLOOD…. GUTS…. HATE… KILL… BLOOD…. GUTS…. HATE… KILL…."

Asa was screaming those words, in cadence with every step taken. The campers repeated the words in a cultish litany.

"BLOOD.. GUTS… HATE … KILL" The Blue Team responded in unison, and this was our anthem as we made our way to lunch.

Jericho had given Harris and me a strip of duct tape that he had stolen from Abner's pickup truck. We slapped it on over our mouths. We were protesting. We passed Asa at the front door of the Mess Hall, and he pulled us out of line.

"BLOOD…. GUTS…. HATE… KILL…" he shouted at us.

We didn't say anything, just stood there with our mouths taped shut.

Asa leaned down, and shouted BLOOD…. GUTS… HATE.. KILL…

Then he ripped the tape off Jericho's mouth. Jericho stared him down, and then tossed a peace sign at Asa.

"Peace and Love… oh… and O.K. USA," Jericho whispered, as he blew Asa a kiss.

"O.K. USA?" what the hell does that mean?

"O.K. USA… that it's our right to protest… so go fuck yourself."

Harris and I just smiled at Asa and flashed the peace symbol.

"O.K. USA, motherfucker," I said.

Then Asa kicked me in the ass, and I couldn't sit throughout the entire meal.

28

For the rest of the afternoon Asa stayed away from us, and we steered clear of him. When we marched into the dining room for dinner Ben was there with us. He stared down Asa, who eventually looked away.

Color War sucks, but I do have to admit that I loved the competition. Jericho and I had become quite the infield tandem at second base and shortstop during the Color War softball game. In the bottom of the last inning, down by one, I singled and Jericho hit a massive home run to win the game. Hardon threw his mitt at Jericho as he crossed home plate... and the umpire, who was also serving as a Color War judge immediately shouted...

"Twenty gigs for poor sportsmanship."

It became an inside joke to us, this word "gig"... we had no idea what it meant, nor where it came from. If Jericho farted I charged him a gig. If I looked at Rachel as she walked into the dining room Jericho punched my arm with three gigs.

We were afforded some freedom after our softball game. We were allowed to watch other groups battling it out, and we were told that we should exhort our Blue team members on, but we snuck off. Harris and The Brain joined us as we got high in our usual place, reappearing just as everyone shuffled back to the bunk for lunch.

That afternoon we marched into the dining room to another mindless military cadence. Asa marched up and down the line as we proceeded to the Mess Hall, vehemently exhorting us on.

Everywhere we go, oh
people want to know, oh
who we are, who we are?
so we tell them
we are the Blue Team
the mighty mighty Blue Team

Most campers tried to keep in step, but most of us didn't care. One long line of campers marching behind the Blue Team banner. And we'd repeat it over and over until we were marching into the Mess Hall where we were greeted by Asa at the door. Once again, we had put duct tape over our mouths and flashed peace signs at all the judges. Asa couldn't whip our asses because Ben was standing right beside him.

As we entered the Mess Hall we were greeted by the girls' team whose cheer was just ending... with a tune... why? Because that's what girls do, they sing. They always sing.

"OH Honey, oh babe, be mine,
Tell them you're blue you're blue, you're blue
Tell them you're blue you're blue you're blue.

It became redundant, this marching into the Mess Hall, in the inane militaristic style that Color War dictated. Straight line, clapping, and cheering some bloodthirsty chant. At breakfast, lunch and then dinner, the stupid single line we marched in, the chanting, the fervor... we couldn't take it anymore... So the next morning Jericho continued to duct tape our mouths, but this time he produced a magic marker from his cubby, and boldly printed an F across his mouth. Jericho scribbled the letter U across my duct taped mouth and then proceeded to print a large K across the tape that covered Harris' mouth.

We marched past Asa who was surveying his troops. We flashed the peace sign at him as we passed. However, our ranks had now grown to four as Ben followed us in with his mouth taped shut, where he printed a large bold **U!** Instead of the peace symbol, Ben flashed the middle fingers and walked by.

Before anyone could say anything we seated ourselves and sat quietly as the waiters spilled out of the kitchen. Chick, a judge during Color War, walked over to the table, whispered something to Ben, and then he smacked me in the back of the head.

"Ehhhh... don't be stupid, kid."

Then Chick walked away. Ben warned us that we might cost our Blue Team the decorum points for the meal. How could that be if we hadn't said anything? I had to do everything to keep from breaking down in laughter.

Halfway through breakfast Asa walked over to our table. He just stared at us, and then he walked behind Jericho and pinched his neck in a vise grip. You could see Jericho was in pain.

"You assholes are not going to cost me Color War," Asa hissed.

"There's a real war being fought, asshole," Jericho spit back, shaking free from Asa's grip.

Their entire conversation was whispered, but loud enough for me to hear.

Ben slowly got up and moved closer to Asa. He was ready to pounce if Asa laid another hand on Jericho.

"The only war being fought is right here... and it's Color War."

Asa had a madman's shit-eating grin spread across his face.

"Camps over in a week, so face the facts. You may be going over there one day so you better pray the real war is over soon."

Jericho was spitting emotion, whispering venom.

"Only morons go."

"My brother is there now. Are you calling my brother a moron?"

"He wasn't smart enough to dodge the war, and he's even a bigger moron if he enlisted , so yeah... he's a moron,"

"Fuck you. He wanted to fight for his country," Jericho shouted as he jumped up into Asa's face.

"Just confirming what I said, he's a moron. Who would fight for this country?"

"At least he's not acting like a fool around young girls, or trying to get them drunk," Jericho whispered.

There was a slap across the face that resounded through the silent Mess Hall. Jericho didn't even budge as an insane glower spread across his face.

"Only girls slap, you bitch," Jericho said.

"Your brother is probably fucking and burning little gook girls right this minute."

Jericho lunged for Asa but Ben jumped between the two frothing animals. Ben pushed Jericho back into his seat and turned to face Asa.

"Move on, Asa. You don't want to hurt this kid."

"You'll get your's, Ben, and so will you, Jericho."

Asa turned and went back to the officer's table, and sat down in solitude. No other officer even asked what the commotion was about. We lost decorum again, but who cared. Jericho had taken a stand and was the better man for it.

It took through rest hour for Jericho to calm down. He was useless in the Color War volleyball game, which we lost.

Now he sat on his bed flipping through his brother's letters, which led him to walk out of the bunk every now and then to suffer silently, maybe shed a tear, though no one could see him do it. We had our big basketball game that afternoon. Mickey Hardon kept taunting us, reminding us how he was going to destroy us on the court. I walked over to Jericho's bed in an effort to distract him from Hardon's blabbering.

"I'm going to throw the game this afternoon. I'm not going to try," Jericho confided to me.

"Why?"

"Asa is our coach. I don't want him winning. He thinks he's such a great basketball player, but that doesn't make him a great basketball coach. Let's see what happens when he can't defeat a team coached by Samson."

"I look at it like this... I'd rather we win and beat Hardon and

Hooky. I'd love to shove their heads into the ground and shut them up so we don't have to listen to them brag when we get back to the bunk. I don't care if we give Asa the victory,"

Jericho thought about this for a moment, and then looked at me.

"Sometimes in life you just have to have a moment that shapes your life forever. It's that feeling of 'fuck it' and 'go for it' and 'what the fuck'... and 'who cares'... know what that moment is? My brother taught me that sometimes you're faced with that instance where you need to say, 'THIS FUCKING SUCKS', and you need to react no matter the consequences. It's your M-F-M! My FUCKING MOMENT.   You realize that your next action may fuck you for the rest of your life, but it's too late, you know you're going to do it anyway. The Vietnam War, this fucking Color War.. asshole counselors... moronic bunkmates... this all FUCKING SUCKS.. After all we're going to be out of camp tomorrow morning on our way to a music festival. I mean, you're still with me, right?" he asked.

"Absolutely. M-F-M. But for once I'd love to stick it to Asa and Hardon at the same time."

"Oh, I think it will happen," Jericho said..

That moment happened to have come with two minutes left in the basketball game, and it wasn't a moment hatched with meticulous planning. No aha moment of recognition that this was a brilliant scheme for achieving our **M-F-M** moment. It was spontaneous and beautiful.

Ben was coaching Harris and the rest of the B team in softball, so he wasn't there to observe what was about to happen in our A basketball game.

It was a close game. Jericho had refused to shoot all game, but was pulling down as many rebounds as he could, and that kept us within points of the White team. My battle with Hardon was a bump and grind affair, and without Asa or Samson refereeing the game I found I was free to play ball. I wasn't being called for every little foul or violation. I flourished. I had scored sixteen points, and held Mickey Hardon to just six. Hardon was clearly frustrated and kept diving into me, picking up his fourth foul with just a minute to play.

I was in a one and one situation and calmly sank both foul shots. We were up by one, when with thirty seconds left on the clock, Hardon took the ball down the court and tried to drive by me. I blocked his shot... total rejection, the ball bouncing off his face right into the hands of someone else on his team who hit the jump shot to put the White team up by a point.

"Fuck you, you're going to lose!" Mickey Hardon shouted as he wiped away the trickle of blood that dripped from his nose as a result of the rejection.

"Just remember how that ball tastes, Hardon," I told him as I ran downcourt trying to position myself under the basket in hopes of receiving a pass and putting up the winning shot. But it was not to be.

Stevie Kohn, who was in bunk seventeen and one of our starting guards, brought the ball down the court. Jericho stood off to the right side at the top of the key, as Asa kept screaming for him to get under the basket. Stevie passed him the ball but Jericho passed it right back, obviously not interested in participating in the last play of the game.

There was no scoreboard clock, just a counselor sitting at the scorer's table with a small hand held clock. We had to estimate the countdown as the timekeeper shouted out "FIFTEEN SECONDS."

" FOURTEEN... "

Stevie got the ball back and kept dribbling, looking to drive to the basket. I kept posting up Hardon from one side of the key to the other, and Hardon kept trying to hold my shirt and keep me from moving freely. I fought him, I kept slapping away his hands. It was a miracle a foul wasn't called on either of us.

"TEN..."

Finally Stevie bounce-passed the ball to me on the right side of the key. I was only a few feet away from the basket, and I started to dribble, pushing Mickey Hardon backwards. I was working my way in for a turn-around jump shot. Then as I was about to spin and shoot I caught sight of Jericho, almost pleading for me not to take the shot.... to blow the game... and I suddenly realized what being a friend was all about. In that instant, that very moment, I knew I could not disappoint him. I stopped dribbling and passed the ball back out to Jericho.

"FIVE..."

Jericho held the ball, and gave Asa the finger. It was either this gesture, or the go fuck you grin Jericho was flashing, that sent Asa into a tantrum.

He stormed up to mid-court screaming "SHOOT IT,... SHOOT IT."

"THREE.... TWO..."

"Fucking shoot it..." Asa pleaded.

"ONE..."

And before the whistle was blown, at the very last second, with his back to the basket, Jericho tossed the ball over his head in a high arc. He never looked back. The ball floated upward toward the hoop as the whistle sounded. Then came the sound of the ball slapping against the backboard, then hitting the front of the rim... and then hitting the backboard again....

"FUCK YOU, ASA," Jericho shouted...

But this was all drowned out as the ball fell through the netting for the winning two points. Pandemonium broke out on the court as the team charged Jericho to congratulate him. He had no idea he had won the game. I turned and faced Hardon who had such a look of despair on his face that I couldn't help myself. I decided to rub in the pain and flipped him the bird.

... "Fifteen gigs for unsportsmanlike conduct," the ref shouted.

"What's the matter, asshole... you too afraid to take the final shot?" Hardon shot back. "You knew I would stuff the ball down your throat?"

I just held up my middle finger, and again the referee screamed, "Another fifteen gigs for unsportsmanlike conduct."

I walked up to Jericho, as he emerged from the jumble of celebrating teammates and he looked at me and we both laughed.

"I can't win, even if I try to lose, can I?"

"I wanted to lose too," I told him

"I know… you had Hardon dead to rights. I knew you were going to make the winning shot… why didn't you?"

"Because you were right, it was better to have Asa lose than to have Hardon win. In the end your defiance was monumental."

"Fuck it, it's just a game," Jericho said as we walked off the court.

With our basketball game over, we sauntered over to the bleachers on the boys' softball field to watch the B softball game. Asa followed us there to check out the results. He had an air of superiority that always accompanies the victorious. He felt that his magical touch could now help bring victory to the B team. Ben was coaching the team when Asa sidled up next to him. He started to exhort encouragement to the Blue team.

Harris was playing left field, and our team was ahead by one run. It must now be said that Harris was not a bad little athlete. He was fast enough to contend with anyone in a race, and he knew how to play basketball. He was too small to really make his mark but when he played with the "B" squads he held his own.

So it was a surprise when Rick Schlaffer, a perennial "B" athlete from the White team, miraculously connected on a lob pitch and sent a screaming line drive towards Harris. There was a man on first and second, and there were two out. This should have been an easy catch, an easy out to win the game. Harris drifted in, instead of backing up. The ball tipped off his glove and caromed past him, allowing two runs to score.

"Fuck! I feel bad for Harris," Jericho said as we watched the White team celebrate. Harris was still running for the ball in a losing effort.

"I swear, if anyone in the bunk says anything to him I may lose my shit," I told Jericho.

"That will be the day... Flanken losing his shit? Will never happen." Jericho laughed.

We wouldn't have to worry about the bunk because Asa took care of our fears. Harris was walking back, with his head down. The ball was held limply in his tiny palm and his glove was about to fall off. Without looking up he made his way to the bench where we were sitting, but Asa intercepted him.

"What's the matter with you?" he yelled, startling Harris.

"I.... I... "

"Fuck the I... you killed us out there. We had the game won. Can't you use your head, or is that wart getting in the way of your sight?"

Asa stood toe to toe with Harris, towering over him. Harris tried to push his way around the counselor, but Asa didn't budge. He started jabbing his forefinger into Harris' tiny chest, pushing him backwards with each thrust.

"You're a loser, a stinking loser. You're going to suck in life. You just took ten points from us because you're so pathetic!"

Harris stood there shaking in his sneakers. He was about to cry. Asa bent over so he was now eye to eye with Harris. At first Asa just studied the camper, but then he began to ferociously bark. He was a mad dog. Suddenly Asa grabbed Harris by the back of his shirt and threw him to the ground, and kicked him in his ribs. "

You suck... you've always sucked. Such an easy catch, you blew the game."

You could hear the pop of air explode out of Harris' mouth. It was amazing he wasn't seriously hurt. Ben, who was consoling the rest of the team, heard the commotion. He ran over to find Harris lying on the ground, A fresh sneaker print could be seen on his shirt. Ben grasped Harris and clutched him to his chest. Harris was gasping for every ounce of breath his tiny lungs could squeeze in. Ben tried to soothe the pain.

In all of the commotion Asa slunk off.

Ben never looked for Asa that afternoon. He spent the afternoon at the infirmary with Harris, begging the nurse to take Harris to the hospital for x rays. The nurse never called for the doctor. Instead she wrapped an ace bandage around Harris' ribs and put a stethoscope to his chest to listen to his lungs. Then she discharged the camper into Ben's care.

At the flag pole that night we were in a stupor. Harris remained in the bunk, and we would eventually bring him dinner. Harris continued to stay in the bunk all night, skipping sing rehearsal. Jericho and I went to sing rehearsal but we couldn't concentrate. We couldn't wait to get out of camp.

It rained all night. We heard the thunder, and the machine gun rattling of rain which pelted the windows. Jericho and I had already packed a few things in our backpacks–extra underwear, socks, shorts and a sweatshirt and sweatpants. We were ready for Woodstock; we were going to leave in the morning.

Reveille blew the next morning and Jericho and I were the first ones out of bed. We flew into the back room and brushed our teeth. We couldn't contain our excitement. With everyone still under their blankets we looked for Ben, but he wasn't in his bed. Neither was Harris. Ben took him to the infirmary in the middle of the night. Jericho and I grabbed our backpacks, made our beds, and walked outside. We stowed everything behind the back end of the bunk, where nobody would look.

As the teams lined up around the flag, Asa and Samson were called out to raise the flag. The entire camp proceeded to put their right hands over their heart in the perfunctory every day salute. We were the exceptions. First Jericho stepped back, and then I followed.

In the distance we could see Ben leading Harris into a car that was parked in front of the Mess Hall. The car spun out, and headed up the road. It was obvious that Ben had finally persuaded someone to take Harris to the hospital for x rays.

Jericho and I stood at ease, with our hands clasped behind our backs. We were no longer going to salute the flag.

"What's this? What's going on?" a voice boomed behind us, rumbling down the hill in a full charge. The ground shook as Joe Geisinger charged toward us.

"Why aren't you saluting the flag? Get your hand over your hearts and salute the flag!" Joe shouted as he pushed me to the ground and stood face to face with Jericho. Joe was snorting like a bull, the vein in his neck bulging and throbbing.

"We have the right not to salute," Jericho told him.

"NOT IN MY CAMP. THIS IS MY CAMP. YOU DO WHAT I SAY IN MY CAMP. NOW I WANT YOU TO SALUTE THE FLAG,"

Furious! Joe's fury bathed over us. I was about to shit in my pants, but Jericho stood firm.

"I have the right not to salute. It's a free country," Jericho told him. There was calm in his voice, not a shred of fear, even as Joe grabbed him by the shirt and threw him to the ground.

"Salute the flag, or you'll never be allowed back at this camp," Joe screamed. His threat only made us laugh because in just an hour or so we would be gone forever.

"No sir, we will not salute the flag anymore. Not till this war is over," Jericho told him.

Joe slapped me in the head, an open palm slap which left a ringing in my ear. He then pushed me to the ground where I joined Jericho.

"You two are done. You're never coming back to this camp," Joe screamed as he turned and charged on, plowing his way into the dining room.

"Our first protest. I'm sure there are going to be many more in the next few years," Jericho said. He was giddy, excited... feeling a part of the peace movement in his own little way.

Breakfast ended, and the Blue team was allowed to leave the Mess Hall first. We raced back to the bunk, took our morning dumps, and made sure our beds were tight and neat. As the rest of the bunk walked in, and clean-up began, Chick walked into the bunk.

"Ben took Harris to get x-rays. I want the two of you to write up what you saw Asa do. I can trust the two of you,"

"Jericho and I have to go to the infirmary. My ears are still ringing from when Joe slapped me"

"Ehhh... that wasn't a slap. That was a love tap. What's your problem?" Chick asked Jericho.

"You saw Joe push me to the ground. My back is hurting. We'll write something for you later."

"We both have golf as our morning competition so we're just going to stay at the infirmary and meet the team on the golf course." I said.

"Okay, good luck. Just remember to write something later. I'm counting on you to give me a detailed report of what happened," Chick said.

It was a good plan. No counselors from our group were needed on the golf course, so we wouldn't be missed. When First Call sounded we waited till everyone left the bunk, took our backpacks and sat on the porch for a second. We made sure everyone was distracted by lineup, and then made a mad dash towards the annexes. The waiters were still cleaning up The Mess Hall after breakfast so we went undetected.

We made it to the pit, and ran to the gate. We climbed over the small stone wall that served as a boundary, and sat down on the grass out of view of the rest of the camp. The air smelled sweeter and felt more peaceful on this side of the wall. We could finally relax. Jericho took out a joint and we started to smoke it.

"Three days of nothing but peace and music," Jericho sighed.

"How long do you think it will be before we're missed?" I asked.

"Oh, in an hour and half, right after the morning activity ends. If Ben is back he'll wonder where we are, and when he hears that Blue lost the golf competition he'll want to know why. That's when they'll come looking. But we should be long gone."

Jericho had it all planned out.

So we sat and waited.

And waited.

We heard First Call blow, and then Activity Call blared over the loudspeaker, and the sound of campers running off to activity echoed off the hills. Jericho looked at his watch with a patience that I could never exhibit. I never broke any rules before, never strayed from proper behavior until I started smoking with Jericho. I didn't know how my parents would react, if they even cared to react. If I was expelled and they received that call from Joe to come and pick me up, they would send a private car.

"What do you think... think you'll call me after camp is over?" Jericho suddenly asked.

"Sure, if you give me your number," I told him.

Jericho laughed. He was beyond mellow.

"I know there's a distance between Long Island and Westchester, but we can always meet in the city,"

"Yeah... like my parents would ever allow me to go into the city..."

"Man, that must suck, not having parents who trust you," he said.

"Oh,.. it's not about trust or anything... they just don't care. They expect me to be the good little boy who never gives them problems. I'm like wallpaper. I'm just there, and they walk past me without ever saying anything."

"So dumbass, if you meet me in the city they'll never know that you left. Right?"

I looked at Jericho and started laughing. Was I really that much of an idiot? All I needed to do was call a cab, grab the train and head into the city. I just never had a reason to think about meeting anyone before. It was a new concept, an awakening.

"I am a dumbass, right?"

"You're going to like hanging with my parents, they're really cool. It's so groovy just to chill with them. And if my brother was home then you'd really have a great time."

"Looking forward to it," I said, and we shook on it.

For once I felt what could only be the feeling of contentment. I never experienced it before, being so at peace with the world. Someone wanted me to be their friend for who I was, and not because my parents had dollars or they wanted to come over and drool over my mother...

And we waited. ...

And waited...

Time seemed to stop as we waited. We both knew that if Jericho's parents weren't here soon Chick would start to look for us, wanting our written report. I wanted to be as far away from camp as possible before the first search party was sent out.

"They'll be here soon," Jericho whispered..

The sun beat through the clouds, setting ablaze the choking humidity that had laid dormant overnight in the dewy grass. The perfect omen that the day would end in a thunderstorm. We didn't bring any water with us, and I could feel my throat tighten. What if we were caught? Would it not be better to just slide back into the bunk and pretend nothing happened?

And we waited.

"You're not worried?"

"They'll be here. This is their thing... they love concerts. They've been to them all, and they've taken us too. It's like a family tradition. We all get high and then go and listen to the music."

Another half hour passed, and now I was getting antsy,... Jericho reached for another joint, but I declined.

"Maybe something happened..... maybe they're not coming."

"They'll be here. Have a toke and relax."

Then Recall sounded, and I knew a decision had to be made. Ben would be back from the hospital, hopefully with Harris. He would realize that we were both gone, the hounds would be set free and we would be hunted down.

"I'm going back," I said as I stood up, a bit wobbly from the sun and the pot. The humidity was getting to me, and you could feel the thunderstorms approaching on the horizon. One of those days.

"Why? Don't you want to go?" Jericho asked, shading his eyes as he looked up at me.

"Listen, I want to go more than anything, but they're not here and a lot of people will be wondering what happened to the two of us. If I go back, at least I can give you a few more hours of cover—tell everyone you're in the infirmary or something. And if your parents do come, and you still want me to go with you... you'll take a chance and come and get me and then we'll sneak out together."

"Promise?" he asked.

"I promise."

Jericho stood up and grabbed me in a bear hug, and then he threw his arm around my neck and put me in a headlock.

"You're the best."

"Just hide somewhere because Ben will be back from the hospital soon, and he may pass by here."

We parted ways, and I looked back sadly because I wasn't sure if Jericho would really come for me or not. I ran through the pit, past the waiter annexes, and then into the bunk just as everyone was undressing for morning swim.

As we lined up for swim Ben could be spotted walking across the campus with Harris by his side. That was a good omen. He told Harris to go in and change for swim, and Harris deftly avoided the glances of every camper as he walked into the bunk.

"He needed x-rays. I just wanted to make sure there were no broken ribs. He's badly bruised."

"That's good. Glad nothing was broken."

"How did you do in the golf tournament?" Ben asked.

"We lost. We were too concerned about Harris. We woke up and you were gone, and then we saw you get into the car. We couldn't concentrate on hitting that little ball."

"Where's Jericho?"

"At the infirmary. We had a little situation this morning with Joe, and he slapped us pretty hard. Jericho still has a ringing in his ears, so he is having it looked at again."

I hated lying to Ben.

But at least this worked.

Harris and I buddied up for swim and took a quick dip. Harris had a horrible black and blue blotch on his chest. He didn't want to talk about what happened. I kept looking up the hill, hoping to spot Jericho waving for me to join him, but there was nothing. We dressed for lunch, and when Ben said he would check in on Jericho I told him that the nurse gave him some salt pills and water and said that he needed to sleep. He would be back in the afternoon. I wasn't sure if Ben believed the story.

The noise level rose perceptibly during lunch. I mean how long can little kids remain silent, but Jericho's empty chair was monumental. It was August 15th, and the first day of Woodstock was set to begin around 5:00 p.m... so even if Jericho's parents were a little late we should be able to get there by the start of the concert. As we walked back to the bunk, rumors abounded about the mammoth size of the Woodstock concert.

Joe was on the warpath. He had no qualms about smacking counselors around and attacked those counselors whose hair was what he considered "too long." Counselors were not allowed out of camp during the week of Color War. The Pit gate was locked, preventing anyone from leaving in a car. It was total involvement for the week. Every counselor had an assignment. The songs for sing were being rehearsed and now it was time to paint the scenery for the final event of Color War between The Blue Country Hicks and The White City Slickers.

During rest hour Joe called a meeting for the counselors down at the boys' HCO. This was a great diversion as Jericho still hadn't appeared, and Ben was stuck down at the meeting. Harris joined me on the bootbox, and we could hear every word Joe screamed at the counselors. It was a warning.

"There's going to be dysentery, and drug overdoses, and you're not going to bring any of that back into my camp. I will break your legs if you leave. I will hunt you down. You will not bring harm to my camp. No one's leaving! If you do, you'll be fired and I'll have you arrested!"

"Can thirteen-year-old boys be arrested?" I asked Harris

"What are you smoking, Flanken? What are you talking about?"

"What if I left camp? Would Joe have me arrested?"

"Now you're being paranoid. Besides, how and why would you be going to that Woodstock thing."

"I'm not. Just wondering."

"Oh, and by the way, where's Jericho?" Harris asked as he gripped my arm tightly. "I know he's not in the infirmary."

I smiled, shrugged my shoulders and acted stupid. And I was stupid. What was I thinking about…. trying to sneak out of camp. Or maybe I should just look in the mirror and say…. THIS IS MY **MFM**! Fuck you to my parents! Fuck you to Asa, Hardon, and Samson. Fuck you to Joe Geisinger who was running this camp like a tyrant.. you have to do this, you have to do that… bugle calls, line ups.. stupid color war chants and cheers…. Counselors who hit you, bunkmates who cursed you up and down, called you an idiot at every move… Counselors who belittled you and made fun of you. Parents who have never sent one letter to you during the summer… not one postcard… and classmates who I wouldn't let befriend me because I knew they were just trying to sneak a trip to my house to see my mom and then go home and jerk off to her images… Fuck you! Fuck you all.

I walked into the bunk, and I was going to pee and then sneak out and meet Jericho, hoping he was still outside the wall, when I heard it loud and clear on WABC radio,the afternoon news break..

"ROUTE 17B IS closed, and traffic is backed up for miles going to the Woodstock festival."

29

They didn't come in the afternoon either.

"Want to talk about it?" I asked Jericho when he walked into the bunk before the counselors returned from their meeting. Harris was the only other one in the bunk who seemed to notice his return.

"Nothing to talk about. Something's wrong. They should have been here by now."

"You heard the news report. They've shut down the roads, maybe they can't get here."

"They would have found a way to go around everything. Maybe they'll be here tonight. We'll just miss the first few acts."

"I'm sure they'll come," but my words fell on deaf ears.

That afternoon our last group event for Color War was the Apache Relay. It was a relay race where everyone in the group was assigned an event, a task, and after completing that event the baton would be passed to the next teammate. They would run to the next assigned event, their assigned event, and complete the task. Then they would pass the baton on. Etc. etc. etc. until all events were completed, culminating in the marathon.

Harris was going to eat a box of cornflakes with his hands tied behind his back and then try to whistle the Star Spangled banner. Jericho was assigned the marathon, where he would have to run from the front gate down to the water ski dock by the second lake. There, he would have to blacken his face with the ashes from a campfire pit. After he rubbed the ashes onto his face and blackened it to the approval of a judge, he would then have to run up the steep Grayson Hall hill and finish down by the Boys HCO shack.

I pictured Jericho waiting at the front gate, anticipating his turn to have the baton passed to him and start his marathon run when suddenly his parents would pull up. Jericho would say "fuck this" and jump into the car without me. I prayed that this wouldn't happen.

The Apache Relay started and I sat patiently on the benches of the basketball court. My event was the foul shot. I had to make five foul shots before I tagged off my teammate.

Unfortunately, I ended up choking. Mickey Hardon was on the other side of the court shooting foul shots for the White team, and even though the baton was passed to me with a ten second lead, I couldn't sink a single shot. I heard Hardon laughing at me when he swished his fourth foul shot, and I had only made two. Suddenly Asa appeared and saw what was happening and he walked right up to me as I was preparing another shot.

"You're blowing this for us. What the fuck is the matter with you? I swear if we lose this I'm going to kick your ass for the rest of the summer," he screamed in my ear.

"Fuck you," I shot back as I abandoned the standard set position for taking a foul shot and instead made a jump shot for my third basket.

Mickey Hardon sank his fifth and final foul shot and was off and running.

"We had a ten second lead going into this event, and you're screwing this up. I knew you were useless. You suck!"

He threw his clipboard onto the ground in disgust and stormed off the court. For some reason I was suddenly calm, no nerves. I sank my next two foul shots, picked up my baton, and ran past Asa. It was a short run to the tennis courts where two of my teammates had to have a successful ten stroke volley without hitting it out of bounds or into the net. I handed off the baton and headed down to the HCO shack where we congregated and waited for the long distance runners to appear.

As it turned out my two team members volleyed like pros and picked up the time lost by not making a single error. Then there was the anxiety-filled moment when everyone was waiting to see which long distance runner appeared first on the horizon. Nobody could match the long distance skills of Jericho, but was he going to show up? Suddenly he appeared over the crest of boys' camp, face blackened, a good fifteen seconds ahead of his rival.

Blue team won the Apache relay and Jericho was hailed a hero. Asa lauded the efforts of Jericho who had an expression of 'I don't give a shit' spread across his face. Then Asa turned to me, jabbed me in the chest and told me that "I was lucky that we won the Apache Relay; otherwise I would have been dead meat."

The 'Rope Burn' and 'Sing' were the only competitive events left in Color War. Then there was the 'Hatchet Hunt'. Actually the 'Hatchet Hunt" was ongoing. It was the search for an elusive hatchet that was hidden in a safe to reach spot somewhere on a neutral site in camp (obviously a wooden replica of the real hatchet was used). It was hidden by the Girls Head Counselor, and every morning and night he would post new clues which were supposed to lead you to the hidden prize. During Free Play we were allowed to search the camp for the hatchet. We were free to roam the camp for thirty minutes.

It was the perfect cover for escape. I followed Jericho back to the wall near the entrance to the pit, and we sat down again with our back to the stones, staring down an empty country road.

We listened to the squealing of children who searched high and low for the hatchet and its secret stash of points. Maybe ten, twenty, or maybe even the extreme thirty points.

"Color War is so stupid," Jericho finally said. "I've always hated this week, but now even more. How can anyone even talk about war when so many kids are dying in a jungle half a world away?"

"I'm sure Asa and Samson would be singing a different tune if they had to fight."

"I heard there's going to be a draft. They're going to pick your birthday out of a large bowl or something and then you're going to have to serve. Unless you go to medical school, or become school teachers, or join the Peace Corp, you're going to have to serve," Jericho told me.

"Well, Asa and Samson aren't going to be doctors, and if they're going to be teachers, well, I'd feel real sorry for their students." I said.

"Or you can go to Canada or something like that. I'm not fighting, that's all I know," Jericho said wistfully, not paying mind to what I'd just said.

"We're thirteen years old Jericho! I'm sure the war will be over before we turn eighteen!"

"You never know."

Recall sounded. I had to talk Jericho into returning to the bunk. We knew that any attempt to escape on Saturday would be made all the more difficult because we would be sequestered in the Social Hall, practicing for Sing. The Rope Burn was about to begin and maybe we would be able to sneak away during that. We walked slowly back to the bunk, with Jericho looking back over his shoulder every few seconds, hoping his parents would materialize. There was no cheering in the distance which was a sure sign that nobody found the hatchet up to this point.

The sun started to set and the entire camp lined up for the Rope Burn. We were bundled up in sweatshirts as it was another chilly August night. Jericho and I were pretty high, having smoked about two joints while waiting for his parents. I could barely feel my feet touching the ground. Harris carried our metal garbage pail from our bunk. I barely realized he was there.

We walked down behind the waiters annexes, almost to the side of the pit, where we were instructed to sit. Blue team side by side with the White team. Rachel and Beth were sitting next to us as we watched the preparation for the Rope Burn. Ellen sat with Harris, and he had given her a branch to help bang on the garbage pail. There was a buzz of excitement that reverberated through my body, tingling my soul. Was it the excitement of the Rope Burn, or being so close to Rachel, or maybe I did believe Jericho's parents were suddenly going to appear and we would make a break for it while Joe and his men chased us down in the Cadillac.

Ed Barnett stood in front of the camp, whistled for silence, and then introduced the counselors who would be participating in the Rope Burn. Samson and Asa, like the other counselors who were involved, wore only shorts and sneakers. Their bodies were lathered with petroleum jelly in an effort to protect their bodies from being burned.

They stood in front of their respective set of poles which stood about twelve feet high. A thick rope was strung tautly between them. They almost looked like two football goal posts. All day long campers were collecting bits of limbs and broken twigs from the woods surrounding the camp, and throwing them onto their assigned piles. Each pile had accumulated about four feet of wood.

"The idea is simple," Ed Barnett shouted. "Each team is given three pieces of paper and three matches to start a fire. Whoever builds the best bonfire and thus burns through the rope first will be declared the winner. If, by any chance, a team fails to start a fire with the three matches, they will be issued a three minute penalty until they receive their next match and piece of paper. Only the counselors are allowed to add wood to the bonfire, but selected campers have been chosen to be runners, to continue to gather twigs and branches from the woods."

Ed Barnett blew his whistle to start the Rope Burn. I was in a zone at this point. I was so high that I just stared in fascination, never realizing that Rachel was talking to me, and that Beth and Jericho were barely speaking to each other.

I watched as Asa and Samson both attempted to create a small teepee of wood as the base, and then delighted in the fact that Samson got his wood to catch fire on the first attempt. Asa was penalized for using up his three matches. After the assessed penalty Asa was finally able to start his fire, but it was clear that the White team had a significant lead.

Then both teams started chanting. White chanted "Burn baby Burn" and the Blue team chanted "Higher and Higher." Harris started to pound on the overturned garbage pail like it was a snare drum and I sensed each pounding beat vibrate through my body. It felt like every molecule of my being was alive, tingling, buzzing. I zeroed in on the fire, watching the White team build a pyramid that helped direct the flames skyward. You could feel the wave of heat glowing around us.

Asa finally got his fire to grow, and now both teams were building flames that were equally tall.

The sun had just set and the last wisps of light were highlighted by the raging, orange, fire. Asa and Samson danced around like bouncing sparklers, the fire reflecting off their slimy coated bodies. I was in a trance. At least twenty minutes had passed as I watched the flames climb skyward.

Finally the flames from both fires began to lick their respective ropes. Both teams were caught up in the frenzy. Blue and White teams were on their feet as the tongues of flame wrapped around each rope, causing them both to smolder. Pandemonium set in. Then both ropes exploded into a fiery kiss of flame. Both ropes shimmered and danced. The Blue team's fire seemed to stall and focus on a singular point in the center of the rope while the White team's flame spread like warm peanut butter on toast, eating away at every strand, every cord.

By now both teams were caught up in the frenzy. Blue and White teams were on their feet as the tongues of flame wrapped around the rope, causing it to start to smolder. Pandemonium set in. Blue and White teams saw both ropes explode into a firery kiss that sent a shiver across the respective ropes. Suddenly the flames started to creep across the White team's rope like warm peanut butter on toast, eating away at every strand, every cord. The Blue team's fire seemed to stall and focus on a singular point in the center of the rope.

Kids were screaming, garbage pails were being pounded, and whistles were being blown in anticipation, but I was a million miles away in my own world. Rachel started to hug me, as she jumped up and down in anticipation of the rope being eaten through by the flames. I was mesmerized by the intensity of the bonfire.

Suddenly, the blue pyre collapsed, and the fire seemed to dissipate.

"Oh shit, we're going to lose," Harris wailed. The Blue team shut down as if sedated for surgery. The White team's cheering reached a feverish pitch. The Blue team's rope was all smoke, no flames. The White team's bonfire was burning hot, and penetrating the rope like a shark chewing on its prey.

Asa was demoralized, and this made me happy. He just stood immobile, watching his rope, praying for a miracle. The reflection of the flame from his dying campfire grew dim against his slimy, jelly-coated body. Samson, on the other hand, was dancing around the fire. It was a victory dance. Raising his hands in praise to the gods of fire who were now eating through the rope, he then dropped to his knees in exaltation. His body mirrored the flames, and he was a dull beacon of light.

It was suddenly over. The White team's rope started to quiver, and move with every fiber being eaten away by the flames until it snapped apart in the middle, each remaining end falling limply against the poles that they were tied to.

Blue team erupted in sadness. Rachel hugged me, crying. Harris put down his garbage pail and sat on it, covering his ears with his hands to deafen the cheers from the victorious White team. When I finally looked around for Jericho I discovered that he was gone.

30

Jericho was truly gone.

His empty cubby and stripped bed punctuated his absence. There was a note on my bed.

"BROTHER DEAD. I HATE THE WORLD. 741-3805. Call me in a few months. Never stop wearing those lime green shorts you have. Thanks for sharing the summer."

I felt a hole in my soul that was so deep I couldn't move. I never felt so alone. For all the vacuous moments of my life this was as black as it ever has gotten. For all the desolate seconds at home when I was being ignored, there was always the comfort of keeping myself busy and making it through another day. But this was new. I never felt I had a friend before, and now he was gone. Snuffed out. Like the friendship never existed.

As the rest of the bunk walked in they stopped for a second in front of Jericho's bare bed as if it was a shrine. I looked at my cubby and noticed that my lime green shorts were slightly askew and I pulled them out of the cubby. There was a slight bulge in one of my front pockets and I reached my hand inside to find a baggie of fresh weed, and some rolling papers. I slid them back inside and made sure nobody had seen what I had discovered.

Ben walked into the bunk, and he looked at me first before he called for everyone's attention.

"Before the Rope Burn I was summoned to Grayson Hall. I met Jericho's parents. Jericho's brother is dead, killed in action two days ago while on patrol."

There was silence in the bunk. Oliver started to sniffle and Mickey Hardon shouted for him to shut up. Ben looked at me and motioned me to follow him onto the porch.

"I guess you were too high to realize what was happening," Ben said softly as he blocked the door, keeping me on the porch.

"How come you never turned us in?"

"What? You and Jericho are the only two normal kids in this bunk. If you felt like you had to get high I wasn't going to stop you."

"He never said goodbye."

"He left you that letter. He didn't have much time. Joe received the call this afternoon and had Abner Dingle pull out his trunk and duffle. I was told to bring Jericho up to Wayne Hall just at the beginning of the rope burn."

"I didn't even hear him leave,"

"He called for you to follow. He thought his parents were there to take the two of you to Woodstock, but you were rooted to that spot. Instead of sneaking out of camp he thought his parents were going to take him out the proper way. He was planning on coming back to get you... but when he saw the look on his mother's face he knew something was very wrong."

"I wasn't there for him," I said as I wiped the snot that had dripped out of my nose. I sat down on the boot box.

"Get back on your beds," Ben shouted as he saw Mickey Hardon and The Brain pressing up against the window to eavesdrop.

There were some things in life I had never encountered. The death of a peer was one of them. I wondered how Jericho reacted, if he lashed out in anger or if he withdrew.

"Look, you had something special this summer; you met a real friend. Not that many people have this experience. You think Hardon and The Brain are friends? They're just a convenience for each other over the summer, but you and Jericho bonded."

"Yeah... The Brain told me as much... but how did you know?"

"Shit, I can tell a lot of things. You just have to learn to read people, Flanken,"

"How bad was it?" I asked.

"Pretty bad. He had a meltdown, screaming and throwing things. I was sent back to the bunk to throw all of his stuff into his trunk and duffle, and then I dragged it all up to Grayson Hall. It looked like his parents had given him something to sedate him... he was calmer. But before they left he said he had to do something and ran off. He said he couldn't face you so he wrote you that note."

"Did he say anything else?"

"Yes, he asked me to tell you that you should be the one to tell Beth. And that you'll always be his Woodstock memory even though you never got there. Oh, and when Joe heard that he nearly blew a gasket. It was quite funny in a dark sense."

"I want to get out of here now," I told Ben.

"Hang in there for another week, it's almost over."

"I hate this place,"

"So do I," Ben confided. "Only one day of Color War is left and then the last week is a breeze. Before you know it, you'll be home."

The rest of the night everyone in the Jewish Mafia, except The Brain, taunted me. The Brain sat on his bed contemplating the events of the day.

"What's the matter? You sad that your homo buddy is gone. I bet the two of you butt fucked each other every day," Mickey Hardon shouted across the bunk when the lights went out.

"The two of you were like lovers," Bugsy shouted, as he sat up in bed, and shined his beacon of a flashlight on me. "I bet you sucked his cock. Did it taste good?"

"Shut up, assholes," Harris shouted.

"Awww... look who's standing up for the faggot... another faggot,' Bugsy shouted and most of the bunk started laughing at Harris.

Oliver stood on his bed, revealing his Mickey Mouse pajamas that were too small on him, causing his fat to jiggle. Hooky turned the flashlight on Oliver, almost blinding him into stumbling backwards.

"What's your problem, you fat turd?" Bugsy shouted from the corner.

"Just leave everyone alone. Jericho's brother died. Don't you have any pity?"

"We don't care," Hardon screamed as he threw a tennis ball across the bunk hitting Oliver in his stomach and making him double over.

Ben walked into the bunk, and the slamming of the screen door sent everyone scrambling under their covers, like this would be our protection. Ben just stood there, making sure that not a word was said. He looked at Oliver who was still wincing from the sting of the ball. Oliver gave him the thumbs up sign and crawled under his blankets.

"I'm in for the evening. No more talking. Time for bed."

It was a weird day, strange day, but it was only going to get more bizarre when the sun came up.

The last day of Color War turned into a full day of Sing rehearsal. We practiced the March, and then the Alma Mater, and then we were introduced to the Comic Song. It really wasn't a song, but a bunch of skits that were linked to a few witty lyrics set to popular tunes. Silly songs that were easy to remember.

Beth sat across from me, and Rachel was not to be found. Beth had no clue that Jericho had left, and when I told her what had happened, she ran off to the bathroom crying.

"I wonder where Jericho is now? How long does it take for a body to come back from Vietnam?" Harris asked between breaks

"I have no clue. I hate war. I used to love playing with those little toy soldiers, had all different types of soldier sets and I would re-create battle scenes, and then in 1965, and I'll never forget that year, I was watching TV. I was re-creating the Battle of the Bulge with this new soldier set, and there on the screen they had a report on Vietnam... and the dead soldiers being carried back from battle.. I looked at reality, glanced at my battle scene and threw all the soldiers away. Never again. No more... what I saw on TV that day made me sick."

Beth finally composed herself and walked back into sing practice.

"I'm ashamed. I'm crying because I miss Jericho, and that's selfish," she said. "I should be crying because his brother died and he must be so upset."

"I miss him too."

"Did he say anything to you before he left?" she asked.

"You were there with me... he just disappeared. Ben said he pulled him away from the rope burn and then he was gone. He did leave this note."

I handed the note to Beth so she could read it.

"Where's Rachel?"

"I don't know... she was told to report to Grayson Hall after inspection, and we haven't seen her since."

Beth read the letter and started to cry again.

I took the note back from Beth because I didn't want to lose the phone number. I knew I was never coming back to this camp, but I knew I wanted to pursue my friendship with Jericho.

At rest hour Ben threw a copy of the New York Times on my bed, with the front page screaming about "200,000 THRONGING TO ROCK FESTIVAL JAM ROADS UPSTATE.'

"How did you get this?" I asked.

"As we walked out of lunch I saw Joe screaming at someone from somewhere on the other side of the Mess Hall so I grabbed the paper from his table. Looks like you missed out on something special. Maybe I should have gone too. Seems like four counselors were fired for leaving camp. I believe they made it to Woodstock. They haven't returned and Joe just had Abner throw all their belongings into garbage bags and he dumped them into the pit."

"You guys weren't going to take me, were you?" Harris asked, as he plopped down on my bed and read the paper.

"We didn't want to get you into trouble," I told him--sort of a white lie.

"You know I want to get out of here as much as you do. I would have gone in a second."

"Want to sneak out now?" I asked Harris, looking at Ben and hoping he would volunteer to drive us to the festival.

"Don't look at me...I need that one last week of salary. But it is a shame... we're so close and yet so far from it."

It was a hot, humid, beyond muggy afternoon and we were sweltering in the canteen for the last sing rehearsal. Sitting side by side, sweating and singing. Everyone was restless and tired from rehearsing the songs. Suddenly there was an explosion of screams, cheering and jubilation that crashed into us from the Social Hall . This was where the White team was rehearsing.

Asa walked in with a look of defeat plastered all over his broad, thin face.

"Your lame buddy found the hatchet for the White team. Way to go, you losers." Asa pointed his bony finger at me. I knew he was pointing at Harris too. The entire Blue Team turned to face us, and even though nobody said anything, their looks could kill.

"Which buddy? We don't have too many friends here," Harris squeaked, but I poked him in the chest as a warning.

"Oliver. That turd, Oliver."

"Well, good for him," I said. I was happy for Oliver.

"You guys are just losers!" Asa screamed as he waved us off in disgust. "There's no way we can win Color War now."

A cry, a groan, followed by a bellow of despair arose from the Blue team as we sat on the Canteen floor. Everyone stared at us, like it was our fault. The only thing we could do was gaze upon the floor, and listen to the female officers spin an optimistic scenario about how we could still win Color War. They tried to get us to sing with vigor and desire but the air was taken out of the Blue team's balloon.

We ended up losing Sing, and thus we lost Color War. Oliver was a hero, and he basked in the glory that he would remember for the rest of his life. He was now under the good graces of Hardon, Bugsy, Hooky and even The Mayor. The Brain sat on his bed indifferent, reading Kafka.

Harris felt the brunt of hatred the entire bunk steered towards us, but I was too numb to feel any pain. I didn't care about Color War, I was numb because I wasn't there for Jericho. It didn't hurt that I had smoked a joint with The Brain before Sing.

Oliver, the picked on. Oliver the meek. Oliver who had to constantly go to the infirmary literally stumbled onto the hatchet. Right after rest hour, just as he reached the infirmary to get some medication, he tripped. He fell face first into the left post of the hand rail leading up to the infirmary... and from that vantage point he spied the small slivers in the wooden post. Taking a slim twig he scored the incision that was made in the wood, removed the cover and voila.... there was the wooden replica of the hatchet. He ran with it tucked under his shirt, wanting to keep it a secret. Then he found Samson, who saved the discovery till later in the day, when the entire White team was assembled for rehearsal in the Social Hall.

Ben headed out that night with the rest of the counselors. Joe Geisinger , every year, would rent a couple of buses to take the counselors out of camp. They would head to a local bar that Joe would rent out for the night. Bramo, Cisco, and some of the specialty counselors would be tending bar, and would pour triple shots for the price of one. After being sequestered all week in camp, the counselors needed a night out, and they reveled in getting so shit-faced that almost half of the staff would puke on the ride home.

Chick was the OD that night, covering all four bunks in the group. I tried to sleep that night, but now had to contend with Oliver mocking me. He took on the personality of the Jewish Mafia and started ragging on me like the others in the bunk were wont to do. Harris tried to sit out on the porch, but Chick forced him back inside.

The second the old man walked back to Bunks 19 and 20 the harassment started up again, but for the first time all summer, they came after me. The Mayor and Hooky sat on top of me, but instead of inflicting any physical pranks, they went right for my stash. Oliver led them there. I tried to fight off The Mayor and Hooky, but they were too much for me, and they had me pinned. Bugsy found the weed that Jericho had left behind and proceeded to the back room to flush it down the toilet. Thankfully the Brain interceded.

"I'll take that," The Brain told Bugsy.

"You want to flush it?"

"Yeah, if you don't flush it the right way the toilet can explode from the water pressure."

Bugsy studied the Brain, wondering if that was bullshit.

"Trust me, I'll take good care of this shit," The Brain told Bugsy. Bugsy had no qualms in handing over the package to The Brain. The Brain stashed it under his underwear in his cubby. I felt a reprieve of some kind.

Mickey Hardon returned with a sock filled with a tennis ball. I was defenseless....unable to knock off the cretins who sat atop me. Hardon started to wail on my body, using the sock like a weapon. It really didn't hurt but I wasn't going to scream for help. Let them believe they were hurting me. When the two glandular morons finally got off me and went back to their beds I was a bruised person. My ego was shot, and I felt the dull ache where the pounding took place.

I fell asleep whimpering into my pillow, not from pain, but from shame. Oliver stayed as far away from me as he could, and nobody bothered Harris for the rest of the evening as he decided to sleep on top of the double decker and wait for Ben to get back and move him.

Everyone had fallen asleep by eleven, but I was wide awake. My mind was racing on how best to achieve revenge. I wasn't going to tell Ben, but I was sure that any black and blue marks in the morning would be a telltale sign. It was close to midnight when I heard the sound of people walking around outside the bunk. Harris heard it too. He jumped down to my bed as I looked out the window to see at least twenty flashlights scanning boys side.

We pulled our sweatshirts on and sat on the boot box. There was a search in process as the flashlights seemed to be scanning for something under many of the bunks. We spied more flashlights flickering on girls side. Suddenly Ed Barnett appeared from behind our bunk and shined his flashlight directly into our eyes.

"What are you two doing up?" he said in a controlled but authoritative voice.

"Couldn't sleep. Heard the noise and saw all the flashlights. What's going on?" Harris asked.

"Nothing, now go back to sleep, " Ed Barnett ordered.

We watched as he squatted and aimed his beam of light under the bunk. After finding nothing, he stood up, realized we were still sitting on the porch.

"Get inside now," he growled.

We sat on my bed and waited till Ed started walking back toward the boys HCO, and then we silently slipped back onto the porch.

"What could they be looking for?" Harris asked as we saw a band of five flashlights move toward the lake.

"Weirdest thing I've ever seen."

We watched the search party scour the boys and girls waterfront area. Then one member turned over a canoe, pulled it into the water and started to paddle out to the middle of the lake.

There was a crackle of walkie talkies which were communicating with the canoe that was heading out into the darkness. We couldn't hear what was being said, but just the fact that there were walkie talkies now involved meant that something pretty serious was going down.

Harris and I dozed off while sitting on the boot box. We were wakened by the gentle prodding from Ben, who plopped down next to us, almost pushing Harris off the box. He reeked of alcohol, and could barely talk.

"What are you guys doing up?" he slurred.

Now that we were awake, we saw that there were even more flashlights leaving firefly traces in the darkness. There was a meeting of about ten flashlights at the boys HCO, and after Ed Barnett said something they quickly dispersed and headed in all directions.

"How was the party?" I asked.

"Awesome... everyone is so shit-faced," he giggled.

The rest of the counselor staff started to stumble through the darkness toward their bunks. It was reminiscent of scenes from all the war movies I ever watched,.... the tired and weary soldiers returning from battle. Some counselors were hoisted and carried on the shoulders of others. Some swayed and stumbled up the steps to their porches where they just plopped down on their respective boot boxes. More flashlights joined the search. Then we saw the unmistakable blue-red lights of a police car. No siren, just the reflections of importance bouncing through the darkness as the car made its way down to Grayson Hall, where it stopped and turned off its engine.

"What the hell is going on?" I asked.

"Well... let's see," Ben started to say, as he gagged and tried to swallow any puke that crawled up this throat. "They served triple shots for the price of one... and I made some new friends from England... cool guys by the way... and then I tried to fuck my girlfriend behind the bar, but she wouldn't have any of it..."

"No, we mean what's going on out there?" Harris finally said.

"Oh man,... scary shit... we were heading into camp and we were singing and fucked up out of our minds, and we pulled into the main gate and the bus stopped. We were the first bus... but we stopped and Joe Geisinger steps on the bus and starts screaming **'SHUT UP... SHUT UP.'** and then he starts slapping our heads and screams again...'**DANGER... DANGER...'**and I scream out 'Danger Will Robinson', and Joe just raced over to me and slapped me in the head and we're all drunk and giggling... but you knew something was wrong as you could see the vein in his neck bulging, about to explode, and we then knew that something was wrong. Then he screams **'WE GOT AN EMERGENCY HERE, NOW SHUT UP'.** He scared the crap out of us, so we stopped talking and the laughter died. Then Joe went to the other bus behind us to scream the same things... and we saw Irv and asked him what was going on and he told us.... "

"What did he say?" Harris asked.

"That... " and here Ben started laughing, "that Rachel's counselor is back on campus...and she brought some friends and we better get back to our bunks because we don't know what she'll do, and shit... and this scared the living shit out of us.,... see.... ssshhhhh... come closer."

Ben wrapped us up in a headlock--Harris under his left armpit, and me under his right pit...

"See, and this is bad news for you Flanken, but see... you know they fired that counselor who was kissing Rachel at the park that day... and up to now Joe Geisinger has been opening any letters that counselor has sent to Rachel. From what I have been told, there was a plan to kidnap Rachel tonight. Seems that counselor was really twisted. Want to know why you didn't see Rachel tonight? Because they came and got her and locked her up in Grayson Hall. She's sleeping there now."

"I don't believe that," I told him. All my dreams of getting more kisses were crushed.

"Believe it. They have proof ... they opened all the letters that were sent to Rachel, and there was this plan that while we were all away at the party Rachel's ex- counselor would sneak onto campus, and whisk Rachel away. They were going to run away together... that's why the police are here, and that's why there's such a major search going on... tonight was the night, but Joe foiled the plot by hiding Rachel away."

"I still don't believe it. She's only thirteen years old, what does she know?"

"You're probably right Flanken, and she's just an innocent victim in all this. She probably didn't even know why she was, .. well basically imprisoned in a room in Grayson Hall all night. She never got any of the letters this counselor sent her."

"So why is it bad news for Flanken?" Harris asked, and only then did Ben let us out of his headlock.

Ben straightened up, and took a deep breath as he tried to make the world stop spinning.

"Flanken," he whispered. It was a serious tone. I looked into his eyes, which were watery and tired. Everything portended bad news.

"Flanken, tomorrow is the carnival. Word of what has happened tonight is going to spread quickly. Your little girlfriend is going to be mocked all day. It's going to be incessant. Everyone who knows.... and it will be many.... will be staring at her and whispering behind her back."

"And you're telling me this because?"

"Because Flanken, tomorrow you're going to be a man and you're going to help her get through the day. She's going to need a friend tomorrow. More than a friend. She's going to need a boyfriend. You need to provide her with understanding, loyalty, and heart. And I know you can do this. While everyone's is laughing at her, you have to be near her."

"Do I have to?" I had no idea why I said that.

"Of course you do. Time for you to be a mensch. Be nice to her and listen to what she has to say. Hold her hand if she'll let you. Pretend that nothing happened."

"You're kidding... right?"

"No, I'm not. Now that Jericho is gone I think you're the only one in this camp who can pull this off."

Ben patted both of us on our knees and staggered back into the bunk where we could hear him collapse on top of the double decker.

We sat on the porch for the next hour. Harris tried to make sense of what Ben had told us. I tried to understand the entire situation. I pondered how Ben had,... in a way... instructed me on how to behave like a man at the carnival. I still couldn't fathom the moment. We watched the flashlights being turned off for the night. The swirling lights from the police car dimmed as it made its way back up the main road and out of the camp. It was time to turn in. I had nightmares all night. I really couldn't sleep.

31

It was 8:30 a.m. Reveille blew an hour and a half later than its usual time. It was called Lazy Morning, and the extra sleep was a gift to the counselors, many of whom were waking up with torrid hangovers.

We were allowed to go to breakfast in our pajamas, and we didn't have to make our beds for the entire day. Color War was over, and we were supposed to come together as unified bunks, but the damage was already done. Oliver now sided with the Jewish Mafia. The Brain seemed more independent. He whispered to me in passing as he went to the toilet that my stash of pot was safe. I kept glimpsing the empty mattress where Jericho used to sleep and felt like the lone survivor on a desolate island.

The morning was spent setting up our booth for the carnival. Little homemade attractions. The Seniors set up a booth where a counselor was to sit under a can that was nailed to a shelf. There was a trigger, and if you threw a softball and hit that target, the trigger would allow the shelf to collapse, dousing the counselor with water. I was hoping that Asa would be assigned to sit in the booth so I could throw the softballs at his face instead of the target.

The attractions became simpler, depending upon the age of the group. For instance, the Rovers, the youngest group, had a racetrack where you would roll four colored dice (red, green, white, blue) and move your color-coordinated horse around a track that had been divided into 20 coordinated spaces. If you were blue and you threw a six, you would move the blue horse six space.

Then there was the ring toss. Pepsi bottles were positioned side by side in a box. You needed to collar at least one bottle by tossing the ring from behind a line. Our group created a marble race which was made in the Boys Arts and Crafts shop. Nails were hammered into a board in a certain pattern, and then rubber bands were attached to the nails creating a maze. When six marbles were lined up at the top of the board, a stick was lifted and the marbles raced down different paths till one crossed the finish line first.

At every event winners received tickets and tickets were exchanged for some lousy prizes at the end of the day.

It was a simple day. Plain, small town America--simple.

The carnival, which started after lunch, was just an excuse for the entire camp to congregate on the great lawn of boys' camp, to mingle, socialize and have fun. Joe Geisinger filtered through the crowd, smiling and grabbing campers in headlocks.

He had survived all that the summer threw at him. Joe Geisinger looked forward to the dark of winter, a season of respite where he could rejuvinate his spirit.

Every crisis was overcome. Woodstock didn't create a Tonkawa pandemic, and there was no exodus of counselors traveling down 17B. He had imprisoned Rachel on the top floor of Grayson Hall, thus preventing her counselor from abducting her.

The story of how Bramo and Cisco remedied the situation would forever be ingrained in camp lore. How they searched high and low, day and night, and finally found Rachel's counselor in Cochecton, sitting at a bar, having a drink with a female friend. What we heard was that Bramo and Cisco politely asked the girls to pack up and go home. Then there were the rumors that they actually gave the women a choice; leave immediately and avoid physical violence, or face jail time. As the story goes, the women finished their drinks and left the bar, never to return.

Ben was right. He knew what Rachel was going to through. The carnival started and the girls started to drift onto boys side. You could sense that the oldest girls and most of the counselors were all staring at Rachel. The gossip spread quickly and Rachel could barely look up as she walked toward me.

"Look, there she is," Bugsy said as he walked past her.

"I knew Flanken had no dick," Hardon sneered as he bumped into Rachel on purpose.

Ellen and Beth had accompanied Rachel to the carnival. Harris joined us. Rachel stood in front of me, and she couldn't look me in the eyes. It felt like everyone was staring at us. We held hands. I saw her fighting back tears. We weren't allowed to leave boys camp, but we made our way to the copse of trees next to the HCO shack and sat down on one of the boulders under the cool shade of the pine trees.

"I don't like girls like they're saying" Rachel said.

"I know."

I put my hand around her shoulders, and she buried her head into my chest. I could feel my shirt getting wet from all her tears as she sobbed. Ed Barnett was going to come over and break it up but Ben intercepted him and whispered something in his ear. The two of them turned and walked away.

"I didn't know what was happening. She was so nice to me. My parents are getting a divorce and she was the only one who would listen to me. She would comb my hair, and hold me when I cried. I just needed a friend," Rachel said softly.

"It's not right what everyone's doing to you," I told her.

"Being locked up in Grayson Hall all night, not knowing why, was horrible. I hated it. Finally someone told me what was going on, and at least that calmed me down because I had no idea why I was pulled away from everyone."

"Well, it's over now, and there are only five full days of camp left, and then we'll be out of here," I told her.

"Will you write to me? Will you see me?" she asked.

"For sure," I told her. The writing part was easy. Seeing her would be difficult as she lived in some far off place called New Jersey.

I held her close. For the first time I felt what it was like to be needed. She sighed and rested her head against my chest.

The rest of the afternoon we spent walking hand in hand, from booth to booth. The Brain was by our side, much to the dismay of the Jewish Mafia. The power of weed. It was the six of us against the camp. We all heard the whispers, the innuendos, and the slurs. We drank soda, ate popcorn, and ice cream, and enjoyed one of the last remaining days of summer.

32

I don't believe there will ever be another summer as eventful as the summer of 1969, and some might say it was a turning point in our culture. Man walked on the moon, and many blamed the intense rains that summer on this event. The Mets were surging and we were promised a possible miracle in the fall. People raved about Woodstock and how it brought together half a million people for a weekend of "peace, love and music." I will always remember how I was just a tad too young, but knew I was on the cusp of the "Woodstock Generation".... and I could taste it, and feel it, and most definitely hear it.

But for me, it was the summer I learned to care about others. I had my first real kiss, and I made my first true friend in life. I realized that I didn't really want to go home to my sterile, lonely life, and that I enjoyed being in the company of others. The last few days of camp flew by quickly, but certain events would change my life forever.

I never got to see Rachel again. Her mother came up and took her home for the summer. I think Joe decided it was best for Rachel to leave early. I never got to enjoy a real tongue kiss.

The Prom took place on the last Wednesday night of the summer. Mickey Hardon, Bugsy and all the other assholes in my bunk got dressed in their button down shirts and fancy boots. I just wore jeans and a t-shirt. I snuck off to our special spot with The Brain and Harris and we smoked a couple of joints. I spent the night talking with Beth, and we commiserated about our lost loves. Beth turned out to be sweeter than I would ever have guessed. She gave me Rachel's phone number. I took it but wasn't sure if I would ever call her.

We finished up our team competition but everyone was merely running through the motions. The counselors didn't care what went on in the bunks, nor on the playing fields. I was tripped while rounding the bases in softball games, and pummeled under the boards in basketball. Harris was routinely punched by The Mayor and Hooky when Ben wasn't around. Asa increased his verbal abuse in a constant stream of sarcastic, nasty remarks, aimed at making Harris cry.

Ben did his best to keep an eye on us, and we spent every rest hour practicing Tai Chi with him. He taught us several new self defense moves. At times Ben seemed to be the only sane person in camp. Yet there was something eating at him, something he was hiding inside. He kept looking around as if he was expecting someone to jump out from behind a bunk and mug him. He wasn't saying much, but he kept a close watch on what the other counselors were up to.

Abner Dingle delivered the trunks to the bunks. Only two days of camp left. He was driving his tractor with a large wagon attached to it. Abner, along with his staff, tossed our trunks to the ground. We were told to open them up, pull out our duffle bags, and air everything out. It was a cloudy, cold day. The gray sky threw a blanket of sadness over the last days. The temperature seemed to drop a degree every few minutes. Wind made the pine trees shiver.

The second Harris opened his trunk, Asa and Samson swooped in and threw him in. Then they closed the lid on him. They sat there smiling, sitting on the trunk as Harris thrashed about inside. He was terrified and he kept banging on the trunk, screaming for help. Everyone laughed at this.

"I wish I had the trunk earlier so I could have shipped him home five weeks ago," Asa proclaimed.

I ran into the bunk and got Ben, who charged outside, leaped over the railings of the porch and pushed Asa and Samson from behind. The two counselors tumbled to the ground as Ben unlatched the trunk and opened it, allowing Harris to crawl out. He was crying and gasping for air, dripping with sweat, and just the thought of being trapped in such a confined area for even ten seconds made me woozy.

"You fucking assholes," Ben screamed, "he could have died in there."

"What's your problem? It was a joke. He's small enough to be shipped home in a trunk so we decided to see if he really fit. We were going to let him out! It's not like it's a fuckin coffin..."

Asa picked himself up off the ground, helped Samson up and then walked over to Ben who was busy consoling Harris. Ben wasn't expecting to be thrown to the ground. "And if you ever touch me again I will fucking kill you," Asa said.

Harris went berserk. He tried breaking away from Ben who was doing everything in his power to hold him back. "I'll kill you!" Harris kept screaming. Harris was breaking down.

I had wondered how long and what would it take to light his fuse. What would make Harris explode? Would I ever let my emotions free? My skin felt like a rubber band stretched to its limits. Maybe that moment would arrive soon. Ben tucked Harris neatly under one arm, and carried him back into the bunk. Harris was kicking and screaming, and refused to calm down.

I looked at all the counselors and campers who were laughing at what just happened.

"You're all a bunch of fucking assholes!" I screamed as I walked into the bunk to help calm Harris.

During rest hour I was called down to the Boys' Waterfront. It was time to finish up my Junior Life Saving course. I had passed the written test, but now came the physical exam. The water was choppy, and I knew it was probably colder than any other day of the summer. The two rafts that created the border at the deep end were pulled in and secured to the dock till the next summer—bound and gagged till they would be liberated once the summer rolled around.

There were about four of us taking the test, and we stood on the dock shivering from the cold. Sy Schwartz walked onto the dock dressed in his baggy bathing suit. His nipples were erect, the cold wind making them stand at attention. He walked up to us and eyeballed each candidate. He was looking to see who showed fear. And I knew that was me, because I was fucking scared. Sy stood only a bit taller than me, but weighed twice as much as I did, his pot belly sagging over his swim trunks.

"You're going first," he sneered as he smelled my fear.

Sy backed away from me, keeping his gaze on my quivering body. My mouth suddenly went dry. Sy lifted his arms, and stood spread eagle, like he was praying to God. Then the waterfront counselors all materialized with cans that boldly stated "CHICKEN FAT."

"Hit me up, boys," Sy said.

The waterfront counselors began to smear a creamy white goo all over Sy's body. They slathered it on, filling every crevice with chicken fat. Or maybe it was Crisco? It didn't make a difference, because when they were done, the waterfront staff had turned Sy into a baby beluga white crisp whale.

"What's all that for?" I finally had to ask.

Sy marched straight toward me, and stood toe to toe.

"You think this is going to be easy? Well it's not, mister. I'm dead serious about this test. If you think I'm going to make this simple you might as well leave now. I'm greased. If you're going to pass the test you're going to have to bring in one greased pig to do so."

Sy turned and sprinted toward the lake and with one mighty leap he did a cannonball into the water. You could see the oil slick from the chicken fat float off his body as he swam about twenty-five yards away from the dock. From there, treading water, he motioned me to commence my test.

I didn't care anymore. If I drowned in the process of failing the test, well... I didn't care. For once, I had somewhat enjoyed a summer. WHAT? Did I really think I enjoyed a summer? Yet it now was all taken away from me. I took a running leap off the dock, and flew through the air. I was making the dive the way we were taught, with arms spread eagle and ready to slap the water, legs splayed apart. The method, the design of the dive, was to enter the water without ever taking your eyes off the victim. I made the perfect splash entry and not a strand of hair got wet.

But the impact of the frigid water made me lose my breath, and I hesitated for a second as I gained control of my body. I was ready. I quickly started to swim out toward Sy, and when I was about five yards away, I dove under the murky water.

We were taught to swim with our head out of the water so we would never lose sight of the victim. When we made our approach, we were to dive underwater and grab the distressed swimmer by the legs, pull them under the water and twist their body around so that when we surfaced we were already in a cross chest carry. The problem was, Sy was slipperier than an eel. I kept trying to pull his legs down but my hands just slid off him.

I finally surfaced, and took a big gulp of air. Sy was laughing at me as he treaded water a few feet away. I dove back underwater and approached Sy's feet, but this time I went for the swimsuit and grabbed the only outstanding member of his body that wasn't greased.

I heard Sy screaming above the waterline, but I held his cock firmly, and pulled him down under, where I twisted him around, released his crushed member, and put him in a cross chest carry. I pushed up to the surface.

Sy fought me every stroke of the way. First he cursed me for grabbing his "shmeckle," and then he struggled to get out of my grip. It was almost impossible to keep my hand from sliding off his barrel chest. I tried to kick into my sidestroke and head back to the dock.

As Sy slipped away I frantically grabbed for his armpit hair. Sy thrashed about and I could feel my grip loosening. I was ripping the armpit hair out of his skin. I dug my fingers into his flabby chest and as I kicked I could feel that hold slipping away again... until I grabbed the only thing I could.

"Fuck. you're ripping my nipple off," Sy screamed.

I was closing in on the dock, my grip now secured.

"You're tearing my nipple off," Sy screamed again.

I wasn't letting go of that nipple. I couldn't keep Sy on my hip because of all that chicken fat. He kept sliding off. The cold lake water had kept Sy's nipples good and stiff and nobody could ever dream that the old man's nipples were one part of his body that needed to be greased for this test.

I was pinching that nipple so hard that Sy had to start laughing. The waterfront staff was laughing so hard that they had trouble reaching a pole out to me so that we could be pulled in. When we were up on the dock, Sy kept asking his staff to examine his left nipple to see if there was a tear.

"Kid, first you grab my cock, and then you nearly decapitate my nipple...."

I was waiting for the bad news.

"Well done, kid.... that was damn smart of you. Didn't mind you grabbing my junk at all... And because my nipple is still here... you pass the test... well done!"

Joe Geisinger didn't want contact sports, or any activity where we might injure ourselves. It wouldn't look good to come home with a broken arm or leg. So no basketball, no softball, no volleyball.... just sitting around doing nothing for most of the day. When I returned to the bunk and changed out of my swim trunks I realized that something was off. I could feel it. Afternoon activity call was about to be blown. We were down two counselors as the two football players left camp a day early. Their first practice was a day away and they needed to get back to school. The poor shmucks were at least ten pounds overweight due to a steady diet of Sunday morning bagels. Suddenly I realized that Chick had disappeared. Asa and Samson stood in front of the group, a 'come fuck with me' grin spread across their faces. They were now in charge.

"So what are we doing?" Mickey Hardon screamed.

"We have a special treat for this afternoon. Special treat as you'll all be going home soon," Asa told us. "And thus enough time to heal," he whispered to Samson.

Ben was about to say something when suddenly the HCO loud-speaker crackled to life.

"Ben, please report to Grayson Hall as soon as possible..."

"Go on Ben, someone needs you," Asa said. He flicked his hands trying to shoo Ben away. Ben stood his ground.

"Now, Ben! They need you at Grayson Hall."

This time you could see Ed Barnett standing outside the HCO shack looking up towards our bunk. He pointed his finger towards Grayson Hall.

"Don't do anything stupid," he said to Asa and he turned and jogged off.

Asa told us to walk out behind the annexes, onto the outfield grass of the softball field. Everyone was sluggish, the heat making us drowsy. Small weary steps, leaning on one another, not knowing what we were about to face. We were told to sit in a square.

"Gentlemen, this will be your ring for the next hour or so," Asa announced as he and Samson paraded around, like they knew a secret.

"We know that a lot of you have had issues with one another this summer, and we figured what would be a better going away present than an old fashioned boxing match to settle one's griev-ances," Samson continued.

Lenny and Spanky reached into a large box they had carried up from the HCO shack, and pulled out two pair of boxing gloves. They threw them inside of the ring where they hit the ground with a dull thud.

"Gentlemen, all you have to do is call out someone's name. If they're chicken they'll back out of a fight, but if they're man enough to face your challenge they'll have one minute to get inside the ring. When the whistle blows you'll have three minutes to work out your anger, your grievances, and whatever else ails you. We will not hold you back. Go for it."

Asa stared at me.

Mickey Hardon jumped out first.

"Harris. I want Harris," he shouted.

I touched Harris on the shoulder, and tried to hold him back. He looked at me with such calm that for some unknown reason I let him enter the ring. I looked desperately around for Ben, hoping he would materialize and stop this charade. This wasn't sport, it was more like hunting. Pick out your prey and make the kill. No consideration for size or weight. They would allow the tiniest camper to match up against the bulvan of the group, and it was all for their pleasure.

Asa was helping Hardon on with his gloves, which were big, thick, leathered, beaten, and cracked. By wearing those gloves there would be no black and blue marks... big stuffed pouches of leather could only knock one silly. Harris brought the gloves over to me, and asked me to help put them on.

"You don't have to do this, you can walk away," I told him. "I'll back you."

"There are certain things you can't walk away from. Everyone dies sometime,"" he said.

"You're not going to die out there," I told him as I slid the first glove on and tried to lace it up.

"No, don't lace it. I know I'm not going to die... it just feels like death has been following me all day. I don't care what happens to me now," Harris said.

Harris was calm and at ease as I slid the second glove on, then he turned and entered the ring. I couldn't decide whether or not to run and find Ben, but I wasn't sure if I would get back in time to protect Harris. I began to ponder if I would have to jump into the ring and protect his scrawny little ass.

"Ready? Let's go, three minutes starting now," Asa shouted as the group started cheering for Hardon, who immediately charged Harris.

"Stop this, can't you?" The Brain asked as he appeared by my side.

I didn't know what to do. I kept looking off in the distance towards Grayson Hall, hoping to see Ben charging towards us to save the day. Harris moved out of the way of the first punch thrown by Hardon, a glancing blow that barely landed on his right shoulder.

"I'm going to kill you for ruining my summer, you little nerd. Now stand still," Hardon shouted as Harris kept moving around the ring.

Mickey Hardon kept charging, but Harris kept moving about. Finally Mickey Hardon landed a second punch. Harris fell to the ground, and licked the blood that began to trickle out of his mouth. Everyone was laughing, and cheering Hardon on, wanting more.

"You still have two minutes," Asa shouted at Hardon.

Harris got up and started to back up, toward Asa. He looked at Hardon, and then the damnedest thing took place, something I might never see again in my life.

Harris shucked off his unlaced gloves and turned to face Asa. He then took two or three steps toward him. It was such a sudden move that Asa had no chance. Harris jump-kicked a direct hit to Asa's balls. Just kicked him in the nuts. He used a move that Ben had taught us. No man can stand a direct kick to the balls, and Asa doubled over in pain. As he fell forward Harris thrust his hand out and connected with a perfect palm heel punch, making a direct hit on Asa's nose. That one thrust, just as we had practiced with Ben, was true. You could hear Asa's nose crack as blood spewed all over.

Asa was rolling around on the floor doubled up in pain, and the entire ring stood there in shock. Out of the corner of my eye, in the distance, I saw Ben running toward us, but there was no time to wait for him. Mickey Hardon was coming in for the kill. Harris didn't notice Hardon charging toward him. Harris was relishing the victory, adrenaline surging through his body. He stood over Asa, and kicked him a second time in the nuts, causing Asa to scream out.

I jumped into the ring and intercepted Hardon's attack. I used my body as a shield. I flipped Mickey Hardon over my body. He flew into the air and came down hard on the ground with a loud thud, and then a groan. I knew I had knocked the wind out of him as he writhed on the floor, gasping for air.

As my rage intensified I felt pleasure. I was acting out, my anger blazing from all the crap that was thrown at me all summer. I watched as Harris kicked Asa in the nuts a third time. Asa covered up between his legs, leaving an opening, so Harris kicked him in the nose again. This blow would ensure surgery for the counselor who antagonized Harris all summer.

I turned and rushed at Bugsy, who meekly backed up. I flew into the air and tackled him. He fell to the ground and I was on top of Bugsy wailing away with fists that suddenly found a reason to scream in rage. Bugsy's nose started to bleed and he started to cry like a little baby.

I was yanked off Bugsy by Hooky and The Mayor, and they tried to wrestle me to the ground but my fury was now uncontrollable. Their fists made contact and I knew my face would be a mess, but I swung wildly, threw elbows, kicked and screamed till the two of them fell to the ground. I reveled in the sight of my three bunkmates crying and groveling on the ground. I turned around to see Samson grab Harris by his neck, lifting him off the ground. He was choking Harris, who flailed wildly trying to escape. Before I could come to his aid Ben charged into the fight and performed a round house kick, making contact right under Samson's ribs. Harris fell to the ground as Samson doubled over. I ran to help Harris up, and watched as Samson slowly picked himself up and charged Ben. It was no contest. Ben stood there calmly and performed a front thrust kick, connecting straight into Samson's chest, causing him to drop to his knees, gasping for breath.

As Asa and Samson lay on the ground groaning, Ben looked up to see Lenny charging him like an overweight bull. Ben was calm, and as Lenny approached he just squatted down and used Lenny's momentum to flip the chubby man into the air. When Lenny hit the ground it felt like an earthquake. Ben held up one finger in a warning for Spanky to stay where he was, and Spanky obeyed.

Ben grabbed hold of Samson's hair and dragged him across the dirt toward Asa. Every time Samson tried to stop him, Ben would stomp down on his hands, causing more pain. Ben stood over the two counselors, who were woozy from the blows. They each tried to get up to attack Ben, but he would just slap them down. It was complete humiliation.

I heard the warning from The Brain. Hardon had regained his breath and was now charging me. No contest. I sidestepped his advance, tripped him to the ground, and pounced on him with a windmill of punches that bloodied his face. Ben had to pull me off Hardon who lay on the ground in tears.

Outside of the moans and groans there was a stunned silence. I joined Harris and Ben in the middle of the ring and we stood staring at the group. Then we looked down to the ground at the defeated . Off in the distance I saw Joe's Cadillac cutting across the field, and I knew that this would not be good news.

Ben lifted up the bloody faces of Asa and Samson and knelt down till he was eye to eye with them.

"Oh, there's one other thing I wanted you to know. My last name... my last name is really SUNSHINE," he shouted for everyone to hear. "Remember that kid you tortured all summer? Well,...that was me." Then he spit in their faces and threw them back to the ground.

Ben had other things on his mind, but first he walked over to me.

"I sort of liked the name Flanken. Going to miss calling you that," he said in passing.

"Sunshine?" was all I could muster, finding it hard to believe that he was the namesake for all that was evil in this camp. Ben just turned and smiled. It was a smile I would always remember. It was a smile that said, "Yeah, once in a while you can make something wrong in this world right again."

It was over in an instant, and yet the ramifications of the day shattered my world. No longer would I ever just sit on the sideline and allow someone to attack or bully an innocent person. I would always be stepping into fights, protecting the innocent. I would never be silent again. I would always stand for what I felt was right. And I prayed that I would never hear or see death again for a long time.

Ben put his arms around Harris, who only let out one sob, and led him toward the Cadillac which had just pulled up. I wanted to walk away with them, but Ben signaled for me to stay behind. Harris tried to be brave, but you could see his shoulders start to quiver as the adrenaline rush wore off, and the rage washed away. Then I saw Joe Geisinger emerge from the car and walk over to Harris. He tenderly hugged him. Chick got out of the car and immediately ordered Spanky, the one remaining counselor who was not injured, to take everyone back to their bunks. I refused to go, and Chick allowed me to stay. Harris was right... he had that feeling.

Abner Dingle's pickup truck was speeding toward us, cutting across the fields. You could see Bramo and Cisco standing defiantly in the open cargo area, holding on for dear life as Abner hit a bump that caused the pickup truck to take flight. Cisco and Bramo had strapped their hands around a roll bar and they were riding like cowboys on a bucking bronco. They pulled up just as the rest of the group started heading back to the bunks. Abner Dingle had a softball bat in his hand.

It was time for Harris to go home, but just before he slid into the Cadillac he turned and smiled at me. He tried to hide the tears, but couldn't. Joe drove Harris back to Grayson Hall. I wanted to follow but Chick grabbed me.

"Let him be, Jason. His Aunt and Uncle are at Grayson Hall waiting to drive him home. His mother has taken a turn for the worse and his father wants him home to spend the last few days with her."

"I want to say goodbye," I told him.

"Another time. Ben has already packed for Harris, and his trunk and duffle are in the back of his aunt and uncle's station wagon. He needs to go home."

"Why Chick? Why did they send him here? Why did they make him come to camp?"

"They wanted Harris to have some fun this summer, instead of seeing her decay every day. She fought it as long as she could and now it's near the end, and he needs to spend the last few days with her. At least he has that."

"I always told him that he was lucky to at least feel the love of his mother for so many years. Some of us never feel that…"

The old man didn't say anything to me, but he turned to Asa, Lenny and Samson, who were still writhing in pain.

"Hey, you scum, get off the ground now before I beat you senseless. Samson and Lenny, go to the infirmary and have them get you to the hospital if you need it."

"I can't walk," Lenny cried out.

"Then crawl to the infirmary. You're not going to get any sympathy from me. Whose stupid idea was it to have the Golden Gloves two days before camp ends. I'd have beaten the crap out of you if it wasn't already done."

"Hey, he broke my nose," Asa screamed.

"Yeah, a little thirteen-year-old boy broke your nose. Who's going to believe that?" Chick laughed. "Oh, and by the way, these three gentlemen need to speak to you about something that happened on the canoe trip? Know anything about that?"

Bramo, Cisco and Abner Dingle closed in on Asa.

Chick put his arm around my shoulders and we walked slowly back to the bunks. It had to be a slow walk, because Chick's bowed legs wouldn't allow him to move any faster. I tried to turn around to see what was happening to Asa.

"Don't," Chick told me, "it's none of your business."

33

One summer, and two deaths. Then, a girlfriend who departed early. One true friend who would always be there for me.

The last day of camp was a silent one. Lenny was on crutches with a hyperextended knee. Samson's right arm was in a sling. Nothing broken, just badly sprained. He would be lucky if he was ready for basketball season.

I listened to Chick that day and never looked back. When Chick and I got back to the bunk Abner Dingle pulled up in the pickup truck with Asa sitting like a limp puppet next to Bramo. Abner got out, walked into Asa's bunk and started throwing Asa's clothing haphazardly into the back of the pickup truck.

The rumor would always be that Bramo and Cisco had meted out some type of physical punishment. Asa didn't look like he was in any worse pain so I doubt they did. But you could tell that he was scared shitless of something. Asa knew he was in trouble and he couldn't bullshit his way out of it. He ended up losing his college scholarship, was thrown out of school and was shipped off to Vietnam. That was the last I heard of him.

On the final evening of camp we lined up for the summer end banquet. Ben stood alone next to Chick. The wounded stood off to the side, quiet and ashamed in defeat. They were no longer invincible, they were no longer gods, and most of the kids in the group could now laugh at them. Samson was impotent without Asa by his side.

The banquet dinner was nothing special, but in typical camp tradition they tried to make it extraordinary. There were small printed menus with words like Hors d'oeuvers, and 'Au Juice' displayed boldly. These were words I had just become familiar with from the one Bar Mitzvah I attended. I tried to make a joke about the words, but The Brain was the only one sitting next to me. Thank God he laughed.

After the banquet Ben took me aside and told me how Asa and Samson, as campers at Tonkawa, tormented and tortured him all summer. When he got home after the summer he hid in his room crying for days. His mother finally took him to seek professional help. It took years of therapy for Ben to get over that summer.

"So no strait-jacket?" I asked.

"Nope. Guess that's just camp lore."

"What did they do to you?"

"Many of the same things they did to Harris, but Harris was much stronger. I was breaking down almost every day. My counselors were pieces of shit. Then one day we went into Honesdale to go bowling. I had two ice cream sandwiches. I didn't realize how ice cream destroyed my stomach. I had the shits. Bus ride home and I couldn't hold it in. Shit all over myself. Asa and Samson tore into me. I was a pariah for the rest of the summer. Those assholes took my stained underwear and ran it up the flag pole. That was it. I banged my head against the bunk wall and ran away."

"Were you hiding in a tree stump for three days?"

"No, I snuck into the infirmary and hid overnight. The counselors were looking for me all night, but I was safe and asleep in the infirmary."

"What did you do then?"

"They had no choice but to send me home. I was a total mess. I took up all types of self defense classes. I was never going to allow myself to be put into a position of being the victim again. I wanted to always be able to protect myself from bullies."

"Didn't you want to get revenge every day?"

"No, I buried that summer. I lost track of those two assholes and tried to forget that summer. As I told you from the beginning, I came up to camp because it was my only free summer before med school. I wanted to get away from the city, and the stress of studying. In the back of my mind I also wanted to make sure nobody was picked on like I was. Then, when I saw Asa and Samson, I knew one day I would have to remind them of who I was. And most importantly, who I am now."

After dinner the entire camp congregated on the great lawn of boys' side. The last night of camp included one final tradition. The 'Burning of the Numbers'. Down by the lake Bramo and Cisco had erected large wire numerals that formed 1969. They were wrapped in some kind of cloth, then doused with gasoline. Bramo then took a torch and lit the numerals till 1969 blazed brightly in the darkness of the night.
Everyone started singing the camp alma mater.

"Hail to the camp we dream of all year
Always its name we shall hold dear..."

Girls were crying hysterically, hugging each other between laughter and tears. We all just looked at them as if they were crazy, unable to understand such an emotional response.

Earlier in the evening, during Free Play, I finished off the rest of the weed with The Brain. On the last night of camp nobody in the bunk bothered me. As matter of fact, everyone avoided me like shit in someone's underwear.
"I don't know why Hardon had it out for you all summer. You're a good guy." The Brain told me as we took our final tokes of the summer.
"I can't understand why you were friends with him."
"I've known him since we were like six years old...shit just happens. "
Oliver tried to be my friend again, but I could never look him in

the eyes after he sided with the Jewish Mafia during Color War. It felt good to walk down the center aisle of the bunk and know that if they didn't respect me now, at least they feared me. I would never feel intimidated again. I discovered the power of standing up for oneself. It was so liberating and seductive.

On the last morning of the summer we rose a half an hour earlier than usual, threw our blankets and pillows into our duffle bags, and zipped and locked everything up for the trip home. Breakfast was a quick affair of rolls and cold cereal. Our waiter said goodbye as he quickly cleaned up the table after we ate. He wanted me to keep him abreast of my basketball exploits, but I knew I would never see him again.

We ran back to the bunks, grabbed whatever we needed for the ride home, and waited out on the porch for the call to head to our assigned busses. I remember how lush and deeply green the boys' side seemed on that first day. Walking on it was like walking on balls of cotton. It glowed with the sparkle of a green neon beacon. Sadly, now, on the last day, it looked muddy and brown, and trampled upon.

Ed Barnett made the announcement over the loudspeaker and we walked to the buses. They were lined up around the circle in front of the Mess Hall, like they were on the first day of camp when we arrived. I walked to the buses alone, with nobody tagging alongside, and I suddenly missed Harris. I never turned around to say goodbye to camp, because I was never going to allow my parents to forcibly send me away again.

I was assigned to Bus 7, and when I climbed on board I was relieved to see that the Jewish Mafia were boarding Bus 3. I looked for a seat… and saw the beautiful, smiling face of Beth and sat down next to her. Girls were crying and hugging each other with such emotion that I thought I was going to be sick.

"I just don't get why they cry all the time at the end of the summer," Beth said as she looked outside the bus to see the hysteria that was taking place.

"Neither do I. All I know is that you do a lot of growing up in these eight weeks."

"I'm not going to miss this place," Beth said.

"Neither will I, but I'll always remember this summer," I said, and then I caught a glimpse of Ben standing outside of my bus, waving goodbye. "And just maybe I'll miss some of the people I met here... just maybe."

The limousine was waiting for me as the buses pulled up in front of the same high school in Queens that we departed from. I sat in silence as the limo driver pulled out, and headed to Westchester without a word spoken between us for the entire trip. Then again, maybe silence was one of the little things you missed after eight weeks of camp.

My parents weren't home, which was no surprise. I let myself into the house through the garage, and surrendered to the delicious scent of an immaculately sanitized house. I turned on my stereo, threw Crosby Stills and Nash onto the turntable, and melted into my bed. I let the magic of the central air conditioning wash away the memory of the muggy and dusty bunks.

I called Jericho about two weeks after I got home. I figured out how to take the train to Grand Central, and then walk to Penn Station for the train ride out to Long Island. I would see Jericho once every two months, and sometimes we'd hang out in the city together. We got high, and met at the Garden for a few concerts. Every year I would go with him to the cemetery and put a rock on his brother's grave, the Jewish tradition to mark a visit.

We grew up as best friends, communicated weekly, and ended up going to college together where we were roommates. I was thankful that my parents paid for my college education, but I was sure that the hidden reason was that they couldn't wait for me to leave home. I couldn't wait either. After college I never returned.

Beth became a nurse at Bellevue Hospital and, of course, she married someone who was a doctor. Jericho received an MBA in Finance, and worked on Wall Street. He did incredibly well.

I desired to pratice law. I struggled though law school, while working as a bartender at night. I wasn't going to accept another penny from my parents. I had accepted their offer to pay for my undergraduate degree as a reparation for the loveless childhood they inflicted upon me. Upon graduation I was officially done with them as they were done with me. When I passed the New York State Bar I joined a prominant family law firm; prenups, divorce, child custody, and what I truly specialized in... Emancipation of Minors.

For a while Jericho and I lived together in Manhattan. A two-bedroom apartment down in Alphabet City, where we met the most incredibly colorful characters since we left Camp Tonkawa. Jericho got married first and I followed him down the matrimonial path a few months later. We both settled down on the North Shore of Long Island, living a couple of towns apart. Jericho had two daughters and I had two sons and we sent them off to day camp, but never to sleepaway camp.

Besides, from what I hear, summer camps aren't what they used to be. Instead of eight weeks, they're now seven weeks, and the cost is double or triple what it was when we attended camp. Bunks are now air conditioned and wired for video games. It is no longer summer camp, where tradition existed and imagination reigned, but more like a vacation for rich entitled kids. The true essence of camp was lost forever.

Plus, I was sure there were no longer any characters in camp like Sy Schwartz, or "Bramo," Chick, or Heshie. Counselors now had to take sensitivity training, which may be the only true advancement in camps these days. It was something that counselors like Asa, and Samson sorely needed.

When my boys were in high school they introduced me to

Facebook. They were embarrassed to do so, but I forced the issue on them. I found Ben, friended him, and found out he had a small family and lived in the Berkshires. He was a doctor at a small hospital, avoiding city life.

Yet, I needed to know one thing—how was Harris. I had googled his name once before, when the internet was just taking hold, but I still wasn't able to make contact. Yet here on Facebook I had no trouble. I searched for Harris and finally found him. He was living in Westchester, and had a family of his own. It was definitely Harris. I could tell by that wart on his nose.

So I friended Harris. No response. I told Jericho and Beth and they told me to send another friend request. I even wrote a quick e mail reminding him of who I was. In his profile it stated that Harris was an orthopedic surgeon. I wouldn't have expected less.

I had given up hope of making contact with Harris when one morning I turned on the computer, and went onto Facebook. There was a message.

"Jason, I never got a chance to thank you. In my deepest moments of despair and loneliness you were my friend. I have tried to forget about the summer of 1969. I was in therapy for years, but I have overcome many things. I see you are still friends with Jericho, and maybe one day we can get together. So thank you for looking me up, for this gives me the opportunity to say thanks for being there for me. Thank you."

I wanted to tell Harris that he showed me what courage really looked like. I thought about what to say, but instead of sending a response I talked to Jericho and we decided to set aside an evening to meet Harris in the city. At that time I would thank Harris. In his way, he taught me many things that summer. He showed me how to stand up against stronger foes, and how perseverance can help you through dark times. And I realized how much sweeter life was with friends. I had to thank Harris in person.

ACKNOWLEDGEMENTS

There will always be a story, but I need to thank Paul Sundick and Rich Schaffer.

Paul Sundick's picture of the war canoes will always remind us of the color of summer, and his videos will forever bring back the memories.

Rich Schaffer, who was never a "B" athlete, is the "oral" history I counted on to confirm the essence of the sleepaway experience

CPSIA information can be obtained
at www.ICGtesting.com
Printed in the USA
BVHW041613051219
565744BV00016B/131/P